Shut Your Eyes

Mandy Lee

Copyright

Shut Your Eyes

First print edition.

.

Dedicated to my mum

Chapter One

I open my palm, watching as the tiny stylised sweet pea flashes in a shaft of light. I've been holding the necklace for an age, reciting Dan's words over and over again: 'Keep it safe. Look at it and think of me ... because one day soon, you'll be wearing it again.' It's my talisman, warding off evil and bringing good fortune. As long as it's with me, as long as I believe in it, I'll be fine. If I had my way, I'd never take it off, but for now I need to keep it buried, along with the truth. Wrapping it up in tissue, I tuck it away in the side pocket of my handbag and sit back, listening as the sounds of the world seep back into my head: a shout in the street, the blast of a car horn, an engine revving. I have no idea how long I've been sitting here. All I know is this – the whirlwind of life with Dan has slammed to a halt, dumping me back in Camden with a hastily packed suitcase.

But I can't stay like this forever. I need to crack through the shock and drag myself back to reality. I focus on the suitcase first. It's sitting by the door, where Beefy dropped it off. And then I move my attention to an empty wine bottle; two glasses, both used; DVDs littered across the floor; the remnants of a chocolate bar. Finally, I notice something just behind the television, a crumpled pair of knickers. I only moved out a week ago and since then the flat seems to have filled up with the chaotic left-overs of Lucy's relationship with Clive. I pick up my mobile and check the time. It's just after six and it's already growing dark, probably because it's raining again. Late July and summer seems to have given up on London. Packed its bags and moved elsewhere. It's certainly moved out of my heart, leaving me with nothing but a grim, familiar ache.

A key scrapes in the lock, making me jump. The time for thinking has come to an end. I steel myself for the job ahead. Until Boyd's dealt with, I'll be living cheek by jowl with deception, and it's not

1

something I relish. I hate secrets.

'What's going on?' Lucy demands, appearing in the doorway. She slings her handbag onto the floor and comes to a halt in the middle of the room. 'Clive texted me. He said you wanted to meet me here. Shouldn't you be at the hospital?'

I shake my head. 'No.'

'Why not?'

Oh bloody hell. How do I begin? I really should have rehearsed this. I'm just no good at ad-libbing.

'Maya, talk to me.'

Come on, I urge my brain. Find something to say. But someone seems to have switched off the light. I'm in the dark.

Lucy's eyes flit to the suitcase.

'And what's that doing here? Why aren't you at home?'

Ah, home. Now there's a word I can use.

'This is my home ...'

'What are you talking about?' She clamps her hands on her hips. 'Your home's in Lambeth. Millionaire's penthouse, wooden floors, walk-in wardrobes, floor-to-ceiling windows, all that shizzle.'

Okay, so it's bombshell time.

'Dan's finished with me.'

I look up to find Lucy staring at me, eyes wide. Working themselves up into action, her lips begin to quiver.

'So,' I continue before she can launch into a rant, 'I'm back here ... for good.'

'But ...'

I wait for something else. When nothing comes, I decide to fill the silence with a little repetition.

'He's finished with me, Luce.'

She scans the room, spots the discarded knickers, quickly retrieves them and stuffs them into her handbag.

'What's happened this time?' she asks, rubbing her hands together.

I clasp my knees, trying to pin down the exact place to start but, like an irritating fly determined to avoid a good swatting, it's escaped. I gaze at my hands, and say nothing.

'Okay, I'll get it out of you sooner or later.' She scans the room again before stating the obvious. 'This place is a mess. I haven't been back here for a few days. I've been at Dan's ... or round Clive's. I'm sorry.'

'It's fine.'

'No, it's not.' She rubs the back of her hand against her forehead.

'I bet there's stuff growing in the sink.'

I stare at her for a moment or two, surprised that she's suddenly blurred. I have no idea what's caused a handful of tears to make an appearance, but I'm thoroughly grateful for their company. They can only help with the charade.

'Oh God,' Lucy groans, leaving the room. Within seconds, she's back, clutching an entire roll of toilet paper. 'Here.' Throwing it onto my lap, she collapses next to me. 'Now, get on with it. What's happened?'

Pulling away a length of toilet roll and blowing my nose, I run through what I'd really like to say: 'Oh, you know, a psychopathic ex-boyfriend trying to kill the love of my life, threatening to harm just about anyone we know if we don't stay apart; the usual sort of crap.' But the truth is out of bounds. After bludgeoning my way into the loop, I've agreed to stick to the party line. Pulling away a second strip of tissue, I dab my eyes, and finally the starting point settles in front of me. Before it can dart off again, I grab it.

'You know I told you I'd done something stupid?'

She nods.

'Well, it was really stupid.'

'How stupid?'

'Ten out of ten stupid.'

'Tell me.'

'His sister ... she came down on Friday night.'

Her eyes expand.

'The one who wrote the card?'

It's my turn to nod. 'She turned up out of the blue.'

'Crap.'

'She wanted to see Dan.'

'Double crap.'

'His other sister's not well ... and I'd offered a way in.'

Her forehead creases. 'How come?'

Ready for the admission, I take in a breath.

'I went to see her ... behind Dan's back. I couldn't help myself,' I explain quickly. 'I went to Limmingham.'

'Triple crap.'

'I only wanted to make contact. I thought I could help. You know ... like we said?'

She shuffles about on her bottom.

'Oh, for fuck's sake, Maya. I didn't think you'd actually do it.'

'It was your idea,' I remind her.

It's bad enough admitting what I've done. I know I've been an

3

idiot, and I really don't need confirmation from Lucy. Anger rubs against my skull, like sandpaper, distracting me from the job in hand.

'Yes, but ... I didn't think you'd actually go through with it.' She blows out a lungful of air. 'This is all my fault. I put the stupid idea in your head.'

And maybe, I'd like to add, if you'd flagged up the fact that it was a stupid idea, I wouldn't have gone through with it. I give myself a good mental slap. This is all done and dusted, not worth arguing over. I need to get back on track, shove the mistakes to one side and deal with the fallout.

'You put the idea into my head.' I hold up my hand to prevent any interruptions. 'But I'm the one who acted on it. If there's anyone to blame around here, it's me. I should never have meddled.'

'So, what happened?'

'He got home, refused to talk to Layla, lost it and stormed out. He took the bike and, well ...' I wave a hand in the air. 'You know the rest.'

'Shit.' I watch her face as she ploughs through confusion, finally latching on to a realisation. 'The accident?'

I nod.

'If I hadn't got in touch with Layla, she wouldn't have come down to London, and Dan wouldn't be in hospital right now.'

'No wonder he's pissed off.' She shuffles about again. 'But he was okay with you. When he woke up, he was alright.'

'And then he remembered. I went too far. There's something between him and Layla, and I can't work it out. He refused to see me this morning, and then he got Clive to do his dirty work.' And this is where the sort-of-truth ends. It's time for the outright lies. 'So, that's it. We're done. Kaput. Finito.'

'Shit.' Lucy sucks at her bottom lip, deep in thought. 'He'll come to his senses.'

And the denials.

'I don't think so.'

'Yes, he will.' She waves a finger at me. 'He'll realise you were only trying to make things better. He's probably off his tits on drugs ... but at some point ... at some point ...'

'He won't change his mind. That's been made perfectly clear to me.'

The finger waving comes to an end.

'Jeez, this is a mess.' She gets to her feet. 'I'll talk to Clive, and then he can talk to Dan.'

'No,' I snap, knowing full-well Clive's not even going to be talking to Lucy for much longer. 'I've crossed a line. It's one hundred percent over.'

'Fuck, is it?' she sneers dismissively.

'Fuck, it is. Leave it, Lucy. I've had enough.'

'This is a disaster.' Her arms flap up and down. 'He's got it wrong. You were just trying to help. So what if you stepped over a line? What sort of fucking stupid line is it? His sister? How bad can she be? I mean, has he met your sister?' The arm flapping stops. 'Of course he has,' she breathes. 'But if he can deal with Sara, he can deal with his own bloody family.'

'It's not that simple. Layla's a no-go area.'

'A no-go area? That's ridiculous.' The arms flap again, faster this time, as if she's trying to take off. 'I'm going to give him a piece of my mind. I'll get Clive to take me over to the hospital and I don't care how crap he feels, I'll make him feel crappier.'

'Calm down.'

'No, I will not calm down. You try to help him, and he dumps you. The man's a twat. I'm going to tell him to his twatty face.'

'Lucy! I don't want you getting involved. Meddling got me into this situation. More meddling's only going to make it worse.'

'We fixed it last time.' She taps her chest. 'Me and Clive. We can fix it again. Yes, we can.'

'You're not Bob the fucking Builder. It's un-fixable, so leave it. He's not the man for me. I'm fed up with all the stupid complications, and the drama and the secrets.' I'm crying again and it's not really surprising. After all, I am fed up. 'Right now, I just want a bit of peace and quiet ... and then ...' I falter. 'I'll move on. Yes, I will.' A sob escapes at the very thought of it. 'I'll find someone else ... eventually. Someone normal ... with no fucking issues. Someone who cleans his car every Sunday, and loves his mum and dad, and watches football on the telly ... and ...'

'Bores you rigid,' Lucy adds knowingly. 'You've just described Tom.'

'Oh shut up.'

I pull away another length of toilet roll and while Lucy sits down again, sliding into a disgruntled silence, I sniff, blow my nose a few times and sob a little more

'What about Boyd?' she asks at last.

'Not him. He's not normal.'

'That's not what I mean and you know it. Boyd's still out there. I know he's been stalking you. Clive told me.'

She waits, obviously expecting me to provide the details. But I'm giving none. I have no idea how much she already knows, and no wish to stoke the fire with unnecessary information.

'So, what's going to happen now? Is Dan throwing you to the wolves?'

'No.'

'We should go to Spain, live with my mum for a few months, take on new identities, work in bars …'

'Stop it.' I cut in. 'I don't need to hide. Dan may be a twat, but he's not a bastard.'

'Well, I don't know about that …'

'He's going to have Boyd dealt with.'

'What? Like taken out?'

'Like warned off,' I correct her, although with Bill's involvement, I'm not entirely sure that'll be the end of it. 'I'm protected. He's not hanging me out to dry.'

'So, where's the protection?'

'Out there.' I point at the window.

'In the back yard?'

'Don't be stupid. Just somewhere out there.'

'You're sure?'

'Absolutely.'

'Well, I'm going to ask Clive about that …' She trails off into silence. Out of nowhere, a cloud of panic envelops her. I can practically see it billowing about her head. 'Oh my God … what do I do about Clive?'

'Nothing.'

Because there's no need. Clive's about to play his own part in this whole sorry masquerade. By the end of the evening, he'll have dumped her and she'll hate his guts. A wave of nausea rolls through my stomach, bringing with it a sudden urge to tell the truth. For a split second, a full and frank admission hovers precariously on my lips … but I swallow it back.

'If I carry on seeing him, it's going make things hard for you.'

'Don't be silly. We're all grown up. I'm not expecting you to split up with Clive just because of this. You don't have to worry about me. I can cope.'

'I couldn't break up with him anyway.'

A second wave. A second urge. In all the time I've known Lucy, I've never seen her fall for a man, not all the way, complete with hook, line and sinker. Please don't tell me she's gone and done it with Clive. Please, please, please …

'I think I'm in love,' she confesses quietly, almost embarrassed, and then a strange expression creeps across her face, half smile, half grimace. It's a little unsettling, as if she's got wind, and she's enjoying it. 'Yes,' she murmurs. 'I'm in love.'

If I wasn't fully aware of the impending romantic doom, I'd be jumping for joy right now. Instead, my heart threatens to break for both of them. They've been sucked into a disaster that belongs to me and Dan. Through no fault of their own, they're about to pay the price.

'He wants to see me tonight.'

'That's nice.'

The strange expression disappears, and I'm relieved … until concern arrives in its place.

'I'll stay in. You need company.'

Actually, that's the last thing I need. An evening with Lucy means a good few hours of acting, and I'm already exhausted by it all. But more than that, Clive needs to play his part as quickly as possible. As terrible as I feel, I need to help the process along.

'No, Lucy. Just go out with him.' I lay a hand on her thigh and magic up a concerned expression of my own. 'He's having a hard time. His best friend's in hospital. He's been under a lot of stress. He needs to see you. And don't try some hare-brained plan. No stupid interventions.'

Guilt flickers in her eyes. I've caught her in the act.

'It won't work,' I warn her. 'Last time, Dan wanted me back. This time … he doesn't.'

We sit in silence for a while, until Lucy finally slopes off to prepare herself for an ill-fated night out and I settle for unpacking my belongings. After dragging the suitcase into the bedroom, I set about stuffing combats, T-shirts, knickers and bras back into the drawers. With the job done, I perch on the end of the bed, gazing at a familiar room that's now woefully empty. There are no photographs on the bedside table, no knick-knacks strewn across the chest of drawers. The covers on the bed haven't been changed since I left, and there's a thin layer of dust on every surface. Neglected and half forgotten, it's the shell of a former life, but for the next few weeks, it'll have to do.

I close my eyes and think of Dan. It's only been a few hours since I last saw him and I'm already desperate to hear his voice again. Before I know it, the tears are back with a vengeance. I wipe them away and shake my head. This will never do. I need to get on with the show.

So, what would a truly heart-broken Maya Scotton do? Drink

wine, that's for sure. Fail to eat anything healthy, another certainty. Wallow in self-pity for a few days, take an inordinate number of baths … and finally go out on the pull. Well, I can easily manage the wine, wallowing and baths, but I've no intention of ever pretending to pull another man. That's a step too far. I'd love nothing more than to bury myself in painting, but seeing as everything's at Dan's apartment, that's currently impossible. I'm sure it'll be shipped over sooner or later, but in the meantime I need to keep myself busy.

In the absence of anything else to do, I opt for cleaning the kitchen, discovering along the way that Lucy wasn't wrong. There are things growing in the sink. In fact, it's a full-blown bio-hazard. I pull plates out of the bowl and scrape them into the bin, wash up every single dirty pot, mug and glass I can find, and wipe over the tops. When I'm satisfied with my efforts, I check the fridge, only to discover it's practically empty. Apart from a lump of mouldy cheese and a half-empty tub of spread, there's nothing. Not even milk. A trip to the local shop is in order.

I grab my purse and keys, open the front door and freeze. My old friends fear and anxiety are standing in the doorway, blocking my exit to the world. I remain motionless, telling myself I've spent far too much time under their spell. They're here now because of Boyd, but I'm not about to let them defeat me. With a deep breath, I shove them to one side and step out into the street.

Two hours later, I'm still chuffed to bits I made it to the shop and back in one piece. Okay, so I might have panicked a couple of times and I might have forgotten everything I went for, returning with four bottles of wine, three bars of chocolate and a slab of cheese. Fear and anxiety came along for the ride, but by the time I got back to the flat they were dragging their heels in my wake.

I'm pottering about in the kitchen again when the doorbell rings. I hear Lucy in the hallway, the front door opening, and I grit my teeth, wishing I could be anywhere else but here.

'Maya.'

Clive's voice greets me from the doorway, and he's not alone. Watching me carefully, as if I'm on the FBI's most wanted list, Lucy's standing by his side.

'Are you okay?' he asks.

I glance at Lucy. What would she expect right now? A good helping of hard-edged bitterness, I expect.

'Of course,' I scowl, coming up with the goods. 'Why wouldn't I be?' I point at the bottles of wine, ready and waiting on the table. 'I'll be drowning myself in that little lot before long. Don't worry about me.' And then, for effect, I add on a touch of break-up nastiness. 'Just worry about your twat of a friend.'

While Lucy baulks, Clive's face remains impassive, soaking up my fake vitriol.

'I'll just go and ...' Lucy hesitates. 'Sort out my make-up. Clive, are you coming?'

'No,' he answers, keeping his eyes fixed on me. 'I'll wait here.'

Lucy beats a hasty retreat. When he's satisfied she's holed up in her bedroom, Clive pushes the door shut, marches over to the sink, turns on the tap and motions for me to join him. As soon as I'm by his side, he pulls me down until my face is practically in the bowl. Leaning on the draining board, he moves in close.

'What are we doing?' I ask.

'The sound of water should mask our conversation,' he informs me seriously. 'If your place is bugged, they won't be able to hear what we say.'

'Did Foultons tell you to do this?'

'No, I saw it in a film.'

He's going totally over the top and I really should tell him that, but we don't have time.

'Are you really okay?' he asks.

'Like I said, I'm fine.'

'So what's all that about?' He motions back to the wine.

'Play acting.'

'Just make sure the truth doesn't dribble out when you're three sheets to the wind.'

'I'll be fine. How's Dan?'

'Same as this morning. Just worried about you.' He touches my arm. 'They're taking good care of him. You need to focus on the show ... and we need to crack on.'

'Are you definitely going to finish with her tonight?'

'Yes.'

'Shit.'

'It needs to be done and it needs to be public.' He watches a pigeon land on the sill outside. 'Just remember what I said. Don't let any other man get his mitts on her. She's mine.' He focusses on me, a little awkward. 'Listen, a couple of practicalities,' he goes on quickly. 'You'll be getting your wages from Fosters. It's not much, but you'll see another payment in your bank account. It's been channelled through a few places, but it's from Dan.'

'For what?'

9

'To keep you going.'

'How much?'

'You'll find out. If anyone asks, tell them Dan bought your last painting. Make out it's guilt money. He'll back up the story.'

'I can't take it.'

'You can and you will. There's a flat up for rent over the road. We'll be renting it through a third party. You'll be watched from there. Twenty-four seven. Whenever you go out, you'll be followed and tracked, discreetly. You'll never be alone. Not for one second.'

I gaze at the running water.

'This is real.'

'Yes, it is.' He fiddles with the tap, reducing the flow. 'And this is making me want a piss.'

We laugh quietly for a moment, and then he grows serious again.

'One more thing.' He's obviously not entirely comfortable with what he's about to say. 'Dan wants you to contact Layla.'

Oh Jesus, I could do without that.

'Me?'

'You're the only one who can do it.' He checks on the pigeon. Missing its footing, it staggers and flies off down the street. 'Sooner or later, she's going to find out about the accident. He doesn't want her showing up out of the blue.'

'But she's his sister.'

'We all know that.' He lowers his head, following the path of the pigeon's flight. 'I don't know why he won't see her.'

'I don't know either.'

'Well, somebody's got to contact her, and apparently you're the best person for the job.'

'Dan said that?'

'Yes. He wants you to pass on the news, make sure she's alright ... let her know she's not to get in touch.' He fiddles again with the tap.

'Great,' I mutter.

'He's sorry ... about the way he reacted to her. I know that much. But he's not ready to meet her yet.'

'What about Sophie?' I ask.

He cocks his head. 'What about her?'

'She's ill. That's why Layla came down. She wanted him to know.'

'What's wrong with her?'

'Breast cancer. They caught it early. Her odds are good, but ...'

Clive rubs his chin.

'Does Dan know about this?'

'I never got to tell him.'

'Fuck.'

'What are you going to do?'

'I don't know. I can't tell him. Not yet. Maybe when he's a bit stronger. He's having another operation, on his leg. After that, perhaps.'

Not for the first time today, I picture the man I love laid up in his hospital bed. No matter what I'm going through, it's far worse for him.

'How am I going to find out how he's doing?'

'You can't. No contact. We're both changing our mobile numbers. This is the last time we can talk for a while. It's going to be hard, but it's only temporary. A few days, a few weeks. Who knows?' He pauses. 'He loves you. I'm to make that perfectly clear.'

Leaving the tap to run, he reaches into his pocket, pulls out a tiny canister and hands it to me.

'What's this?'

'Mace spray. Just in case.' He reaches into his pocket again and gives me what looks like a small black key fob. 'And this is a personal alarm. You can't hide away here. You need to be out and about. If you're worried at any time, press the button.' He touches it lightly. 'You won't be alone.'

I examine the alarm. I can only hope it's never needed.

'We stuck to the story with the police,' Clive goes on. 'I don't know if they bought it, but there you go. We're searching for Boyd. Bill's coming over from Bermuda. He knows a few people.'

I think of Bill: on the surface, nothing more than a bright-eyed, harmless old man. But there's a dark undertow, complete with shady connections ... and the iron will to use them.

'I don't want anybody bumped off.'

'Nobody's being bumped off.'

We're interrupted by a banging door. Clive turns off the tap. A hint of panic flashes across his eyes.

'Ready for your performance?' he asks.

'Bring it on.'

We straighten up in unison.

'What the fuck are you two doing?' Lucy demands.

'I was feeling a bit sick,' I blurt quickly. 'Clive was helping me.'

'But ...'

Another ring at the doorbell causes all three of us to start. I'm grateful for the distraction. Lucy clearly doesn't believe a word I'm saying, and to top it off, she's just clocked the mace and the little black fob.

11

'I'll get it,' I announce.

Dumping my new possessions on the worktop, I make my way out into the hall and pull open the front door. I'm faced with an overly-happy delivery man, clutching a huge bunch of red roses.

'Maya Scotton?' he chirps.

'Yes.' A sliver of ice runs through my veins.

'These are for you. There's no card.'

Before I can tell him to sling his cheery hook, the roses are thrust into my hands. Without another word, Mr Happy gets back into his van, slams the door and starts the engine.

'Well, these aren't from Dan.' Clive cranes his neck over my shoulder, eyeing up the van, making a mental note of the company name. 'I'll look into it.'

'You won't find anything. He'll have covered his tracks.'

We both know who I'm talking about. Convinced he's won the latest battle, Boyd's making it obvious he's still around.

'They're going in that thing,' I announce, stepping out onto the pavement. Thank goodness the neighbours are busy with home improvements. There's a skip right outside our flat. In the most public way possible, I'm going to let Boyd know he certainly hasn't won the war. Far from it. With a dramatic flourish, I make a show of dropping the roses into the rubble.

Chapter Two

I hear a cough and take another furtive peek at the man who's currently examining a seascape. He's been here for almost as long as I have, picking over one painting after another. It's three days since I last saw Dan and I'm already descending into paranoia. My brain's on the rampage, wondering whether he's one of my protection team or some low-life Boyd's employed. With his slicked-back hair, brown corduroy jacket, striped polo shirt, neatly ironed jeans, and brogues, I settle for the third, most realistic option. He's nothing more than an innocent art lover, working his way through every single canvas in the place. Disregarding him, I look out over Frith Street, watching the bustle of Friday night in Soho, wishing I could return to a simple life, where everything was exactly as it seemed. But for now, at least, I'm lost in a world of pretence, conscious of every single movement, every last word, doubting everyone and everything. A car rolls past, slowly. Black and sleek with darkened windows, it pulls to a halt for a moment outside the gallery, and then moves on. My thoughts run riot again.

I close my eyes, summoning up the dream that's visited me for the past couple of nights. I'm back with Dan. I don't see him, but I smell him, taste him, feel him keenly, as if I'm wide awake and he's right there with me. My senses lap it up: the touch of his lips, his breath against mine, the delicious, tortuous waves of pleasure building inside as he thrusts. It's a nightly elixir that keeps me going. I can only hope it comes again tonight, and every night until we're reunited.

I hear the bang of a door and open my eyes. Lucy emerges from the kitchen, carrying a wine bottle and a couple of glasses. She casts a disdainful glance in the direction of the mysterious visitor and joins me at the front of the gallery.

'Right, I'm done.' She places the glasses on the table. 'It's Saturday. Let's get blasted.'

I stare at her in silence, wondering why the fact it's Saturday makes any difference. Ever since Wednesday night she's been on a mission to forget. An hour after flouncing out of the door with Clive, she staggered back in alone, transformed from a loved-up lust-puppet into a weeping, self-pitying shambles. Four bottles of Pinot Grigio just didn't stand a chance. Inevitably, three evenings have now disappeared under a mountain of used tissues, a thousand unanswerable questions, and even more wine.

'Why don't we go upstairs first? I'd like to see my new studio.'

After all, that's the main reason I'm here. My clothes have already been moved back to Camden. There wasn't the space for the canvases and paints. It was Lucy's idea to store them in a spare office above Slaters, the Steves' suggestion I use it as a temporary studio until the sale goes through.

'Later.' Opening the wine bottle, she fills the glasses. 'Drink.'

Eyeing up the wine, I silently wonder how much more I can take. Dragged along in Lucy's boozy wake, my brain's fried and my liver's threatening to implode.

'Where are the Steves?'

I pick up the glass. Reminding myself that a real post-break-up Maya Scotton would have slugged back the lot by now, I gulp down a mouthful and wince.

'Downstairs. Faffing.' Lucy slumps next to me. 'I texted Clive.'

'Not again, Luce.'

'I couldn't help it.'

Honestly, I could give her a good shake. Nothing too violent. Just a quick 'snap out of it' shake, followed by a well-meant slap on the cheek. After all, by my calculations, this is the fourth time she's texted Clive. I stare at my mess of a friend, deciding she's like a pinball, mercilessly flung from one flipper to another, veering between anger, despair and desperation.

'He's only going to think you're a head case. Leave it.'

'I can't.'

'Why not?'

She shakes her head. 'Denial?'

'You didn't ask him to give it another go? Please tell me you didn't.'

'Well ...'

'Oh, Lucy. Did he reply?'

Of course he didn't. I already know that.

14

'He hasn't replied to any of them.'

'You're developing stalker tendencies.'

'It's not my fault I fell for him.'

Biting back the urge to scream, I decide it's time for another flick of the flippers. I can't deal with misery and desperation, not right now.

'Give up on being pathetic,' I suggest. 'Go back to anger. It's much more fun.'

'Is that where you are?'

'Not sure.'

Picking up her glass, she takes a gulp of wine and gazes out of the window, watching a loved-up couple as they amble past, hand in hand.

'Bastards. I'm too depressed to be angry.'

'Just give it a go. For me.'

She rolls her eyes. 'He's a shit.'

Not good enough. Way too half-hearted for my liking.

'You need to go that extra mile. How about he's a womanising shit?'

'Still sounds a bit lame.' She gulps back more wine.

'Okay, a lying, ruthless, heartless twat of a womanising shit?'

Her lips curl upwards. It's not much of a smile, but at least it's a start.

'I'll drink to that.'

We chink glasses and finish off our drinks.

'He's a bastard,' she exclaims, with a little more gusto. Leaning forward, she grabs the wine bottle and refills our glasses. 'In fact, he's a big bastard.'

'Excellent.'

I might just have got her on a roll.

'He's a big bastard shit,' she affirms, cranking up the volume.

'Fantastic.'

'An even bigger shit than Dan ... and that's saying something.'

I wince.

'An accountant ... called Clive. What the hell came over me?' She's got that mad dog look in her eyes now. 'He's the king of shits,' she half-shouts. 'The shitmeister!'

'Keep your voice down,' I hiss.

'Why?'

'There's a punter over there.'

'And? He's a man. Therefore he's a wanker. They're all a bunch of wankers.'

15

Oh Lord, I've set off something here, opened up a Pandora's Box of sweariness, and I'm not entirely sure I can keep it under control.

'Too loud,' I warn her. 'And too much swearing.'

'I can do much better than that.'

Oh, I know she can ... and that's what I'm scared of.

'They're a bunch of cun ...'

'Enough,' I snap loudly before she can finish.

'You wanted me to get angry.'

'Yes, but not with him. He might be about to buy a painting.'

'He's not buying anything.' She motions her glass towards the visitor. 'Look at his shoes.'

I check on the shoes and shrug. I have no idea how Lucy's learned to rate potential buyers based on their footwear.

'What's wrong with them?'

'Brogues,' she sneers, slamming her glass on the table. 'He's biding his time before he goes to Ronnie Scott's. Jazz hands.'

Splaying her fingers and waving her hands about, she laughs insanely.

'Have you told her yet?' Big Steve demands, appearing at the top of the stairs.

Lucy presses her lips together.

'Told her what?' I ask.

Saying nothing, Big Steve lowers himself onto the opposite sofa. Within seconds, there are more footsteps on the stairs. Little Steve joins us, collapsing into place next to his partner. Lucy picks up the wine bottle and shakes it. I have no idea why. It's clearly empty.

'Told her what?' I repeat.

'The sale's fallen through,' Little Steve grumbles.

'I'm sorry, Steve.' I've no idea which Steve I'm aiming my apology at, or why I'm apologising at all.

'You haven't told her, have you?' Big Steve glowers at Lucy.

She shakes her head.

'I was getting round to it.'

'Getting round to what?'

'Dan. He was the buyer. But he pulled out this morning.'

'Let's just say his name's dirt around here.' Little Steve grimaces. 'Don't get me wrong. I feel for the poor man.' He swats a hand through the air. 'But why throw away everything decent in your life?'

'We were all sworn to secrecy,' Lucy explains sheepishly. 'He put in an offer soon after he met you. He wanted it to be a surprise.'

'And now it's all gone to rat shit.' Little Steve purses his lips. For the time being, he says nothing else. Instead, he gazes into space as if he's contemplating all the evils in the world.

It gives me time to wonder what on Earth possessed Dan to put in an offer so soon. Was it to please me, to showcase my work? Or was I nothing more than a catalyst, inadvertently triggering some half-formed plan to move on with his life? Maybe it was a measure of his commitment to me, his faith in us. I have no idea what caused it, and no way of finding out ... not yet. But whatever it was, I shouldn't be surprised. Rushing headlong into things is just his way – a simple fact I've come to understand.

'Oh well,' Big Steve sighs, knocking me out of my thoughts. 'We've got someone else interested now, but I'm not holding out much hope.'

Someone else?

'Who?' I ask.

'An American chap.'

'That's what you said last time.'

'And this time it's true,' Lucy confirms. 'It's a real American chap. He's got a couple of galleries in Manhattan.'

'Well ...' I press on, trying to say all the things I ought to. 'That bodes well. At least he knows his art from his arse.'

Little Steve shakes his head. 'Dan knew this art from his arse.' He motions toward Brogue Man. 'He was going to keep Slaters going as it is. Lucy in charge. But this new bloke. Jesus, who knows?'

Another miserable silence ensues and I make the most of it, getting back to the job of trying to make sense of it all, quickly coming to the obvious conclusion: buying Slaters right now would be a step too far. Dan can't be seen to have anything to do with me, but there's no way he's pulling out completely. This new buyer must be some sort of holding arrangement. Don't believe what you see, I remind myself, and don't believe what you hear. It's all part of the charade.

'Right then.' Big Steve claps his hands. 'Maya's come to see upstairs. We'd better get on with it.' He touches Little Steve on the arm. 'You stay here, my love, and keep an eye on that one.' He nods to the art lover.

'You'll have to go through my back passage,' Little Steve laughs. 'It's terribly grim and grotty. Good luck.'

Feeling a little unsteady on my feet after the wine, I follow Big Steve and Lucy down to the basement office and through a mysterious door at the back. Tentatively, we navigate a path past several musty cardboard boxes, and climb an ancient, rusting spiral

17

staircase that takes us back up past the ground floor, to the space above.

'So, this is it.' Big Steve pushes open a second door. 'Barry's office.'

He steps into the 'office', followed by Lucy. Bringing up the rear, I inspect my surroundings: a long room, complete with wooden floor, windows at each end and another door at the back. Originally whitewashed, years of neglect have left the walls slightly discoloured, the paint peeling off in places.

'You've got a separate entrance here.' Big Steve nods at the door. 'Very dangerous steps down to the back. They're a death trap. Barry used them, but he's an old daredevil.'

'Who's Barry?'

'A theatrical agent. This was the hub of his empire. He mostly dealt with has-beens, but he's retired now. He put it up for sale and he who shall not be named saw the opportunity to expand.' He pauses, raising an eyebrow. 'Anyway, Barry's willing to hang on for another buyer. Nobody wants a room like this on its own, but linked to the gallery, it's a sure-fire sale.'

'Is the American interested?'

'Yes, but you can use the place for now. Barry's fine about it. He'll let us do anything. Oh look, he's left a present.' Scooting over to a wall, he lifts a calendar away from a screw. 'Kittens. He's left it on March. That's bad luck. What is it now? July?'

Big Steve flips the calendar to the correct month, and I wander round the room, noting the fact that my painting gear's stored at the front, a couple of crates in one corner, canvases lined up against a wall. My triptych's there, arranged in order and begging to be finished. Doing my best to ignore it, I turn away, assessing the potential. It's roomy, that's for sure. And the light's good enough. All in all, it's a bright, calm space. I could definitely work in here. Until everything's sorted and I can go back to my studio in Lambeth, this will do just fine.

'Lucy tells me you haven't painted since the accident.'

I shake my head. Lucy's standing in front of the triptych now, unusually quiet. I move to her side, fixing my attention on the left-hand canvas. Pleasure. And then the right. Pain. In a flash, it all floods back, the night he stood me in front of these pictures, understanding me completely, telling me I deserved to be loved. I home in on the centre panel, all too aware of a stabbing sensation in my stomach. My throat's constricting and tears are threatening to betray me. I knew this would happen. The moment I laid eyes on it, I was bound to fall to pieces. Struggling to keep control, I study his body: the muscular form, the taut chest, the mop of blond hair, his face turned towards pleasure.

'You need to finish this,' Lucy murmurs. 'I know it's painful, but ...'

'I agree.' Big Steve adds. 'Creativity's a wonderful thing. Good for the broken heart.'

A few moments pass in silence.

'So,' Lucy breathes. 'You'll work here?'

'Yes.' My eyes are still fixed on Dan. In spite of all my previous reservations about the triptych, I'm almost excited. It's the right thing to do. I need to paint again because apart from Dan, it's the only thing that makes me feel alive. And what's more, while I'm finishing off the triptych, I'll feel as if he's with me.

'Good. Starting on Monday, we'll come into work together. I'll know you're painting ... and I'll know you're safe.'

With my agreement in place, we close up the room and wind our way back down the staircase, through the passageway, the office and back up to the main floor of the gallery. While the Steves slope off to the kitchen, Lucy slumps back onto the sofa and I join her.

And then it happens. Slowly, very slowly, Brogue Man inches towards us. I watch him out of the corner of my eye.

'Nice paintings,' he says.

'Yeah, they are,' Lucy agrees, barely paying attention. 'I don't suppose you're buying though.'

'I might do.' He checks his watch.

'Ronnie Scott's,' Lucy whispers out of the side of her mouth. 'What did I say?'

'Well, I'd better go. Are you two off out tonight?'

'Who wants to know?' Lucy demands.

'Me. That's why I'm asking.'

'We weren't planning on it,' Lucy snarls.

'Oh.' He shuffles about a bit. 'You should. There's a new bar down the road. Really nice. Mangans. Good music.' He winks at me. 'You'd like it.'

Half an hour later and much against Lucy's wishes, we're sitting in Mangans, a distinctly upmarket wine bar. Reclining on a plush sofa and fighting for space with a bunch of cushions, we nurse two glasses of wine that have set us back nearly twenty pounds.

'Rich people.' Lucy scowls at the clientele. 'Rich people everywhere.'

19

She's right. We really don't fit in here. I scour the room, taking in the super skinny women and super smart men, and then I spot him, standing out like a sore thumb – the 'art lover' from Slaters. Propped up on his own collection of cushions, he's busy reading a newspaper.

'Why did we come here?' Lucy demands. 'This is shite.'

'It's posh.'

'Posh shite.'

And I'm not prepared to leave, not yet. For a start, there's no way I'm about to abandon a glass of wine that cost the best part of a tenner. But more than that, I'm determined to find out exactly why the brogue-wearing jazz fan wanted us here.

'I like it,' I mutter.

'Really? It's bloody expensive, and there's no totty, and oh God, it's him.' She nods toward Brogue Man. Finishing his wine, he folds his paper and gets up. 'He's coming over. Make him go away.'

'Evening ladies,' he smiles. 'I told you it was nice.'

'Thanks for the tip-off.' I raise my glass.

'My pleasure.'

'So,' Lucy growls. 'Are you the owner? Or are you just trying to get into our knickers?'

'Neither. I just thought I'd pass on the recommendation.'

'Well, thank you. You can go now. We're lesbians.'

Brogue Man holds up his hands.

'I'm sure you are. Have a lovely evening.'

Almost as soon as he leaves, music kicks into life and warmth floods right through me. I recognise it immediately. The soaring strings are unmistakable. It's the very first song Dan played for me, on our very first date. I was right to follow my gut. The strange visitor to Slaters has lured us here so Dan can give me a message.

'What the hell is this?' Lucy demands, searching the air as if she can actually spot the chords.

'Ray Charles. 'You Don't Know Me'.' With a shaking hand, I put down my glass.

'It's miserable.' She turns to the bar and shouts. 'Can't we have something a bit more upbeat?'

'Shush,' I reprimand her. 'You're being rude again. Drink your wine.'

'Two pounds a gulp,' she complains, sliding into a bad-tempered silence.

Grateful for an end to the moaning, I listen to the song's progress, content in the knowledge that he's reminding me, in the only way he can, that nothing's changed. He's still there and he still loves me.

20

The rush of warmth subsides, quickly replaced by an onslaught of emotion. I've been teetering on the edge all day, and before I know it, I'm sobbing.

'What's wrong?' Lucy demands.

'Nothing.' I wave a hand at her. 'Just leave it. Please.'

While she plunges even further into a foul mood, I sob some more. And the next song doesn't help matters much. By the time Eva Cassidy's finished singing 'True Colors', I've dug out my handbag's entire supply of tissues, abusing them all to within an inch of their lives. I'm about to pay a visit to the toilet in search of a fresh supply when another song begins. It's something I don't recognise.

'What's this?' I ask, convinced that Dan's selection is already over.

'Mumford and Sons,' Lucy replies, bursting unexpectedly into her own fit of tears. "I'll Wait for You".'

Contentment creeps back onto my face and I give it free rein. I smile into space, at my uber-expensive glass of wine, and even at Lucy – although she doesn't notice. Finally, I smile at the man sitting at the next table. And then I focus on his face, registering the broken veins on his nose, the sallow skin and sunken eyes. There's something distinctly unsettling about him. He's paying me far too much attention, watching my every reaction with indifferent, scientific interest. At last, with a nod of satisfaction, he downs the last of his beer, stands up and leaves.

Chapter Three

It's dark, pitch black. But I know the feel of his body, the soft warmth of his skin, the hard muscles beneath. He's above me again, pinning me down while his cock moves inside, slow and unhurried, rubbing at the underside of my clitoris, the walls of my vagina, causing everything to flutter, quiver, and quake.

'Dan?'

He says nothing. Instead, he seals his lips around mine, delivering a perfect, possessive kiss. In an instant, all too soon, I'm caught in the throes of an intense orgasm that jolts me back to consciousness. Fighting for breath, my crotch still throbbing, I reach out and run a hand over an unused pillow, the cold half of the bed sheets, expecting to find him next to me. But all too quickly, memory puts me firmly in my place.

He's not here.

Wide awake now, I spend a few minutes gazing at the ceiling, conscious of the ache that's plagued me since I last saw him. In the short time we've known each other, he's become my drug of choice. The nightly dreams bring me a tiny dose, but they're never enough. And now he's been torn away from me, I'm suffering the consequences: a constant need consuming every waking thought; a craving that's never going to end.

An addiction.

Never a good thing. Body and brain conspiring to self-destruct in a desperate hunt for pleasure. I lean over, retrieving the necklace from its new hiding place in my bedside drawer. Is that what I've got with Dan, I wonder? Does the pleasure blind me to everything else? I watch as the silver chain slips through my fingers, shocked at the turn in my thoughts. There's no way I'm ever going to give up on him. I know that for sure. But while I'm stranded in the eye of the storm, before we're reunited and logic and reason are engulfed in his presence again, I'm determined to get some perspective.

I place the necklace back in the drawer and gently close it. Then I reach for my mobile, switching off the alarm before it kicks in. It's almost five o'clock. Sunlight's already playing against the curtains. Time to get up and get on with it, because today I'm on a mission. Today I'm going to Limmingham.

The journey to Liverpool Street is bad enough, nerves jittering with every bump in the road, but it's not until I'm finally disgorged from the taxi that the heebie-jeebies really set in. My heart rate triples, palms grow sweaty and my legs turn to blancmange, threatening to give way at any moment. Willing myself to get a grip, I hand over a twenty and make my way inside the station, focussing on the job in hand.

I find a cash machine, insert my card and tap in the PIN. As soon as the balance flashes in front of my eyes, I catch my breath. Thirty thousand pounds. I squint, lean forward, and check the balance again. Yes, there's no doubt about it. Thirty thousand pounds. A ridiculous amount of money. It makes me wonder just how long Dan thinks this is going to drag on. Resolving to spend as little as possible, I take out a hundred and queue up to buy a ticket to the east coast.

As soon as I reach the front of the queue, I become conscious of someone standing behind me, uncomfortably close, possibly making a mental note of my destination. I check on my shadow, discovering a middle-aged man who's dressed in jeans, a white T-shirt and a denim jacket. Clearly fit, he's an ideal candidate for Team Dan, and he gives me a small smile. Feeling reassured, I grab the ticket and weave a path through the crowds.

Under the bright lights of the station, I buy a takeaway coffee, head to the platform and step onto the train. Settling myself into a fairly busy carriage, I place the coffee on the table and rummage through my handbag, stopping to fiddle with the mace and the personal alarm, hoping I'll never need to use them. When I'm done, I dig out a magazine I've borrowed from Lucy.

It's not long before the train pulls out. As the clutter of central London thins out into the sprawl of the suburbs, I scan my fellow passengers, registering a family at the far end, a pair of elderly ladies gossiping, an unkempt youth; a rough type, barely washed. The door behind me slides open, and I'm joined by my shadow from the ticket queue. He takes a seat a few rows away and stares out of the window. Turning my coffee cup on the table, I do the same. Eventually, I go back to the magazine, distracting myself with a good dose of celebrity gossip. I'm doing my best to focus on an article about some reality TV star when we pull into Limmingham.

Determined to fight the paranoia, I shove the magazine back into my bag and without looking back, make my way out of the tiny station. Avoiding the sea front road and the inevitable throngs of tourists, I navigate the back streets of town, past Victorian terraces and huge, opulent family homes. They soon give way to the modest, modern housing estate where my parents live. A quick visit to Mum and Dad is in order before I get down to the main business of the day.

I find the back door open, as usual, and the kitchen empty. They're in the living room, Dad asleep in an armchair and Mum stuck deep into a book. As soon as she spots me, she gives a jerk, dropping the book to the floor.

'Oh, for goodness sake,' she cries out, clapping a hand to her chest. 'Are you trying to kill me?'

Dad's roused. An eye slides open.

'Maya, what are you doing here?'

'Just visiting.'

'Oh, Lord,' Mum gasps. 'I wish you'd give us some warning.'

'Why don't you lock your back door?' I ask. 'Then you won't have people turning up out of the blue in your living room.'

Rolling her eyes, she pats the space next to her.

'Roger,' she snaps. 'More tea. Now! And fetch the biscuits.'

'I can't stay long,' I apologise, sinking onto the sofa next to Mum.

'You never can these days. What's brought you up here?' She checks over my shoulder. 'And where's Daniel?'

Without any further ado, I launch into my fabricated tale of woe, eager to get it over and done with. By the time Dad returns with the tea tray, I've come to an end and judging by the expression on his face, he's clearly been listening in from the kitchen. He places the tray on the coffee table, points back to the door, mumbles the word 'biscuits' and disappears again.

'So, that's it then,' I summarise, watching him go. 'Me and Lucy are free agents.'

'Both of you?' Mum asks, picking up her cup and saucer.

'Yes.'

'They've both dumped both of you?'

I gaze out of the French windows. It's begun to rain. I really should have brought an umbrella.

'Yes.'

24

She leans forward, grimacing, as if she's just drunk ditch water.
'But why?'

'It's personal, Mum.'

'It's because of this place,' she decides quickly. 'That's it. It's because you're from here, and he can't stand the memories.'

I shake my head. 'It's nothing to do with that.'

'So, what is it?' Her lips are wobbling now. 'I thought you'd found the one. I thought you were going to get married. I thought … Oh, I don't know what I thought.'

She waves the teacup in front of her face, and begins to cry. Oh great. That's all I need. I thought she'd opt for righteous indignation. I never expected tears.

'Mum, it didn't work out, that's all. You know what it's like.'

'No.' She shakes her head. 'I don't know. Roger … Roger was the only one. How can it not work out?'

'It just didn't.'

'And I thought he was such a lovely boy. I can't believe it.' Putting down her cup and saucer, she wipes her eyes. Her face clouds. She's obviously moving on to anger. 'If I could get my hands on him, I'd …' She bites her lip. 'I'd rip his bloody testicles off. He's an idiot. He's lost the best thing he's ever found.' She waves a finger. 'I know he's poorly and he's in hospital, and you shouldn't speak ill of the …'

'He's not dead,' I interrupt.

'I know that, but he's not worth it, Maya. That's what you've got to remember. It's not you. It's him.'

I cross my arms and stare at the tea tray, biting back a little anger of my own. It's not him at all. And he is worth it. And one day I'll be able to explain. Suddenly, I'm gripped by a need to defend the man I love. It's a good thing Dad appears in the doorway, clutching a biscuit tin.

'Roger, Dan's finished with Maya.'

'And Clive's finished with Lucy,' I add.

'Has he? Oh.' And that's it from Dad. Lowering himself back into his armchair, he opens the tin. 'Ginger nuts, malted milks, bourbons and custard creams. No digestives.'

'Your daughter's life's falling apart and all you can think about is biscuits?'

'Well, you've got to go on eating.'

He offers the tin to me. I wave it away.

'Explain,' Mum orders. 'Explain why he's dumped her.'

Dad's eyebrows wiggle. 'How can I explain?'

'Well, you're a man, aren't you? You should know what goes on in

25

men's brains.'

'I'm not so sure about that.' He helps himself to a custard cream. 'You trained it all out of me.'

He's about to get a good verbal mauling from Mum when the phone rings.

'That'll be for you, Audrey,' he says. 'The daily call. Pam from the reading circle.'

'Oh, for God's sake.' Rising to her feet, Mum stomps into the hallway, answers the phone and launches into a muffled rant.

'Are you alright?' Dad asks, biting into his biscuit.

'I'm fine.'

'If there's anything I can help you with ...'

'I don't need any help, Dad.'

He doesn't seem convinced.

'You're still my little girl. If you need anything ...'

'Honestly, I'm alright.'

He pops the rest of the biscuit into his mouth and chews thoughtfully.

'It's a shame,' he says at last. 'I liked him, I really did. I suppose it just wasn't to be.' He rummages through the tin and pulls out a bourbon. 'You'll find someone else. Don't worry. But you deserve the best, Maya. Remember that. Someone who can give you everything you need.'

'I don't need much.'

'Love, respect and friendship. Everyone needs that.'

'Have you heard from Sara?' I ask, eager to change the subject.

'She's losing her house, moving in with us for a while.'

My mouth falls open. I knew it was difficult for Sara, but I didn't know things had got this bad. I have no idea how Mum and Dad are going to cope with my sister and her feral boys.

'That's going to be interesting.'

'It'll be a bloody nightmare,' Dad grins. 'Temporary though. She's moving back to Limmingham, looking for a job, and then she'll rent. The kids are going to use your old bedroom.'

'Well, I'm not going to need it.'

'Staying in London then?'

'Of course.'

He bites into the bourbon and pulls a face, probably because he's never understood why I went to live in the capital. As far as he's concerned, it's full of ne'er-do-wells.

The telephone receiver's slammed down.

'Oh, here she comes. Have a biscuit. You're getting skinny.'

He thrusts the tin at me again. This time, I help myself to a malted milk and stare at it.

'Bloody Pam,' Mum almost spits. 'Going on about bloody books.'

Through a mouthful of bourbon, Dad gives out a sigh.

'She runs a reading circle, Audrey.'

'Well, there's no need to go on about bloody books at a time like this. We've got real life going on here. Oh, Maya.' She clasps her hands to her chest. 'You haven't got a job. You gave up your job.'

'I'm an artist, Mum. That's my job.'

'How can it be a job? What about security?'

I suppose I could tell her about the ridiculous sum of money that's recently landed in my bank account. That's security enough.

'I've sold another picture. I've got enough to keep me going. I need to focus on painting. I need to take a chance.'

Mum's face puckers.

'I've got to go,' I add quickly, before she can tell me that my painting's never going to amount to anything. 'I'm meeting someone. A friend.'

While Mum eyes me with more than a good dose of suspicion, I collect my handbag and make for the door.

'I'll see you soon.'

The rain hits me as soon as I step outside. Retreating just long enough to borrow an umbrella, I finally head off, relieved to escape my parents' attentions.

I choose the coast route this time, emerging onto the main stretch, crossing the road and following a cliff-top path down the hill, past the crazy golf course, bowling green and ornamental gardens, towards the centre of town. When I reach the first building, I pause. Holding the umbrella in one hand and grabbing the steel railings with the other, I look out over the North Sea. It's overwhelmingly grey beneath a darkening horizon. An endless mass of cloud rolls in, dragging the rain in its wake, but none of this seems to have dampened the spirits of the August holidaymakers. The beaches below are still busy with people sheltering from the showers beneath umbrellas, coats and beach tents. I smile at the grit of the British, determined to make the most of it, come what may.

'Penny for them?'

Jolted out of my reverie, I turn to find Layla standing by my side.

'They're not worth that much.' I'm transported back to Dan's kitchen garden, to the softness in his blue eyes when he asked me the very same question ... and I gave the very same reply. I shake the memory out of my head. I've got to think straight. I can't afford to be

27

distracted. 'How are you doing?'

'Not bad.'

Gripping her own umbrella, she stands fixed to the spot, clearly unsure of what to do next. It's up to me to give a little reassurance. Stepping forward and angling my umbrella to one side, I give her a one-armed hug.

'Shall we walk?' I ask.

'Why not?'

In silence, we take the slip road down to the promenade and walk southwards, past shops and arcades and cafés, all of them busy. I have no idea what Layla's thinking about as we move on, but I'm wondering exactly how to give her my news … and I'm dreading her reaction. By the time we reach the pier, the rain has stopped, and both of us have closed our umbrellas.

'Let's grab a bench.' I nod towards the Victorian hotels and flats that line the top of the cliff. 'How about up there?'

With a nod, Layla gives her agreement. We climb a steep, winding path back up to the top of the cliffs, and find a bench overlooking the sea.

'Prepared for everything.' Opening her handbag, Layla pulls out a tissue and wipes the seat. 'You don't want a wet bum.'

'Certainly not.'

I settle myself next to her, arranging my handbag and umbrella on the bench, and the thoughts in my head. I glance up at the sky where the clouds have parted now, albeit temporarily. And then I gaze out to sea again. Ever-changing under a restless sky, it's mutated into an olive green-grey, streaked with strips of deep blue.

'Oh, look at that.' Layla points to the right, where a rainbow's kicked into life above the cliffs. 'Make a wish.'

I wish for this to be easy.

'Happy families,' she observes, turning her attention to the beach. The promise of a tiny scrap of sun has lured the crowds back out of the cafés and beach huts. Already there are children paddling, making sandcastles, kicking balls about on the sand. 'I often wonder what goes on behind closed doors when I see people like this.'

'That's pretty cynical.'

'Is it any surprise? My dad was good at putting on an act in public, but once we got home …' She shakes her head. 'I'm sorry. I shouldn't go on about him.'

'Why not?'

We slip back into silence for a moment or two. A seagull wheels through the air in front of us, in search of a lunchtime chip.

'There are plenty of normal, happy families out there,' I press on, determined to be positive. 'You've got one of your own now.'

She smiles. 'Yes. But I'm determined. My kids are getting the best upbringing I can provide. All the love and care and attention. It's the best way to undo the past: break the cycle. But I suppose it's not always that easy.'

She's thinking about her brother. I know it. And even though we're fast approaching the inevitable, I'd like to put it off for a little longer.

'How's Sophie?' I ask.

'Starting chemo. I'm going over to visit next weekend. Should be interesting. We've talked on the phone, but I haven't seen her since she moved to Wales. She's talking about moving back to Limmingham. I think she's finding it hard on her own out there.' She pauses before going on, tentatively. 'And Dan?'

I clasp my hands together and say nothing. Out of the corner of my eye, I can see we've been joined by my shadow from the ticket queue. He lights up a cigarette, leans against the railings and stares at the pier.

'I'm so sorry about what happened, Maya. I wasn't thinking.'

'There's no need to apologise.'

'I shouldn't have turned up like that. Did you sort it out with him?'

I falter, fiddle with the umbrella. The moment has finally arrived.

'There's something I need to tell you,' I begin, searching for exactly the right words and finding nothing particularly helpful. 'He's had an accident.'

Too blunt, by far. I watch as shock takes hold of her face. Lips part and eyes widen. Before she panics, I need to allay her fears. Speaking quickly, I fill her in on what happened, tell her there's no need to worry, reassure her that her brother's alright. For all I know, I could be talking complete and utter bollocks, because the truth is I have no idea how he is at the minute. I'm simply working on assumptions. The shock seems to deepen. It's joined by confusion, along with a good dash of anger, and I know exactly why that's arrived.

'I'm sorry I didn't call you. I just couldn't … I should have called you. I know that.' And I also know I'm babbling. 'He's your brother and you had a right to know, but after what happened, I thought I should get his permission first, but he was unconscious and I had to wait, and I thought you had enough to deal with.'

'It's okay.'

'It's not, Layla. But I was caught between a rock and a hard place.'

She shakes her head.

'It's alright. I understand.' Reaching into her handbag, she pulls out a fresh tissue and wipes her eyes. 'But he's alright now?'

'On the mend. Past the worst of it. It's just broken bones. He'll be fine. He's still in hospital ...'

Absent-mindedly, she taps her umbrella.

'I should send him a card ... so he knows I care.'

'No. Listen to me. This isn't a good time for you to make contact. You need to be patient.'

'You're right. What am I thinking of? If I send him a card, it'll only end up in the bin.'

And now, out of nowhere, I'm angry with Dan. For the life of me, I can't work out why he won't face his sister. She's just about the nicest person I've ever met and as far as I know, she's never done anything to merit his contempt. I swallow back the irritation, reminding myself I have no right to be angry. After all, I'm not in possession of all the facts.

'I could give it to you,' Layla suggests. 'You could wait for the right time.'

I shake my head.

'I can't.'

'Why not?'

'We've split up.'

She stares at me, perplexed.

'He finished with me,' I explain. 'Because of what happened. Because I got in touch with you. When he woke up, he put an end to it.'

'Oh God.' She raises a hand to her mouth. 'Oh no, Maya. What have I done?' The poor woman. If it's not bad enough that her brother's in hospital and his relationship's apparently in tatters, she's now convinced the entire mess is her fault. 'I only wanted to make things better ... for all of us. We all feel like there's something missing. I know we do. Something here.' She touches her chest and drifts into thought. 'That bastard.'

For a split second, I think she's referring to Dan, but then she pulls a photo out of her handbag.

'He caused a lot of pain.'

She hands it to me. A picture of a man. Thick-set, dark-haired and bleary-eyed, he's smiling at the camera ... but I can see the cruelty in his eyes.

'My dad. You see the resemblance?'

It's obvious. While she has the same bright blue eyes as Dan, the rest of her features are clearly influenced by her father.

'Two peas in a pod,' I murmur, without thinking. 'No wonder Dan lost it.'

She blinks at my words, and I wish I could take them back.

'Why?' she whispers. 'That's all I ever wanted to know. Why did he treat us that way? Why was he such a pig? I never got the chance to find out. None of us did. I should have talked to him in those last few weeks. He was different then.'

'Different?'

'Quiet … miserable. You could almost see the shame in his eyes.'

'He was dying.'

'I don't think it was that. He changed after he got beaten up. He said he didn't know who'd done it, but I think he did. I think he finally realised he was a low life piece of shit. I should have made the most of it.' She becomes silent for a minute. 'It doesn't matter now, does it? He caused all that pain, fucked everything up, and now I've fucked it up even more. I'm sorry.'

Tears well in her eyes. I search through my handbag for more tissues and hand them to her, knowing exactly what's going to happen next. My brain's just flicked the 'fuck-it' switch and my mouth's planning on letting me down in style. I'm losing the will to deceive, because it's exhausting. And besides, I can practically see the guilt gnawing away at my companion. If I leave her like this, she'll only end up jumping on a train to London and ambushing her brother. I need to take a leap of faith and put her lifeline back in place. Hopefully, she'll believe me, find some comfort from the fact that nothing's ruined, and maybe discover a little patience. Whichever way it goes, I feel like I've got no choice.

'Okay.' Leaning in to her, I speak out of the corner of my mouth. 'I'm going to tell you something very strange now.'

She blows her nose, suppresses a sob and narrows her eyes.

'I don't want you to say a word,' I warn her. 'And I don't want you to react. I want you to just carry on as if you're upset. Do you understand?'

She frowns.

'I mean it, Layla. I'm not supposed to be telling you this. You're going to think I'm mad, but I'm not, and this is the truth. So just listen and say nothing. I've not really split up with Dan. It's only temporary and it's all an act.'

Leaving out my sister's involvement, and Jodie's too, I tell her almost everything, from Boyd tracing me, through his surprise

31

appearances, to what he did to Dan. I give her a moment to let it all sink in before I explain the upshot of it all.

'Boyd's told Dan to stay away from me. If we see each other, if we go to the police, he'll do something else. Don't worry, you're perfectly safe,' I lie, noticing the alarm in her eyes. 'He's only after me and Dan. We don't know what he's capable of, so we have no choice at the minute. We have to go along with it. So, officially, we've split up. Dan's ended it. And we need to make everyone believe that.'

'Have you been drinking?' she asks, goggle-eyed.

'I wish.' I fix her with a resolute stare. 'I'm not mad and I'm totally sober. This man tried to kill your brother. It's important you tell no one. I'm not supposed to talk about it, but you need the truth. And now I've given it to you, you need to keep it safe.'

She's still not convinced, and I could do with some proof. I look around. Thankfully, my shadow's still leaning against the railings.

'See him?' I nod in his direction. 'I think he's my protection. He'll turn round in a minute and check on me.' I open up my handbag and show her the contents. 'This is mace and that's a rape alarm. Dan's making me carry them. He wanted me to come and talk to you. You were going to find out about the accident sooner or later, and he's not ready to meet you.'

She twists the tissues in her fingers. A seagull lands by her feet and begins to pick at a discarded, soggy chip.

'But he will be one day. I know it.'

She locks eyes with me, as if she's searching for evidence.

'It's all true. On my life. But whether you believe me or not, you need to keep this quiet.'

She blinks a few times, then nods.

'Until this is all sorted, I can't go anywhere near him. I can't contact him. I can't talk to him. And it's killing me. But if I can do it, then you can do it too. I need you to be patient this time. I need you on my side.' I take in a deep, jittery lungful of sea air. 'Promise me, Layla. Say nothing. And don't text me or call me. I think Boyd's tapping my phone.'

The possibilities flash through her eyes.

'I won't,' she confirms at last. 'You can trust me.'

'Well, I'm relying on you. Just don't let me down.'

It's early evening. I'm on another train, nursing yet another coffee. As we wind our way back to London, I gaze at my reflection, wondering who the hell I'm looking at. This morning's nerves have disappeared. I've defied fear and I've defied Boyd. I haven't hidden and I haven't run. I'm certainly not the woman I used to be.

But why is that?

The answer comes immediately.

Dan.

An addiction? Yes. Without a doubt. But so much more than that. Since he first exploded into my life, I've been high on adrenalin, high on excitement and high on lust. And I wouldn't have it any other way. After all, if I hadn't lost myself in the madness, if I hadn't nudged aside the doubts, then I would never have fallen in love with the man beneath the veneer. And he's a man who gives me everything I need: love, respect and friendship, support, encouragement, protection, fidelity. The list is endless, each component worth its weight in gold. And mixed together, the final result is priceless – a one-off work of art, just like the necklace. It's because of him that I'm finally becoming myself, finding a strength I never knew I had. I study my reflection again. That's who I'm looking at. The Maya Scotton I always wanted to be.

And now I feel a little sick, a little foolish. I sit back, watching as the fenlands slip past and questions tumble about in my mind. Can I really trust Layla to keep quiet? Or have I just woven a massive weakness into the web? Now that I've realised, with absolute clarity, what I've found with Dan ... have I really just put it all at risk?

Chapter Four

Marooned in chaos, I've decided that today's the day for sorting things out. My poor combats and T-shirts must be completely confused. After living it up in a penthouse walk-in wardrobe, they're back in their usual downmarket surroundings, languishing in my bedroom alongside their snooty Harrods counterparts. Over the past few days, I've been slowly unpacking, half-heartedly opening one neatly taped-up box after another and rummaging through the contents, finding everything perfectly folded and rolled. Gina's obviously been roped in to organising the move. If she could see what I'm doing at the other end, she'd have a coronary. With the wardrobe now at bursting point, I move dresses and skirts from one place to another, sling shoes into a corner and make a pile of handbags under the window. I'm just glad the evening gown hasn't re-appeared. There's no room for eight thousand eight hundred pounds-worth of silk in a pokey Camden flat.

I open up the next box, temporarily halted by the fact that it isn't filled with clothes. And then I rifle through it, pulling out the laptop Dan gave me, the Kindle from the flight to Bermuda, a whole host of silly things I've hoarded from childhood and finally, my jewellery box. Lifting the lid, I discover the sweet pea earrings, jumbled in amongst a pile of cheaper jewellery. Reuniting them with the necklace, I place them carefully in their own section of the jewellery box, and leave the box on top of the chest of drawers. Finally, I pull out a small packet. It has my name written on it, in handwriting I don't recognise. I open it up and find a message from Clive.

'I can't sort out the CDs. Don't know which are yours and which are Dan's. He's told me to send you this for now. Track one. Eat this note as soon as you've read it!'

I pull out the CD, a compilation of John Lennon songs, and home in on track one, 'Woman'. Dan's favourite song. Immediately, the tears begin to flow.

'You're crying over a CD?' Lucy remarks from the doorway.

'It's just dusty in here.'

She laughs: a hard, I've-had-enough type of laugh.

'You see?' She points at me. 'This is what men do to us, the bastards.' Folding her arms, she surveys the semi-organised chaos through semi-focussed eyes. 'I'm cooking dinner,' she announces. 'And then we're getting off our faces.'

'But it's Tuesday.'

'And? What difference does it make?'

She slams the door behind her, leaving me to stew. I've already had enough of post-break-up Lucy. Sober, she's a nightmare. Drunk, complete hell. Hung-over, a strange mixture of the two. What I need now more than anything else is a serious detox, but judging by the way she's slurring her words, I'd say she's already made a pretty good start on the 'getting off your face' thing. A quiet evening in with a cup of tea is the last thing on the cards.

She's sitting at the kitchen table, surrounded by bowls and packets, empty tins and reams of onion skin. Right in front of her, a bag of flour seems to have exploded, sending its contents far and wide. On the hob, a pan filled with a strange, gooey mixture sits next to the frying pan. I take a couple of nervous steps forward, fixated on the goo. I'm not entirely sure what it is, but it's brown and lumpy and I suspect there's some sort of meat in there. It all smells a little odd. I turn back to Lucy. Wine glass in hand, she's currently eyeing up an aubergine.

'What's going on?' I ask, tentatively.

'Cooking.' She slams down the glass and picks up a knife.

'Is that what you call it?'

'That's what everyone calls it.' She points the knife at the half-destroyed bag of flour. 'Ingredients.' And then at the hob. 'Heat source. Cooking.'

'And what do you think you're cooking?'

'Moussaka.'

A serious case of trying to run before you can walk. And when it comes to cooking, in Lucy's case she's barely at the crawling stage. This is a full-blown disaster in the making, worse than anything I'd expected. Self-pity and anger, swathes of alcohol, hours of ranting. They've all been a given. But I've never foreseen this new-found obsession with transforming herself into a domestic goddess. She

35

refills her glass, taps her phone and grabs the aubergine.

Gloria Gaynor begins to blare out. 'I Will Survive'.

'Do you really think this is wise?' I shout over the din.

'I'm working to a recipe,' she shouts back, waving at an ancient, tatty book that's half hidden underneath the chaos. 'What could go wrong?'

Everything. That's what I'd like to say. But I'm already in fear of my life. In a strange sort of trance, my flatmate begins to slice into the aubergine. And then she begins to sing along with Gloria … in a loud, defiant, totally out of tune voice.

'When your life falls to pieces, Maya, you've got to find a hobby. And my hobby is cooking.'

'Shit.'

I watch as the aubergine's hacked and stabbed and sliced. When she's finished, she pushes back her chair, carries the chopping board over to the hob and sets about flinging the bits into the frying pan, adding industrial quantities of oil along the way. I move over to the window, pull back the net curtain and gaze at the row of terraced houses across the street. I've no idea which one's being rented. I've noticed no movement over the last three days, and despite Clive's reassurances, I'm not entirely sure anyone's installed there yet.

At last, the song comes to an end and thankfully Lucy's too preoccupied with frying the hell out of vegetables to select another.

'What are you looking at?' she demands.

'Nothing.' I drop the curtains and sit down at the rickety table. 'Couldn't you find a different hobby?'

Flipping the aubergine slices with a spatula, she shakes her head.

'What about knitting?' I ask.

'What about it?'

'It's less dangerous for a start.'

'Bollocks to knitting.' She retrieves her glass and swigs back more wine.

'So,' I venture. 'This is moving on, is it?'

'No.' She turns up the heat on the pan of brown goo. 'I think this is me distracting myself from the fact that any human being with a penis is a penis.'

And that confirms it. She's finally moved out of shock. Bypassing denial, she's gone straight for anger, and this is going to be a painfully long night unless I can find some sort of diversion. Perhaps I should make a start on the 'look at me, I'm moving on' stage of the exercise. After all, it's what any heart-broken twenty-something would do: gather their wits, slap on the make-up and get on with it.

'Maybe we should go out,' I suggest, silently terrified of what's happening in the saucepan now. The brown goo's begun to bubble, violently.

'What for?'

'Dinner? And then perhaps we might enjoy ourselves.'

She grimaces in disgust.

'If you think I'm going to flirt, you can forget it.'

'Enjoying ourselves doesn't necessarily mean men.'

'Because I'm not picking up another of those bastards,' she goes on, ignoring my words of wisdom. She waves the spatula, sending dollops of oil across the linoleum.

'That's not the intention.'

Deciding I'd better clean up the mess before someone goes arse over watercress, I collect a dishcloth, drop to my knees and begin to scrub. As soon as I make a start, I realise that getting this close to the kitchen floor is a huge mistake. It should carry a public health warning.

'We could just go out and dance.' And drain some of that pent-up frustration out of you, while we're at it.

I'm pretty sure she's about to tell me to get stuffed when the doorbell rings. She gives a start and stares towards the hall.

'Who's that?' she demands.

'I don't know. I can't see through walls.'

'Probably another bunch of roses from McPsycopath.'

'And they can go straight in the skip.'

Leaving Lucy with her pots of dubious matter, I go out into the hallway, preparing myself to tell some feckless flower deliveryman to take the roses and stick them where the sun doesn't shine.

I tug open the front door, open my mouth, and clamp it shut again, silenced by the sight of Skinny Lily Babbage posing on my doorstep in a ridiculously tiny grey dress, topped with a white jacket. For a few seconds, my heart trips with excitement. I'd love nothing more than to throw my arms around the woman and hug the life out of her, probably breaking a few bones in the process. And then I'd love to grill her for news on Dan. But I can't, I remind myself, because Lily Babbage is on the wrong side of the smokescreen ... and I need to get into character.

'What do you want?' I snarl.

She rearranges the designer handbag on her arm.

'I want to talk.'

'There's nothing to talk about.'

'There's plenty to talk about.'

From the way she's looking at me, her thin lips set into a line, it's perfectly clear she's not about to cave. Maybe it would be easier to beg.

'Please, Lily. Just leave it.'

I begin to close the door, but she's surprisingly quick for a stick insect. In an instant, the handbag's wedged in the doorway, and so is a distinctly expensive shoe.

'I've waited as long as I can.' I've never seen her hazel eyes so hard, so determined. 'And before you start, Dan's definitely not sent me this time. And I need to have my say.'

I pull back the door and roll my eyes.

'Go ahead, but be quick. I'm busy.'

'You two are made for each other.'

'Is that it?'

'No, it's not.' She waves a manicured finger at me. 'You're the fucking love of his life, and he's making a huge mistake.'

As nonchalance is the name of the day, I take a moment to battle back the surprise. It's not easy. Never in a million years did I ever expect to hear the F word coming out of that refined little mouth.

'And I'm not prepared to stand by and let this happen,' she continues. 'I've only waited this long because I thought he'd change his mind, but the stupid sod's still digging his feet in. Now, let's talk.'

We exchange glares, real from her side, fake from mine. I can't risk Lucy getting involved in this. In her current state, I'll never hear the end of it. No, I need to keep Lily out of the flat.

'Wait a minute,' I growl. 'I'll get my jacket. Let's go for a walk.'

Skinny Lily narrows her eyes, thinks for a moment, and then nods. As soon as she removes the stiletto and the handbag, I slam the door on her.

Making a detour to the kitchen, I find Lucy pouring more oil into the frying pan.

'Jesus, these things soak up the fat,' she virtually spits. 'What a load of sodding effort for a stupid, sodding moussaka.'

'How long until dinner?'

'Dunno.' She tips even more oil into the pan. 'An hour? Two, maybe? Three?' Giving up on the oil, she downs another mouthful of wine.

'I'm just nipping out for a while.'

She squints at me.

'Where to? Who's at the door?'

'Nobody. A salesman. He's gone. I'm going to get more wine. If we're staying in, we're going to need it. I thought I'd go up the High

Street and get something nice ... to go with the moussaka.'

I wave at the hob and Lucy stares at me as if I've completely lost it. We both know the moussaka's going to be an unmitigated disaster, and no amount of fine wine's going to make it remotely edible.

'Fair enough.' She picks up a spoon and stirs the goo.

Leaving Lucy to it, I grab a jacket and my handbag, and slip out of the front door. I motion for Lily to follow and walk to the end of the road, listening to the sound of her designer heels clacking against the pavement.

'Coffee?' I suggest.

'Why not?'

Before long, we come across the first café on the High Street, a small, ramshackle affair that seems to have been thrown together with no planning whatsoever. Pushing open the door, I'm greeted by a wave of warmth, the aroma of coffee and the dark eyes of a surly barista. I gaze around at a gathering of mismatched tables and chairs, walls adorned with flyers and tatty posters and a huge, ornate, gold-framed mirror near the window. Noting we're alone, I order cappuccinos while Lily settles herself in the window seat. After a good deal of faffing, the surly barista presents me with two cups of coffee, each one decorated with chocolate sprinkle heart. I hand over the money, take the cups to the table and sit opposite Lily. With the huge mirror directly behind her, I'm going to be only too aware of every last bit of my bad acting.

The door swings open again, letting in a draught of cold air along with another customer. Anxious now, I watch as he orders a coffee and sits close by, checking his mobile. He's in his forties, greasy-haired, dull-eyed and sporting a podgy stomach. A prime candidate for team Boyd.

'So,' Lily begins, a little too loud for my liking. 'What's going on?'

'We're having a coffee.'

'Don't be facetious, Maya. You know what I mean.'

'Of course I do.' I pick up a teaspoon and slice it through the heart, destroying it completely.

'I know he ended it this time.'

'He did.'

'Why?'

'Ask him.'

'I did.'

'So, what did he say?'

'He told me to mind my own business.'

Typical Dan, explaining nothing.

'Well then, you should do what he says.'

Her perfectly made-up face mutates into a scowl.

'He was in love with you, head over heels. I've never seen him like that before.'

'Things can change.'

'Things can change?' she repeats incredulously. 'Maya, he went from wanting to marry you to nothing. Zilch. Nada. What happened?'

Trying to dupe Lucy is one thing. A self-obsessed flat mate, lost in an alcohol-fuelled ride through break-up land, is an easy thing to deal with. But Lily Babbage is something else. Totally fixated on her task, as sharp as a razor and most probably an expert in reading micro-expressions to boot, she's locked into a thoroughly sober mission – to reunite Daniel Foster with Maya Scotton.

'I did something I shouldn't have done,' I state, careful to keep my tone flat, willing my face to stay absolutely still.

Her eyes flicker.

'You cheated on him?'

Good God, she's got a low opinion of me.

'No,' I glower.

'Then what?'

Wrestling my face under control, I continue. 'It's not my place to tell you. It's between me and Dan.' But that's clearly not enough. Two perfect vertical lines have appeared between her brows. I'm going to have to give a little more. 'I did something he can't forgive, and that's that.' And then, for good measure, I add on the next bit with an apathetic shrug. 'He'll find someone else.'

Just the idea of Dan ever finding someone else delivers a wave of disgust to my gut. He's mine, all mine, and no other woman's ever getting her hands on him ... ever.

'So, you're giving up then?'

She picks up her cup. Extending her little finger ever so slightly, she takes a tentative sip, winces and lowers the cup again, revealing a tiny coffee moustache.

'There's no point in fighting. Not this time. It's well and truly over. That's all I'm prepared to say. It's private.' I force out a dramatic sigh. 'Frankly, I'm surprised you've waited this long to come and harass me.'

'Dan told me not to, and so did Clive, but I've run out of patience.'

'Already? It's only been three days.'

And now I can't help myself. The first contact with someone

who's still in his orbit, and I'm overwhelmed by the need for news. I'll just have to do it subtly, in a way that doesn't arouse suspicion.

'How is he?'

Well, bugger it. That's not subtle at all.

Lily's eyes flash. 'Ah, you still care then?'

'No ... I mean yes. Of course I do. I want him to be alright, but that doesn't mean I want him back.'

She raises an eyebrow and I'm swallowed by panic. Am I giving the game away? Yes, probably. And that means only one thing: I need to come up with something else, and I need to come up with it now. Opening my mouth, I begin to ramble.

'I can't live with him, Lily. I just can't deal with him. He hides too much, and he certainly can't deal with me. I wanted him to be more open and he couldn't do it.' I sip at my coffee. 'So, back to my question. How is he?'

'Recovering,' she answers, keeping her gaze levelled on me. 'He's in plaster now. Both arms, left leg. He had another operation on his right leg yesterday.'

'It went well?'

'They're happy with the results.'

She turns her cup on the table, and I know there's something else.

'I sat with him afterwards.' She eyes me closely. 'I don't know what sort of pain relief they were giving him, but it must have been pretty strong stuff.'

I pick up a teaspoon and tap it against the side of my cup.

'It certainly loosened his tongue.'

The teaspoon stops moving. Sitting absolutely still, I wait for the next bit.

'He kept asking for you.'

A prick of panic at the back of my brain. I drop the spoon. Here's me, doing my level best to deceive the world and its dog. And there's Dan, blabbing it all out under the influence of grade A narcotics.

'Now, why would he do that?' She leans forward, catching the edge of her jacket in a pool of coffee. 'Why would he dump the love of his life, and then ask for her ... again and again.'

'No idea.' I falter. 'His brain was obviously scrambled.'

'Well, that's what Clive said.' She leans further forward. 'But I've got another idea. He's made a mistake. The biggest mistake of his life.'

'Too bad for him.'

'I think he wants you back.'

'It's too late. What's done is done and all that shit.'

'Oh Maya. You know, you're really crap at the hard bitch act.'

I shrug.

'It's not an act. He's burnt his bridges.' I try out a smile. Jesus, this is killing me. 'Even if he has changed his mind, I'm not taking him back.'

Lily sits back. Running her fingers around the edge of her cup, she probes me with those dark eyes. At last, she seems to reach a conclusion.

'Wooden acting, a thoroughly terrible script ... and an awful storyline.'

'Pardon?'

'This show. I'm asking for my money back.'

I say nothing. My heart's beating against my rib cage. Please don't tell me I've already been rumbled. I've only just started my acting career, and I already seem to be on the verge of crash and burn. I take another sip of coffee.

'Let's not go on about it.' I wipe my mouth with the back of my hand. No matter what else is going on, I'm not going to make a fool of myself with my own coffee moustache.

'What else is there to go on about?' Lily demands.

'How about you?'

'What about me?'

'You were seeing someone.'

'Still am.'

'Lucky you.'

She shrugs off my attempts to change the conversation.

'I'll get you and Dan back together. I'm determined. I'll just give him a while, and then I'll start to work on him.'

Oh Lord, that's all he needs.

'Don't,' I snap. Because he's got enough to deal with. 'You know what he's like. Once he makes up his mind, that's it.'

'And he can get things wrong,' she snaps back.

I roll my eyes.

'He's messed me about once too often, Lily. You can say what you like and think what you like, but I'm telling you, I'm done with him.'

She leans down, opens her handbag and pulls out a notepad and pen. She scribbles down a number, tears out the page and hands it to me.

'Here you go.'

'What's this?'

'My number.' Pursing her perfect little lips, she shoves the pen and notepad back into her bag. 'For when you change your mind.

Just get in touch.'

Without another word, she gets up, pushes back her chair and makes an exit, leaving me to stare at my reflection. My hair's all over the place. My skin's pale. Too much booze, not enough sleep, endless worry about Dan, a constant fight against the growing ache inside. No wonder I'm a mess.

'So, that went well,' I tell myself, remembering all too late that I'm not alone.

The man at the next table looks up from his mobile, holding eye contact for a few seconds before he too gets up and leaves.

I stop off for wine and make my way back down the High Street, peering over my shoulder every now and then, eyeing every single stranger who passes me. The man in the café is playing on my mind. It may be a fact that Dan's never very far away … but then again, neither is Boyd. Shifting about in the shadows, he's the cat and the mouse in this game, and it hits me again – wherever I go, whatever I do, I need to be constantly on guard.

I hear the music even before I reach the front door. Sliding the key into the lock, I'm greeted by a wall of sound, and a further wall of smell. I find Lucy slumped on a chair, a half-finished glass of wine in her hand, her head dipped. I can't hear it above the sound of Adele's 'Someone Like You', but I know she's crying. Her shoulders are practically vibrating. I hit the stop button on her mobile and switch my attention to the frying pan. The brown goo's transformed into a congealed, blackened mess – and it's on the verge of catching fire.

'What is this?' I ask, turning off the gas.

'It was lamb,' she sobs, lifting her head. 'And now it's a mess.' She blows out a breath. 'Everything's a mess.'

The urge to tell her the truth is almost overwhelming. I'm torturing my best friend by holding it back, and I hate myself for doing it. But judging by the state of her, if I let her know that Clive's not lost, she'll be off to see him in a heartbeat.

Very carefully, I prise the wine glass out of her hand, ease her off the chair and guide her to her bedroom. Once she's tucked up in bed, I fetch the John Lennon CD from my bedroom, take it to the living room and slot it into the CD player. Locating track one, I lower the volume and listen. I know the song well. In each verse, Lennon struggles to say those three little words until finally, they come spilling out into the open, again and again.

Dan's talking to me through music. He's done it before and he'll do it again. He loves his woman … and he always will.

43

Chapter Five

A good five hours of painting done today. Oblivious to the world and pausing only for cups of tea, I've been caught in a trance. But now I'm exhausted. It's time to stop for the day. Perched on a stool, brush in hand, I stare at the calendar. Complete with three kittens in a basket, all glassy-eyed, October stares back at me. I lean over, flipping the calendar back to August and September, where I began to mark off each day with a blob of paint, a practice I quickly abandoned when I realised so many of the bloody things were slipping past. Since then, I've paid little attention to time, barely noticing when it switched up a gear and took the fast lane. But today, of all days, it's not willing to be ignored.

'Happy fucking birthday,' I mutter, thinking of the three cards sitting at home, one from Mum and Dad, one from Sara, and one from Lucy. I'm not surprised there's nothing from Dan. After all, since the songs were played at Mangans, there's been absolutely no contact. For some reason – and there must be a good one - he's opted for silence.

I get up, move to the window and watch the clouds scudding across the sky. Two months in limbo. Two whole months since I last saw him. I can barely believe it. I've watched summer retreat and autumn quietly take its place, breathing a last rush of colour through the trees: red, gold, bronze and yellow. It's in full force now, but it won't last long. The leaves are already losing their grip on life, spiralling to the ground in ever increasing numbers.

I've spent the days here at Slaters, burying myself in painting. Nights and weekends, holed up in Camden, slugging back unhealthy quantities of wine, suffering through Lucy's new-found obsession with cooking, and half-watching an endless stream of soppy films. It's an uninspiring story, punctuated by the odd outing to a pub and regular deliveries of roses, all quickly consigned to the neighbour's skip. And all the time the ache has grown, consuming every part of me. There's no relief from it, not even in sleep. Over the past few weeks, Dan's presence has faded from my dreams.

No wonder frustration's a constant companion, plaguing every waking moment and blitzing me with countless questions, unending possibilities. It's prompted me to search the internet, and that hasn't helped matters. I've found nothing apart from a brief article about the CEO of Fosters recovering from a motorbike accident, and rumours of expansion. More than once I've picked up the phone to call Lily, always stopping before I go too far. It's a bloody miracle I've somehow managed to keep a hold on faith, clutching at it like a comfort blanket. But it's tattered now, worn and fraying at the edges. I'm beginning to doubt my own memories of what happened, the promises he made. I'm beginning to doubt everything.

I hear a door bang down below, the sound of voices in the stairwell. Giving up on the grotty Soho back street, I take my place back on the stool, and survey the room. Propped up at the far end, the triptych's finished, waiting for a suitable home. And it's lured me in a new direction, away from landscapes, further into the world of figure painting. I've been working on a series of self-portraits. Gazing repeatedly into an old mirror and using larger canvases, five feet by three, I've begun to mark out my time in isolation.

The first portrait's leaning against a wall next to the stairwell. I'm sitting on a couch, wearing a long grey dress, legs curled up beneath me, gazing out of an open window at a vibrant blue sky. Summer light floods in from outside, playing against the rough texture of an olive-green wall and illuminating my face. It's partly an experiment in still life, partly an exploration of composition. Leaving the space uncluttered to the right, I've focussed the details on the left-hand side. Beneath the window and next to the couch, there's a wooden three-legged stool, adorned with a simple jam jar filled with pure white sweet peas, all glowing against the shadows. I'm more than pleased with the end result, how the lines draw attention to the flowers, how I've captured the texture of a red throw on the couch, the delicacy of the sweet peas, the sheen of the glass jar.

And now I've moved on to a second picture. This time I'm wearing a black dress. On the floor in front of the couch, with my knees pulled up to my chest, I'm staring straight ahead, into nothing. The window's still open, but the light's weaker, colder, barely touching the uneven plaster of the wall. The jar of sweet peas remains on the stool, the flowers faded, limp and lifeless.

'Amazing work.'

I'm startled by a man's voice. It's deep and low, laced with an American accent. I find the owner standing in the doorway. Immaculately dressed in a tailored grey suit, he's tall and perfectly proportioned, with thick black hair that's a little overlong, giving him a rakish edge. His charcoal eyes sparkle with mischief. I take it all in, acknowledging the fact that he probably sends women wild in the head and weak at the knees ... but he doesn't have that effect on me. There's no quickening of the heart, no sharp intake of breath, no twinges down below. Thanks to Dan, I'm immune.

'I'm sorry ...'

'Gordon,' he beams, revealing two rows of perfect white teeth. 'Gordon Finn. Pleased to meet you.'

Striding forward, he holds out a hand. I slip my fingers into his, allowing him to squeeze the life out of them, while I wait for more information, but nothing arrives. He just carries on beaming and squeezing.

'Can I ask what you're doing up here? I don't mean to be rude. It's just that ...'

Just that what? I wonder. Just that you might be some hired nut-job coming after me on Boyd's behalf? Well that's a ridiculous notion. For a start, hired nut-jobs don't wear beyond-the-radar-expensive suits. And secondly, nobody comes up here without being shown the way by Lucy, or one of the Steves.

'I'm just taking a look around.' He releases my hand. 'Lucy said it was okay.'

Then I realise. He's American. Some American chap. It's been ages since I last asked about the gallery sale. The new buyer was being difficult, finding problems at every stage, and the longer the process dragged on, the more pissed-off the Steves became. Eventually, I thought it best to keep quiet. But now he's here, the prospective owner of Slaters. And there's a distinct possibility he's acting for Dan. A frisson of excitement kicks off in my gut. For the first time in weeks, I'm being offered a tiny scrap of hope, and it's my full intention to grab it.

'You're thinking of buying this place?'

He wanders down to the far end of the room, shoes clacking against the floorboards. 'No,' he says crisply, eyeing up the triptych. 'I am buying this place.'

'And you're only visiting now?'

'I'm a busy man.' He peeks out of the front window and returns to me. 'The owners were prepared to wait. I made them an offer they couldn't refuse. Don't let me hold you up.' He takes a few steps back, and then homes in on my current painting. As if someone's slipped a handful of crushed glass into his super expensive underpants, he's incapable of staying still for one minute. 'And that is amazing work.' He turns to the first portrait. 'And so is that. And the triptych ... well, that's phenomenal.'

Ignoring my quiet 'thank you,' he returns to the three canvases. Folding his arms, he chews at his bottom lip, taking in one panel after another before leaning in to examine the naked male torso in the middle.

'Daniel Foster,' I announce, watching him closely for any sign of recognition.

He straightens up.

'Who?' He seems genuinely perplexed.

'Daniel Foster,' I repeat, this time with a dash of uncertainty. 'My ex-boyfriend. Do you know him?'

'Should I?' From the frown on his face, it's pretty clear I've just asked a completely ridiculous question. 'Is he an actor? Or a model? He's certainly got the perfect body. Great abs. I wouldn't mind a set of those. He's got to be a model.'

'No.' I smile. Disappointment's sidling its way into my head. 'He's not an actor ... or a model. Just my ex-boyfriend. I thought you might know him.'

'Never heard of the guy.'

We lock eyes for a few seconds and while I have no idea what he's checking for, I'm busy hunting down a crack in the performance.

'Hello,' he says, tipping his head forward.

'Pardon?'

'Are you actually trying to read my thoughts?'

'No. Of course not.'

He shrugs.

'Well, I can confirm, absolutely and without any shadow of a doubt, that I do not know Daniel Foster.'

I open my mouth. I'm on the verge of asking for a 'cross your heart and hope to die', but that would be childish. While I'm still clinging on to a scrap of dignity, I'd better stay in control.

'So, what makes you think I know him?'

We lock eyes for a second time and I see no cracks, no flaws. Confident it won't be shown the door, disappointment takes a seat and makes itself thoroughly at home. Mr Finn's telling the truth.

'No idea.' I've gone too far. This random rich American thinks I'm an English lunatic. I need a decent excuse for my ridiculous

47

suggestion. 'He pulled out of buying this place. I thought he might have tipped you off.'

'My agent tipped me off. She doesn't know him either.'

'Oh.' Embarrassment floods through me. It's definitely time for a little back-tracking. 'I'm sorry. I'm a little out of sorts today.'

'Well, it is your birthday.'

'What?' I blink in disbelief. 'How did you ...'

And now I can't quite work out what I'm seeing. His eyes glimmer momentarily. He glances at my lips. I blink again, wondering if that's attraction on his part. It's impossible to tell. The expressions on his face move quickly too. I can't work out where one begins and another ends.

'Your friend downstairs. Lucy. She warned me the artist in residence seems to be in a foul mood. Birthday-related. Beware.' He shuffles from one foot to the other, finally returning to the triptych and leaving me relieved. At least he's not examining me. 'So this is you?'

'Yes.' The heat rises in my cheeks.

'And it's about?' He waves at all three panels.

'It's ...'

Oh God, no. I can't go into that.

'She's in pain.' He points at the left-hand canvas, and then at the right. 'And she's experiencing pleasure. And your Mr Foster's in the middle, making his choice.'

I'm totally exposed, and I've only got myself to blame. Mr Finn's spent less than five minutes in my company and he already knows what I look like naked. And on top of that, he'll have guessed plenty about my sex life. If I'm not a deep shade of crimson by now, I must be at least bright pink.

'I'm loving your style, Miss Scotton.'

Oh Jesus, I seriously hope he's talking about my painting. I seriously hope this isn't flirting because if it is, he's wasting his time.

'You know my name?'

'Sure.' He goes back to studying the pictures. 'So, what do you know about me?'

'Not a lot. Well, you're American, and you're probably rich. And your name's Gordon.'

'You don't miss much.' There's something about the way his lips have parted now. And the glimmer's back. Oh God, he is flirting. 'I also own a gallery in Manhattan. Forty-fourth Street. We specialise in avant-garde material.'

He wanders round, examining the walls, floor and skirting boards, stopping by the window at the front to take in the view of Frith Street. Then he crosses the room, peering out of the rear window.

'So, what are your plans for this place?' I ask. Because Slaters is anything but avant-garde.

'Plans? Well, subject to permissions, this needs to be blocked off.' He gives the back door a gentle kick. 'New windows, a complete refit and, of course, we need to open up a staircase to the ground floor.'

'I didn't really mean that.'

'No?'

'I meant the art work.'

'Oh, that.' Giving me a toothy smile, he scans the room. 'We'll just carry on.'

With a shrug, he thrusts both hands into his pockets. For a man who apparently owns galleries in Manhattan, he seems pretty clueless. Whatever's going on here, I need to dig further.

'Which artists do you favour?' I ask.

'The ones I've seen downstairs.' He notes the incredulity in my eyes. 'I'll be honest with you. This isn't my comfort zone. I'm branching out. I've always loved London, always wanted a foothold here. This is perfect.'

'You're not going to change Slaters?'

'If it ain't broke, why fix it? Landscapes, seascapes. It works.' He looks at the triptych and then at me. 'But you're outgrowing this place, Miss Scotton. That's clear to see. We have an opportunity coming up in New York, an exhibition devoted to the subject of sex.' He pauses. 'Just sex. All forms of sex. We're calling it, well ... Sex.' He raises both hands in the air, palms upwards, as if he's apologising for stating the obvious. 'I'd like to exhibit this.'

It hits me all at once: a strange brew of amazement, excitement, pride and disbelief.

'But why?'

'Because it's wonderful.'

And now a touch of fear.

'It's too personal. If I display this, if I go public, then I'll have to talk about it.'

'Almost certainly.'

'I'm not sure I could do that.'

'Why not? Are you ashamed of who you are?'

'No.'

I bristle. Because I'm not entirely sure I'm being honest. Am I ashamed? And if so, then what am I ashamed of? That I'm different? A kinky freak? Or is it something else, something hidden away deep

MANDY LEE

inside?

'The truth is ...' I hesitate. 'I wouldn't know what to say.'

And maybe that's it. If I'm ashamed of anything, perhaps it's my own confusion, the fact that I've never really worked out how I came to be who I am.

'Then think it through,' Gordon answers. 'Why hide your true self? It can cripple you, believe me.' He gives me a knowing look and I wonder what he might be hiding. 'Show yourself to the world. Set yourself free and liberate your talent.'

'That's what he wanted.' I gaze at the centre panel.

'Then he sounds like a wise man.'

I turn back to Gordon. He's deadly serious. Any signs of flirting, if that's what it was, seem to have disappeared.

'He may not be with you,' he says. 'Not now ... but you'd do well to follow his wishes.'

My lips tremble. They're about to ask why, but before they get a chance, Mr Finn's talking again.

'Tell me, why did you specialise in landscapes?'

'I don't really know. I suppose I was fascinated by the world. Colours and light.'

'Were they less personal to you than these?'

I stare at Dan's form, and it becomes clear. Every time I set a brush against canvas, it's nothing but personal.

'There's always emotion,' I explain as best I can. 'When I painted the sea, I felt free. When I painted the woods, I felt safe.'

'It's like Picasso said: painting's just another way of keeping a diary. But you need to learn to let go of your creations.'

'I let go in the past ...' I stumble to a halt. What else can I say? I sold a picture to a certain Scottish maniac who used it to find me again? I'm being silly and I know it, and Mr Finn, whoever he is, is being eminently sensible.

'Take control of your career, Maya. There's too much talent here.'

I twirl the paintbrush in my hands.

'I will.'

'Good.' He claps and I give a start. 'So, let's cut to the chase. I'm serious about displaying the triptych, but it has to be available for sale. I'm guessing it's already done its job.'

'Yes, but ...'

'Then move on. This is a real opportunity for you. I'll get it shipped over to the States. The exhibition's next week. I'd like you to attend the opening night.'

My thoughts snap to attention. Exhibition. New York. Planes. Big

50

scary things. I can't do it. Not without Dan.

'Me?'

'Well, you did paint this.' He arches an eyebrow.

'But ...'

But what, I wonder. This is a real opportunity, probably the biggest opportunity of my life. Am I really going to let fear get in the way?

'You should be jumping at this chance,' he presses. 'Why are you still hesitating?'

'Because she's a scaredy pants,' Lucy intervenes, kicking open the door and swinging a champagne bottle in each hand. 'And she doesn't like planes.'

'Witchcraft,' I murmur, eyes wide.

'Technological wonders,' Gordon counters. 'I'll pay for the flights, of course. And the hotel. Won't cost you a penny. You can bring Lucy. Would that ease the pain? How about a couple of seats in first class?'

'Maya,' Lucy gasps. 'We're doing this.'

'But ...'

This is all moving too fast. I can barely keep up.

'New York. The Big Apple. The city that never sleeps. I've never been to New York. We're doing it. Fucking hell, Central Park, that big thing you go up ...'

'Rockefeller?' Gordon asks, bemused.

'I don't know,' Lucy breathes. 'No! Empire State ... and ...' She's almost bouncing now. 'That statue.'

'Liberty,' Gordon laughs. 'Set yourself free.'

'But ...'

I don't even know why I'm making a noise. No one's listening. Lucy's caught up in a New York reverie, and Mr Finn seems determined to fill us in on details of a trip I've not even agreed to.

'Plenty of sight-seeing. Anything you like. But don't forget the exhibition. We need to get Maya noticed. A couple of interviews. Maybe a feature in a magazine. Yeah, I think we've got a new star on the rise.'

He moves over to Lucy. She's still grinning from ear to ear like a lunatic. He motions to a bottle. She lifts it.

'Moët,' she announces.

'Very nice,' Gordon comments.

'It cost a bomb.'

'No problem.'

'I've got change.'

'Keep it.'
'But it's over a hundred.'
'Treat Maya to dinner.'
'No,' I interrupt. 'And what are those for?'
'You,' Gordon informs me, as if it's perfectly obvious. 'Something to take the edge off. A little birthday present ... from someone who'd like to see you happy. Now, I've got to go. Dinner at The Ivy.'

With no further ado, he disappears through the doorway, taking the steps back down to the gallery and leaving an uneasy silence in his wake.

I glare at Lucy.
'I can't go to New York.'
'Are you a complete fucking moron? He wants to push you.'
'Yeah, but why?'
'Because of your talent.'
'You think? Champagne, Lucy. He's bought me champagne.'
'And?' She watches me. 'Oh, you think he ...'
'Champagne. Dinner. New York. He's chucking money at me. And he couldn't take his eyes off that.' I nod at the triptych.

'God, you've got an overblown sense of yourself. Ever since Dan, you think you're some sort of sex siren.'
'He wants to get into my knickers, and that's a fact.'
'You're in full control of your knickers. Another fact. And don't think the flying thing's going to get you out of this. You've already flown and you can do it again. You and me are going to New York,' she growls, waving a champagne bottle at me for good measure. 'And that's another sodding fact.'

Chapter Six

I really should have chosen the other queue. It's moving far more quickly than this one. It's taken half an hour to almost reach the front, and now I'm here the customer ahead of me is taking his time, changing his order over and over again. I'm sorely tempted to kick him up the backside and tell him to get on with it, but that wouldn't be the right way to go. Instead, I settle for rubbing my hands together, trying to work a little life back into them while I politely wait my turn. A couple of ancient radiators are no match for a London winter. After a morning's work in semi-Baltic conditions, my fingers are numb and I'm glad of a chance to escape.

After a quick sandwich and a mug of tea, I'll return for the afternoon session, watched over by Barry's ridiculous calendar – November's kitten wrapped up in a tiny, kitten-sized scarf and posed next to a vase of cheap red roses. Every time I look at them, I think of Boyd. At least once a week, the roses have continued to arrive. I'd love nothing more than to tear November out of the year, but I won't be beaten. Besides, December's only a few days away. I've already had a quick peek. I'll be passing the time in the company of a pair of kittens disguised as reindeer, curled up next to a fake poinsettia.

'Can I help you?'

I'm yanked out of the kitten trance by the grumpiest woman in the world. Clutching a bread knife, she glares at me from beneath a hairnet. I swallow hard, temporarily forgetting my order, fixated on a pair of lips that seem to be curling into a sneer.

'Prawns ...' I stammer.

'Just prawns?'

'No, no ...' I shake my head. 'Prawn salad on white ... no, brown.' And now I know why the previous customer was so indecisive. I've got the distinct feeling this woman's silently planning my demise.

53

'And BLT on white.' My voice jitters with nerves. 'Extra mayonnaise please. My friend's not on a diet.'

Ignoring my pathetic attempt at humour, she sets about preparing the order while I watch an endless parade of downcast faces passing by the window. Winter's thoroughly staked its claim on the city, stripping it bare of colour and imposing a reign of cold, grey misery. Why the rest of humanity has descended into a mire of gloom, I have no idea. I can only vouch for myself. Still no contact. Still no news.

And faith's at breaking point.

'Your phone's ringing.' Grumpy woman points a knife at me.

With a start, I pull my mobile out of my pocket and check the screen. Lucy.

'How's it going?' she demands.

'I'm being served now.'

'You need to get back here.'

My God, I knew she was hungry, but I didn't realise she was this desperate for a bite to eat.

'I can't help it. There was a queue and ...'

'Never mind that. There's a woman waiting for you. Posh sort. Wants to talk.'

For the first time in weeks, my heart quickens. Lily Babbage. Now, there's a 'posh sort' if I've ever seen one. And if she's come to see me, then I could be in for some news.

'What does she look like?' I ask eagerly, watching as two huge wrapped sandwiches appear on the counter in front of me.

'A high-class prostitute.' Lucy cackles. 'Skinny. Red hair.'

It's a brief description, but enough to banish any further excitement. My heart's still racing, but now it's all down to anxiety, because unless Lily's opted for a radical change of hair colour, I'm pretty sure my visitor is a certain kinky madam.

'Nine pounds eighty,' grumpy woman says gruffly.

Absent-mindedly, I reach into my pocket, pull out a twenty and hand it over.

'What does she want?' I ask.

'She'd like you to clean for her.'

'What?'

'She wants to talk to you about painting something for her, twat brain. Why else would she be here? Now get the sandwiches and get back, pronto. She practically stinks of money.'

Grabbing the lunch, I flee the delicatessen, ignoring the bad-tempered calls that follow me. I didn't collect the change, and I don't care. I've got more pressing matters on my mind.

54

Half-running along Frith Street, and nearly dropping the sandwiches in the process, I arrive at the door to Slaters within a minute. Coming to a halt, my pulse racing, I edge forward and peer furtively into the front window. My suspicions were correct. There she is, facing away from me. Perfectly poised on a sofa, it's Claudine Thomas. Taking in a gulp of wintry air, I steel myself for the job ahead. Whatever reason she's got for being here, it won't be pleasant. I'll have to kick her twisted backside out of the gallery before she gets a chance to spill her venom.

I mount the steps and enter the gallery as quietly as I can. The Steves are out for the afternoon, choosing a camper van, and Lucy must be downstairs. For the time being, we're alone, and thank God for that. Approaching her silently, I register the fact that her shoulders stiffen. She knows I'm here, but she doesn't turn. As I move in front of her, dumping the sandwiches onto the coffee table, she watches me out of the corner of her eye, her lips curling upwards, just a little.

'You need to leave,' I open.

'I'm a customer.'

'Bollocks.'

'Nice language.'

'Fuck off, Claudine.'

'I'm not going anywhere.'

Slipping an arm across the back of the sofa, she makes herself comfy. And despite my best intentions, curiosity gets the better of me.

'What are you doing here?'

'Didn't your little friend tell you?'

'She passed on your bullshit. What's the real reason?'

'I'd like you to paint something for me.'

As if.

'Ian's sent you.'

'What makes you think that?' Her eyes glint like gem stones, hard and unforgiving even when they're filled with light.

'He set up the ambush at The Savoy,' I remind her. 'You were clearly in on that. You're in contact with him.'

'Haven't seen him for a while.'

'He's sent you. I know it.'

'You're wrong. The fact is, I asked Isaac to find out where to contact you. He's good like that, Isaac. Looking after my every need. In fact ...' She waves at the window. 'He's coming to fetch me in a while.'

'I haven't got time for this. Get out.'

'It's not your gallery. As I understand it, a certain Mr Finn's in the process of buying it.'

She's digging for information, I know it, and I'm about to give her none. In an instant, I make my decision: if she's not going to leave, then I certainly will. Swivelling on my heels, I make for the door and before I know it, I'm back out in the bitter air, walking fast down Frith Street, pushing my way past meandering tourists ... and Claudine's voice is following me.

'Haven't you seen the pictures?'

I keep going.

'Don't you want to know what Dan's been up to?'

I quicken my pace. Of course I want to know, but not from her.

'I've got them here.'

And that does it. Sodding curiosity. It always wins the day. I turn to face her, ignoring the obvious fact that this can't end well. I've been starved of information for weeks and I'm feeling reckless. Like an addict desperate for a hit, no matter where it comes from, I crack.

'What pictures?'

She pulls a magazine out of her handbag.

'They're in here.' Dangling the bag on one arm, she fingers through the pages. 'At the back. Society section. I'm surprised you haven't seen them.'

'I don't read magazines,' I lie.

'Well, you should. All sorts of interesting things. Like this.' She thrusts the magazine at me, opened at the desired page. 'An article about one of London's most eligible bachelors,' she explains quickly. 'Daniel Foster. Apparently, he's made a good recovery from his little accident, and now he's back at work.' She pauses, examining my face before she drops her bombshell. 'He went out last Friday night. He's dating again.'

I knew this would happen. He warned me it would. Fighting back the urge to scream, I snatch the magazine out of her hands. Slowly, I focus on the page in front of me, a mass of writing accompanied by two photographs. Nausea rises in the pit of my stomach.

'In fact, he's dating that woman.'

A perfectly manicured index finger lands on the first picture, moving slightly to reveal him. Dressed in one of his black suits, he's smiling straight into the camera, an arm curled protectively around a woman's waist, holding her close, too close for comfort. She's slim, petite, brunette. Nothing like me. I don't recognise her, but according to the caption, she's an actress. The finger moves to a

56

second picture. This time he's laughing, both arms around her now, facing her full on, eye to eye. And she's touching his cheek ... lovingly, tenderly. 'What the fuck do you think you're doing?' The words rumble at the back of my head, threatening to spill out into the open. 'Get your fucking hands off my man.'

'She's a stunner, isn't she?' Claudine asks.

Yes, she is. I can't deny it. And I'd love to slap her stunning little face into the middle of next week.

'Looks like he's moved on.' She studies me closely. 'A friend of mine was at the same party. Apparently, he was all over this woman, barely able to control himself. But then again, I suppose it's to be expected. He's gone a while without a shag.'

Don't believe it, I tell myself.

Breathing quickly, on the verge of panic, I examine the photographs one more time, deciding that they're just too convincing.

Whatever you see. Whatever you hear about me. Don't believe it.

'Now you know how I felt. I always thought he'd come back to me, but he didn't.'

'Don't even think you're on the same level,' I sneer, shifting my attention to the opening of the article. My vision's already blurred with tears and shock. I can't read a word of it. 'You were never in a relationship with him.'

'Not the way you'd define it. But to have him, and then to have him reject you, well, that's painful, isn't it?'

I need to get away from here. I need some time to think, and I can't do that with Claudine's words digging into my brain.

'They're quite a match. Very much in love.'

Whatever you see. Whatever you hear about me.

'We're in the same club now, the I've-been-fucked-and-fucked-over-by-Daniel-Foster Society.'

Don't believe it.

'Would you like a handkerchief?'

'Not from you.'

She shrugs.

'So now you finally see what a bastard he is. You meant nothing to him. He used you.'

Don't believe ...

'Whatever he said, all those wonderful words, they were just lies. Because that's what he does. He lies.' Still watching me, she bites her bottom lip, her eyes gleaming. 'Did he tell you he loved you?'

I open my mouth, temporarily unguarded, and she catches the

answer in my expression.

'Did he tell you he'd be there for you ... forever? Did he tell you he'd wait for you?'

She's digging again, rummaging for information. And just in case Boyd has sent her, I need to protect myself.

'Nobody's waiting for anyone,' I say crisply, wiping away the tears with the back of my hand. 'It's over. It's been over since the accident, and you know that. Now take your poison and fuck off.'

A black Bentley draws up next to us. Instinctively, I move away from the kerb. It's become a habit in recent weeks.

'Oh, just in time,' Claudine chirps. 'Here's Isaac.'

The driver's window rolls down and Isaac's droopy face appears, his lips struggling to raise themselves beneath the handlebar moustache.

'Did you get what you wanted?' he smiles.

'Yes,' Claudine replies breezily, turning back to face me. 'I wanted you to paint a picture for me, Maya. I wasn't lying. And you did. A lovely picture. A real work of art. Thank you. I enjoyed it very much.'

I'm on automatic pilot. Dropping into Slaters to retrieve my handbag, I dump the magazine in the bin and make my excuses for the day. I spend a while wandering aimlessly through Soho, pretending to study the shop windows for a good hour or so before I take a seat in the Square and pretend to study the mock Tudor pagoda instead. Eventually, I wander up to Tottenham Court Road, and navigate the maze of tunnels to the Northern Line. It's a short tube ride to Waterloo. Emerging from the station, I walk along the embankment, finally reaching my target – fifteen floors of darkened glass, the headquarters of Fosters Construction.

Lost in a swarm of bodies, I look up at the top floor. He's up there right now, and in all probability, he'll be fully aware that I'm lurking outside. So, is he looking back down at me? And if he is, what's on his mind? Perhaps, like me, he's paralysed with longing. Or perhaps, if Claudine's right, he's simply wishing I'd vanish. After all, this break's given us both thinking time and while it's only confirmed my need for him, maybe he's come to a different conclusion. Maybe I'm too much of a liability, not that special, utterly replaceable.

I check my phone. Just after five. No wonder the Embankment's filling up. On top of the droves of tourists, rush hour's throwing an endless stream of workers into the mix. Without a clue what I'm doing, I leave the Embankment and begin to wander the back streets.

Before long, I find myself in a lane behind Fosters, pinned down by inertia, leaning against the corner of an office block.

'What the fuck are you doing?' I whisper to myself, answering my own question immediately. 'Stalking, you bloody idiot. You're a stalker.'

I should go. I know I should. But I stay in position. A need to see him has dragged me here, and now it won't let me leave. And logic must have given a helping hand, because he might have made a good recovery, but I'm willing to bet a long walk home's still out of the question. He won't be using the revolving doors at the other side of the building. He'll either emerge from the garage, driving himself, or he'll be chauffeured home. As I settle in for the wait, palpitations flutter through my chest. I have no idea how long I stand rooted to the spot, fixated on the doorway across the street, but I'm about to call it a day when a car pulls up at the rear entrance. I withdraw slightly, peering round the edge of the building.

And then, he appears.

I get my first view of Dan in almost three months and immediately, I'm a quivering, quaking mess. Good God, I'm pathetic. Like some crazed teenager, spying on her latest crush. Relieved there's no limp, no obvious sign of his injuries, I watch as he walks toward the car. He hands his briefcase to the driver, stands by the open rear door and without any warning, looks my way.

Yes. He definitely knows I'm here.

My pulse races. I'm frozen to the spot.

Move, I tell myself. Just bloody well move.

But I can't. Even from this distance, he's got me mesmerised. I need a sign, one little sign that everything's okay. But there's no smile, no warmth in those eyes, just a hard edge of nothing. Finally, he turns away, speaks to the driver and manoeuvres himself into the back of the car.

I'm released from his hold.

Reeling back against the wall, I begin to shake.

'Shit, shit, shit.'

If he really is moving on, he'll hate me now. I am a liability. A bloody big one.

It's a couple of minutes before I manage to get my body back under control, and then I make my way back to the embankment. In a blur, I negotiate a path through the evening crowds, heading for Gabriel's Wharf, where I finally come to a halt in a tiny coffee shop. I place my order, settle myself at a metal table in the courtyard and with my cappuccino delivered, take a few absent-minded sips, staring at the shops, the mural, the South Bank Tower.

And then, as if waking from a deep sleep, I realise I've come back to where it all began. Before he went to Edinburgh, he brought me here and warned me to ignore the gossip. But should I ignore it this time round? He's given up on Slaters, apparently given up on selling Fosters, and now there's a distinct possibility he's given up on me. Overwhelmed by frustration, blind faith isn't enough any more. The time has come for something concrete. I need proof.

I take my mobile out of my pocket. Surely it wouldn't hurt to talk to Lily. Tapping in her contact, I wait impatiently, wondering if I'm about to throw up. It's a good few seconds before she answers.

'Hello?'

'It's Maya.'

There's a long pause. When she speaks again her voice is different, brittle, almost hollow.

'How are you?'

'Fine.'

Why have I just opened with that? I'm not fine at all. And that's precisely why I'm calling.

'It's been a while.'

'I know. But you said ... you said to call if ...'

'You changed your mind.'

'Yes.'

'So, you're not fine at all.'

'No,' I admit, my voice cracking. 'I need to contact him.'

I hear a dainty sigh.

'Have you got his new number?' I ask.

'Of course I have.'

'Can you let me have it?'

Another silence. She's thinking.

'I don't think that's the right thing to do.'

'But you said you wanted to help.'

'And it's been a long time.'

'I know, but I miss him,' I blurt. 'I really miss him. It's taken me a while to realise. I was just so angry when he dumped me, but now ... I just need to talk to him. I need to give it a try.'

'Maya. You're too late.'

I crash to a halt.

'Why?'

'He's seeing someone.'

'No.' The word's out of my mouth before I know what's going on. And before I can get a grip on matters, more follow suit. 'He's not.

Not really.'

'He is,' she insists. 'I met her a few days ago.'

I let my head fall, rub my free hand over my face, remind myself that nothing gets past Lily Babbage. He must be putting on a damn good show ... if it is a show.

'Maya?'

What the hell. Why not let her in on the ruse?

'We didn't really split up.'

'What?'

'It's all a pretence. There was somebody ... somebody who made threats. I can't tell you any more. He told Dan to keep his distance. This is just acting, Lily, until he's dealt with this person. Dan said we'd just go through the motions.'

'You're not making any sense.'

'It's true. God, don't tell anyone.'

For a few seconds, I listen to her breathing. At last, she speaks again.

'Are you thinking straight?'

'Of course I am.'

'It's just ... well, this is all a bit far-fetched.'

'You don't believe me?'

'I'll talk to Dan about it.'

'No.' My heartbeat accelerates. 'Don't tell him. I'm not supposed to say a word.'

'Then what am I to do?'

'I don't know.'

Suddenly, I seem to have no energy. I'm sick of it all. All the waiting and silence and frustration. And not one scrap of hope.

'He's with someone else now. He's happy. I'm sorry, Maya, but I don't think it's appropriate for me to be involved any more.'

'No, Lily, you've got to believe me.'

'Perhaps you should see a doctor,' she cuts in quickly.

'I'm not making this up.'

'I'm just as upset as you are about the split, but I can't force him to take you back. His feelings have obviously changed.'

'But ...'

'Maya ...'

'He promised me, Lily. He was even selling the company.'

'He's not selling the company. He'd never sell Fosters. Listen to me. This story in your head ... that's all it is ... a story. You're kidding yourself. You need to let it go.'

The phone goes dead. I stare at it in desperation, then throw it into my handbag and gaze into space instead.

It can't be true, not after everything we've been through. He'd never treat me this way. I pick up my coffee and take another shaky sip. He'll know I'm here now, drinking the best coffee this side of the Thames, and waiting for him. He'll know I'm upset and he won't be able to help himself. If I sit here long enough, he'll turn up and lock me in with those bright blue eyes, and they'll soften with love, and then he'll tell me everything's going to be fine.

Putting down the mug, I gaze up at the trees, their bare branches scratching against the sky. Oh, don't be a fool, I tell myself. Think about it. All the evidence stacks up. The article. The ice in his eyes. Lily's words. You can sit here all night and he'll never show, because he's done with you. He just hasn't got the balls to admit it. Wise up. Lily was right. You are kidding yourself. A tremor of shock erupts at the base of my chest, surging up through my throat. I swallow back as much as I can, but a sob manages to escape from my mouth. I shake my head and close my eyes.

I'm falling, crashing … and I need to go home.

Abandoning the coffee, I get up and head for the embankment wall. The evening crowds pass by, oblivious to the chaos in my head, the tears streaming down my cheeks. I lean over and stare at the Thames. Black and unforgiving, it moves on relentlessly, just like the rest of the world.

Any comfort I had unravels … completely and irrevocably.

Chapter Seven

Gusts of wind skitter down the road, catching the last of the autumn leaves, along with a few handfuls of litter, and casting the whole lot into spirals. I shiver, look down at the roses in my hands. Yet another bunch from Boyd. Stepping forward onto the pavement, I hurl them into the skip.

'Are you going to pay for that?'

My neighbour scowls at me from his doorstep.

'I'm sorry ...'

'Well, it's going next week. You'll have to find somewhere else to dump your flowers.'

He slams the door, leaving me alone with my embarrassment. I've been caught red-handed, making unauthorised use of a skip. But worse than that, it's five o'clock in the evening and I'm dressed in my pyjamas, probably looking dishevelled to say the least. After a restless night, I shied away from Slaters, telling Lucy I felt under the weather, and cocooned myself from the world. I've spent the entire day on the sofa, knocking back one mug of tea after another, flicking through an endless selection of daytime television crap, and relentlessly raking through the facts. Closing the front door, I head for the kitchen. Lucy's due home soon. The least I can do is prepare dinner. I heat up the oven, pop in a frozen pizza, open a bottle of white wine and set the rickety table.

The front door opens and bangs shut.

'Evening,' Lucy grunts, dropping her handbag on the floor. 'Friday night. Let's get pissed.'

'Bad day?'

'Shit day. Gordon's back. I had to go through the accounts with him. And yours?'

'Had a bath. Watched telly. Cooked a pizza.' And that reminds me. 'Oh shit, the pizza.'

In a panic, I tug open the oven door, dismayed at the sight of a blackened disc in front of me.

'Bugger.'

We stand together, staring at the burnt offering.

'We're crap,' Lucy breathes. 'It's official.'

'It is official.' I switch off the oven. I really ought to get that slab of charcoal into the bin, but it's still smoking. 'I've had enough.' And the devil inside wants to play. 'No more moping, Lucy. No more feeling sorry for ourselves. We're going out … on the pull.'

'We are?' she gawps. 'But I thought you were ill.'

'Not any more.' I prod the pizza, burning my finger in the process. 'I need to get back on my bike. And you need to get back on yours.'

'Seriously?'

'Seriously.'

'But …'

'What?'

She thinks for a moment, giving me one of her should-I-really-say-this looks. I don't know why she bothers. She always says it in the end.

'I saw the magazine,' she ventures nervously. 'The one you dumped in the bin. I saw the article.' She swallows. 'I knew you weren't over him. You were like me, hoping he'd made some huge mistake, hoping he'd come back.'

In a strange moment of intimacy, I see it all in her eyes: the raw grief of losing Clive, her sadness for me. And I just can't help myself. I throw my arms around her, pressing her into my chest and giving her the biggest hug of her life.

'You're a wonderful friend, Lucy. I love you.'

'I love you too,' she mumbles into my breasts. 'But please don't hug me. This shit's going to make us both cry.'

I release her and step back, taking in a gulp of air and coughing it back out again. There's a distinct taste of burning in the room.

'You weren't ill today, were you?' she asks.

'No.' I shrug. 'I was brooding.'

'It's always the hardest part. When you find out they've moved on.'

A huge understatement if I've ever heard one. In fact, I never knew it was possible to feel this messed up. The inside of my head's not a good place to be at the minute. A landscape of complete desolation, there's nothing familiar left in place.

'I know.'

'So, tonight ... maybe it's not the best night to get back on your bike. Perhaps we should stay in.'

I smile at her. She may be a ditzy idiot, but my best friend's definitely got my back. The trouble is, my back, along with the rest of me, just doesn't want to stay in.

'There's never been a better night, Luce. Trust me.'

She stares at me, disbelief quickly giving way to mild excitement.

'Well, if that's the case, I know exactly where we're going.'

'Where?'

'Back to Soho. The Mill. More bikes than the Tour de France.'

I stare at her blankly.

'It's a metaphor ... I think. Anyway, Gordon's seeing some friends there tonight. And we're invited. I didn't think you'd be interested, but ...' The excitement grows. 'He wants to treat me for working so hard today.' She pouts dramatically. 'Free entry courtesy of the new boss. We're on the guest list. No queueing. Straight in. VIP area. Complimentary bubbly.'

And Gordon. A man who seems to have a crush on me, which I wouldn't normally mind, but when all's said and done – and in spite of all my brave allusions to cycling – I'm not entirely sure I'm ready for any shenanigans. It's going to take a good few months to shake the big kahuna out of my system. And besides, all I really want to do is get drunk, dance and lose myself in oblivion.

'Come on, Maya. I'll give you a make-over. Little black dress. You're going to look the dog's bollocks.'

Before I know it, I'm dragged from the kitchen into my bedroom and squeezed into the black dress I bought for my first exhibition at Slaters. Refusing point blank to let Lucy anywhere near me with her make-up bag, I apply eye shadow, eyeliner and mascara. Finally, I open my jewellery box and find myself gazing down at the sweet pea necklace and the matching earrings. Somehow, I still want to wear them. But I can't. Instead, I opt for my grandmother's Yorkshire jet and close the box, resolving to leave all thoughts of Dan behind.

Three hours later, after a meal in a Greek restaurant and an unknown quantity of ouzo, we're staggering through the streets of Soho. Oblivious to the fact that my world's already swaying and I need a little rest, Lucy keeps going while I grab hold of a lamp-post and steady myself. I hear a cough, and follow its direction, peering down a set of steps at a man in an open doorway.

'Coming in?' he asks, lighting up a cigarette.

'What is it?'

'Don't you know?'

'Well, no.'

Seeing as there's no sign and I'm not telepathic, I could really do with some sort of clue. He moves aside, letting in a couple.

'Kink,' he says.

'No thank you,' Lucy answers for me, back by my side. 'She's had quite enough of that.'

But I'm already hooked.

'We could give it a try,' I suggest.

She shakes her head.

'Let's do this the usual way.' Taking hold of my arm, she drags me further along the road. 'Dancing. Booze. Maybe a snog. I don't fancy being manacled to a wall and fucked by a geek in a gimp mask.'

A few more unsteady steps and we arrive at The Mill. Heading straight to the front of the queue, Lucy gives our names, and we're waved in. We drop off our coats and make our way into the main atrium, coming to a joint halt, stunned by the space around us.

'Fucking hell,' Lucy squeals. 'Why haven't we been here before?'

To be honest, I have no idea. It's amazing, like some sort of modern cathedral, a showcase of architectural wizardry, illuminated by a kaleidoscope of colour. Crafted in steel and marble and black glass, it's sleek, industrial ... beautiful. Girders twist above my head, forming a vast, imposing dome, while half way up, a gallery circles the room, lined with silver arches. At the far end of a packed dance floor, a steel platform apparently hovers in mid-air: a futuristic pulpit, the DJ's station. Finally, I lower my gaze to the bars, and then a labyrinth of seating areas in front of me

'Wow!'

Lucy drags me into the throng of sweaty bodies, ordering me to stay next to a podium while she wanders off in search of champagne. Feeling distinctly woozy, I do as I'm told. Loud thumping dance music fills my head, the bassline of something I don't recognise reverberating right through my body. I gaze out over the dance floor. Bathed in a storm of flashing light, shapes intertwine and merge until I'm not sure what I'm seeing.

A hand slips around my waist. Instinctively, I withdraw and find Gordon standing next to me.

'Hey,' he smiles. 'You made it.'

'So I did,' I smile back. 'How did you find us in here?'

'Saw you come in.' He nods upwards. 'I've got a pod.'

And razor sharp vision, to boot.

'Really? Can you take medicine for that?'

He laughs.

'Oh, that British sense of humour. Gets me every time. No.' He puts an end to the laugh, a hand on my arm and points up at the gallery. 'A pod. Up there. Come and meet my friends.'

'In a while.' I retreat from his touch. 'I'll probably dance first.'

Or shuffle about in a daze. Or worse than that, go completely mad and fling myself around like a whirling dervish on acid.

'I'll leave you to it then. It's the VIP area. Join us when you're ready.'

As soon as he's gone, Lucy appears out of the gloom, wielding two glasses of champagne.

'It's free, remember!' she shouts. 'Get it down you.'

Slugging back her champagne, she eyes the room, in search of more. She's certainly on a mission to get wasted tonight, and why should I stop her? There's no point in trying to keep Lucy on a tight leash. If Dan's moved on, then in all likelihood, so has Clive.

Don't believe it.

The words spring out of nowhere, returning to taunt me, doing their level best to make me feel like a wavering idiot. But they fail. Instead, I'm angry. Seriously angry. With Dan for his lack of communication. With Boyd for fucking up my life. But most of all, with myself for sitting on a crappy see-saw of trust and doubt.

'What's wrong with you?' Lucy demands, wafting her empty glass at me.

'Gordon's here,' I reply quickly. I'm not about to give up the truth. 'He's got a pod.'

'Looks like you've found your ride then.'

'I am not riding him,' I shout.

'So, which one would you ride?' she asks. 'How about him?' She nods towards the bar. 'Bloke in the pink shirt.'

I follow the direction of her gaze, spotting a flash of pink.

'Not for me.'

'Okay,' she shouts. 'Pick a man, then. Any man. Which one would you shag?'

None of them, I'd like to answer. But I'll go along with Lucy's game. I scour the room, squinting through the gloom and finding nothing. My attention wanders back to the nearest bar. One after another, faces appear out of the shadows, and disappear again. Dark meshes with light. Shadows move and collide. And then, like a flare over No Man's Land, a blinding flash illuminates the scene. It lasts for no more than a couple of seconds before we're plunged back into darkness. But it's enough. I blink, not entirely sure of what I've just seen. It can't be. Out of a sea of faces, one in particular, so achingly familiar. My entire body sparks into life. I focus on the spot and wait for the next flash. It's not long in coming … and my suspicions are confirmed.

Dan.

He's here.

Finally making contact.

In an instant, everything malfunctions: brain, heart, lungs, stomach. With my legs threatening to give way beneath me, I begin to move.

'Where are you going?' Lucy asks.

'Nowhere. Stay here. I'll be back.'

Still clutching my glass, I weave an unsteady path through the crowd, homing in on my target. A strange concoction of fear and excitement floods through me. On top of the alcohol, it's a potent mix. I'm breathing quickly now, and the shakes are back. At last, he's right in front of me, seemingly unaware of my presence. Dressed in black jeans and a white shirt, open at the collar, he's leaning back against the bar, gazing up at the dome, looking ridiculously delicious. He turns to the woman next to him. She's slim, petite, wearing a short black dress, and she's facing away from me, but I know exactly who she is: the woman from the magazine. He places a hand at the base of her spine, leans over to whisper in her ear.

She laughs, and I freeze.

I have just enough time to realise I'm in shock when the anger surges back at full force. Without another thought, I close the space between us and tap him on the shoulder. He pivots quickly. I have no idea what sort of reaction I expected, but what I get needles me in the gut. There's no surprise on his part, and no warmth either.

'What the fuck's going on?' I seethe.

He studies me for a moment, cold and detached.

'I'm enjoying an evening out.'

Well, what a coincidence. He's enjoying an evening out in exactly the same nightclub as me … with another woman.

'You fixed this up.'

He narrows his eyes.

'Lucy's invitation here tonight,' I press on. 'You fixed this up.'

I catch the beginnings of a sneer.

'I have no idea what you're going on about.'

'Gordon.'

'Who?'

'Of course,' I laugh, realising he doesn't need anyone to tell him where I am. 'My phone. You're still tracking it.' I bite my lip. Tomorrow, I'll go out and get a new mobile. New number. Everything.

'This is because of yesterday.'

He stares at me, giving nothing away.

'You made yourself perfectly clear,' I tell him. 'There's no need for this. No need to go parading your latest piece of skirt in front of me.'

And that does it. The latest piece of skirt moves in close, staking her claim on Dan.

'What's going on?' she asks, as smug as you like, and I know exactly why. I've sported that look on plenty of occasions. He's fucked the living daylights out of her. I know he has.

'Nothing.' He raises a hand. 'Don't worry about it.'

'And who's this?' I demand.

'None of your business.' His eyes harden.

'Oh, it is my business,' I laugh. 'You and me, we never came to an end, Dan. Not officially. You owe me an explanation. So, what's going on?'

'What does it look like?'

'You told me to wait.'

He grimaces, clearly irritated.

'Things can change.'

'Oh, I get it. Every day's a new beginning.'

'It's over. Face it and move on.'

Out of nowhere, a burly creature appears at Dan's side.

'Is she bothering you?' Beefy asks.

'Yes.'

'Want me to sort it?'

He nods and turns away. Grabbing hold of his shirt, I force him back to face me.

'Do you really mean that?' I demand.

Without a flicker of emotion, he doesn't reply.

'You ...'

'What?' he snaps. 'If you can't deal with it, get out of here.'

It's an automatic reaction. I throw my champagne in his face. He baulks, stares at me in surprise, and then nods at Beefy. Out of the corner of my eye I know there's another burly creature behind him now, nightclub security.

'Miss, you need to leave.'

'I'm not leaving. It's a free fucking country. Pig,' I sneer at Dan. 'You told me to wait for you.'

'You're deluded.'

'Deluded? I did exactly what you told me to do … and this is how I get treated?'

We glare at each other for a good few seconds. I watch his eyes carefully, unsure of what I'm seeing. Is that hatred? Regret? Or is it pain? An apology? It's hard to tell, what with the flashing lights obscuring the truth. When he eventually speaks, the words push me completely off balance.

'Fuck off, Maya.'

The next breath nudges its way from my lungs, inch by inch, emerging in short, sharp spurts. I stare at his mouth. No way did it just say that. The bastard deserves a slap, and I give him one, good and hard across the cheek. He barely reacts.

'You'll need your necklace back then.'

'Keep it. It's nothing to me.' He speaks to his companion now. 'Let's get out of here.' Grabbing her arm, he practically drags her towards the exit.

Temporarily paralysed by rage and disbelief, I watch them go. If anyone's deluded around here, it's Dan. No one talks to me like that and gets away with it. I glance up at the dome, realising that I am in a cathedral, a massive, overblown shrine to shallowness and self-obsession, where fatuous arses come to worship themselves.

'Fucking idiot,' I mutter, deciding that the biggest arse of all is about to get his come-uppance.

Erupting into action, I march towards the exit, following Dan's path and catching up with him outside where he's waiting by the kerb, a protective arm around the bitch brunette. As soon as he sees me, his face breaks into irritation.

'What's happened to you?' I shout, approaching him, half conscious of the fact that there's still a queue for the club, and I'm about to provide some free entertainment. 'Where's the Dan I know?'

'Gone.'

'Why?'

Letting go of the tart, he wheels round.

'Because I came to my senses,' he snarls. 'Because I realised you went too far.'

'I contacted your sister. You forgave me for that.' I jab my finger at his face. He grabs hold of my wrist and pulls me in close.

'The first time, yes. But then you went and spoke to her again.'

'You asked me to.'

'I didn't ask you to fill her head with nonsense.'

'What?'

70

'You told her this was all a sham.'

My mouth opens.

'Did you think I wouldn't find out?' He pulls back. 'You've been rumbled. She wrote to me, told me everything about your little visit to Limmingham. Apparently, you and me are getting back together.'

He waits for my response, but all I can do is flounder, unable to believe what I'm seeing, what I'm hearing.

'I ... I told her that in confidence.'

'Well, you shouldn't have. She can't keep a confidence, especially one as misguided and fucked up as that.'

'Fucked up?' Tears cloud my eyes. 'You promised me ...'

'It's amazing what you'll say when you're high on morphine. You should have got the message by now, Maya. We're through.'

I hear the words, and they confirm everything. The ground gives way beneath my feet, threatening to suck me into the darkness. But I'm not going easily. The grip on my arm tightens, firing me up into a fury.

'And you didn't have the balls to tell me?' I demand, glaring at him.

'I've got the balls to do anything, but I'm not stupid. No contact. Not even for that. I'll protect the people I care about. But you? You fucked up once too often. I'm done with you.'

Almost as soon as I'm released, a chunky set of fingers close around my arm.

'Miss, you need to leave.'

Obviously terrified of what I might do next, Beefy's startled, bird-like eyes are fixed on me.

'Fuck off, Beefy. I've got as much right to be here as him.'

I struggle, only to find I'm held tight in a grip that's certainly vice-like but curiously gentle. I look at Beefy's hand, and then at Dan. The expression on his face says it all. He's disgusted by my behaviour. But I just don't care. Dismissing him, I inspect his latest conquest, a self-satisfied cat that's clearly had the cream. It's enough to light a fuse, and I'm not surprised when I turn back to Dan and hear myself shout.

'Do you know what you are? An arrogant, fucked-up shit! The biggest fucked- up shit to walk this planet since ... I don't know when. A manipulative, lying, selfish bastard! That's what you are!' There. That should do it. I've set the record well and truly straight. And now I address the queue. 'Ladies and gentlemen!' Steadied by Beefy's hand, I wave a hand at Dan. 'I give you Daniel Foster. A man with a big cock and a massive bank balance. Handsome, isn't he?

71

But, ladies, don't let that fool you. Keep your distance, because this,' I point an accusing finger at him, 'is one huge fuck-up of a disaster zone!'

'You're making a fool of yourself.'

I'm halted in my tracks by the creamed-up feline. How dare she dump her ridiculous opinion on me?

'And you'd better be careful,' I tell her. 'Don't believe a fucking word he says. He'll tell you he loves you, he'll tell you he needs you, he'll tell you you're the best thing since sliced bread, and then he'll dump you. Good fucking luck!'

The grip on my arm tightens a little.

'Come away,' Beefy urges me.

'Leave her,' Dan orders. 'The job's done. We're going.'

A black limousine draws up at the kerb. He opens the back door quickly and motions for Little Miss Smug to get in. She complies. Stunned, I watch as without another word, Dan joins her and slams the door, disappearing behind darkened glass. Finally releasing me, Beefy installs himself in the front passenger seat and the car pulls away.

An icy wind whips at me. I shiver, focus my attention back at the queue and register a row of faces, all fixed on me, none of them offering sympathy. I'm about to tell the whole lot of them to fuck off when Lucy appears at my side.

'What was that all about?' she asks. 'What was he doing here?'

'Giving me proof,' I grumble. 'As if I needed it.'

I check the faces surrounding me. Suddenly, I'm not so sure I'm being shadowed any more. After all, if the man hates me that much, then why would he have me protected? And suddenly, fuelled by alcohol and disgust, I really don't care. If Boyd's out there waiting for me, he can have me. In full-on self-destruct mode, I retreat inside the club and head straight to the cloakroom. Lucy follows close behind, making a call on her mobile as I shrug on my coat, still shadowing me as I stomp back outside.

'Leave me alone, Luce,' I shout, launching into a brisk march.

'No way,' she pants, struggling to keep up. 'You're drunk and you're angry.'

'No shit!' I whirl round on the spot. 'And do you know what? I don't want anything anyone's got to offer in that shit-hole.' I point back to the club. 'I'm going somewhere else.'

'Where?'

'Mind your own sodding business. Go back to the cattle market.'

I don't have to stagger far to find what I want. Within seconds,

I'm heading down a set of steps. The man's still there, standing in the doorway, smoking yet another cigarette.

'I thought you'd be back.' He moves to one side.

'Maya, what are you doing?' I falter at the sound of Lucy's voice.

'What does it look like?'

'If you go in there, you'll get pissed on.'

'Well,' I laugh, 'I've already been shat on. What difference is it going to make?'

I disappear into the shadows, edging my way through a gloomy corridor that leads to a bar. Surveying the room, I'm surprised to find it's not a dungeon, and I'm not surrounded by sweaty naked bodies, and I haven't heard a single groan. In fact, it's just a normal bar, filled with seemingly normal people, doing what normal people do in bars, drinking and talking. And they're all fully clothed, not a gag or a flogger in sight. A wave of drunken disappointment washes through me. The doorman must have been stringing me along with all his talk of kink. I head for the counter, propping myself up next to a tallish, blond-haired man. He greets me with a blue-eyed smile, and yet again I'm thinking of Dan.

'Are you okay?' he asks.

Of course not, you prat.

'Why do you ask?'

He points at my face. 'You've been crying.'

'I stubbed my toe,' I lie. 'And now I need a glass of wine.'

'Allow me.'

Remaining silent, I watch as he orders the wine and slides it under my nose.

'I thought this was a kinky club.' I slug back a mouthful.

'It is.'

'But ...'

'Rooms at the back,' he explains. 'That's where all the action takes place. New to this?'

'Not exactly.'

'On your own?'

'Yes.'

I scan the bar. No sign of Lucy. I can only assume she didn't dare enter this den of filth. And I'm glad. The last thing I need right now is her gabbling in my ear like Jiminy Cricket. Focussing back on my blue-eyed companion, I realise that the reckless part of my brain has thoroughly taken the helm. 'He's nothing special,' I tell myself. 'But he'll do.' I watch as he sips at his pint. He doesn't seem to be about to push things any further, so I guess it's all down to me.

'Will you show me the ropes?' I ask.

He raises an eyebrow.

'Talk about going in at the deep end. Maybe not rope … not yet.'

'Well, what do you suggest I start with?'

He purses his lips, thinking for a moment.

'I'd say a light spanking, but if stubbing your toe made you cry, I'm not sure you'd enjoy it.'

Seriously? Do I actually look like a kink virgin? I lean forward, swaying slightly.

'Oh, I like a good spanking, but I've done that, been there, worn the T-shirt. And now I want something more.'

'Which is?'

I hold my breath. I know exactly what I want. I'm feeling pain and craving pain. And I want to take it to the extreme.

'Whips. I want whips. Do they have whips here?'

He opens his mouth.

'Trust me, you don't want to be whipped.'

I blink into his face. I definitely just heard those words, but the lips didn't move and there was something distinctly American about that accent. I turn slowly, only to find Gordon standing behind me.

'What would you know?'

'Quite a bit, actually,' he says breezily. 'I once spent an entire week with my butt cheeks on fire. It wasn't pleasant. Now, I don't know why you're jonesing for agony, but let me tell you something. It's not what you need.'

'And I don't need you telling me what I don't need. And anyway …' I prod him in the chest. 'What are you doing here?'

'Lucy came to get me. She wants me to take you home. I've got a ride waiting outside.'

'I'm staying.'

'You shouldn't.' His eyes flash with something I can't quite understand. 'Now, let's go.'

'I don't have to do what you say,' I slur. 'You're not actually my boss or anything.'

'No, I'm not. But I'd like to consider myself a friend. Whatever happened back there at the club, this isn't the answer.'

'Oh yes it is.'

He shakes his head. 'You won't feel that way in the morning.' He pauses. 'And I won't take no for an answer.'

He holds out a hand, and I stare at it. I'm exhausted and drunk, and in actual fact I'd love nothing more than to climb into bed and curl up in a foetal position. With no further complaints, I give in, letting him lead me back outside and guide me to a car. Lucy's already in the front, sitting next to the driver. I slide into the back, with Gordon at my side.

'You okay?' he asks.

'What's it to you?'

'Maya!' Lucy barks. 'Don't be so rude. What's got into you?'

'Men.' I look out of the window, unable to focus on anything. The booze is really kicking in now. 'They all think they can boss me about, and they all want the same thing. A good fuck.'

'Maya!'

'Well, it's the truth. He wants to fuck me.' I wave a hand at Gordon. 'Knights in shining armour. They've always got a hard-on underneath all that chain mail.'

'Well, this particular knight in shining armour doesn't fit your generalisation,' Gordon argues. 'He just wants to see you through your front door, make sure you're okay, and then be gone.'

I laugh.

'Oh come off it. Sex. That's all men ever want. And when they get what they want, they chuck you in the bin and move on to the next conquest.'

'What makes you say that?' he asks.

'My ex,' I mutter, hating the sound of the word in my mouth. Daniel Foster, my ex. A man who belongs to the past. 'He's changed his mind and wriggled out of it. He just never had the fucking balls to tell me straight. Lucy was right. Men are shits.'

I close my eyes, descending quickly into a stupor. I don't know whether I dream it or imagine it, or if it's real, but I feel a finger brush against my cheek and hear Gordon's voice again.

'Don't believe it,' he says quietly, his words almost lost in the rumble of the engine. 'Hold on.'

75

Chapter Eight

We stagger into the arrivals hall at JFK. Immediately, we're greeted by a chauffeur and escorted outside to a black limousine.

'We've had some pretty heavy snowfall,' he informs us. 'I hope you've brought your thermals.'

I glance at the snow – heaped up at the kerbside, piled against bollards and bins – and then I thank Lucy for checking on weather reports, insisting we bring our thickest coats.

'Get in the car,' she urges me, breath clouding in front of her face. 'I'm freezing my knackers off.'

Satisfied with my achievements so far, I settle in for the next leg of the journey. Apart from one slight hiccough, I've managed to stay relatively sane on yet another trans-Atlantic flight, not an easy task with my travel companion bouncing and babbling at my side. Luckily, after a few glasses of wine, she became almost bearable, even drifting off to sleep for a couple of hours and leaving me in peace. But now she's conscious again, and practically vibrating with excitement. I can only hope it's a short drive into Manhattan.

Before long, the suitcases are loaded and we're rolling out of the airport, along snow-lined freeways, through suburbs, past houses, shops, industrial estates. I sit with my face practically squashed against the window. This is my first real taste of the United States, and I'm determined to make the most of it.

'Fucking hell, Maya! Look at that!' Lucy taps me on the arm and points out of her own window. 'There it is!'

I lean over, as far as I can, sensing the first pin-pricks of excitement. In the distance, I make out the jagged skyline of Manhattan, a forest of skyscrapers wrestling for supremacy, sharp-edged against a cold November sky. Squinting a little, I locate the unmistakable silhouette of the Empire State Building but as soon as it appears, it's gone again, hidden behind a jumble of buildings. I'd carry on searching for it but the limousine dips into a tunnel and anxiety sparks into life, playing havoc with my heart rate until daylight greets us again, and we emerge onto the streets of Manhattan.

Suddenly, the world's transformed.

I've seen it plenty of times in films, but I'm stunned by the reality of the city. With our limousine bouncing along uneven roads, I watch as New York slips by in the late afternoon sun. At first, it's a blur, an attack on my senses, one iconic image instantly replaced by the next: a swarm of yellow taxis, steam rising from manhole covers, a subway entrance. Down-at-heel tenements give way to brownstone townhouses, up-market office blocks and a jumble of shop fronts. I begin to make sense of it now, quite inevitably looking up and taking in the mishmash of architecture, an intricate patchwork – stone, brick, steel, glass – a crazy collection of angles and heights, an eclectic mixture of styles, the new squeezed in next to the old, every possible space filled, everything reaching skywards. Nothing seems to match, but in amongst all the clutter and confusion, everything seems to fit. Finally, with an aching neck, I focus on the busy sidewalks. Swathed in thick scarves and hats, New Yorkers go about their daily business, apparently oblivious the magnificence around them ... but I'm mesmerised by it all.

Before long, the road widens out. Skirting a roundabout, we join the traffic at the edge of a park. Beyond the railings, a thick white blanket lies heavy on the ground, and there's not a soul around. Too cold, the driver tells us. Minus sixteen with the wind chill. Anyone with a scrap of sense has stayed inside. We take another left, pulling up outside a hotel, clearly a cut above with its darkened glass doors, gold embossed signage and black canopy. Gordon's made absolutely sure we're in the lap of luxury.

'Where are we?' Lucy asks.

'Central Park, ma'am. East Side.'

'Bloody hell ...' Clasping her palms to her cheeks, she's in a state of shock.

While the chauffeur collects the luggage from the boot, a doorman steps forward and opens Lucy's door. We climb out into icy temperatures, catching a blast of wind that rolls in from the park. It steals my breath for a split second, almost freezing me on the spot. Fortunately, we're ushered straight inside by the doorman, leaving a bell-boy to deal with the cases. While Lucy checks in, I marvel at the marbled entrance hall, soaking up an overdose of Art Deco magnificence before we're guided to our suite on the twelfth floor.

'Jesus,' Lucy cries as the door swings open and we step inside. 'I feel like the Queen. I've died and gone to heaven.'

Well, I'm pretty sure heaven's not quite as sumptuous as this. Even after my time with Dan, I don't think I'll ever get used to this level of opulence. While the bell-boy offloads our luggage in the bedrooms, I explore the suite with Lucy: two bedrooms, two en suites and a sitting room the size of a football pitch. Forgetting to tip the bell-boy, we're lost in a daze, admiring massive sofas and chunky furniture, appreciating gigantic beds and luxurious soft furnishings, exchanging numerous 'oohs' and 'aahs' over twinkling chandeliers and expensive art work. Finally, we stand together by the window in the sitting room.

'This is weird.' I gaze out over a snow-covered Central Park. 'Are we really here?'

Lucy pinches me. 'Yep. It's all real.' She surveys the scene. 'A marathon journey, but definitely worth it.'

'Definitely.'

'We're living the dream, Maya. And well done, you. Only one panic attack.'

Yes, just the one. Shortly after take-off, I lost control of my breathing and burst into a fit of tears. But never mind. Digging my head into Lucy's chest for a good half an hour got me back on a fairly even keel.

'Are you okay?' She examines me closely. 'I mean, you know … what with the Dan thing.'

'Of course.'

But I'm not entirely sure about that. It's going to take a whole lot longer than a week to get over the man. And so far, I think it's safe to say I've made a complete pig's ear of the process. Spending the last few days locked away in Camden, I've cried an ocean, carried out the inevitable post-mortem, and come to the only conclusion I can – I've fucked up on a grand scale, and lost the only man I ever really loved.

'We've got an hour.'

'I know.'

As if I need a reminder. In his wisdom, Gordon's shipped us over on the very same day as the exhibition. And now, utterly knackered from the flight, I need to get ready, put on a positive face and present it to the world.

'Did you pack anything posh?'

'I'm not a complete idiot.'

Although I've opted for scruffs for the journey, I've packed a selection of Harrods dresses for New York. On more than one occasion, I'd been on the verge of carting the whole lot off to a charity shop, but now I'm glad I never got round to it. I need to look the part for the next couple of days, but as soon as this trip's over, they're all off to help out a good cause.

'You'd better make an effort for the exhibition,' she warns me. 'I'll do your make-up.'

'I can manage, thank you.'

'Did you bring jewellery?'

'Yes.'

But not the sweet pea necklace. That was carefully packed and despatched back to Lambeth three days ago. Despite the fact he told me to keep it, I had some clearing out to do.

'Right then.' Lucy claps her hands. 'Let's get this show on the road. See you in a bit.'

We go our separate ways. I take a shower, pull a brush through my hair and dry it off before emptying out my suitcase, choosing a simple black dress for the night and opting for stockings underneath. The usual bare minimum of make-up completes the preparations, along with the Yorkshire jet earrings. I'm examining myself in the mirror, thinking of how I wore the very same earrings on my first date with Dan, when Lucy bursts into my room.

'Are you ready? Gordon's downstairs in the lobby, waiting for us.'

'Yes. All ready.'

Grabbing a clutch bag and my coat, I follow Lucy to the lift, noting that underneath her coat, she's squeezed into a purple cocktail dress.

'This is going to be a brilliant night,' she says. 'I can feel it in my water.'

'I bet you can.'

I wish I could feel it too, but I'm as frozen as the streets outside. Despite spending an entire week in a slough of self-pity, I haven't moved on an inch. When all's said and done, I'm still imprisoned by shock, simply going through the motions. The door slides open onto the lobby where Gordon's waiting for us at the reception desk.

'Good evening, ladies. Looking delicious.'

'Thank you,' Lucy giggles. 'You too.'

He lifts an eyebrow.

'Ready for your big moment, Maya?'

'As ready as I'll ever be.'

I follow Gordon out into the night. Another ride in the black limousine through snow-lined streets brings us to the gallery.

Glowing with warmth and light in contrast to the dark avenue, a glass frontage stretches out before us. It's busy inside. Very busy. My pulse trips while my brain enters meltdown mode. I've been through this before, at Slaters, but it's different this time, on another level entirely. Taking a few deep breaths, I remind myself that I can do this. I can cope.

It only takes a couple of minutes to extract ourselves from the car and make it into the building, but by the time I'm inside, I'm already half frozen.

'Fuck,' I gasp, forgetting myself for a moment. I shake off my coat into an attendant's hands, straighten out my dress and scan the room, only to discover I'm surrounded by very arty types ... and they're all staring at me. A great start. 'Oh. I'm sorry.'

'It's okay.' Gordon touches me on the back. 'This is Maya Scotton, everyone.'

Still shivering, I'm guided through the crowd, introduced to one important person after another, asked repeatedly if I've had a pleasant journey. At last, I'm set free and I move on, taking in the space around me. It's ultra-swish: marble floors and plain white walls, adorned with a sea of canvases depicting naked bodies in one pose or another. I examine them all, one after the other, and at last I come to the triptych. It's spread out in its own area, spaced and lit to perfection. Several groups are standing in front of it, deep in conversation, motioning to it every now and then. Uncomfortable with the world scrutinizing my innermost thoughts, I falter. But I'm quickly recognised, thrust into a mad whirlwind of conversation, and questioned about my work. It's a thoroughly awkward experience, and I'm amazed I manage to keep control of my answers. Yes, it's a personal exploration of preferences. The man in the middle? No one in particular. Indulging in a little deflection, I bring the conversations back to the mechanics of painting, explaining how I wanted to tie the three canvases together, giving only the briefest over-view of what I was trying to explore. It seems to keep them content.

I decline a glass of wine, opting for juice instead. Lucy appears by my side.

'I'm knackered,' I chunter. 'This is relentless.'

'Don't worry. You're doing brilliantly. They're loving you. Just take a look around.'

She waves at the gallery, and I see her point. Most of the guests seem to have gravitated towards my canvases.

'You deserve this, Maya.'

'Thank you,' I say quietly. 'You know, if Dan's done nothing else for me, he got me here. He was a catalyst. He got me painting again ... and believing.'

'In what?'

'Myself.'

'Now, don't get big-headed.'

We smile at each other.

'Well, here's to Mr Mean and Hot and Moody.' I raise my glass, and so does Lucy. 'He may have screwed me over, but he also flicked the switch.'

'Ah, here's the artist,' Gordon announces, approaching me with an extremely hip and trendy woman on his arm. Squeezed into a tight tartan dress, she's all tiny fringe and bright red lipstick and supreme self-possession, the polar opposite of me.

'May I introduce Mindy Summers? She's going to interview you.'

Oh shit.

'Okay.'

I sense a knot of unease in my stomach and it's nothing to do with Mindy Summers or the impending interrogation. There's something strange in the look Gordon's giving me now, a mixture of pride and admiration ... and something else. Oh yes, I've definitely fallen into the sights of yet another millionaire. Maybe I should just tell him he's wasting his time, that I'm determined to give his sort a wide berth from now on, that he can stick his Lear jets and luxury apartments where the sun don't shine.

'We've got a quiet space set aside for you.'

Taking hold of my elbow, he guides me to the back of the gallery. I seat myself on a velvet-covered bench and Mindy Summers sits opposite me. Gordon stands back, with Lucy at his side.

'You're not watching,' I tell them both.

'Why not?' Lucy demands. 'It's all going to be public sooner or later.'

Mindy Summers pulls out some sort of recording device. Switching it on, she consults her notes and then levels me with a gaze that tells me she's totally in control.

'We'd like a picture if that's okay.'

Oh, and a sexy voice to boot. All New York and sassy.

'Of course.'

'Our photographer's out front. I'll call him in when we're ready.'

'Fine.'

'So ... I'd like to start with the triptych, if that's okay.'

'It's the logical place to begin.'

81

'Can you explain the ideas behind it?'

Bugger it. Can I?

'I just wanted to explore something personal.'

'Sexual?'

'Yes.'

'And?' she prompts.

'Like I said, it's personal.'

'And like your friend said, you're making it public.'

'That doesn't mean I have to explain,' I snap. 'People are free to make their own inferences.'

'Maya.'

Gordon's voice interrupts us. I look up at him.

'What?'

'Give us a moment, Mindy.'

Urging me to my feet, he puts a hand to my back and nudges me into a corner.

'What's the matter with you?' he demands, more than slightly agitated.

'She's being nosy.'

'She's a journalist. That's her job. These people can boost your career, but you need them on your side. Be helpful, not difficult. Work with them, not against them.'

'But I don't know what to say.'

'Then think on your feet. And be honest. Don't be afraid to show the real you.'

'The real me?'

'That one.'

Reluctantly, and with a few deep breaths, I resume my place on the stool.

'Okay,' I begin. 'I'm sorry. I'm a bit jet-lagged. What was the question?'

'I asked you to explain a little about the triptych.'

'It's about pleasure ... and pain.'

'Masochism?'

'I suppose so.'

'You're into it?'

I catch a glint in her eye and for a split second, I wonder if she's into it too.

'A little.' I swallow. 'I met someone. He introduced me to it.'

'He inflicted pain on you?'

Good God, yes. Mental pain. Heaps of it. But I'm not about to go there.

'It wasn't abuse,' I explain quickly. 'Let's get that straight right from the start. It was consensual. I always had the option of stopping it, but I didn't. Because I liked it.'

'Liked?'

'Maybe that's the wrong word. I don't know. It gave me something.'

Miss Summers readjusts her position, leaning forward slightly.

'I'm interested.'

I'm sure she is.

'I'm not a freak. There are plenty of people indulging in this sort of thing.'

'Oh, I know.'

The bright red lips part, but no more questions come out of them. Instead, she waits for me to elaborate. I have no idea what to say next, and then suddenly I find myself mimicking Dan's explanation, clinging on to his words.

'Some people like the adrenalin rush. Some people use it to block things out. And then there are some who do it because they think they deserve it.'

'And you?'

'A mixture of all three.'

Good grief, did I just say that? Well, judging by the anticipation that's currently lurking beneath that ultra-short fringe, it seems I did. Okay, so I'd better move on, explain a little. For a few moments, I flounder, struggling to find the right words. Finally, something begins to slip out, something I recognise ... and I think it might be the truth.

'I loved the adrenalin, feeling alive, alert, in the moment. When you're in the moment, nothing else matters. It's exhilarating.'

'And blocking things out? Deserving it?'

I focus on the floor, wishing I'd just stuck with the adrenalin thing, because now I've backed myself into a corner.

'Oh, I get it. You want to know about the tortured artist. Yes, I'm screwed up, but then again most of us are.'

She laughs.

'Oh, I know. But right now, I'm interested in this particular screwed up artist. This is amazing work, Maya. I want to know what brought you to paint it.'

What brought me to it? Panicking now, I check with Gordon. He nods, prompting me to go on.

'Say it as it is.' He smiles gently.

Easier said than done when you've avoided the truth for your

83

entire life. So, where do I begin? I need to dig back in time, before Dan, before Tom, before Boyd. Further back.

'Some people are blessed with self-confidence,' I begin, 'right from the start. Some people are born with it. Some have it bred into them.'

'And you?'

'Neither. I wasn't naturally self-confident. There wasn't much in my upbringing to encourage it. I was a loner, didn't have many friends, never felt confident with boys, that sort of thing. I didn't understand why I didn't fit in. I just carried on, hoping there'd be something better one day, hoping I'd find somewhere I felt at home.'

In Dan's arms. That's where I finally felt at home.

And now he's gone.

'But you had your talent.'

'I wasn't even sure of that. My parents praised my art. They knew I was good, but they never really thought I could make a living out of it. They said I'd be better off getting a proper job, settling down. I'm not blaming them. It's not their fault. It was just the way they'd been brought up. The only people who really encouraged me were my art teachers.' I sigh. 'Look, there was no big trauma in my childhood. It was just life that made me that way.'

I'm not about to mention my sister's part in all of this. She's going through enough without being vilified in the press. And besides, I've always known that's not the whole story.

'I was different, and not particularly happy to be different. I could have tried to change, but the truth is I never wanted to. I wanted to read and paint and be on my own. I was too sensitive, constantly in touch with my own shortcomings.'

'Maybe that's part of being creative.'

'Maybe. For some people. But it leaves you vulnerable.' And maybe I'm getting to it now. 'I fell into a relationship, a while before this one.' I motion to the triptych. 'He made me feel special, but then it turned abusive. I ran away. And then there was another. It was dull. I kidded myself I was in love, but I wasn't. I was just doing what my parents wanted me to do, blindly sleepwalking into oblivion. I wasn't even painting. I should have got out of it, but I didn't. He did me a favour in the end. He called it a day. So, it was one failure after another and when you're weak, it's difficult to break the cycle. I suppose that's what I was blocking out. And part of me wanted to be punished for my own stupidity.'

'So, this man here. Is he number one or number two?'

'He came afterwards.' I pause, tears welling in my eyes. 'Like I said, he introduced me to pain. It started off with the rush, but he saw what I was doing. He knew I'd be addicted ... for all the wrong reasons. He told me I didn't deserve to be punished. I deserved to be loved.'

'A happy ending?'

'Not exactly.' I give her a bitter smile. 'We're not together any more. But I'm stronger now, I think. I know where I'm going, what I'm doing with my life.'

I come to a halt. Mindy Summers stares at me, clearly noticing my distress.

'Thank you.' She switches off the recorder. 'I've got enough.'

More than enough. For the first time in my life, I've opened up completely. And now I just want to curl up in a dark room. I feel a hand on my arm.

'It's time to go,' Gordon tells me, helping me to my feet.

With guests politely ushered out of the way and photographs taken of me sitting in front of the triptych, trying to look deep and meaningful, Gordon makes our excuses and guides me and Lucy back outside to a waiting car. A short, silent journey and we're back at the hotel, waiting for the lift in the lobby.

'Did I get it wrong?' I ask at last.

'No, you got it absolutely right,' he replies, his face brightening. 'You were honest, a natural.'

'I thought I'd done something wrong. You got us out of there pretty quickly.'

'Job done. No need to hang around. Besides, I'd like a chat. I'm staying in the penthouse.'

'Here?'

'Sure.'

'Oh.'

'I've got a little something for you.'

His face is at it again, throwing out one expression after another before I can pin down exactly what's going on.

'I'm a bit tired.'

I manage a yawn. There's no way I'm going up to the penthouse with Gordon. I may well be exhausted, but I can still spot a seduction in the making.

'You'll be fine when you see what I've got.' He winks. 'Just give me a few minutes to get things ready, then come on up. It's important. Believe me. Goodnight, Lucy.'

He steps into the lift. The door slides shut and he's gone.

'Well, that's me told,' Lucy grizzles. 'I'm not invited.'

'And I'm not going up to the sodding penthouse.'

'Yes, you are.'

'He's going to try it on.'

'No, he's not.'

'He just winked at me.'

'And? Just go up there and see what's going on. It could be anything. He might have sold the triptych. He might have a commission for you. If it's business, then great. If Gordon tries to get his wicked way, then you're more than capable of knocking him back.'

The lift arrives again.

'Alright,' I mutter, stepping in and pressing the button for the top floor. 'But I'm telling you now, I won't be long.'

Chapter Nine

The lift opens onto an entrance hall. I thought our suite was amazing, but this is something else, the Art Deco theme at its simple and super-expensive best. I take in the marbled walls, a red leather chair, a side table topped with two massive urns, but it's the doors leading through to the rest of the suite that really grab my attention. Slightly ajar, they're fashioned from dark wood, adorned with straight symmetrical silver lines that fold in on themselves, creating a maze effect. I spend a moment or two admiring them, increasingly aware of music playing in the background, and more than slightly anxious that this is all part of a grand seduction plan. I glance back at the lift. The doors have already closed. I should really press the call button and beat a hasty retreat, but if Lucy's right and Gordon's doing nothing more than setting himself up as my patron, I need to give him the chance.

I edge toward the doors, nudge them open and sidle into a vast living area. Softly lit by table lamps, decorated in creams and browns and complete with the obligatory luxurious sofas and expensive tables, it's an Art Deco dream. Although it's getting late, the curtains remain open, framing a breathtaking view of Central Park in all its glory. Drawn straight to the window, I drop my handbag and take a few steps forward. Coming to a halt in front of the glass I gaze out at the skyline of the West Side, hypnotised by a thousand lights twinkling from a thousand apartments, listening to the soft rise and fall of guitar strings. At last, I recognise the song. It's Snow Patrol. 'Shut Your Eyes'.

Caught in the magic of the moment, I hardly notice it at first. But slowly, I become alert to my own reflection in the glass. And my heart beat catches, falters, returns with a vengeance ... because I'm not alone. There's a figure behind me.

I open my mouth, sense the beginnings of panic, inform myself that I must be dreaming because this just isn't possible.

'You took your time,' he says, his voice rich and deep and velvety.

I stay exactly where I am, fixated on the window. I can see him clearly in the darkness, the tousled hair, the black suit over a white shirt, tie-less and open at the collar. Hands in pockets, head tipped slightly to one side, he's looking straight back at me.

'Dan?'

I get no further. In a fluster, my body launches into its habitual Daniel Foster fiasco. Bones turn to jelly, muscles to blancmange. My pulse races and my lungs shrink to a fraction of their normal size. I'm not entirely sure whether I'm breathing in or breathing out ... or even breathing at all. I'd urge my brain to deal with the mess, but there really is no point. It's currently pre-occupied with the question to end all questions.

'What the fuck?' I murmur, letting it into the open.

He takes his hands out of his pockets and moves closer. I fizzle with anticipation. I can smell him now, that signature scent of his, fresh and clean. He slips an arm around my waist, watching me for a few seconds before he leans in, gently skimming his lips across my skin. I feel his breath against my neck and fizzle some more ... shortly before I come to my senses.

'Stop.'

He pulls back at my command, and I jolt with surprise. This isn't the Dan I know. He'd just carry on, regardless of complaints.

'Let go of me.'

Again he complies, backing away a few feet and keeping his eyes firmly fixed on mine. I'd like to ask him what's going on, but I'll have to figure out the whole 'personality transplant' thing after I've dealt with the anger. It's already sparking into life.

'Who the fuck do you think you are?' I growl. Swivelling on the spot, I note the fact that he looks ruddy gorgeous, and then remember he's an arrogant prat. 'You treat me like dirt and come back for a second helping?'

'There's more to this than meets the eye.'

'Of course there is. I suppose you've locked me in.'

'Naturally.'

'Why break the habit of a lifetime?'

'It's not the habit of a lifetime. I've only taken to false imprisonment where you're concerned.'

He moves forward slightly, causing a frisson to travel down my

88

spine. I hold up a finger in warning.

'Do not lay a hand on me.'

'I won't. I promise. Not until you want me to.'

'Until?' I gasp incredulously. 'Like it's ever going to happen.'

I give him a damn good glare, knowing full well I already want both of his hands on every part of me. It's quickly followed by a damn good mental slap. I will not cave in to lust. Not this time.

'I don't know what you're up to,' I tell him, 'but I'm out of here.'

I begin to move and so does he, quickly positioning himself between me and the doors.

'Look.' He holds up a hand. 'I know you think I'm a huge fucked-up disaster zone. You made that perfectly clear. But you need to hear me out. All I'm asking is five minutes of your time.'

'Demanding, not asking. There's no asking when you're the one with the keys ... unless you're lying again.'

I spot a hint of panic in his eyes.

'Just five minutes,' he repeats. 'And then ... possibly ... the rest of your life.'

I blink, barely able to believe what I'm hearing. The man who totally withdrew from me, who paraded his latest conquest in front of my eyes and then told me to fuck off, has actually changed his mind? Well, apparently so. Reaching into his pocket, he produces the sweet pea necklace and offers it to me.

'This thing doesn't know whether it's coming or going.'

I gaze at the necklace, and then at his hand. I'm pretty sure it's shaking.

'Keep it.'

'It's yours.'

'I don't want it.'

'It belongs to the woman I love.'

I force out a laugh.

'You don't love me. You're plain lazy, Dan. It doesn't work out with Little Miss No Tits so you're down to recycling your ex.'

'You were never my ex.'

'Yeah, whatever.'

I wave a hand in the air. After the weeks of torture, I should be relieved, but I'm not. I should be swooning into his arms, but I'm far too busy weighing up the practicalities of kneeing him in the nuts. Hell hath no fury like a woman scorned, especially in public, and if he thinks he can just pick up from where we left off, he's in for a massive surprise. He takes another step forwards, smiling gently and causing my fury to double in size. 'No contact!' a voice cries out at the back of my head. 'You'll lose all sense, and he'll get exactly what he wants.'

'I said don't touch me,' I sneer, astonished when he comes to a halt.

'Somebody's pissed off.'

'I wonder why.' I stare at him. 'Where's Gordon?'

As if I need to ask. It's suddenly completely clear. Gordon's been in on this all along.

'You've got me to yourself, and you're worried about Gordon?' He shakes his head incredulously. 'He's gone home.'

'But he's staying here.'

I point at the floor.

'You don't really think he needs to rent out a room in this place? He's got an apartment on the West Side.'

'But I thought ...'

'He was coming on to you?' He laughs, his eyes glimmering in the lamplight. 'No chance of that. Gordon's one hundred percent gay.'

My thoughts slam into a wall of confusion. Surely not. No, no, no. Gordon Finn can't be gay. I would have picked up on the signs.

'You're kidding me.'

I'm gawping now, a bit like a landed fish.

'I'm not. He's more likely to try it on with me than you.' A frown appears. 'You weren't attracted to him, were you?'

'Of course not.'

'Because I wouldn't be too happy about that.'

'I didn't fancy him.'

I've no idea why I'm defending myself. I'm about to tell him as much when the glimmer returns, dancing mischievously through his blue irises and setting off a delicious quivering sensation between my thighs.

'But you came up here to see him.'

'He said he wanted to talk.' I've had enough. It's time to turn the tables. 'And anyway, why am I the one getting an interrogation? You've got a few things to explain yourself, mister.'

'Such as?'

'Such as? Well, why this, for a start? Why lure me up here without letting me know what was going on?'

'We didn't want to take any chances.'

'Bloody rich. You've been keeping me in the dark ... again. You didn't trust me.'

He takes another shifty step toward me. And I take one back, pointing at him.

'Stop right there. You didn't trust me, did you?'

'We couldn't let you know what was going on. Foultons advised ...'

Oh, that again.

'I don't care what Foultons advised. You promised.'

'I know, but we had to keep it simple. Lucy might have found out.'

'I could have dealt with that.'

'You've had enough to deal with.'

'Yes,' I shout, making him start. 'I've had plenty to deal with. Weeks of shit, thank you very much. You didn't get in touch with me, you pulled out of Slaters, you didn't sell Fosters, not one word of reassurance, and then ...' I splutter, pointing at him again, 'you went and got yourself another woman.'

He takes another small step.

'Stop!'

'Never.'

Well, that's more like it. Determined to get what he wants, the old Daniel Foster hasn't completely disappeared.

'Leave me alone.'

'Impossible.'

'I wait three sodding months for you and the first time you see me, you talk to me like I'm ... shit on your shoe.'

'Interesting phrase.'

'What?'

'Every time I've ever had shit on my shoe, I've never bothered talking to it.'

'You're not funny.'

'If you say so.'

He's moving again, inching forward little by little until he's close enough to touch me. I'd edge further backwards but I seem to have a sofa behind me now. If I end up on that, he'll be on top of me before I can take a breath.

Suddenly, he grabs my arm. Curling long fingers around my flesh, he tugs me in close and seals his mouth against mine. Immediately and without the slightest hesitation, I let myself down, kissing him back with a vengeance and enjoying every single second of it: the softness of his lips, the touch of his tongue. It goes on for an eternity, giving me more than enough time to realise what's going on. He's lost patience with being patient, and now he's reverting to the usual battle plan – shock and awe.

'It was all an act,' he breathes, when he's finally had his fill.

'Well, it was a fucking good act,' I breathe back. 'You were all over that tart like a rash.'

'Enough of the clichés, Maya. It was an elaborate ruse.'

'Elaborate ruse, my arse. You were enjoying it.'

'Trust me. I wasn't.'

'Did you kiss her?'

'No.'

'Did you fuck her?'

'Certainly not.' A hand comes to my buttocks, pressing me into his crotch. 'This thing belongs to you.' And judging by the feel of it, he's primed and ready for action. 'Are we through with the ranting yet?' Keeping me tight in his grip, he searches my face for signs of an answer.

Finally, my brain clicks back into action.

'Condescending twat. Just because you kissed my face off, it doesn't mean we're good. I've got plenty more ranting to do yet. Now get off me.'

With a shrug, he releases me, steps back and makes his way towards a bar.

'Okay. But would you like a drink while you're at it?'

Astounded by his sudden nonchalance and silently amazed he's still in full possession of a sexy walk, even after everything he's been through, I watch as he carefully places the necklace on the counter.

'You're asking for it, Mr Foster.'

'I'll be begging for it before long.' He lifts a bottle. 'This is a seriously nice Pinot, by the way.'

'And you're a serious piece of work.'

'Thank you.'

He pours a glass and brings it over to me.

With a petulant sneer, I take it.

'Don't throw that over me,' he warns. 'It's expensive stuff.'

'I can do better than chucking a glass of wine at you.'

'I know you can.' Beating a hasty retreat, he lowers himself onto a sofa, smiles and straightens his jacket. 'To be perfectly honest, I kind of banked on you falling into my arms as soon as you saw me. I obviously got that bit wrong. You're angry. I get it.' Every last bit of playfulness evaporates. 'I'm sorry I didn't get in touch and I'm sorry for the way I treated you, but you need to understand two things: none of it was real ... and all of it was necessary.' He holds my gaze. 'So, if you'd like to join me ...' He pats the space next to him. 'I'll explain the details. And then you can forgive me. And then you can fall into my arms.'

'I wouldn't bank on it.'

92

'Oh come on, Maya. It's inevitable.'

And you know it, a voice niggles at the back of my head. Totally inevitable. Within the next half an hour, you'll be writhing around on some luxury Art Deco bed with Mr Foster seeing to your every want and need. I sip at the wine, watching as he leans back and crosses his legs. I catch a wince, just a slight one.

'Are you in pain?' I ask. In the midst of the confusion and anger and lust, I've pushed all thoughts of the accident right out of my mind.

'No,' he answers crisply.

'But you winced.'

'My pants are too tight.'

'There isn't a millionaire on the planet whose pants are too tight.'

'I'm an exception to the rule.'

From the steely glint in his eyes, I can tell I'm not about to get the truth. He's working to his own agenda, and I'll just have to add 'obvious signs of discomfort' to the list of things he can explain later. Warily, I take a seat on the opposite sofa and set down my glass on the coffee table.

'Well?' I open.

'Where shall I start?'

'The beginning's a good place.'

His eyes flicker.

'So it is. Okay, let's go back in time. I had music played for you in that wine bar. Remember?'

I nod.

'I wanted you to know I was there, that I was thinking about you. I had somebody drop by to Slaters to reel you in.'

I flick back through the memories. The brogue-wearing jazz fan. Massive cushions. Expensive wine. Music.

'He bribed the barman to play a few songs, our songs, with a little addition. 'I'll Wait for You'.'

'Nice touch,' I mutter reluctantly.

'And what harm could it do? That's what I thought. Turns out I'd made the first mistake.' He pauses. 'Boyd smelt a rat.'

And now I'm thinking of broken veins and sunken eyes, an idiotic smile aimed in the wrong direction.

'There was a man in there. He was watching me. I didn't know whether he was one of yours or one of theirs.'

'One of theirs,' Dan confirms. 'That night, Boyd contacted Clive. He wanted to know what we were playing at.'

'It was my fault. I made it too obvious.'

'It was my fault. I shouldn't have put you in that situation. You couldn't help reacting the way you did.' His lips twitch. He's half-teasing me. And why wouldn't he? After all, I may be a little prickly at the minute but despite everything that's happened, I'm utterly and completely in love with this man ... and he knows it. 'Clive did his best to smooth things over but Boyd wasn't convinced. So, I didn't contact you again. I didn't dare.' His eyes search mine for understanding. 'Are you with me so far?'

I nod again, already convinced I've grabbed the wrong end of the stick. In fact, if I'm not much mistaken, I've grabbed the wrong stick altogether.

'I know it was hard for you.' He watches me closely. 'Trust me, I conjured up endless ways of getting messages to you and every single time, I thought better of it. I couldn't take any chances. I can't tell you how many letters I wrote with broken wrists. It takes forever, you know.' He pauses, raising both arms. 'They're okay now, by the way. Thanks for asking.'

Suddenly, I'm washed through with shame. I should have asked before.

'You're better then?'

'Physically fine. Bones heal, but this thing.' He touches his chest, just where his heart is. 'This isn't feeling too good right now.'

'But you winced. I saw it.'

'Underpants,' he says sternly, dismissing my concern. 'Now, let's address a few facts here.' He draws in a breath, and goes on briskly. 'We tried to track Boyd, but it's been impossible. He's used a different mobile every time, and then dumped it. I got a new phone, a new number, and so did Clive, but somehow Boyd always managed to get in touch again. I had no idea what he was capable of or how he was getting his information. I pulled out of Slaters because there was no way I could keep it a secret. If I'd gone ahead with the deal, Boyd would have found out.' He uncrosses his legs, winces again and leans forward. 'I've known Gordon since university. We haven't been in touch that often, so he was an ideal wing-man. Seeing as I couldn't buy Slaters, I asked him to step in and keep it safe for me.'

'You're still buying?' I ask. In spite of a good infusion of endorphins, confusion and jet-lag are still doing their best to scramble my brain. I'm not being too quick tonight.

'Of course.' He cocks his head to one side. 'I'm going to need something to keep me occupied when Fosters is gone.'

'You are selling it? But I thought you were expanding.'

He laughs.

'Rumours of expansion. Nothing concrete. Fosters needs to be in a good position when the time comes. In reality, I've been working on the sale behind the scenes. It's a long process. The Board are in on the deal, but it's top secret for the time being. We can't have anyone smelling weakness.'

'I thought you'd changed your mind.'

'Why would I do that?' He gets up, heads straight for the window and looks out over Central Park. 'I've made the right decision,' he says quietly, 'and I'm sticking by it.'

I sit in silence, stunned by it all.

'And just in case you're thinking I'm a rich, up-his-own-arse twat ...' He turns back to me. 'I'm doing my best to sell Fosters as a going concern, trying to protect as many of those jobs as possible, but beyond that I can't be responsible for everyone who works there ... not any more.'

He takes off his jacket and throws it over the back of a chair.

'Norman's finally retired, by the way.'

'He has?'

He nods. 'Betty's not too happy about it. He's under her feet all the time now. Jodie's started her beauty course. I'm happy to report there have been no more drug sprees. And lately, she's even taken to wearing things that aren't pink.'

At the thought of the pink princess, my face relaxes and my lips curve upwards.

'Bingo.' Satisfied he's nearly there, he moves back toward me, slowly. 'I knew you'd come round.'

'Big head.'

'I love you, Maya. I never stopped loving you. I never stopped thinking about you. The last few weeks ... they've been torture for both of us.'

My breathing becomes shallow again. I'm melting under his gaze, on the verge of getting up and throwing myself at him. But before I do, there's one final matter that needs a little explanation.

'So, about what happened at the nightclub?'

He rubs his forehead, closing his eyes for a second.

'It was the last thing I wanted, but it had to be done ... and it had to be convincing.'

He edges past the coffee table and sits next to me, his hand brushing against my thigh. My body tingles. We're getting close to the end game. He's homing in for the kill.

'Things had been quiet for a while,' he explains. 'Foultons were busy protecting you and me, searching for Boyd. Bill's contacts got involved, but we couldn't find him. I got out of hospital, went back to work, did what I needed to do. And then things went a little pear-shaped.'

I look up. His eyes have darkened now.

'The day before I saw you at the nightclub. I got a call from Boyd. He said he knew what we were up to, and I had to put it right.'

'How did he know?'

'He wouldn't say, but ...'

'Me,' I interrupt, flushing with embarrassment. 'Turning up at Fosters.'

'No, I don't think so.' He lays a hand on my leg. 'And I don't blame you for it. I know about Claudine's involvement.'

'You do?'

'You were followed, every single minute of every day. I had reports.'

My thoughts stumble over themselves. So, if it wasn't my mad stalking episode, then it must have been the ridiculous phone call to Lily.

'Did you hack my mobile?'

'It was tracked, not hacked. Who you call and what you say is your business. I trusted you to make the right decisions.'

And he must already know I made a wrong decision. If he didn't listen in on my phone call, then Lily must have told him about it herself. I'm about to admit to a huge bout of stupidity when he floors me with something else.

'It was the letter. I'm sure of it.'

'What letter?'

'The one from Layla. She did write to me.'

'Oh shit.'

He squeezes my thigh, gently.

'She apologised for what happened, said she hoped I was okay, and told me about Sophie, who's moved back to Limmingham, by the way. And then she said she knew the truth, that the split was a sham.'

I let my head fall into my hands.

'I didn't want to tell her. Honestly, I didn't. But she went to pieces. I'm sorry, Dan. I made her promise not to say anything. I made her promise to wait.'

'It's okay. I understand.'

I look up again to find him smiling.

'She's my sister. Maybe we both inherited the impatient gene.'

'But still ...' I opened the bag and let the cat right out of it. How could he possibly understand?

'Sophie's ill. Layla's had a hard time of it. I can see why you told her.'

'Did you write back?'

'No,' he answers quickly. 'I'll make contact when I'm ready.'

And this isn't the time to quiz him on that particular matter. Instead, I move on with something else.

'But how would Boyd know about the letter?'

'It arrived at the penthouse. I was down in Surrey. Normally, the concierge keeps my post secure, but he was on holiday. The stand-in didn't quite understand procedures. The letter was downstairs in the lobby, in a pile on the desk. It had been there for a few days before I picked it up.'

'Had it been opened?'

'Maybe. It's hard to tell, but it's the only thing I can think of.'

I let out a quiet sigh of relief. He definitely doesn't know about the phone call. I could tell him now, but I'd rather not. I'm already feeling like a prize idiot and I can't really see what difference a confession would make. Whether it's down to Layla's letter or Boyd tapping my phone, the damage has already been done. And whatever Dan says, it's been done by me. All we can do now is deal with the fallout.

'I had to do something,' he says. 'And I had to do it quickly. That's why I rigged up the meeting at the club. That's why I made a show of it. I just hope it did the trick.'

'I'd be amazed if it didn't.'

'I never wanted to hurt you, Maya, but I couldn't let you know the truth. There was no safe way to do it. I can play the heartless bastard. I've had years of practice. But if you'd known what was really going on, would you have been able to play your part so well?'

'I could have had a damn good try.'

He laughs, his eyes dancing.

'Your acting isn't up to much.'

'Well, I'm an artist, not an actress, not like Little Miss No Tits.'

'I love it when you're jealous.' He bites back a grin. 'I'm assuming you're referring to my so-called girlfriend.'

I can't help it. My lips pull back into a sneer. I must look like a rabid dog.

'That woman was paid a significant amount of money,' he explains. 'Provided by Foultons. Fully vetted. Back story. The lot.'

'Really?'

'Really.' He shakes his head. 'You lost faith.'

97

'And can you blame me?'

'Don't believe a thing you see. That's what I said.'

'And I tried. But it took so long.'

He leans in, ever so slightly, and drapes an arm behind my head. I want the talking to stop now, but we're not finished yet.

'Why did you go to that club?' he asks.

Oh God. Of course he'd know about that, my desperate search for an escape. I know he understands. It was because I'd been rejected, because I felt useless. I needed to let the pain rush through me, and simply forget it all.

'I cracked,' I admit, feeling small and pathetic.

'We're only human.' He skims a fingertip against the back of my neck. 'What do you think this is? All this cloak and dagger crap? This is me cracking. I can't take it any more, not being with you.'

The finger circles slowly, and I close my eyes, soaking up the glorious sensation of his touch.

'But he'll find out.'

'Not if I can help it.'

'He'll know you're here.'

'No, he won't. Officially, I'm in Bermuda. It's all a risk, but we couldn't go on the way we were. Look at me, Maya.'

I open my eyes and what I see sets a glow in my heart. Contentment. Tenderness. Pure love. Yet again, I've been the queen of difficult, but he's battered against my defences, and broken them down.

'Can we get to the bit where you fall into my arms now?' He gives me that boyish grin. 'Please?'

'Oh, why not?'

I sink against his chest, allowing his arms to close around me, relieved that after all this time I'm finally back where I belong. In a split second, the floodgates open. I begin to cry, spilling out all the anger and frustration in one fell swoop. And through it all he holds me tight, smoothing my hair, rocking me gently, occasionally pulling back to kiss my forehead and tell me everything's going to be fine. Finally, a handkerchief appears in front of my face. With a sob, I take it and put it to good use. When I've sorted myself out, he stands and urges me to my feet. Signalling for me to wait, he goes back over to the bar and picks up the necklace. Turning my back to him, I hold up my hair, allowing him to place the sweet pea back around my neck. He seals the clasp.

'That's where it belongs, Maya. Don't ever send it back to me again.'

'I won't.' I face him.

'Tell me you love me. I need to hear it.'

'I love you.'

'And I love you too. Never forget that. You and me. We're for keeps.'

He pulls me into his arms, holding me for an age before he delivers another perfect kiss.

'How long have we got?' I ask.

'Not long enough.' He touches the sweet pea. 'Two days. It's all I could manage. Have you got your mobile?'

I nod to my handbag.

'You need to ring Lucy. Tell her you got lucky with Gordon.'

'But he's gay.'

'And firmly in the closet, perfectly happy to provide an alibi.'

'But me and Gordon?'

'Yes, you and Gordon. You're a terrible slapper. Did you know that?'

'Takes one to know one.'

'Touché.' He saunters over to the handbag. 'Tell Lucy you'll be spending the next couple of days with your latest conquest. He's insisting on it. Tell her not to worry. Gordon's arranging for her to be picked up tomorrow morning by one of his people. She'll be shown the sights of Manhattan, wined and dined and all that. Lap of luxury. Money no object.'

He picks up the bag, places it on a side table and opens it.

'And Boyd?'

'If he finds out about Gordon, he's got his confirmation that we're over.'

Rummaging through the bag, he pulls out a receipt and an empty crisp packet.

'And then he'll start on Gordon.'

'Let him try. The big G's got his own security team. We're talking billionaire territory. No one can get to him.'

'But our family, our friends.'

'He told us to keep apart. He didn't tell you to keep away from other men. Worst case scenario, he'll just try to threaten Gordon. Good luck to him.'

'Lucy's going to go mad.'

'She'll soon forget.' And now he pulls out a clump of tissues and gives me a disapproving glance. 'Gordon's man's a bit of a looker by all accounts. He'll keep her happy.'

'Don't tell me ...'

'Strictly no shenanigans.' He rummages some more. 'He's under strict orders to be a perfect gentleman. Clive wouldn't be too impressed with anything else. We're not the only ones who've been waiting, remember?'

'You really are sneaky.'

'It's one of my strengths.'

At last, he manages to locate my mobile.

'Now, Miss Scotton ...' He holds it out to me. 'It's time to piss off your best friend.'

Chapter Ten

I'm still reeling from Lucy's ear bashing when Dan takes the mobile from me and lays it on the coffee table. With a glint in his eyes, he leads me through the suite to the master bedroom.

Like the rest of the penthouse, it's top-notch, everything luxurious, antique, solid. I'm surrounded by a range of dark wood furniture: a wardrobe, a chest of drawers, a cream sofa and over by the window, two armchairs next to an occasional table. But without a doubt, the centrepiece of the room is the huge bed, complete with a slatted wooden headboard. Draped with rich cotton covers and a cream silk throw, it's sprinkled with an array of cushions in a range of deep browns and reds. And behind it, along the entire length of the room, windows give out over Central Park. I'm gazing in awe at the scene when I feel his hands around my waist.

'Nice dress,' he murmurs into my ear. 'Where did you get it?'

'Harrods, I think.' His lips brush against my neck, just under my ear lobe. 'I was a bit drunk at the time.'

He laughs and turns me to face him.

'You are a bad, bad woman. One of the many reasons I love you.'

'Are you going to draw those blinds?'

'No. Nobody can see us.'

'But Boyd ...'

He places a finger on my lips.

'Isn't out there in the park, isn't over on the West Side, isn't here full stop.'

We lock eyes for a few seconds before he draws me in for a long, deep kiss. While one hand comes to rest between my shoulder blades and another on my buttocks, I drift away into a dream world, forgetting Boyd, tracing my palms across Dan's biceps, up his shoulders, finally clamping them across the back of his neck. I'm

101

knocking on the door of my own personal promised land when, in the midst of it all, a simple fact bubbles to the surface of my brain.

Shit.

I haven't been taking my pill for the last week, not since the nightclub incident. After Dan's apparent rejection, I couldn't see the point.

Double shit.

I really should tell him, because I'm willing to bet he's not come armed with condoms, and seeing as he's not supposed to be here I have no idea how he'd manage to get hold of any at short notice. Within a matter of seconds, I've made a rash decision. I won't fill him in on the situation because I'm fired up on lust. Instead, as soon as I'm out of this place, I'll get myself to a pharmacy for the morning-after pill.

He releases me and steps back.

'Stay exactly where you are.'

I do as I'm told. After all, I know the deal … and I like it too. Fizzing with anticipation, I wait as he circles me, slowly, surveying my body. At last, he reaches out and trails a finger lightly down my bare arm. A spark of electricity erupts at my core. I close my eyes, throw my head back and groan.

'Head up,' he whispers into my ear, behind me now. 'Eyes open.'

His hands come to my waist and hold me firm.

'You've lost weight.'

'I've been on a wine diet. Broken heart and all that.'

'You need to eat, woman. I love your curves.'

Releasing me, he takes hold of the zipper, patiently draws it down and slips both hands inside my dress, running warm palms across my skin, easing the fabric away from my shoulders until it drops to the floor. The spark of electricity erupts again. This time, it's joined by others. Flinging themselves around my crotch with wild abandon, they're already transforming me into a melting, quivering mess.

'Oh good Lord,' he breathes.

'What?'

'White knickers, black bra.'

'Shit.'

Instinctively, I try to bend down to retrieve the dress, but I'm stopped immediately and urged back up.

'If there's one thing I've learned over the years,' he says, wheeling me round. 'When a woman goes out to get laid, she always wears matching underwear.'

His eyes flash with amusement.

'So, here's your proof. I wasn't planning on fucking anyone else, including Gordon.'

'I'm sure he'll be relieved to hear that.'

He reaches round, unclasps my bra and draws it away. With a smile of appreciation, he throws the bra to one side and cups my breasts for a moment before leaning down to seal his lips around my right nipple. He sucks gently, licks and sucks again. A sudden flood of heat in my breast quickly spreads through the rest of my body, wrenching the air out of my lungs, causing mayhem in my stomach and homing in on my crotch. Trying to steady myself, I grab his shoulders. Immediately, he releases the nipple and lowers himself to his knees. Slipping an index finger into my knickers, he tears them away, leaving me in nothing but stockings and suspenders.

'Hello again.' He smiles at my crotch, parting my pubic hair. 'Long time, no see. How have you been?'

'A bit bored actually,' I answer on its behalf.

He raises an eyebrow. 'Really? You didn't indulge in a little finger action?'

'Well ...' A blush rises in my cheeks. 'Maybe a little.'

'Vibrator?' he asks, tenderly smoothing a fingertip across my labia.

I shake my head.

'Never owned one.'

'Good God, woman. We'd better put that right. I'll buy you one for Christmas.' His eyes darken. 'And then I'll use it on you.' He kisses my crotch. 'Get your backside on that bed.'

Again, I follow orders and by the time I'm in position on my back, he's standing again, watching me

'Right,' he says, growing serious. 'I need to get this out of the way.'

'Get what out of the way?' I sit up.

He wavers.

'I'm a little different.'

'What do you mean?'

Keeping his eyes fixed on mine, and clearly uncertain of himself, he unbuttons his shirt. He slips it from his shoulders, drops it to the floor ... and waits. A silence extends between us. Finally, I break eye contact and look down, past the broad shoulders, the perfect chest and the six-pack, finally coming to rest on a scar that appears just above his waistband, crossing the lower half of his abdomen. Although I try not to react, I take in a sharp breath.

'Does it bother you?' he asks.

'No. It's just bigger than I thought.'

'Well ... they didn't exactly have time to be careful.'

'It makes no difference to me.'

'It's not the end of it.'

Slowly unbuckling his belt, he lowers his trousers to the floor, steps out of them and straightens up, presenting himself for inspection. Apart from the scar on his stomach, everything else is exactly as I remember. After a few weeks laid up in hospital, he must have been determined to get himself back into shape because he's as close to perfection as he's ever been. I'm about to tell him I see no difference when he turns to the side.

'How about this, then?' He nods down at his right leg.

I follow the direction of his gaze. Focussed on the lower part of the leg, but travelling up a little past the knee, the scars are vicious this time.

'It's a mess.'

I hear it in his voice and see it in his eyes. I'm not the only one who's been dealing with anger and frustration. For the time being, lust has flown straight out of the window. All I want to do is throw my arms around him, give him the reassurance he needs, but as soon as I begin to move, he raises a hand to stop me. No sympathy. All he wants is acceptance.

'Damaged goods.'

'You're not damaged. You're perfect in every single way.'

'Far from it.'

'Perfect for me. I don't care about the scars. They're part of you now ... and I love you, everything about you, every last imperfection.'

'I've got a few.'

'You had a few before the accident. It didn't stop me then, and it won't stop me now.'

Because each one of them is a mark of his suffering, proof that regardless of all the slings and arrows thrown his way, he's always been determined to pull through and make something better of his life. I gaze at him in utter admiration, noting that his breathing's quickened a little. His lips part, and I wonder if he's about to say something else, but as soon as it arrives, the moment's gone. Maybe it's time to inject a little humour into the situation.

'I'm willing to bet your cock's still in full working order.'

'It certainly is.' He smiles. 'A fact I'm about to prove.'

'Better get your pants off then ... seeing as they're too tight.'

'Absolutely.'

He takes off his underpants, his cock springing free, erect and ready to go. Straightening up again, he doesn't move. Instead, he stays exactly where he is, standing at the end of the bed, studying me.

'Lie back down. Show me your body.'

With my heart rate zooming off the chart, I do as I'm told, raising my arms above my head and wrestling for every single breath as his gaze moves from my face down to my breasts, further down, across my stomach, to the stockings. At last I can't take it any longer.

'Just get on with it.'

He bites back a laugh.

'Do you know what Winnie the Pooh said?' he asks.

'Pardon?'

'Winnie the Pooh?'

'Fuck Winnie the Pooh.'

'What an awful thing to say. I'd rather not, if you don't mind.'

I giggle.

'So, what did Winnie the Pooh say?'

'Although eating honey is a very good thing to do, there's a moment, just before you begin to eat it … I think it's called anticipation.'

'And I think you've anticipated enough.'

'Fair enough.'

He climbs onto the bed, manoeuvring himself onto his side next to me. Still making no contact, he leaves just enough space between us for me to feel the warmth of his body. Propping his head on his right hand, he rests his left arm along his side.

'But just a little more. Fucking hell, woman, I've missed you. How can that happen? How can you miss someone like they're a part of your body?'

'I have no idea. Just touch me. Please.'

He surveys my body again, enjoying the view.

'Where?' he asks at last.

'What?'

'Where do you want me to touch you?'

Oh God. What to say? My skin's effervescing.

'Anywhere. Everywhere.'

'Not good enough. I need specifics.'

And I need his hands on me now. I opt for an obvious start.

'Breasts.'

'Which part of your breasts?'

'Dan …

'Specifics,' he warns me.

'Nipples.'

He reaches over and takes hold of my right nipple, gently squeezing and tugging, slowly elongating it, causing me to moan. Satisfied with my reaction, he lets go, swirling an index finger around my areola, again and again. I moan some more.

'Enjoying that?'

'God, yes.'

'And now?'

'The other one,' I stammer. 'Do the same.'

'Magic word?'

'Now.'

He pulls back, removing all contact, and I squirm in disappointment.

'Try again.'

'Please.'

'That's more like it.'

He moves to my left nipple, repeating the process, watching my every reaction.

'Now, where shall I go?'

'Down,' I falter. 'Run your fingertips over my stomach.'

'Like this?' he asks, following my instructions. He splays his fingertips and touches them lightly against my skin. Starting just below my breasts and skimming downwards at a snail's pace, he leaves a trail of superheated flesh in his wake.

'Exactly like that,' I gasp.

He traces a path back up my stomach, stopping beneath my breasts, and then down again.

'And now?'

'Along my sides, and then inwards ... to that place.'

Eyes still firmly locked on mine, he moves his hand to my flank, laying his palm flat against my skin, and cocks his head.

'Which place?' he asks, trailing the palm downwards.

'You know ...'

'I'm afraid I have no idea.'

His eyes glimmer. He's teasing me.

'You know.' My breath jitters as he moves back up, down again. 'My lady garden.'

The hand's removed. He takes hold of my chin.

'I don't deal in euphemisms, sweet pea. Say the word.'

'My ... you know.'

He laughs.

'Say it.'

'Clitoris ... ah.' I squirm and close my eyes. I haven't got a clue why this makes me feel so embarrassed.

'Well done.' Releasing my chin, he brushes his fingers through my pubic hair. His index finger finds my clit and begins to circle, lazily. 'You know, for a woman who swears like a trooper, you're remarkably coy about your own body. It's just a word. There's no need for shame or embarrassment.'

'I can't help it.'

'Oh yes you can.'

I open my eyes to find him staring down at me, stern and tender all at once. His finger finds exactly the right spot and my muscles come alive.

'This is about intimacy, Maya. Feeling ashamed of nothing. Knowing what turns us on and why, what we like to give and receive, where we shouldn't go.' The finger continues to move, creating a bundle of heat just behind my clitoris. 'This is about knowing each other like no one's ever known us before, creating a bond so tight, no one can ever break it.'

'Well, if that's the case,' I manage to breathe, fired up by his words. 'I want your fingers inside my ... oh.' I'm temporarily halted by a ripple. 'My vagina,' I rasp. 'Right inside it ... and your thumb on my clitoris ... and I want you to suck my nipples while you're doing it.'

He smiles broadly.

'There, it's not so difficult, is it?'

His fingers enter me. One, then two, then three. He pushes deeper, rubbing against the underside of my clit and dispatching fireworks through every single nerve ending. At the same time, his thumb works at the outside. The fingers move, changing position slightly, finding another super-sensitive spot and bringing me right to the edge. And all the time, he watches me, gauging my state, stopping as I begin to quake inside.

'Oh no,' I whimper.

'Oh yes.' He begins again. 'Let's drag this out. So, that's the fingers inside the vagina and the thumb on the clitoris. What was the other thing?' A glimmer passes through his eyes. His lips twitch with mischief. 'Oh, I remember.'

Still working at my clit, he takes my left nipple in his mouth, licking and sucking. And before long, I'm quaking again. He's giving me pleasure ... pure pleasure. 'But how much?' my brain screams. 'Because you know what this man's capable of. He can pleasure you to death if that's what he's in the mood for.' And judging by the way he's trailing his tongue around my nipple right now, I'd say that's exactly what's going on. I have no idea how long it carries on, the fingers and thumb thrumming down below, his lips and tongue working at my nipple, but before long, I'm on the verge of becoming a sexual fruitcake.

'Bite,' I groan.

He comes to a halt, fingers still inside me, and raises his face to mine. Readjusting his position slightly, he brings his right palm to the back of my head and his left leg over mine.

'No.'

'But it's what I want.'

'And it's exactly where we shouldn't go.' He gazes at me, silently urging me to remember the night with the cross. 'Not now.'

Not now? But, does that mean not ever? I open my mouth to ask but he claims it before I can say a word, kissing me deeply for an age while he goes back to working at my clit.

'I give you an inch and you take a mile. I'm taking over again. I don't want you getting too big for your boots.'

'Controlling bastard.'

'Got me in one.' He brushes his lips across mine. 'A controlling bastard who's currently controlling you.' To make his point, he presses his leg against mine and tightens his fingers against my head. 'Keep those arms exactly where they are. I think it's time I allowed you an orgasm.'

'Thank bloody Christ,' I half shout.

He shakes his head, admonishing me.

'No noise, no movement, no distraction. I want you to soak up the sensation. Understand?'

I nod, my mouth clamped firmly shut.

'And I want your eyes on mine. Don't close them. Don't look away.'

I nod again.

Holding me in place, he picks up the rhythm down below. A ball of warmth rises quickly in my groin. It expands, shimmers, pulsates ... and then implodes. My muscles clutch at his fingers. A wave of ecstasy thrusts to the top of my vagina, and beyond. I jitter and judder beneath him, reach up and run my right hand across his shoulders, his biceps ... and then, quite inexplicably, I howl.

'I'm sorry,' I pant when I've finished. 'I couldn't help it. I just couldn't.'

'You're forgiven,' he laughs. 'I've never heard anything quite like that.'

'But I broke the rules. Big style.' A delicious idea occurs to me.

'I'd say that deserves a spanking.'

And that does it. A surge of adrenalin shows up at the party. But it doesn't stay long. He shakes his head again.

'No.'

'Oh, why not?'

'Because I say so.'

'But ...'

'Shush.' He puts a finger to my lips. 'You've got a memory like a sieve. Who's in charge here?'

'You are. But only in the bedroom.'

'And wherever else I decide to fuck you senseless.'

'But ...'

'Any more arguments and I'll indulge in some serious torture. And not the painful type either. You wouldn't enjoy it. If I were you, I'd just do as you're told.'

Leaving me to quake a little more, he repositions himself again, this time parting my legs and kneeling between them. He smooths both palms across my stomach, down to my thighs, stopping at the tips of the stockings.

'I love these stockings. Silk?'

'Of course. I've gone up in the world.'

He unclips the right stocking, patiently unrolling it, trailing his fingers across my skin and kissing the insides of my thighs. When he's removed the stocking, he moves to my left leg, doing exactly the same. Finally, unfastening the suspender belt, he casts it to the floor but keeps the stockings on the bed. And then he straddles me again.

I gaze up into a pair of glistening blue eyes.

'Are you going to fuck me now?' I grin.

'When I'm good and ready,' he grins back, retrieving the first stocking and dangling it above my head. 'Patience. Give me your hand.'

Gently, he brushes my hair away from my face before he sets about wrapping the stocking around my left wrist. With a knowing look, he leans over me, urging my arm upwards and fastening the stocking to the bedpost. While he concentrates on making sure the bindings aren't too tight, I grab the opportunity to examine the scar again, up close.

'Comfortable?'

'Yes, thank you.'

He repeats the process with my right hand.

'I've been looking forward to this for months.' He finalises the knot. 'And I intend to make a fucking meal of it. Have you seen enough of the scar?'

What? He's noticed?

'I didn't ...'

'Maybe I should blindfold you, take your mind off it.'

'No,' I blurt quickly. 'I want to see you.'

'Then behave yourself. If you're going to fixate on anything, fixate on this.' He points down to his erect penis, and then he touches my chin, angling my face towards his. 'They're just scars. That's what you said. I'm still perfectly capable of driving you wild.'

'Do your best.'

'Oh, I will. Trust me, you're going to be a deranged shell of a woman by the time I've finished with you.'

'I can take anything you've got.'

'That's fighting talk.'

He leans down, sealing his lips around mine and delivering a long, deep kiss. At last, he pulls away and smiles down at me. He's totally in control, and he knows it. Moving again, he parts my legs wider than before, and kneels between them.

'Am I allowed to make noises now?' I ask.

'Why not?'

He touches my vagina, moves the finger up to my clit, and back again. I buck at his touch. A palm comes to rest on my stomach, pushing me back into place. His eyes glint darkly.

'I'm going to remind you what you've got with me, and you're allowed to make all the noise you want, because I want to listen to your sweet moans while I make you come ... again and again and again.'

'I might howl again.'

'I don't care.' He leans down, smoothing back my pubic hair and blowing against my labia. 'Just don't beg me to stop.'

'Why not?'

'Because it's pointless. I'm not going to stop.'

'And if I do beg?'

His lips curl up at the corners.

'Then I'll gag you.'

A squeak escapes my mouth as he places a hand on each of my thighs and leans in. I feel his tongue at my anus, warm, soft and wet. He licks a path along the length of my perineum and then across my labia, probing softly between the folds. Spending an age there, he laps against the bundle of nerves before moving to my vagina, circling it, moving out and in, over and over again. And then his tongue penetrates me, as far as it can go, tasting me. A moan erupts from my lungs as he withdraws, moving back to my clit. And then he works at me again, slowly at first before picking up the pace. My insides knot. Muscles heat, twinge and contract.

'Oh God.'

I'm exhausted, completely disconnected from time, fighting the urge to beg him to get on with it, and definitely covered in a sheen of sweat. At last, he puts an end to the sweet torture, allowing me to trip over the edge into a long, all-consuming orgasm that explodes at the back of my vagina, undulating outwards in rich, deep ripples. Wave after wave of contractions rip through me, causing me to arch my back from the bed. Somehow, I manage to look down at him. With his mouth still on my clitoris, bringing me back from the high, he watches me, evidently pleased with himself as I writhe and pant and tug at my bindings.

'How was that then?' he asks when he's finished.

'Not bad,' I tease, trying my best to get my breathing back under control. Aftershocks of ecstasy are still rippling through me. I'm sliding into a post-orgasmic fuzz.

'Not bad?' he queries.

'Uh huh.' I wriggle. 'Quite nice.'

Arching over me, he begins to skim his mouth across my flesh, every last inch of it. His lips leave a trail of tingles in their wake. I light up again under his touch, pulling at the bindings, wanting nothing more than to feel him now. But he's got me exactly where he wants me. I'll just have to wait. He pauses, raises his head and smiles at me. And then he leans back in, running his nose along my sternum, licking me here and there, sucking gently, tasting my sweat.

'You do know this is my favourite hobby?' he asks.

'Not knitting?'

He laughs.

'No. Not knitting. Not any more. Driving you insane with pleasure.'

'I'm already there.'

My insides are sparking still, every single muscle twitching. I'm filled with an all-consuming calm. I close my eyes, drifting away ... and he's moving again. Suddenly, he thrusts his fingers back into my vagina, swirling them round before withdrawing them, quickly. I open my eyes to find him arched over me.

'Taste this.'

I open my mouth and accept the fingers, sucking greedily at them.

'A good chef tastes the dish as he goes along. I'd say you're pretty much ready.'

He removes the fingers and nudges my legs further apart. Never breaking eye contact, he lowers himself on top of me, steadying himself on his right arm and sliding his left hand under my buttocks. He nudges his cock against my vagina, once, twice, before he probes inwards, filling me completely. Slowly, he withdraws and drives in again, adjusting his position, sending spasms right to my core, a warning that I'm not going to last long. And then, buried deep inside, he comes to a halt. I can feel him keenly now, every tiny movement as he grinds his crotch against mine. At last, he begins to thrust, keeping to a steady, unhurried rhythm, prolonging the pleasure for both of us. A wave of energy gathers force in my muscles and I arch my back away from the bed, eager to be as close to him as possible.

'I love you, Maya,' he whispers, his breathing ragged. 'Stay with me.'

He withdraws to the edge, and confusion skitters through my brain. I have no idea why he's saying this now.

'Why would I leave?'

'Because I don't deserve you.'

He drives in again. The wave swells.

'Don't ever say that. Of course you do.'

I struggle against the bindings. Dear God, I want to hold him, I want to hold him so tight, I want to squeeze my love into him and reassure him I mean every word. I open my mouth to tell him I love him, but I get no chance. My breath's knocked straight out of my lungs as he increases the power and the tempo. Again and again, he withdraws and thrusts, his left hand tightening at my back, the other moving beneath my shoulders and securing me in its grip. He pounds into me, slamming against the back of my vagina, relentlessly, holding me in his gaze as I groan and gasp with each punishing movement. Before long, the pressure builds inside. I'm on the verge of losing it when his pupils dilate and his breathing comes apart. He thrusts harder than ever, finally emptying himself inside me.

'Fuck, Maya. Fuck!'

Flickers of pure pleasure fire through my groin. I come again, shaking violently in his grip while he collapses on top of me, pinning me down with his weight. Neither of us moves. He makes absolutely sure of that. Instead, we lie locked together, perfectly still, soaking up the after-shocks. He digs his head into my neck, his favourite place, taking time to regain control before he pulls out of me, raising himself to his knees and unfastening the stockings. I watch him move above me, captivated by the power of his body, his gorgeous face, those bright blue, copper-flecked eyes. Right now, I'm the luckiest woman on this planet, and I don't care what all the other lucky women think. I'm right, and that's that.

When he's done, he rolls onto his back, beckoning for me to join him, and I cuddle against his chest, loving the feel of his arms around me. This is my own personal space, my sanctuary, and I know it so well: the smell, the contours, the warmth of his skin. Drifting off into post-coital haze, I smile to myself, happy in the knowledge that everything's perfect, only half aware of something a little strange.

He's shaking.

Chapter Eleven

W hen I wake up, he's gone. Half-convinced it was all a dream, I roll over and smooth a hand across his side of the bed, reassured by the crumpled pillow next to mine, his scent lingering on the sheets. And then I see the chair, my stockings strewn across the back of it, more evidence that last night was no dream at all. Every moment was real. And true to his word, he made a meal of it. After resting for a while, he used the stockings again, tying my hands behind my back and ordering me onto my knees for an amuse bouche which I willingly delivered. And that was nowhere near the end of it. Back on the bed, he bound my wrists to my ankles and took me to the edge of insanity ... over and over again.

I look out of the window. The sky's threatening more snow. But what does it matter? I'm cocooned in this apartment with the man I love, and the outside world can't touch me.

Utterly contented, I stretch out on the cotton sheets and yawn. And then I rest a palm on my stomach, remembering the risk I took last night, an idiotic risk. If Dan's sperm are in as much of a rush as the rest of him, I could easily be pregnant by now. And seeing as I acted without his consent, I need to deal with the possible consequences as quickly as I can. But for the time being, I'm going to brush my worries under the super expensive rugs and enjoy every second of this reunion. Rising from the bed, I head into the bathroom, sort out my tousled hair, rinse my face and brush my teeth, using the only brush I can find, probably Dan's. Back in the bedroom, I pull on his shirt from last night. And then I go in search of him.

As soon as I enter the sitting room, my senses are ambushed by a marauding army of roses. I blink, shake my head and scan the room. They're everywhere, organised in a range of antique vases: a variety

114

of colours – reds, pinks, white, yellow – filling the air with a sweet fragrance. And there's music too, just loud enough for me to be able make out the song, and it's one of my favourites.

I'd be swooning over his romantic gesture, if there weren't currently a voice grumbling at the back of my head, demanding to know why he's chosen roses. Deciding there must be a damn good reason, I focus in on him. Dressed in a black T-shirt and sweat pants, he's standing by the window, his back to me, gazing out over Central Park. I cross the room. As soon as I'm within touching distance, he turns, smiles and opens his arms.

I step right into them.

'About time you got up. I've had this song on repeat for the last half an hour. 'New York Morning'.'

'Elbow. My favourite. You remembered.'

'Of course.' Pulling back, he touches the end of my nose. 'But just for the record, I still prefer arse.'

Holding each other, we spend a minute or two listening to the song. And while the words spiral through my head, I reach up and urge him in for a long, lazy kiss, digging a hand into his mop of hair, holding him firm, never wanting to let go. But when the song comes to an end, it's time to come back to reality. Releasing him, I watch as he retrieves a remote control from his pocket, aims it at a cabinet and presses a button.

'It's a great song, Maya.' He tosses the remote onto a sofa. 'But I can't listen to it again.'

Now the room's silent, my attention returns to the flowers.

He notices.

'What's the matter?'

Seriously? After tracking my every movement for the past few weeks, I'm surprised he needs to ask.

'Roses,' I say glumly, and even though I don't want to poison the moment, I have no choice. 'Boyd sent me roses. Lots of them.'

'I know.' He runs a hand down my arm. 'I wanted to stop it, but I couldn't. I'm sorry.'

'So why ...'

'Why have I filled the penthouse suite of a hotel with them?'

I nod.

'Because I got a good deal.'

'Dan.' I prod him lightly.

'Okay.' He tips his head forward. 'Because they're the classic flower of love and romance ... from me to you.'

Floundering in confusion, I wander round the room, taking in the floral chaos. Roses belong to Boyd, and Dan knows that. If he wanted me to melt in his arms with no discussion, then he should have sourced a vanload of sweet peas ... not roses.

'Why should he own them?' he presses on, as if he's heard my thoughts. 'Why should a rose make you think of that piece of shit?'

His hands come to my shoulders. He pivots me round to face him, cupping my cheeks in his palms.

'I'm taking control, taking them back, making them ours,' he explains, deadly serious now. 'I don't want you thinking of him when you see a rose. It's not fair on the roses.' He keeps my face in his hands, his eyes piercing me right to the soul. 'I want you thinking of this, of you and me, of how much we love each other.'

My lungs have gone again, the sheer weight of his love causing them to malfunction on a grand scale. I can barely breathe. But he's completely right, and I'm a fool for thinking he was being ignorant. We need to reclaim the roses.

'Are you okay with that?' he asks. 'Because if you're not, they'll go straight out of the window.'

Wrestling my lungs back under control, I spend a moment entertaining a delicious image: the unsuspecting, well-heeled people of the Upper East Side showered by roses from a hotel window. I can't help but smile.

'I'm alright with that,' I confirm.

'Good. Time for breakfast then.'

He motions to the dining table. Over by the window, it's been laid out ready with delicate china, expensive cutlery, a teapot, a coffee pot and a sprinkling of roses. At the centre of it all, a silver platter glimmers in the morning light, the domed lid still in place.

'I hope you didn't use room service. You're not supposed to be here.'

He shakes his head.

'Gordon's family own this hotel. He fixed up all the meals. They're being left in the lobby. When we're done, we leave the dishes out there to be collected. I'm flying under the radar.'

'You can't even trust the hotel staff?'

'Can't trust anybody. The roses were dumped out there too. It took me bloody ages to sort them out.'

Grabbing hold of my hand, he guides me towards the dining table, pulling out a chair for me before he takes his place opposite.

'Dig in.'

While he pours a cup of tea for me and a coffee for himself, I decide it's time to bring us both back down to Earth. We seem to have slipped off into la-la land, but the roses have kicked my brain into action, reminding me there's a huge threat hanging over us.

'This is all wonderful, but what about Boyd?' I ask. This is the second time I've infected the room with his name. 'Are you going to find him?'

'We're working on it. He'll be dealt with soon enough.'

'Dealt with?'

'Dealt with,' he repeats definitively.

There's something about the ice in his eyes that leaves me feeling distinctly uneasy. Aware that I'm being watched, I pick up my teacup and take a sip. My thoughts are whirling, and I'm pretty sure he can see it in my face. He promised he wouldn't go too far, but now that Boyd's showed the true depths of his depravity, I'm wondering if it's a case of second thoughts.

'Those people Bill was talking about ...' I begin.

'Aren't particularly nice. But then again, neither is Boyd. Drink your tea.'

I put down my cup. I'm not finished with this. Not yet.

'You said you wouldn't have him ...' Unable to say the word, I trail into silence.

'Killed?' he asks bluntly.

We stare at each other for a few seconds. He's asking for my blessing. I'm sure of it. And after what Boyd's done, I shouldn't be surprised. If I were hard enough, I'd simply leave Dan to get on with whatever he's planning. But I'm not hard enough. I couldn't live with a man's death on my conscience. Even a man like Boyd. I shake my head, just a little.

'It's okay,' he says quietly. 'He'll be warned off. That's all.'

'Warned off?'

'Words won't do the job, Maya. You know that.'

I tap the side of my cup and stare at a rose.

'I won't be personally involved. It's not a good idea. But we need to let him know we mean business.'

'Fine.'

When I glance up again, he's already focussed back on me. We exchange a long, silent look of understanding across the table before he finally speaks again.

'So, that's the crap out of the way.' His face lightens a little. 'I've got you all to myself for a few hours. I don't want to waste time.'

'Understood.'

He lifts the lid on the platter, revealing a mound of hot food. French toast, crispy bacon, tomatoes, scrambled egg.

'Would you look at that? Shall I be mother?'

'Go ahead.'

Picking up the serving spoons, he shovels a pile of bacon onto my plate.

'Well done on the exhibition, by the way. You were a star last night. Gordon told me all about it.'

Oh God, the interview.

'Everything?' I ask.

'Everything.'

So, maybe that's why he veered away from pain last night. No spanking. No biting. Now that I've confirmed the whole lack of self-esteem thing, perhaps we're going pain-free forever. I can only hope I'm wrong. Picking up a fork, I watch as a dollop of scrambled egg joins the bacon and sense an unwanted slump of disappointment. It's partly down to the threatened cutback on mild masochism, but more to do with a realisation I've just had. Suddenly, it's clear. What I thought I'd achieved myself was simply part of the ruse.

'You were behind it all.' I prod the bacon. 'The exhibition. I thought I'd done it off my own back.'

He slides a tomato onto my plate and pauses, holding the spoons in mid-air.

'You did,' he reassures me. 'Gordon wouldn't have agreed to showing the triptych if he didn't think it was brilliant.'

'Really?'

'Really.' He goes back to dishing out the food, adding a couple of slices of French toast onto my meal before he begins on his own. 'He's willing to help but he's got his limits. The truth is he's smitten with your work. All the attention you had last night, all the admiration – you earned it all. I couldn't have set that up if I tried.'

I look out of the window. More snow is falling now, smothering the park. It's freezing outside, but try as it might, the cold can't reach me. Even without high-end double-glazing and a state-of-the-art heating system, I'd still be glowing with warmth. It's true. None of those people would have faked their admiration for my work, and Gordon wouldn't risk his reputation as a favour for Dan. A smile creeps across my face. Maya Scotton, the artist, has finally made her mark.

And she needs to apologise.

'I'm sorry.'

'For what?'

'Being a difficult arse.'

'You're just being yourself.' Satisfied with his own massive plateful of food, he lays down the spoons. 'I wouldn't have it any other way. Besides, I can be difficult too.'

'And I wouldn't have it any other way.'

He glances at my side plate, chews at his bottom lip.

'When you're the big I-am in the art world, and I'm an art gallery-owning ex-CEO of a building company, will you still love me?'

'How could I ever stop?'

He hesitates.

'Tell me something,' he says, picking up his knife and fork. 'When we first met and I behaved like a total prick, making one mistake after another, you stuck with me. Why did you do that?'

'I must have seen the possibilities. It's like when people go and look at a house, when they're thinking of buying it.'

His forehead creases. He's clearly not following.

'Some people can't see past the furnishing and decoration,' I explain further. 'Other people see the potential. They see what's at the heart of it.'

'And that's you?'

'I think so.'

'So, I'm some shabby old house?'

'Very badly decorated, complete with appalling furniture, shag pile carpets and a disgusting avocado bathroom suite.'

'I think you've extended that metaphor far enough.'

He looks at me some more, totally relaxed now, and a hint of devilry creeps into his eyes. Shaking himself into action, he cuts a slice of French toast.

'Eat,' he orders.

I pick at a piece of bacon and slip it into my mouth.

He tuts, pointing his knife at my plate.

'Use the napkin.'

'I'm alright.' I munch on, happily.

'I said use your napkin.'

Well, this is weird. After all this time, Daniel Foster's finally decided to reveal he's a stickler for good habits at the table? Well, if he has, then he's on a hiding to nothing. I'll eat my own way.

'I'm really not a napkin kind of girl.'

His face straightens. His eyes steel over. He speaks again, his tone low and determined, emphasising each word.

'Use ... your ... napkin.'

'Stop being so bloody bossy.'

'Use the sodding napkin.'

'For fuck's sake.'

119

With a huff, I pick up the napkin, hear the clink of metal and immediately catch sight of a ring on the side dish. My heartbeat triples.

'What's this?' I ask, waving my napkin over the ring.

'Uh?' As if nothing out of the ordinary's going on, he tucks into his scrambled egg.

'This?' Holding the napkin in one hand, I point at the ring with the other.

'Oh, that?' He leans forward, squinting at my side plate. 'Looks like a ring.' With another shrug, he shovels up a second forkful of egg.

'What's it doing here?'

The egg disappears into his mouth. He chews, swallows, and licks his lips.

'Dunno.'

'Dan?'

With a sigh, he puts down his knife and fork, and picks up the ring.

'Maybe it's the maid's,' he suggests, turning it in the light.

'Of course it is.' We're playing another game of silly buggers, and I'm definitely going to win. 'But it's expensive. She's a careless woman leaving it here.'

'Definitely a careless woman,' he muses, examining the ring as if he's never seen it before. 'I'd say it's made of platinum. Perfect for the woman who prefers silver to gold but deserves to be treated to something really special.'

'The maid's a lucky woman.'

'And careless to boot. That's a diamond in the setting.' He squints again. 'In fact, I'd say this is a one carat diamond, flawless clarity, D grade, completely colourless, excellent cut.'

'You're jewellery expert, all of a sudden?'

'Yes I am,' he says chirpily. 'It was one of the things I researched on the internet from my hospital bed. I also learned all the flags of the world.'

'Really?'

'Absolutely. Go on. Test me. Slovakia.'

'Bollocks to the flags of the world. Let's discuss the jewellery situation.'

'Okay.' He focusses on the diamond again. 'I'd say this was acquired from Tiffany's Fifth Avenue flagship store. It must have cost a bomb. Very simple though. Very classy. Just like you.'

'Simple?'

'I don't mean, you know, lacking up here.' He taps the side of his head. 'Although you are a bit slow sometimes ...'

'I think that's enough of the insults, shit head,' I cut in. 'You'd better call the concierge and get the ring back to the maid.'

'Maybe later. I quite like it. I wonder ...'

He motions for my hand.

'What?'

'I'm sure she won't mind if we just muck about with it for a bit. Try it on.'

Feigning nonchalance, I offer him my right hand. He shakes his head and points at my left hand. I offer him that instead. He tries the ring over my thumb, shakes his head and moves on to my index finger, middle finger, and finally my wedding finger.

'Oh, would you look at that?' He slips it on and taps the diamond. 'Perfect fit.'

I pull back my hand and stare at the diamond.

'What do you think?' he asks.

'It's bloody lovely.'

'Keep it on.'

'But it's the maid's.'

'She won't miss it. I bet she's got a drawer full of the things.'

Seemingly done with the ring situation, he goes back to his breakfast. I'd do the same, but it's difficult to play along with a game when your heart's racing at a million miles an hour. Instead, I admire the ring, watching as light flickers through the diamond.

'So,' I venture at last. 'Does this actually mean we're engaged?'

'What?'

'Engaged? That thing you do before marriage.'

'Oh that.' Putting down his knife and fork, he takes a swig of coffee. 'I suppose so. Is that a problem?'

'Not really. I just think I might have preferred to do this the traditional way. You know, the romantic way.'

'Oh, are we thinking inside the box again?'

'Probably.'

'So, what's the traditional way? The romantic way?'

For a split second, I wonder if he actually knows the traditional way for anything. After all, he's hardly had the most conventional of upbringings. But then again, he's no idiot. In another split second, I decide he's stringing me along for the heck of it.

'Well, first you have to propose, and then I have to say yes, and then you put the ring on my finger. And you need to do all of this on one knee.'

'Mmm.' He seems to think for a moment. 'I did propose … more than once if I remember rightly.'

'Fair enough,' I mutter, recalling the fact that he did indeed propose, prompted by a mad outburst in front of a Chinese billionaire, on three different occasions. And each one of them is seared into my brain.

'And you did say yes,' he reminds me.

'When?'

He sits back, distinctly smug.

'When I was in hospital. I heard you.'

'You did?' I know exactly what he's going on about. My gushing acceptance at his bedside. I thought he was asleep. Clearly not. 'Are you sure you weren't hallucinating?'

'Absolutely.' He points at my hand. 'And now I've put the ring on your finger.'

'But you weren't on one knee.'

'The one-knee thing. That's important?'

'Yes.'

'Not two knees?'

I hold up a finger. 'One.'

'Why's that?'

'I don't know.'

'It's just that I'm sure it's more comfortable on two knees.'

'Dan.'

'Okay, okay.' He holds out his hand, palm upwards. 'Give me the maid's ring.'

Obediently, I remove the ring from my finger and hand it to him. Pushing back his chair, he comes to my side of the table, smiling down at me all the time. And then he lowers himself onto one knee. It's only slight, but I catch another wince.

'Bloody hell,' I gasp, remembering only too late that he's still recovering. 'Get back up again. Your leg.'

'Sod the leg. I'm alright.' He settles himself and holds up the ring.

I stare at it, and then I stare at him.

Bloody hell, it's happening. He's actually doing it. The man I love is right in front of me, and he's on one knee, presenting me with a mega-expensive Tiffany engagement ring, and he's about to say the words. For some reason, I want to clap and squeal and laugh like a maniac. But that might ruin the moment. Instead, I adjust my position and face him, doing my very best to seem all dignified

'Now … Maya Scotton,' he begins.

'Yes, Daniel Foster?'

'A few months ago, you walked into my life wearing a ridiculously short skirt.'

'I did.'

'Be quiet. You'll ruin my train of thought.'

'Sorry.' A giggle escapes.

'The first time I ever saw you, I only saw your backside and as you know, it gave me a massive hard-on. I'm pretty sure I fell in love with you right then.' He arches an eyebrow. 'Well, I fell in love with your backside, that's for sure. And then I heard your voice – and yes, you were pretty rude to me ...'

'You were rude to me too.'

'Oh yes. So I was. Be quiet.'

'Sorry again.'

'Where was I? Ah, yes. So, after I'd fallen in love with your backside, I then fell in love with your incredibly rude voice. And then your face, the first time I ever saw it.' He coughs. 'And your boobs. When you poured water down your incredibly tight blouse. Anyway, enough of this ...' He waves his hand, as if he's trying to wave away the triteness. He becomes serious, but it doesn't last for long. 'Maya, you and me, we're meant to be together. Always. We're like cheese and wine ... strawberries and champagne ... Batman and Robin.'

'Batman and Robin?'

'I'm struggling here. What I'm trying to say is we're perfect for each other, in our own imperfect ways. I fell in love with you as soon as I met you and I fucked up big time, but you gave me a second chance, and a third ... and a fourth. When I came at you full-on, you didn't run away.' He rolls his eyes. 'Well you did a bit, but you always came back.' He slows down, emphasising every word. 'You believed in me. You looked past the appalling furniture and the shag pile carpet and the disgusting avocado bathroom suite. You saw the real me ... and you saved me.'

He takes a jittery breath. Good God, Daniel Foster's actually nervous? He thinks I'll say no?

'I love everything about you, Maya ... apart from your cooking.' He shakes his head. 'Oh, for fuck's sake. Will you do me the honour of being my wife? Because I love you. I fucking love you. I can't exist without you. I need you and I want you. I'll make you the happiest woman in the world, ridiculously happy, so happy, ordinary people are going to think you've lost it. You might even get committed.'

'Finished?'

'Think so. Maybe.'

He frowns, clearly convinced he's just made a hash of the whole

123

thing. But my God, he hasn't. My heart's on fire with happiness.

'Say it again.'

'What? All of it?'

'No, just the marry me bit.'

A small, relieved smile creeps across his lips.

'Maya, will you marry me?'

I make him wait for a few seconds. He gazes into my eyes, the blue whorls filled with hope.

'Yes,' I breathe finally.

'Well, thank fuck for that.'

He slips the ring back on my finger, stands and draws me to my feet.

And then he kisses me … thoroughly.

Chapter Twelve

I step out of the shower and inspect myself in the bathroom mirror. Wet hair, tangled and matted; green eyes, slightly glassy from lack of sleep; a little thinner than usual. Still nothing special, nothing to shout about.

'Don't think that,' I whisper, needing to hear the words spoken.

I'm still struggling to understand how it all happened, how I went from lonely, friendless misfit to this: a successful artist engaged to a thoroughly wonderful man. I can't help the confusion. After all, in my eyes, I'm still that awkward, oddball child. I raise my hand and examine the ring. Simple and beautiful, just like everything in our world, it's a symbol of Dan's commitment to me, a sign of his belief. And now I need to repay him. I need to believe in myself because that's what he wants for me. It's a journey I've started on, and I've still not reached my destination, but one of these days, I'll get there. I know I will.

After towel-drying my hair, I tug a brush through it and wander back into the bedroom, glancing at the rumpled covers on the bed where we spent the entire morning, cuddling, talking, filling each other in on what we've been up to over the past few weeks … and making love. A quick freshen-up was definitely in order. I'm just surprised he didn't join me in the shower. Instead, suddenly preoccupied, he opted to make himself a coffee.

Pulling on a fresh shirt from the wardrobe, I send Lucy a quick text, the third one today.

Are you okay?

I don't know why I'm bothering. I scroll back to the first text.

How's it going?

Ignored.

And then the second.

125

Are you still angry with me?

Also ignored.

I wait for a minute or two, hoping she's calmed down by now and forgiven me. When nothing comes, I finally give up and go in search of Dan.

The living area's deserted, breakfast dishes cleared away and roses glowing in the bright New York winter light. I hear water running in the kitchen and go to join him, quietly padding across the floor in bare feet. I find him at the sink, hands clenched on the worktop, shoulders stooped, head down. At first I can't make out what's going on, but then I spot an open bottle of tablets in front of him.

'Dan?'

He jolts, switches off the tap and straightens up, suppressing a grimace.

'What's going on?'

'Nothing.'

'So, what's this?' Before he can stop me, I grab the bottle and examine the label. 'Codeine?'

'Like I said, nothing.'

He moves to the breakfast bar and sits on a stool.

'Nothing?' Still holding the bottle, I turn. 'This isn't paracetamol, Dan. It's strong stuff.'

He stares at me, doing his best to bring down the mask. But it isn't working, not today.

'Don't give me the hero act,' I admonish him. 'You're in pain.'

'It's not that bad.'

And that's a lie.

'I want the truth.'

He draws in a breath.

'Okay, it's my leg.' The words catch as he exhales. 'It's not worth talking about. I'm fine.'

'Oh, stop it.' I slam down the bottle next to the sink. He jolts again. I'm furious, but not with Dan. I'm angry with the man who's caused all of this. 'Stop it now. I need to know.'

He says nothing, and he doesn't need to. It's all there in the pallid skin and taut lips. And I can hear it too. His breathing's shallow, uneven. Two things are completely obvious: the man I love is suffering, and this isn't the time for anger.

'Why didn't you tell me last night?' I ask, softening my tone.

'It wasn't this bad last night,' he admits, adjusting his position on the stool.

126

'But you showed me the scars.'

'They're difficult to hide.'

'And you thought you could hide the pain?'

He watches as I move towards him, halting just out of his reach. And then he fixes his attention on my throat, avoiding all eye contact.

'I don't want you keeping things from me,' I go on. 'It doesn't protect me and it doesn't stop me worrying. It only makes things worse.'

'I know that.'

'So, why didn't you say anything?'

'I thought I could manage it.' He pauses, still staring at my throat. 'I was scared ... still am.'

'Of what?'

He clamps his lips together, refusing to answer, but he's already gone too far. There's only one thing that scares him and I know exactly what it is.

'You thought you'd lose me. You thought I'd give up on you.'

His eyes meet mine. He seems shattered now, almost despondent.

'You've already dealt with enough of my shit.'

'True,' I answer briskly. 'And just for the record, I'm thoroughly prepared for more. How bad is the pain?'

'Bearable. Mostly.' He runs a hand through his hair.

'The truth, Dan.'

I move closer and touch him on the arm.

'Okay.' His eyelids flicker. 'It's worse in the mornings. There are days when I can barely get out of bed.'

'Like today?'

He nods.

'Days when I want to shut myself away, and I'm not exactly a pleasure to be around.'

He lowers his head again, as if he's totally ashamed of his confession. I stop him in his tracks. Placing a finger under his chin, I coax his head back up and wait for his eyes to meet mine.

'How often?'

He closes his eyes. 'There's no pattern.' He blows out a breath. 'But it's not been this bad for a while.'

I make a decision.

'It's all the sex.'

Panic appears in his eyes.

'No.'

'We'll have to cut down.'

'Maya, I'm not doing that.'

'And I'm not walking away.'

'Well, you should.' He falters, breathes deeply again. 'It's not fair on you. I'm not the man you fell in love with. I shouldn't have asked you to marry me.'

I'm stunned. I can barely believe what I'm hearing. We've been engaged for half a day and he's already trying to pull out? I'd give the man a damn good slap if he wasn't in agony.

'You bloody idiot,' I growl.

And then I stop. Mouth open, I stare into his face. If I'm not much mistaken, he's on the verge of tears … and I'm not having that. This is self-doubt, pure and simple, the very same thing I saw in the mirror a few minutes ago. And as far as I'm concerned, it can take a hike … because it's outstayed its welcome.

'You really are a piece of work, Dan. You made me an offer and I accepted. That's called a contract and you're not getting out of it. I didn't fall in love with Mr Perfection or Mr I'm-always-in-control. I fell in love with you.'

He frowns a little. Clearly, I need to set a few things straight.

'Okay, so you can be a little overbearing and bossy, and you're always in a rush to get everything done, but I can deal with that.' I wave a hand. 'The truth is, underneath it all, you're kind and thoughtful, funny and intelligent, caring, protective, loving, faithful …'

I stall.

'Run out of adjectives?'

'Yes, but I'm not finished yet, not by a long shot.' I point at him, panicking slightly because although there's plenty to say, it's all jumbled up in my head. In the absence of any clarity, I opt for the first ridiculous things that come to mind. 'You look after me and I like it. You're a bloody good cook. You tidy up after me and never complain. You let me have the remote control when we're watching telly. You buy me knickers and tampons …'

A smile hovers on his lips.

'You fell in love with me because I bought you tampons?'

'Of course not.'

Oh dear, I really am making a prime mess of this. I need to home in on something a little more substantial.

'You understand me and believe in me. You want me to be happy. You want me to be myself. You love me because I'm me, and that's priceless. That's the man I fell in love with, and he's still in here.'

I prod the side of his head. The smile deepens. I'm almost there. Just a little stroke of his ego, and I'll have him locked down.

'And I'll tell you something else. He might have a few scars and he

128

might be struggling with pain right now, but he can still deliver the best orgasm known to womankind.'

He gives me a can't-disagree-with-that kind of look.

'And just in case he's in any doubt, he's still a bloody gorgeous sex god.'

Life flickers back to his eyes.

'I couldn't even think about another man after you. It'd be like swapping an Aston Martin for a Ford Fiesta.'

'Ford Fiestas are very reliable.'

Well, at least he's joking again.

'Oh shut up.' Standing between his legs, I take his face in my hands. 'I'm not giving up on you, and that's that. Capiche?'

'Capiche,' he whispers.

Thank God. Crisis averted for now. I motion him into my arms and hold him for an age, gently running a hand across his back. At first, the tension's obvious. I can feel it in his taut muscles, the occasional shiver, the quick rise and fall of his chest. But gradually, the muscles relax, the shivers die away and his breathing returns to a regular rhythm.

'I fucking love you,' he mumbles at last.

'And I fucking love you too.' I pull back, smooth his hair and almost lose myself in those eyes. 'Is there nothing you can do about the pain?'

'The pills help ... eventually. And physio.' He thinks for a moment before he reveals the facts. 'It's where they put the plates in. They can take some of them out, fuse the bones in places. It might help.'

'Then that's what you'll have done.'

He shakes his head.

'It's another operation. Another six weeks in plaster. I haven't got time ...'

'You'll make time.'

He stares at me.

'I'm not going back on crutches, not while Boyd's around. If I need to deal with him, I want to be able to move.'

'But you don't need to deal with him. You said so yourself. You've got Bill's people. You've got Foultons. Forget about Boyd and get yourself sorted.'

'When the time's right.'

I know him well enough to realise he won't back down on this.

'Fair enough, but as soon as Boyd's out of the picture, you're having that operation. And then if you're still in pain, we'll find ways to deal with it ... together.'

He nods. His eyes soften.

'The pills are kicking in.'

'Good.' And I know something else that might help. 'Because we're having a bath.'

I step back.

'But you just had a shower.'

'And you've been sweating your bollocks off all morning. I want you cleaned up before we go in for more.'

'But ...'

'No arguing. We're bath virgins, Foster. It's about time we had a soak.'

I gaze in despair at the mountain of unruly suds obscuring the huge, round, sunken tub. It's been almost half an hour since I turned on the taps and it's finally ready. At least I think it is. After pouring in far too much expensive hotel bubble bath, I'm now presented with something that looks like an over-the-top Ibiza foam party. I've no idea where the water level is.

'We're not going to be able to see each other in that,' Dan remarks, curling an arm around my waist. 'I could just take a quick shower and see you in the bedroom.'

I lean back against his chest.

'Okay, so I misjudged the bubbles.'

'No shit?'

'Get your clothes off and stop complaining. It'll be romantic. Erotic ... probably.'

I break his grip and move away, making it perfectly clear I mean business. With a reluctant shrug, he removes his T-shirt and throws it onto a vanity unit. The joggers follow quickly. I take a moment to ogle his body in all its naked glory. Resisting a sudden urge to drag him back to the bedroom, I pull the shirt over my head and let it fall to the floor.

'Now, that's erotic.' Coming towards me, he wraps me in his arms, brings a hand to my buttocks and presses me in against his crotch.

'In the tub,' I order, determined to see this through. 'Now.'

As soon as I'm released, I navigate a path down the marble steps into the water, relieved that at least I've managed to get the temperature right. Dropping to my knees, I shuffle to the far end and position myself on a ledge. Past the mountain range of suds, I can just about see Dan. He's still standing at the side.

'What's the matter?' I laugh. 'Haven't you ever taken a bath?' Immediately, I curse myself for my own stupidity. That's not something you ask of a person who was banned from the family bathroom as a child.

'Of course I have.' He steps into the water, hesitantly. 'A few years ago. I've just never taken a bath in a giant, deformed meringue.' He shrugs. 'I'm a shower man really. Quick and efficient.'

'Well, I'm going to transform you into a bath man. What do you think about that?'

'Try your best.'

Picking up on my reference to our first walk together, he smiles as he lowers himself into the water, immediately disappearing behind a wall of foam.

'Maya,' he calls. 'Are you still there?'

'Yes,' I call back. 'Follow the sound of my voice.'

'I think I'm going snow blind.'

'Stay with me. You can do it.'

The water surges, bubbles move and part, and there he is, edging towards me on his knees, complete with a soapy beard.

I snigger.

'Hello Santa.'

'Hello.' Deepening his voice, he widens his eyes. 'Have you been a good girl this year?'

'I'm afraid not.'

He moves up close, slipping a hand around my back and pulling me onto his lap. A tidal wave of bubbles escape the bath.

'Oh dear, what have you been up to?'

'Kinky sex. Lots of it,' I announce proudly. 'I've even had anal.'

'Naughty.' He taps the end of my nose. 'No presents for you.'

The arms tighten, and I'm drawn in for a kiss, bubbles tickling at my chin. When he's done, he piles foam on top of my head.

'There you go. A crown for my queen.' He pecks me on the lips.

I can't help but laugh, content that he's relaxing, forgetting the worries, having fun.

'Any sign of the soap?'

I shake my head. 'I last saw it about half an hour ago. I could go in search.'

His grip tightens.

'No way. We might never find each other again.' He sweeps a hand through the water. 'Bingo.' He holds up a sponge. 'This'll do. Let's clean you up, you filthy woman.'

Before I can remind him I've already showered this morning, I'm swept around, temporarily disorientated by a haze of white foam and swishing of water. Within seconds, I find myself back on his lap.

Only this time, he's settled onto the ledge, legs stretched out, and I'm held in place against his chest, facing away from him. His left hand comes to my inner thigh, urging my legs apart before it clamps back across my stomach. Resting his chin on my shoulder, he sets about sliding the sponge along my thighs, firmly here, softly there, lulling me into a world of pleasure and taking full control of the situation.

'So,' he murmurs into my ear. 'Where do you want to get married?'

I try to look at him, but I'm held tight. I can only see his chin, and that's nowhere near good enough. I need to see the rest of his face, judge his expression, because I can't tell anything from his voice. I need to know if he's serious, if he's really asking me what I want, or stringing me along while he sorts it all out behind my back.

'I get to choose?' I ask.

'Why not? But I'd like to point out that Bermuda's the perfect location.'

Although I can hear the humour in his voice, I'm not entirely sure he's joking. I know what Bermuda means to him, but it's off the cards. It's too far away. I want everyone to witness our wedding day, everyone who's near and dear to us, including Sara. And if that's going to happen, then it needs to happen in England. There's only one choice. It's the perfect, obvious decision. I'd love nothing more than to get married at our new home.

'Thoughts?'

The sponge comes to my groin, tickling across my labia. Closing my eyes, I give out a tiny groan. If I'm not careful, he'll have me mesmerised, hypnotised and caving in to his will.

'In England,' I murmur. 'Surrey. At the house.'

I'm half expecting him to come back at me with another delicious touch of the sponge and a quick 'Are you sure?' But his answer comes immediately.

'Done.'

'Done?' This time I turn so quickly, he doesn't have a chance to hold me in place. I fix my eyes on his face and what I see there perplexes me even more. He's deadly serious.

'And dusted,' he adds. 'When?'

I narrow my eyes and think again. The Daniel Foster I'm used to would want this tied up as quickly as possible, but I'm in no rush. I'd like to savour the build-up. I'm going to test this apparent change of character a little further. If he's faking, then he won't be able to keep it up for long.

'Next summer.' I watch his face for signs of impatience, and find none. 'When the sweet peas are out.'

His lips curve upwards.

'Perfect.' He kisses me again.

Leaning my head back against his chest, I decide this is too good to be true. There's no way Mr Foster's asking me what I want, and then simply giving it to me. I'm going to test him a little more. He touches the sponge along the length of my right thigh, in and out, finally reaching my crotch again. Pressing it firmly against my clit, he sends me into a spin. At the same time, his left hand comes to my right breast, gently tugging at my nipple.

'I want my family there,' I manage to breathe. 'And yours too. Your sisters.'

'We'll cross that bridge when we come to it.'

The sponge has gone now. Fingers are working at my clit, slowly, patiently. Fighting back the surge of warmth in my groin, I resolve not to let him distract me with pleasure.

'I suppose you've made a start on the studio.'

I tilt my head back, to one side. He touches his lips against my ear lobe.

'I'm waiting for you to look at the plans. No rush.'

'And the decorating?'

'Your home. Your choices. I've done nothing.'

'Really?'

'Really.'

And now seems to be just the right time to ask about the personality transplant.

'What's going on?'

The finger stops.

'What do you mean?'

His arms relax, allowing me to face him. I readjust my position, straddling his lap and holding his shoulders. He brings his hands to the small of my back.

'Well, if I'm not much mistaken, you're listening to me and taking my lead.'

'That's because my future wife gets whatever she wants.'

'But I thought you got whatever you wanted.'

'And all I want is you. I've already got it.'

'Seriously? No more bull-dozing?'

'Well,' he smiles, 'maybe just a little ... here and there.' He becomes serious. 'But habits can change and they will change. I've already made a start. How am I doing?'

'Very well. But seriously, what have you done with Dan?'

'He's right here. Like you said.' He taps the side of his head. 'It just turns out you can teach an old dog new tricks.' He wafts the same hand through the bubbles, lazily, watching them part and drift. 'I've learned a lot over the past few weeks.'

'Such as?'

'Lobsters never stop growing and they taste with their legs.'

I wrap my hands around the back of his neck, forcing him to look at me.

'Your life came to a crashing halt, and that's all you learned?'

'Good God, no. I also discovered that cows can sleep standing up, but they can only dream lying down. The internet's a very useful thing.'

'Joking aside.'

'Joking aside,' he repeats, serious again. The hand returns to my back. 'When something like that happens, they say it changes you. I never believed it, but it's true. I almost lost everything when I crashed that bike. Every day's precious, Maya. I need to slow down and smell the roses ... and the sweet peas.' He traces a thumb across my forehead, down my cheek. 'It made me think about what's important, and what's not.' He brushes the thumb across my lips. 'I love you. You gave me my life back, and I want to make you happy. That's all that's important to me now, and I'll do anything to make it happen. I won't always get it right, but I'm going to give it a damn good try.'

I shake my head in disbelief.

'You remember asking me what this was?' he asks. 'In the lift?'

I nod.

'Asset stripping. Those were the words you used. And you remember my answer?'

'Mergers and acquisitions.'

'Working both ways.' He points at my chest, then his own. 'We're in the process of merging, acquiring each other ... and that involves change. You're adapting to me ... and I'm adapting to you. This is a partnership, equal in every way.' He thinks for a moment, his lips twitching with mischief. 'Apart from the sex.' An eyebrow lifts. 'That's all mine.'

He makes his point immediately, urging me up with one hand and reaching down with the other to position his cock at my vagina. Keeping his eyes locked on mine, he guides me down, carefully, holding me in position as he enters me, and then nudges his crotch further until there's no more space. My insides quiver, in anticipation of what's to come. While one hand supports my left buttock, the other comes to the middle of my back. Buried deep inside, he stays absolutely still, savouring the moment.

'I love being like this,' he murmurs. 'Completely together.'

I slip my hands around his shoulders and lower my face to his. He opens his mouth, his soft lips accepting mine, and draws me in as close as we can get. We're totally connected now, body, soul and mind.

'Ready to make some waves?' he asks.

'Always.'

He lifts me again, dispatching ripples of water across the bath and heat through my groin. I'm almost at the tip of his penis when his grip loosens, and I sink.

'Hold on,' he warns me.

The hand comes away from my back. Anchoring himself against the side of the bath, he thrusts upward, slamming his cock into me with all the force he can muster.

My muscles spasm, and I can't help it. I give out a squeak of delight.

'Kiss me, and don't stop.'

I do as I'm told, kissing him with a passion while he urges me up, releases my body and slams into me, repeating the process over and over again. We slide into a rhythm, complementing each other's movements until we're both at the edge. With waves and bubbles sloshing about us, my muscles contract, clutching at him as I ride through an orgasm. Almost immediately, he groans into my mouth, and comes inside me.

'Shit,' he breathes when I finally break the kiss. 'Why have I never done this before?'

He draws me in, wrapping his arms around me as we tremble our way back down from the high.

'Baths,' he muses. 'I think I'm converted. They're very pleasant.'

'And erotic.' I remind him, dolloping a mound of foam on his chin and sculpting another soapy beard. 'How's the leg?'

'Fine.'

And this time, I believe him. We sink into silence, admiring each other.

'I know why you wouldn't spank me last night,' I say at last.

He blinks slowly. 'I'm not exactly a fan of pain right now.'

My disappointment must be clear to see.

'What's the problem, sweet pea?'

'I suppose you'll want to get rid of the spanking bench.'

He laughs, and his answer gives me a speck of hope.

'I don't think so. A spanking bench is like an exercise bike. Multi-purpose. We can always hang the washing on it.'

Chapter Thirteen

He's on his front, still asleep, his face relaxed and turned towards me, an arm draped across my midriff. Lost in thought, I trace a finger across his cheek, forehead and chin, loving the feel of his morning stubble. After the whirlwind of the last few months, a sense of calm has finally settled over me, permeating every last part of my being. From the initial onslaught when I could barely see past his outer layers, through the ups and downs, the misunderstandings and secrets and revelations, I can only thank God that my body took the helm because if I'd left logic in charge, I'd never have got to this point.

He takes in a breath and stirs. His eyelids flicker, then open. Immediately, he secures his attention on me.

'Morning, sweet pea,' he whispers.

'Morning, shit head,' I whisper back. 'Your mobile's just pinged.'

He rolls onto his back, stretching out to retrieve the phone.

'Lily.' Still sleepy, he slips it back onto the side table.

'What does she want?'

'The usual. We're building some apartments. North side of the Thames. She's buying the penthouse.' He yawns. 'And she's a pain in the arse, always calling me over there to query the details.'

'I didn't know you could get one-to-one consultations with the boss.'

'You can't, normally, but she can't stand the site manager, and well ...'

'She's a friend.'

As if he's just had the most wonderful idea in the world, he turns back to me, eyes glimmering with promise, and draws me into his arms. But behind the smile, I detect a hint of discomfort.

'Your leg's hurting.'

137

'A little.'

And that's not surprising, seeing as we were at it until the early hours.

'Too much sex.'

'Never,' he says sternly. 'I told you, Maya. I'm not laying off.'

'Well, you'd better take some pills then.'

'In a while.' He pulls me in tight. 'You can distract me for now.'

His lips close around mine, silky-soft and warm. As if the world's about to end, he kisses me long and hard. It must be at least five minutes before he decides to come up for air.

'So, what's on the cards today?' I ask, gasping for breath.

'Sex. Lots of it. And another bath. Maybe not so many bubbles this time.'

'How about a bit of small talk?'

He bites my fingers.

'Bollocks to small talk. I haven't brought the cuffs.'

'We've got the stockings.'

Or what's left of them. In unison, we glance at the chair. Once again, the stockings have been strewn over the back. Only now, after last night's heavy-duty usage, they're beginning to look a little dishevelled.

'So we have.' He seems to think. 'And I still don't know your favourite biscuit.'

I giggle.

'You're going to have to torture it out of me.'

'Oh yes,' he says dreamily, threading his fingers through my hair. 'Small talk. I reckon we could fill an hour or two with that.'

We sink into another comfortable silence, gazing into each other's eyes. I could lose myself in those irises. They're a darker blue this morning, the flecks a deep gold. I could spend forever looking at them, but the hours are slipping away and before long I'll be starved of their company.

'Are you okay?' He traces a finger down my cheek, picking up on my concern.

'I just want to stay here. I don't want to go back to reality.'

'You and me both.' The same finger skims across my mouth. 'We'll sort this out, I promise. And next summer, we'll get married … surrounded by sweet peas.'

'The deal's completed then?'

His lips twitch. He takes in a breath, as if he's resigning himself to something.

'Not quite.'

'What do you mean?'

'I mean, I need to give you a full and frank disclosure. You need to know exactly what you're getting into.'

I thought I already did. My sense of calm eyes up the door.

'Well, that sounds serious.'

'It is.'

Flummoxed, I stare at him, wondering what on Earth he's going to come up with next. So far we've had the secret past and the secret wife. I'm pretty sure it can't get much worse than that, but I should have guessed there'd be more.

'No more secrets … please.'

'It's not exactly a secret. It's just something I haven't told you yet.'

'You hoard fridge magnets.'

He laughs.

'Got me in one.'

The laugh subsides. While his lips straighten, his eyes continue to dance with pleasure.

'Come on, Dan. What is it, really?'

'It's about money.'

'If you lose it all tomorrow, I'm not going anywhere. As long as we've got a roof over our heads and food in the cupboards, I'm happy.'

'You think I'm on the verge of going broke?' He can't help himself. He laughs again. 'Priceless.'

'Well, why else would you bring it up?' I ask, impatient now for him to get to the facts.

'Because you need to know about the assets you're taking on.'

'No, I don't.'

'Yes, you do.'

'Go ahead, but I'm not interested.'

'I'm rich.'

It's my turn to laugh. He might as well be informing me that he's a man, complete with two arms and two legs, and all the other things a man usually has.

'Well, d'uh … I could have guessed.'

'I don't think you know how rich.'

'I don't care.'

'I don't doubt it. But you need to know.'

And by the look on his face, I'd say there's no way I'm going to wriggle out of this.

'Go on then.'

He blows out a breath.

'I don't believe in putting all my eggs in one basket, unless we're talking a relationship – this relationship – because all my eggs are right here, in this basket.' He squeezes my waist. 'Well, I suppose technically speaking, you're the one with the eggs.'

'Get on with it,' I urge him, resolving not to think about that right now.

'Okay.' Another breath expelled. 'Construction can be a fickle business, so I've always had a back-up plan. Just in case.'

Fine, so he's popped a little money in the bank, bought a few premium bonds.

'I've got a pretty extensive property portfolio. I own a lot of places along the Thames. They're rented out,' he pauses, checking my reaction, 'to other rich people.'

'Right,' I say tentatively, but I still have no idea why this is so important.

'And I have an apartment here. In Tribeca.'

Now, there's a surprise.

'You've got an apartment in New York?'

'Yeah,' he says dismissively, almost embarrassed. 'I bought it a few years ago. It was cheap.'

'This is mad.'

'Along with the house in Surrey and the apartment in Lambeth, in terms of assets I'm worth about two hundred.'

He falls silent. All I can hear is the sound of my own breathing.

'You're not talking thousands, are you?'

'No.' He picks at an imaginary piece of fluff on the sheets. 'When I sell Fosters, you can double that, at least.'

Fucking hell, my brain gurgles.

'Four … hundred … million?' I ask, dragging out each word.

'Yes.' He winces at the admission. 'And a few more in the bank.'

'But you …'

He waits, watching me, eyebrows raised, and when I don't go on – largely because I have no idea what I'm about to say – he fills in as many gaps as he can.

'I support Lily's charity, and a few others. I could do more. I just haven't thought about it yet. What with Fosters, I haven't had time. And yes, I have nice things, but I don't go over the top. I don't need to. I've got nothing to prove.'

'But four hundred million. Why does anybody need to be that rich?'

'They don't,' he answers. 'I suppose I just didn't fancy ever going back to sleeping in an outhouse. And maybe I went a little over the top along the way. So ... now you know what you're getting into, not that you're getting out of it. You're going to be a very wealthy woman, and I want you to help me decide what to do with it all.'

I pull back a little, on the verge of hyperventilating. I knew that marrying Dan would mean the end of money worries, that I'd be free to paint for the rest of my life, but this is ridiculous.

'We'll need a pre-nup.'

At lightning speed, he rolls me onto my back, pinning me down by the wrists and bringing his face close to mine.

'There will be no pre-nup,' he tells me, eyes steely. 'If I fuck up, you get to take me to the cleaners.'

'Are you planning on fucking-up?'

'No. Are you?'

'No.' I raise my chin defiantly. I can't believe what I'm about to say, but I need to inject a little realism into this madness. 'But what if I do?'

'Then you still get to take me to the cleaners.'

'So, if I'm understanding this right, you're putting yourself straight into a lose-lose situation.'

'I see it as a win-win situation. And just for the record, neither of us is ever going to fuck up.' He grinds his cock against my crotch, driving me crazy. 'I have absolute faith in this. Failure's not an option.'

And it's not. Whatever problems we come across, we'll see them through together. If we can get through the present crisis, we can get through anything. I reach up and touch his cheek. He kisses my fingers before he goes on.

'With that sort of money, you need to be cautious, and I want to keep you safe.'

So, that's what he's getting at. Even after Boyd's gone, he'll still want to protect me. And I'd like to know exactly how far this is going to go.

'Which means?'

'Increased security at the house, new gates, a permanent guard, nothing obtrusive.'

'I don't want to be tailed all the time.'

'I know. It doesn't exactly bring out the best in you.'

He widens his eyes, and I know what he's referring to – my little trip to Fosters, a mobile in the Thames, a surprised Mr Sun, and a quick one in the lift.

'I'll try not to go over the top,' he says. 'But we'll need to take care. I'll make no decisions without consulting you.'

141

'You'd better not,' I warn him. 'So, that's it?'

'I'd say so. Deal completed. Where do I sign?'

'Wherever you like.'

'How about here?' He kisses me on the mouth. 'Or here.' He moves to my throat, skimming his mouth across my flesh. Goose pimples prick into life. 'Or maybe a little further down the page.'

Releasing my hands, he readjusts his position, sweeping his lips over my sternum, up to my right breast, stopping to lick at my nipple and setting off a rush of tiny tremors.

'About half way down,' I prompt him.

His lips move again, across my midriff, my stomach.

'Here?' he asks, stopping at my tummy button and running his tongue around it.

'Further.'

'Oh ... I see.'

With a wicked glint in his eye, he moves further down, his lips barely touching me now. But I can feel his breath, warm and enticing, leaving me super-sensitive wherever he goes. He stops at my crotch this time.

'Can't see a dotted line.'

I close my eyes as his tongue comes to my clitoris. I buck at his touch.

'Better date it too.'

The tongue's removed, coming back into contact with my skin half way between my vagina and my back passage before licking a line back up to my clit.

'You're wet, you filthy woman.'

'Is it any wonder?'

I get another mischievous look, and then he begins to work at me with his tongue. Slow, lazy movements encourage the knot of nerves to send out a host of messages through muscles, sinews and skin. I'm about to let out a shameless groan when I hear a bump.

We both give a start.

'Who's that?' I ask.

'The maid?' He gets up quickly and pulls on his joggers. 'Maybe she's looking for her ring.' Slipping on a T-shirt, he waves back at the bed. 'Stay there.'

He opens the door and peers round the edge.

'Gordon,' he exclaims. 'What the fuck are you doing here?'

Gordon's voice wafts through the apartment.

'Good morning, love's youngish dream. We need to talk.'

Dan backs into the bedroom.

'You'd better get dressed and come out here.'

'Get dressed in what?'

'I don't know,' he shrugs. 'Make it up.'

He disappears. Desperate to get out there and hear the latest news, I spring up from the bed and scan the room for possibilities, discovering nothing but the stockings and yesterday's shirt.

'How the hell am I supposed to make it up with that?'

Tugging open a wardrobe door, I search through Dan's selection of clothes: jeans, T-shirts, joggers, a couple of suits, more shirts. Finally, my fingers light on a dress ... my dress. He must have hung it for me. Pulling it on, without any form of underwear whatsoever, I rush out to join the men.

'Hey.' Installed on a sofa, Gordon sips lazily at a cup of coffee. 'How's it going?'

'I don't know,' I answer, readjusting the dress. 'You tell me.'

'I've sold your triptych.'

'What?'

'Sold.' He examines his nails. 'To a very influential collector based in this wonderful city. He loved it, wanted it and snapped it up. There were other offers, but they didn't stand a chance. There's also a lot of interest in any similar work you might produce. You'd better get busy.'

'Jeez.'

He turns to where Dan's busy examining today's breakfast. Evidently Gordon brought the trolley in with him. Lifting the lid on the platter, Dan picks up a slice of bacon and pops it into his mouth.

'Good enough?' Gordon asks.

'Same as yesterday, minus the ring.' Dan replaces the lid and sets about pouring drinks.

'Ah, the ring. Do you like it, Maya?'

Flopping onto a sofa and careful not to give Gordon a flash of my crotch, I raise my hand and display the diamond. 'I love it.'

'Well, that's a relief. We had people from Tiffany's come over here. Simple, classy and silver. That's all he knew. They showed him a selection and he panicked. I had to step in, give him the gay perspective, generally save the day.'

'You did a good job.'

A cup of tea appears under my nose. I take it.

'We said tomorrow morning, Gordon.' Holding a coffee, Dan sinks onto the sofa next to me. 'What's going on?'

'Clive called this morning. Your Mr Boyd just raised his ugly, Scottish head.'

In spite of the sunlight pouring in through the windows and the warm touch of the heating, an edge of cold seems to enter the room.

'What's he done?' Dan asks, a frown settling on his forehead.

'Nothing major. Don't panic. Clive ran into him. Or should I say, he ran into Clive.'

'Is Clive okay?'

'Sure.'

'So, what happened?'

Placing his cup on the coffee table, Gordon sits back and begins his story. 'Mr Boyd follows Clive home from work, catches up with him outside the Financial Times building. He wants to know what's going on.' He pauses, narrowing his eyes before he continues in one of the worst Scottish accents I've ever heard. 'Och, what's Maya doing in New York and where's that Mr Foster? I know they're up to something. Och, I do.'

'And Clive said?' Dan asks, uneasily.

'Fuck off!' Gordon almost shouts, switching to one of the worst English accents I've ever heard. 'But Boyd doesn't like that.' He reaches out and makes a fist. 'He grabs hold of Clive and demands the truth.'

I hear Dan sigh. Any minute now, he's going to snap. Clearly oblivious to his friend's irritation, Gordon presses on with his dramatic rendition.

'Clive tells Boyd he doesn't have a clue about Maya, but Dan's in Bermuda. And then he says, what the fuck does it have to do with you? Apparently, Mr Boyd doesn't take too well to this.' He waves a hand in the air. 'And then they have a little dust-up.'

'A dust-up?' Dan asks. 'They had a fight?'

'Yup. And needless to say, Clive came out on top. He was in the boxing club at Cambridge, Maya. Did you know that? A man who can crunch numbers and knuckles. You don't mess with Clive Watson, trust me.'

'But Boyd's suspicious?' I venture.

'And that's why I'm here. It's time to bring this secret rendezvous to an end.' He focusses on Dan. 'I need to take Maya out on the town, and you need to get back to Bermuda.'

Saying nothing, Dan slides a hand over mine. This is the last thing either of us wants.

'He's right,' he says. 'We need to throw Boyd off the scent.'

'Completely off the scent,' Gordon adds. 'Maya's my girlfriend now.'

'But you're gay,' I blurt, regretting the words as soon as they leave my mouth.

Gordon stares at me, steely for a moment, before his face breaks into a grin.

'I sure am.' He flaps a hand. 'But as far as the outside world's concerned, I'm a mystery wrapped in an enigma.' With a dismissive shrug, he gets to his feet. 'My parents wouldn't understand. They're stuck in the dark ages.'

'But you said ...'

'Show the real you?' He waves a finger at me, and tuts. 'Do as I say, not as I do. I may be a homosexual, but I'm also a mendacious, grasping, power-hungry homosexual.' He straightens his suit. 'My parents are never going to change, and I want my inheritance. What are you gonna do?'

'But that's wrong ...'

'Get used to it, Maya,' Dan interrupts. 'Gordon's happy to stay in the closet. He likes his luxuries.'

'You know me so well.' Gordon smiles proudly. 'Unlike the paparazzi.' He takes his cup over to the trolley. 'They just can't work me out. They're constantly sniffing for a story, so we're going to give them one. My people are tipping them off as we speak. We're going to leave this hotel arm in arm, all freshly fucked and loved-up.'

I look to Dan for help.

'You'd better go with it.' He squeezes my hand.

'I'm not kissing him.' Oh God, another badly-thought-out blurt. 'Sorry, Gordon.'

'That's okay,' he laughs. 'And just so you know, I'd rather kiss a gibbon's ass than kiss you.' He claps his hands together. 'Okay, Sunday in the Big Apple. What shall we do?'

I shake my head. I have no idea what to do, no wish to go sightseeing, no enthusiasm for anything apart from spending time with Dan. Leaning forward, I place my cup on the table and slump back again. Ignoring my dejection, and obviously in his element, Gordon pushes on with the plans.

'Dan, I've organised a private jet to take you back to Bermuda. You'd better get packing.'

Rising to his feet, Dan nods glumly.

'Why are you going back to Bermuda?' I ask.

'I need to fly home from there. And we can't both show up back in London at the same time. I'll have to stay with Bill for a few days.'

'I'll wait downstairs for you, Maya. You've got half an hour.' Gordon hesitates, surveying my dress. 'You wore that the other night. You might want to go and change.' He purses his lips. 'And a

145

pair of panties wouldn't go amiss.' He winks at my crotch, and makes his way to the lobby. 'And make-up too,' he calls back. 'If you're stepping out with me, you need to look like the dog's testicles.'

'The dog's bollocks,' Dan corrects him.

'I love you Brits,' Gordon laughs. 'You talk so weird.'

I stay where I am, crossing my legs and listening to the swish of the lift door. Finally, we're alone again. Only now it's different. The spell's broken. Reality's nudged its way into our bubble. Holding out a hand, Dan beckons me to get up. I rise and step into his arms.

'Every single sodding time,' I grumble against his chest. 'Why can't he just leave us alone? I'm sick of this.'

He pulls back and smooths my hair.

'I'll come home soon.' He watches the slow progress of his hand before fixing his eyes on mine. 'And then I'll find a way for us to meet each other ... if it kills me.'

'Don't say that. Be careful.'

'Of course.' He lifts my hand, admiring the diamond. 'You'd better hide this.'

'For how long?'

'I don't know, and that's the truth.' His palms come to my cheeks. His eyes glimmer, completely earnest. 'Remember the song I played for you when you got here?'

'Snow Patrol.'

'"Shut Your Eyes".' He pauses. 'Do it.'

I laugh.

'What? Now?'

'Yes. Now.'

With a smile, I comply. I have no idea what he's planning. I'm about to open my eyes again when I feel a hand at the nape of my neck, soft and tender, another around my waist. He draws me in close and I feel his breath against the side of my face.

'Trust.' He brushes his lips against my earlobe. 'However long this takes, don't lose your faith. If I don't get in touch, there's a reason. I'll tell you everything when I can. Every time things get too much for you, just shut your eyes and think of your sanctuary ... of you and me.'

Chapter Fourteen

I lean back on the stool and examine the latest canvas. Still only a sketch, it's a third and final self-portrait – outdoors this time, freed from the constraints of the room, I'm sitting on a bench in front of a wall, surrounded by a shower of sweet peas. With my head turned slightly to the right, my eyes are fixed on someone or something just outside the frame. Tomorrow, I'll build up the base coat: grey-green and ochre for the wall, white for the dress. I look back at the other pictures, realising I've moved from hope in the first, through the darker shades of despair in the second, finally arriving at faith.

I put down my pencil and rub my hands together. After spending the morning adding touches to the second canvas and the afternoon sketching out the third, my fingers are stiff with cold. The addition of an extra heater in the studio doesn't seem to have made much difference, but it doesn't matter. Whatever discomfort I have to endure, it's nothing compared to Dan's. And I can see an end to it all now. Soon enough, I'll be back in Lambeth.

I check the calendar, doing my best to ignore the demented reindeer kittens and the gaudy poinsettia. It's Thursday, almost a full week since the exhibition, and now I'm back in the midst of a London winter New York seems a world away. I shut my eyes, not for the first time, and think of the snow, the skyline, Dan's reflection in the window. Suddenly, I'm warm again.

My mobile pings. A text from Lucy.

Get your arse down here now.

I check the time. Almost five. Time to go home. After cleaning up, I change into a clean pair of jeans and a jumper and make my way downstairs, through the gloomy back passage, into the basement of Slaters. Dodging past a clutch of boxes in the office, I come back up to the main floor where the Steves are sprawled out on a sofa, the evening glooming behind them.

'Here she is,' Little Steve announces. 'The millionaire magnet.'

'I'm not a millionaire magnet.' I sink onto the sofa opposite.

Big Steve's eyes twinkle with mischief.

'Okay, billionaire magnet,' he says. 'You can't deny it. We've seen the photos.'

Great. Lucy must have shown them the collection of paparazzi pictures floating around the internet, a strange memento of a day spent with Gordon. It's all a blur in my head now: leaving the hotel arm in arm with New York's most eligible bachelor, lunch in a swanky restaurant, a spot of shopping on Fifth Avenue, a freezing cold jaunt around Central Park in a horse-drawn carriage, dinner in yet another swanky restaurant, followed by a night's sleep back in the penthouse. While Gordon stayed in the second bedroom, I returned to the bed I shared with Dan, wrapping myself in cotton sheets and comforting myself with his lingering scent.

'And Lucy's told us all about your disappearing act. She's not best pleased.'

As if I don't already know. A bad-tempered reunion on Monday quickly escalated into a full-blown row. I must have apologised at least twenty times, getting nothing in return apart from a cold shoulder that lasted through a six-hour delay at JFK and the entire flight home. When we arrived back in Camden near to six o'clock on Tuesday evening, reduced to zombies, we went our separate ways to bed. By the time I got up on Wednesday morning, she'd already gone to work. By the time she came home, I'd already gone back to bed. At least today, my first day back at Slaters, she's finally decided to speak to me again, albeit grudgingly. First contact came this morning. Riding the Tube together, I heard her grunt something about cooking risotto for dinner … but then again, that's probably just her idea of revenge.

'Tell me about it. I don't know how many times I can say sorry.'

'Give her time. She'll cool down … eventually.'

'Maybe.'

'Oh, she will. She can't be on the wrong side of the boss's girlfriend.'

I must seem confused now because he feels the need to explain.

'We've signed on the dotted line. Gordon officially becomes the new owner of Slaters next week.'

I can't help myself. I'm thinking of Dan's version of completing the paperwork.

'Look at that,' Little Steve laughs. 'Dreamy smiles. She's thinking about her man.' He claps his hands together. 'Now, we're having a retirement party a week tomorrow. Covent Garden. You and Lucy are coming. No complaints. And the lovely Gordon too.'

'What?'

'I've already asked him, and he's already confirmed.'

Now, that's going to be interesting. A gay man, pretending to be straight at what's going to be a thoroughly gay retirement do.

'Won't it be a little odd?' I ask. 'I mean, you hardly know him.'

Little Steve brushes off my question with a flip of a hand.

'Some of our punters are going to be there. He needs to meet them.'

I suppress the urge to shake my head.

'Now, tell me you're coming,' he pouts. 'If you don't come, I'll cry for a week.'

I doubt that, but I nod anyway.

'Yes, I'll come.'

'Wonderful.' He snakes an arm round the back of Big Steve's head. 'Right, sweetie, it's time to lock up. I want to go home and binge watch Orange is the New Black.'

'I'm with you,' Big Steve agrees.

A door bangs at the rear of the gallery. There's a clattering of heels on wood. Lucy appears, clutching our coats.

'I've had a shit day,' she announces. 'Where did you two disappear off to?'

'Shopping.' Little Steve examines his fingernails. 'We found a camper van.'

'Well, thanks a lot,' Lucy growls. 'Two fucking hours with Shih Tzu Man ... on my own. Two hours of halitosis.'

The Steves chortle in unison.

'Yeah, very funny. He's spent another six grand, by the way.'

'Excellent,' Little Steve chuckles.

'Excellent? His dog ran riot and shat on the floor, and then ... then, he only fucking asked me out.'

'I hope you said yes,' Little Steve counters, mustering all the seriousness he can. 'He's very well-heeled.'

'Piss off,' Lucy snarls. 'If he's that well-heeled, why doesn't he have his breath sorted out? I've had enough.' She points at me. 'And don't think you're forgiven. We're going out on the lash and I'm only taking you because there's no one else.'

Oh God, no. An evening of heavy drinking is the last thing I need. It's bound to end in another argument, a handful of badly-judged, drunken admissions, and then, quite inevitably, the obligatory tears.

'You've got work tomorrow,' I remind her.

'What do I care?' She hurls my coat at me.

'You're cooking risotto.'

'Fuck the risotto. Do you really want your teeth cemented together? Coat. Drink. Now.'

Without any further ado, I stand and shrug on the coat. I've had just enough time to grab my handbag when I'm yanked sideways and dragged into the streets of Soho.

'Hang on a minute,' I moan, grabbing hold of the railings to anchor myself. 'Let me sort myself out.'

She pauses, lets go of my arm, moves back a little and proceeds to shuffle impatiently from one foot to the other while I button up my coat and look at the darkened sky. It makes me think of the darkness hanging over my life. Boyd could be anywhere. Anxiously, I check over my shoulder, reminding myself of Dan's promise. I'm being protected every single minute of every day. I just wish it were more obvious.

'I don't really fancy a drink,' I say at last, watching as Lucy's features crumple in disgust.

'You're no fun any more.' She edges to one side, allowing a group of men to pass by. While I ignore them, she eyes them up, obviously deciding they're not worth the bother. 'You're getting all sensible.'

And maybe I am. A few months ago, I would have gladly joined Lucy on a binge, drinking my own body weight in wine, and flirting with anything possessing a heartbeat. But now, I'd love nothing more than to cuddle up in Dan's arms, watch a film together, and maybe indulge in a little small talk. When he's back in my life and I'm officially part of a couple, I'll have a ready-made excuse to avoid the bars. And with Clive back in her life, maybe Lucy might calm down a little too. But for now, with no excuse, I need to come up with something, and quickly too.

'How about a little shopping?' I suggest, stunned by my own words. Jesus, I must be desperate to say that, especially at this time of year.

'Shopping?' Lucy's mouth falls open. Evidently she's as surprised as me.

'Shopping,' I hit back.

'But it's nearly Christmas. The shops are heaving.'

'I know that. How about Liberty?' I opt for the only shop I can really stomach. At least it's quirky and different and old. I might be sufficiently distracted by its eccentricity to avoid a full-on meltdown. 'I need to get a few bits for the family.'

'Bits?' Lucy snorts. 'From Liberty? Exactly how much money have you got?'

'Plenty.'

She puckers her lips. If I'm going to get anywhere, I need to knock her out of her foul temper. Another apology might do it.

'Look, Luce ... I'm sorry about New York. I really am.'

'You dumped me.'

'And I'm ashamed of myself. I don't know how many times I've told you that. I shouldn't have done it. I just got carried away.'

'Bang out of order.'

Oh, I've had enough. I'm in the mood to give it to her straight.

'Gordon said you'd have a chaperon, and I thought you'd have a blast. I texted to see if you were alright.'

'You gave up pretty quickly.'

'Whatever. You didn't reply. Not once. I thought you were enjoying yourself. Anyway, it's done now. Forgive me. Please. I can't go on like this. You're my best friend.'

'Your only friend,' she corrects me.

We spend a good thirty seconds exchanging glares before the next idea lands in my brain.

'Look ... I've got a lot of money at the minute. He-who-shall-not-be-named left it in my account before we split up.'

That sparks her interest.

'How much?'

'None of your business.'

'Ball park?'

'Lots.'

She readjusts her handbag.

'You should give it back,' she mutters, glancing at a passing couple.

'No way. Not after what he's done.' And now, I'll dangle the bait. I just bloody hope it does the trick. I'm beginning to freeze. 'I could always treat you to something in Liberty. A peace offering?'

That does it. Her features soften, lips rise into a begrudging smile, eyes widen and I swear she's begun to vibrate with excitement. The prospect of shopping, married with a nice, tasty bribe is far too much for her to resist. In an instant, all thoughts of alcohol are banished. With a squeak, she pounces on me, links her arm through mine and urges me to move.

'What's the limit?' she asks.

'There isn't one.'

With Lucy taking the lead, I'm practically dragged along Frith

Street, past Soho Square and through a succession of minor streets. Before long, we reach Liberty's unmistakable mock-Tudor façade, take the main entrance and come to a halt in the atrium. While Lucy examines the displays, poking at bags and threading scarves through her fingers, I gaze up at the four storeys rising above me, each one a dark timbered gallery illuminated by soft light tumbling from the chandeliers above.

'Let's go up to Homewares,' Lucy suggests. 'They've got cooking stuff.'

'Why would you want cooking stuff?'

'D'uh ... to cook with.'

She beckons me to follow her, navigating a path to the right, through the Jewellery department, before climbing a creaking wooden staircase. Giving Women's Clothing a wide berth, we climb another flight of stairs, and then a third, finally reaching Homewares.

Impressed that my heart's opted for a mild tango rather than a full-blown quick-step, I stand still, taking in the random displays of teapots and tiles and trays indiscriminately arranged on a jumble of tables and shelving units. Immediately, Lucy begins to mooch, leaving me to my own devices. Vaguely aware of Christmas music playing in the background, I head to the right of the gallery, past a display of Liberty-print dressing gowns. Wondering how on Earth this can be classed as Homewares, I'm stopped in my tracks by a rail of tiny pastel-coloured clothes. A young couple pause in front of me, the man waiting patiently while the woman examines the outfits. It's when she turns, revealing a huge baby bump, that my brain kicks into panic-laden overdrive. Dragging my attention in her wake, she moves off to the right, into a small, brightly lit room. Little Liberty. I shuffle forward and peer through the doorway, coming face-to-face with a display of cots and blankets and bibs.

Babies.

Shit.

Babies.

An abject failure to deal with a more than slightly pressing situation.

Babies.

'You bloody idiot,' I scold myself, raking through the past few days.

What with Gordon's company and the paparazzi attention, I didn't dare visit a pharmacy in Manhattan, deciding to seek one out at the airport instead. Only there wasn't a pharmacy at the airport, at least not one I could find. After returning home to Camden and sleeping off the effects of the trip, I woke yesterday morning certain it was already too late. True to form, I blanked it out, a tactic that's worked pretty well for me in the past. But it's not the right tactic now. Fixing my attention on a display of teeny-tiny boys' clothing, I realise I've been a first-class idiot. I need to seek some advice, and quickly too.

'What's up with you?' Lucy demands, snapping me out of my reverie. 'Getting broody?'

I swallow, hard.

'No way.'

'Let's go through there. Kitchen department.'

Taking hold of my arm, she hauls me past a display of clocks, through a timber archway into another section, this one arranged around a balcony above the main light well. Plates, cups, saucers, teapots, bowls: they're everywhere – set out in piles on tables, displayed in cabinets, even perched precariously on chairs.

'Christ, I'm crap at presents.' Edging forward, I scan the wares. 'I never got Dad anything for his sixtieth.'

'You were a bit distracted at the time.'

And I'm distracted now. By visions of nappies and baby wipes. Closing my eyes, I shake them out of my head.

'So, what are you getting?' Lucy touches a plate.

'No idea.'

'Who are you buying for?'

'Mum, Dad, Sara.'

'Gordon?'

'What do you get for the man who's already got everything?'

I pause, eyeing up a range of teacups, decorated with flowers. If I'm not very much mistaken, I've just spotted a sweet pea. Suddenly excited, I head for the display and pick up a cup. It's crafted from delicate porcelain, and yes, adorned with sweet peas, curling around the body of the cup and twisting up the handle. I examine the rest of the display. Amongst the teacups and saucers, there's a matching teapot, a sugar bowl and a milk jug. Perfect.

'Is there something special about that cup?' Lucy asks.

'No. It's just pretty, that's all.'

She picks up another, turns it over and draws in a breath.

'Twenty-five pounds.' She puts it back down, carefully, and waves at the matching teapot. 'I can't imagine how much that is.'

'I'm getting this for Gordon,' I announce. 'Hold these. I can't see any baskets.'

I pass two cups and saucers to Lucy and equip myself with a teapot and a milk jug.

153

'He's American. He won't know what to do with it. They're all coffee, coffee, coffee ...'

'I'll educate him in the ways of tea.'

Which is a downright lie. In actual fact, the tea set's for Dan. As yet, I haven't managed to locate a teapot in the apartment, and we can't carry on like that. He may well be a coffee man, but I'm sure I can convert him with this little lot. Wandering further through the department, I choose a biscuit tin for Dad, and wedge it under my arm. And then serendipity runs dry, leaving my brain to descend into its usual shopping-panic mode.

'So, what do you want?' I ask.

Lucy shakes her head.

'Dunno.'

'There are some electric mixers over there.'

She seems terrified.

'Oh, I don't know. Electric mixers. That's a bit serious.' She shrugs. 'Let's leave it for now.'

Relieved of the tea set and biscuit tin by a helpful assistant, we skirt further round the gallery, finally arriving at a luminous sign that informs us we're entering the Bath House. A few more steps and I'm surrounded by oils and body butters, shampoo and lotions, candles and vanity bags. And there's soap too. Mounds of the stuff – in all colours and sizes – laid out on tables and shelves and baskets and presentation boxes.

'Soap.'

'Yeah, soap,' Lucy echoes. 'You can't go wrong with soap.'

I'm pretty sure you can, even if it is expensive. But for now, it's all I've got.

'So, when are you seeing Gordon again?' Lucy asks, delving through a flowery display.

'He's got a tight schedule, but he's sorting something out.'

'I suppose you'll be swanning off to New York all the time now.'

'Maybe.' I pick up a hand-made bar, light blue with a whale at its centre. 'That'll do for someone.'

I choose two more: one with a starfish, the other a shell. When I'm finished, I look up, focussing straight on a man at the next table, and an uneasy feeling surges through my gut. There's something not quite right about him. He's well-dressed, not one of Boyd's obvious lackeys, and he's currently examining a tub of body butter. But that's not the issue.

'I'm sorry,' Lucy murmurs absently.

'For what?'

154

'Being a bad-tempered cow.'

I raise an eyebrow, surprised she's finally chosen to apologise here. Maybe it's the calming effect of aromatherapy oils.

'I don't blame you.'

'But we've never fallen out like this.'

'I know. And we won't do it again.'

I take another peek at the man. I'm sure I've seen him before. I just can't put my finger on the exact place.

'I didn't have such a bad time,' Lucy admits, picking up a bar of soap and sniffing it. 'Most of it was a blast.'

'Most of it?'

'My chaperon was fucking gorgeous.'

I pull my best 'Wow, what a surprise' sort of face.

'He took me everywhere. Round the Statue of Liberty in a helicopter, up the Empire State Building, ice-skating at the Rockefeller. I can't complain.'

But she will. In fact, she's already building up to it. Her eyebrows have sunk and her bottom lip's sticking out. I look over her shoulder, relieved that Mr Familiar's moved on now. He's over at the far end of the room, talking to an assistant. Placing a hand on her back, he guides her out of the department.

'He was lovely. Bloody fit,' Lucy goes on. 'And I thought he fancied me. And then we went out on Sunday night and ...'

'And?'

'Nothing.'

She chucks the soap back onto the table, causing the whole display to wobble. I wince.

'Careful.'

Ignoring my plea, she picks up another bar and carries on talking, this time in some terrible sort-of-American accent. 'I'm so sorry, Lucy. Oh my gahd, this has been so rad and everything, but I need to take a rain check.' She wafts the soap in the air and scowls. 'And off he pops. No number. Nothing.'

I can't help smiling. No shenanigans, as promised. Clive's going to be relieved.

'What's so funny?'

'Nothing.'

'You're smiling at my bad luck. That's a foul thing to do to your friend.'

'Sorry.'

She throws the second bar of soap back into the display. It wobbles again.

'Gordon's a crap name by the way, much worse than Clive.'

Ooh no, she shouldn't have done that, shouldn't have mentioned the 'ex.' Her bottom lip begins to tremble.

'I'm fed up with being single.'

'It's never bothered you before.'

'Well, it's bothering me now. I'm twenty-seven and I want a relationship. And not with Shih Tzu Man. I thought … I thought … Clive …'

No, no, no. Not again. I thought the New York experience might have eased the pain, but it only seems to have made things worse. Her eyes have reddened, and tears have made an appearance. Biting her lip, she picks up yet another bar of soap, and I'd say there's a distinct possibility this one's going to end up being hurled across the shop. Eager to avoid a scene, I move around the table, prise it out of her hand and put it back in place.

'It's not fair,' she sobs.

'Lucy. Just be patient. One day, the right man's going to show up. He's out there waiting for you.'

And his name, I'd like to add, is Clive.

'Yes, but he won't … he won't be like Clive.'

No, he won't be like Clive at all … because he actually will be Clive.

I roll my eyes, suspecting she's about to launch into one of her 'I really miss him' rants and decide it's time to make an exit.

'Come on.'

I guide her to the till, identify myself as the prospective owner of the tea set and biscuit tin, present the three bars of soap and settle in for a wait. I've just about managed to kid myself that the Clive crisis has passed, when it starts up again.

'He didn't mind it when I tried to cook.' Watching my hoard of presents reappear on the counter, she blinks away a tear. 'He always tried his best to eat it. And he didn't mind the mess. I think he was the one, Maya. We could have got married. We could have shopped here for bits. But now it's just you and me.' She begins to sob again. 'You and me.'

Shrouding the teapot in bubble wrap, the woman behind the counter eyes up my friend, clearly deciding she's a lunatic.

'Calm down.'

'I can't.' She wipes the back of a hand across her eyes. 'I've lost so much. He was lovely. Really funny. And bloody good at sex.'

'Oh …' I gasp.

I really don't want any further information on that particular matter. I check on progress with the wrapping. The teapot's done, and now the assistant's making a start on the cups. Only she's slowed down a bit, and there's a mischievous glint in her eyes.

'You don't need to wrap them so carefully,' I tell her, waving a hand.

'But they're lovely.' She smiles slyly. 'We don't want them chipped, do we?'

'Very attentive,' Lucy continues, oblivious to her audience. 'Know what I mean?'

I open my mouth, and close it again, not entirely sure what to say.

'He'd go down on me for ages.' A sob and a sniff. 'Ages.'

'Oh,' I breathe, watching as the milk jug gets the bubble wrap treatment.

'Magic tongue.' She sticks her own tongue out and waggles it.

Suppressing a snigger, the assistant stows the tea set in a bag, and makes a start on the biscuit tin.

'No, don't wrap that.'

'But ...'

'It's fine.' I grab the soaps and dump them in the bag. I try to do the same with the biscuit tin, but the bloody woman's not parting with it easily. 'Bag it,' I snap. 'How much?'

'Two hundred and forty-three pounds.' She produces a second bag and slips the tin into it.

'For a tea set, a biscuit tin and three bars of soap?' Lucy demands.

'I can afford it.' I hand over my card.

'I suppose you can,' Lucy muses. 'One millionaire dumps you and another steps right into his place. How do you do it?'

I'm presented with a card machine and tap in my PIN.

'Luck,' I announce.

'Bollocks to luck. Has he got an accountant?'

'Probably.' PIN accepted, I pop the card back into my purse, grab hold of the bagged biscuit tin, and thrust it at Lucy. 'I think that's enough shopping. We're going home.'

'No,' she whines. 'I want a drink.'

'And you're getting a drink,' I inform her. In fact, she's getting so much wine, she'll be wallowing in a tongue-tied, drunken stupor by eight o'clock, if I have any say in the matter. 'At home,' I add, picking up the second bag. 'I'm not letting you inflict any more of your crap on the unsuspecting public.'

Casting an apologetic smile in the assistant's direction, I march out of the Bathroom section, hardly caring if Lucy's following me. I'm stopped in my tracks by a young girl. She thrusts out a hand, and I look down, sucking in a sharp breath. She's holding a single red rose.

157

'From an admirer,' she says awkwardly. 'He asked me to give you this.'

'Who?'

'I don't know. He's gone now.'

My stomach reels. I have no doubt it was Mr Familiar. And wherever I've seen him before, he's definitely working for the opposition.

'It's so romantic,' the girl smiles dreamily.

'No, it's not.' Lucy appears at my side. 'It's from her stalker. No offence, but you'd better sling it in the bin.'

Chapter Fifteen

'You should go to the police,' Lucy calls after me.

'No.'

'Why not? He's stalking you.'

I come to a halt. After making our way up Regent Street, we've finally reached the madness of Oxford Circus. And now, unless we take a diversion via the backstreets, I'm going to have to negotiate a route through the hordes of shoppers. I check to the right, registering the crowds, the gaudy window displays, the Christmas lights shimmering against dark skies. My pulse begins to race.

'The police,' Lucy insists, catching up with me.

'Leave it.'

'Leave it? That's what you always do.'

Because that's my modus operandi. Bury it for now, tuck it away in some dusty compartment at the back of my mind, and deal with it later. Trouble is, the compartment's currently full to overflowing, its contents spilling out into the open. Despite Boyd's intrusion, nagging images of baby bumps and expensive cots refuse to leave my head. There are some things that just can't be tucked away. Narrowing my eyes, I scan the shop signs. There's bound to be a chemist somewhere.

'Boyd's being dealt with. Trust me.'

'Is he?' She looks around. 'How? And I don't see any protection, by the way.'

I close in on her.

'It's here. Somewhere. Now, stop going on about it. I need a chemist.'

'What for?'

'Thrush.'

Without another word, I pitch myself into the Christmas mayhem, heading toward Tottenham Court Road. Along the way, I find what I'm searching for, and head into the harsh light of a chemist. While Lucy takes herself off to examine the make-up, I sidle up to the pharmacist's desk. A middle-aged, suited man emerges from the back office and I stare at him, panicking.

'I've had unprotected sex,' I mutter out of the side of my mouth, leaning over the desk.

'Have you?'

'Yes.'

'Oh.'

We spend a few seconds nodding at each other before I realise he's waiting for a little more guidance.

'I don't know what to do. I need help.'

He becomes business-like.

'When did this happen?' he asks.

I count out the days on my fingers, starting from Friday.

'Five … no six days ago.'

'Okay.'

'Okay?'

'Well, it's too late for the morning after pill. Five days is your limit.'

'Five?' My mouth hangs open. 'Shit.' If I'd had my head out of the stupid sand, if I'd done my research, I could have dealt with this yesterday.

'Five days tops. But it's best to take the pill the morning after, hence the name.'

'Oh.'

There's no denying it. I'm a first-rate idiot. But maybe, just maybe, I'm a first-rate idiot who wasn't ovulating six days ago. That's my only hope.

'When is your period due?' the pharmacist asks.

When is my period due? I have no idea.

'I don't know. I had my last period a couple of weeks ago … I think.'

While my brain descends into chaos, a strange noise escapes from my mouth, something like a cat being strangled. I stare at him, blankly.

'Okay,' he says at last. 'I think you might want one of these.' Disappearing for a moment, he returns with a pregnancy testing kit. 'It's sensitive, but best to use it on the first day your period's due, if you can work it out.'

'Oh God.' Urgently, I scan the shop. There aren't many people in here, but any of them could be working for Boyd, or Dan. And I don't want either man catching a whiff of this. 'Put it in a bag, quickly.'

He does as he's asked, swiping the kit over a scanner and swiftly hiding it.

'Good luck,' he whispers conspiratorially, handing it over.

'Thanks.' I thrust the kit into my handbag and pay. 'I'll need it.'

It takes forever to reach Tottenham Court Road, and longer than eternity to force our way onto a Northern Line train. Laden with shopping bags, we ride the Tube back up to Camden, both of us standing, wedged in between strangers and clinging on to the grab handles for dear life. While Lucy examines our fellow travellers, I slip into yet another baby trance, brightly coloured tiny outfits flitting in front of my eyes, the pregnancy testing kit burning a hole in my handbag, and the same two questions pinging about in my brain.

What if I am pregnant? What do I do?

I'll need to tell Dan. Because from now on, we make all decisions together. I swallow hard, realising that for me at least, this particular decision's already made, no matter how Dan feels about it. I've made a mistake and I'll deal with the consequences, nappies and all. I swallow again. He'll back me up. I know he will. But it's a sure-fire certainty he'll put an end to the charade, hauling me back to the apartment in Lambeth and locking me away like some prize possession. And then what will Boyd do?

By the time we've emerged onto Camden High Street and staggered back to the flat, I'm agitated beyond belief, in need of some certainty, and determined to sit down and work out exactly when I'm due on. Leaving the shopping in a corner of the living room, I withdraw to my bedroom with my handbag, sit on the end of the bed and breathe deeply. I'm about to go in search of pen and paper when Lucy appears in the doorway.

'What's the matter?' she asks.

'Nothing. The crowds. They've got to me, that's all. Go and slob on the sofa. I'll get us some wine.'

'Where from?'

'Corner shop.'

She hesitates.

'I should go. We both know who was behind that rose.'

'And I'm not about to let him know he's won ... because he hasn't.' I open the handbag and rummage around for my purse, careful to bury the test away from view. The whole pregnancy issue is going to have to wait. Before I do anything else, I need to deal with Lucy.

'But ...'

'Just go and find a film for us to watch. I'll be fine.'

I wait until she's gone before I make a move. Steeling myself for the task ahead, I get up and make my way into the hall.

'I won't be long,' I call, opening the front door.

As soon as I'm outside, the cold makes its move, pouncing on me with a vengeance. I slam the door, fasten up my coat and scan the road. Nobody around. Nothing apart from a couple of parked cars. I check on the row of houses on the opposite side of the street. I still have no idea which one's being used by my protection team, but there's no sign of life. All the lights are off.

Taking my time, I walk towards the shop, aware of the distant rumble of traffic, the clack-clack-clack of my heels, my breath catching against the air. I hear a laugh, glance over my shoulder, note the silhouettes of two men about fifty metres behind, and sense a shiver in my spine. They've appeared out of nowhere, and now they're walking in my direction. My heartbeat accelerates as I round the corner, and stall. Outside the shop, only a few feet away, three more men are loitering by the newspaper sign. One of them lights up a cigarette and eyes me with interest. I look down, quicken my pace, and edge past them into the shop.

I nod a greeting to the owner and tell myself there's nothing to worry about. Heading straight down the first aisle, I turn and come back up the second, halting in front of the wine section. I'm searching for Pinot Grigio when I hear the shouts. Muted but vicious, they come from outside. I step back, peer through the meshed window and catch sight of wild-eyed faces, fists thrown in the air.

'What's going on?' I ask.

'Bunch of idiots,' the shopkeeper replies, as if it's an everyday occurrence. 'Looks nasty. I'll call the police. Stay in here. I'll lock the door.'

Great. That's all I need. Local thugs, tanked up on cheap lager, slugging it out on the pavement. Determined not to let it get to me, I fix my attention on the wine. At last, I reach out and select a bottle.

'I wouldn't go for that one.'

The voice grates against my ears. A Scottish lilt. A drunken slur. I've heard it all before. A swell of nausea rises in my stomach. My throat constricts. I fight to see straight, to stay upright.

'Turn around, Maya.'

I can feel him now, his body against mine. It disgusts me. Clutching the bottle tight, I concentrate on my breathing. In. Out. In. Out. Keep it going, I tell myself. Deep and slow. Fight your way through the shock. Stay in control.

'I said, turn around. Look at me.'

No. I won't. I won't give him the satisfaction. Instead, I make no move. I should stay silent too, but I can't help it.

'I don't want to look at you. You make me sick.'

He slides an arm around my waist. I recoil at his touch, but the arm tightens.

'I'm logging it, you know. All the disobedience. You'll pay for this.'

I'm sure I will ... if he ever has his twisted way. I peek at the shopkeeper, knowing I should scream for help, but my brain seems to have lost touch with the rest of my body. The breathing's already come apart, and I've begun to shake.

'I'm not going anywhere with you.'

'Not tonight, but there'll come a time.'

I glance at the door, silently begging for help to arrive.

'They've been held up, your men. But not for long. I know you're being protected. I've watched for long enough. Had this little plan in place for a while. Thanks for giving me the chance to use it.' He pauses. 'How was New York?'

'None of your business.'

'Meet someone?'

'I said it's none of your business.'

'That's what Mr Watson said.'

Suddenly, I'm forced round to face him. I clamp my lips together, pushing shallow, jittering breaths through my nose. He brings his face close to mine, dark eyes swimming with venom. I almost retch at the stench of whisky, but I'm quickly distracted by the outcome of his set-to with Clive: a bruise on the chin, a swollen lip, a grazed nose. Totally satisfied, I smile.

'Mr Swanky Pants, was it? Is that why you're smiling?'

I remain silent.

'He's out of the country. I wonder where he is.'

'I wouldn't know.'

'Perhaps ...' He slides a finger down my cheek and I freeze. The smile takes off. 'Perhaps he's been sampling the delights of the Big Apple.' The finger comes to a halt under my chin. 'Or maybe he's been tasting other forbidden fruit.'

He directs his gaze to my crotch.

I feel sickened.

'I've no idea where he is. You're wasting your time. I've met somebody else.'

'Mr Finn? Oh, I saw the photos. Nicely staged.'

'There's nothing staged about them. Give up and fuck off.'

'Language.' The finger moves to my mouth.

'Seriously.' I pull my head away. 'I'd fuck off right now if I were you. When the police get here, I'll report you for harassment.'

He grabs my chin, giving me no option but to lock eyes with him.

'Oh, no, don't do that. You remember what I said. I don't like the police. Nosey bastards. They bring out the worst in me.' Letting go of my chin, he reaches out, picks up a bottle of wine and examines it. 'And I'll tell you what else brings out the worst in me.' He puts the bottle back. 'You keep throwing my flowers away.'

I clench my teeth, resisting the urge to punch him on the nose. I'd love to add to Clive's bruises, but I'm not sure I'd make much of an impact.

'That's because I don't want your shitty flowers,' I seethe.

'Ungrateful little bitch. There'll come a day when you'll take everything I give you. And I mean everything.' His eyes flash with threat. 'You need teaching.'

'I don't need anything from you.'

'The police are on their way,' the shopkeeper calls, waving his mobile in the air.

'And sadly, that means I've got to go.' Boyd grimaces. 'I'll be watching you, lady. Every single move you make. Don't forget that. And when the time's right ...'

He leans in, looking at my lips.

Instinctively, I draw back.

'We'll be together again.' With an empty smile, he leaves, pushing past the shop owner, unlocking the door and disappearing into the night.

My heart thuds. I'm close to hyperventilating. Staring at the open doorway, I drop the bottle and barely hear the sound of breaking glass. I have to go. I need to be home. The shopkeeper says something, but I can't focus on the words. Within seconds, I'm through the door and out on the pavement. A police car draws up next to the kerb, but they're already too late. The fight's broken up and the men have gone, dissolved into thin air. And I should do the same. If Boyd sees me talking to the police, God knows what he'll do next. Hastening my step, I half run, half stumble back to the flat. It takes at least three attempts to get the key into the lock, but once inside, I slam the door, lean against the wall and shut my eyes.

At first, my brain's fuddled by terror, but then, ideas gradually begin to emerge from the turmoil. He'll know. There's no doubt about it. Three thousand miles away in Bermuda, Dan's bound to have been given the news and he'll already be working on what to do next. I just have to be patient. But should I tell Lucy? That's the thing. It doesn't take me long to decide I should. Boyd's closed in on our territory, and she deserves to know the truth. When I've finally managed to wrestle my body back under control, I stumble into the living room where Lucy's curled up on the sofa.

'Did you get the wine?' she asks.

'No.'

'Why not?' Her eyes widen. 'What's up? You look like you've just seen a ghost.'

'I have.' I slump next to her, lean forward and put my head in my hands. It's only now the tears arrive. 'Boyd ...'

'What?'

I feel her hand on my back, steadying me. When she speaks again, her voice has softened.

'I told you not to go. What happened, Maya? Tell me.'

Between sobs, I force out a garbled account of the corner shop ambush. Yet again, Lucy insists on calling the police. I'm only saved from another argument by a ring at the doorbell.

'Wait there,' she orders. 'I'll get it.'

I'm expecting another bunch of roses. That would be right up Boyd's alley, scaring me shitless and then ramming his point home. But when Lucy reappears, she beckons Gordon into the room.

'Hey.'

'What are you doing here?'

'Just passing. Thought I'd surprise you.'

'And I've told him what happened,' Lucy interrupts. 'I've told him about Boyd, seeing as you probably haven't got round to it.'

Moving further into the room, Gordon fixes his attention on me. I've never seen him so serious.

'You okay?'

'Yes.'

'You don't look it.'

'She won't call the police.' Lucy complains. 'Tell her. She's got to. He's stalking her. It's out of control. He's dangerous.'

'I'm being protected,' I remind her.

'Oh, really? Well, if you ask me, Dan's fucked off and taken his protection with him. He's hanging you out to dry, Maya. He doesn't give a shit. Go. To. The. Police.'

'No,' Gordon interrupts. 'If Maya doesn't want police involvement, then you need to honour that.'

'But ...'

'Enough, Lucy. I'll fix this. I'm taking her with me tonight.'

'What?' I sit up straight.

'You're coming back to my hotel. I need to know you're safe.'

'But what about Lucy?'

The last thing I want is to abandon her again, and the last thing I need is another fall-out.

'I'll have someone come over and watch this place.' He glances at Lucy. 'You okay with that?'

She gives him a meek nod. Clearly, she doesn't dare argue with her 'new boss.'

'I understand, Maya. It's alright. Go with Gordon. I'll be fine.'

Without another word, she retreats to the kitchen, leaving us alone. Gordon takes a seat next to me and slips a hand over mine.

'You're shaking.'

'Dan sent you, didn't he?'

He nods and leans in to me, lowering his voice. 'The bush telegraph's mighty quick these days. Got a call and came straight over.'

'I don't want to go to a hotel.'

'You'll want to go to this one. I'm in the Royal Suite at The Goring.'

He lifts an eyebrow, as if he's just told me the most amazing thing in the world, as if I'm expected to squeal with delight. But I'm not impressed. I have no idea about The Goring, and I don't care how posh it is. I want to stay here.

'Besides,' he adds before I can say anything. 'You've got no choice. We're under orders.'

'Dan?'

'Correct.' He surveys our tiny living room. 'Lucy's safe here,' he reassures me. 'I don't actually need to get anyone to come over. The truth is, Dan's guys are watching from over the road. As soon as you left your apartment, they followed.'

'And look what happened.'

'Tonight was a mistake. It won't happen again. They weren't exactly expecting an ambush outside a liquor store. From now on, we're stepping up protection, increasing the numbers ... and keeping you close.' He gets up. 'Now, may I suggest you pack an overnight bag? I'd like to return you to the lap of luxury.'

I do as I'm told, say goodbye to Lucy and follow Gordon out to a black Bentley waiting at the kerb. The driver opens the rear door and takes my bag. Without a word, I get in.

'Straight to The Goring,' Gordon orders, settling next to me.

'Maya, this is Carl.' The driver installs himself in the front. 'He works for Foultons, but to the outside world he works for me. Show your face, Carl. Just in case Maya didn't catch it.'

The driver turns and nods. I do my best to register his features. Dark-haired, blue-eyed, early thirties perhaps.

'He's packing,' Gordon whispers out of the side of his mouth.

'Packing what?'

'You know.' Like an over-excited little boy, he makes an imaginary gun with his hand. 'And he'll be driving you for the foreseeable future. You go anywhere, you ride with him. No public transport.'

'Even to work?'

'Even to work. This is Carl's number.' I'm handed a card. 'Store it on your mobile. Call him whenever you need to travel.'

The Bentley pulls away and I slip the card into my pocket. Riding in silence, I gaze out of the window, seeing nothing but darkness. It's everywhere: waiting behind the flash of a headlamp, lurking in the depths of a side street, hovering in the clouds above – an unstoppable, overpowering force. As we push further into Central London, even the glow of streetlights and shop fronts can do little to banish it.

'Dan's still in Bermuda,' Gordon says at last. 'I'm to tell you he knows what happened, and he loves you. But he says you already know that.'

My lips curve into a smile.

'He's making arrangements to come home.'

'Tonight?'

A tremor of excitement passes through me.

'Maybe.'

'Have you talked to him?'

'Not directly. He's gone through Bill.' His mobile buzzes. Pulling it out of his pocket, he squints at the screen and holds it to his ear. 'Talk of the devil. Bill, what's going on?' He listens intently for a minute or so while Bill talks incessantly at the other end of the line. 'Okay. I'll let her know.' Dropping the phone back into his pocket, he stares at the back of the driver's head.

'What is it?'

'A development.' He looks at me. 'I need to fill you in. Boyd got away this evening. He had a car waiting. But we've got hold of one of his men. Bill's contacts are having a little chat with him.'

I'm flooded with the same sense of unease I felt in New York. In spite of his reassurances, I wonder if Dan's really taken heed of my wishes.

'Problem?' Gordon asks.

Yes, there's a problem. But how to say this? Bluntness is probably the best option.

'Will they hurt him?'

'Not unless it's necessary. And I'm sure it won't be.' He puts a hand on my knee. 'Money's mightier than the sword, Maya, and a damn sight quicker too.'

But I'm still not happy. Bill knows some unsavoury types, and I can't imagine them resisting the urge to use a fist.

'I don't see why Bill has to be involved.'

'Foultons provide security,' Gordon explains, nodding at the driver. 'Intelligence, that sort of thing. But they don't like to get their hands dirty. Bill's contacts are more into enforcement ... where necessary.'

'And if they find Boyd, what then? Will they kill him?'

He shrugs. 'I have no idea.'

The lights of a shop window dance past, catching Gordon's face for a few seconds, but failing to lift the shadows.

'I've told Dan I don't want that.'

'After everything Boyd's done? By all accounts, the man's an animal.'

'We're not sinking to his level.'

He stares at me now, as if I'm mad, his eyes darkened to pitch, and suddenly it's clear. Money can buy just about anything, apart from a decent, fully functioning moral compass. I look out of the window again, wondering if I can make my point some other way.

'I don't want to be an accessory to murder and I don't want Dan in that position. I just want Boyd out of our lives, with no threats hanging over us ... from anywhere.'

He says nothing, and I take his silence as acquiescence.

'I want you to contact Bill for me. I want you to make sure his people don't do anything stupid. They're just to scare Boyd off.'

'But this is an opportunity to end to it ... properly.'

I'm too worn out to argue any more.

'I'm not changing my mind,' I inform him. 'Just make sure Bill gets my message.'

I crash land in yet another penthouse suite. Another plush hotel. This time I'm cocooned in Edwardian luxury: heavy curtains, silk walls, expensive mahogany furniture, well-stocked bookshelves, antiques, a grand piano. I'm guided into a drawing room, offered coffee by a footman, and decline. I've had enough of today. All I want is to put an end to it, to sleep it all away. I'm shown to my bedroom and with my bag delivered, Gordon checks on me once last time before I'm finally left alone.

Immediately, I take myself to the en suite and sit on the toilet, gazing into space, wondering if I should try the pregnancy test. But there's no point, not until I'm sure when my period's due. Feeling utterly exhausted, I look up, focussing on an oil painting of Queen Victoria hanging on the opposite wall.

'My life's a mess,' I tell her.

'I know,' she seems to answer with a disapproving glare. 'And we are definitely not amused.'

Chapter Sixteen

'Maya.'

Soft lips brush against mine. I already know it's him. His scent is unmistakable. I open my eyes, finding his face right in front of me, those familiar blue irises so vibrant, I wonder if I'm dreaming.

'You're here?' I ask, fuddled by sleep.

'Yes, I'm here. And I love you.'

I don't have time to tell him I love him back. Before I know it, his lips secure around mine, kissing me slowly, tenderly, and I'm back in my sanctuary, our special place. I shut my eyes, soaking up the quiet intimacy. He's back, and any vestige of tension dissipates immediately.

'I don't love this sheep though.'

Ah, the sheep. I found it on my bed last night, all part of the strange quirkiness of the Royal Suite, I'm sure. I must have grabbed hold of it in my sleep, because now I'm clutching it tight.

'I'm not into cuddly toys.'

'Good.' Gently, he prises it out of my hands and tosses it on the floor. 'Nothing takes my place.'

'I've missed you so much.'

'I've missed you too.' He gazes at me for an age before he speaks again, a boyish grin on his lips. 'I tried a bath on my own. It was no fun.'

I blink, rub my eyes and look to the window. The curtains have been drawn slightly, allowing morning sunlight to pour through the gap.

'Are you okay?' he asks.

'I'm fine.'

I shuffle into a sitting position, blink some more, and take a moment to admire my fiancé. Dressed in an outfit that always has

170

me salivating – jeans and a black T-shirt – he's sitting by my side, a little tired, but as delectable as ever.

'I just got here.' He nods to his suitcase, dumped next to the door. Clearly, he's come straight from the airport. 'What happened with Boyd?'

Okay, so we're down to business. I focus back on his face, melted by the concern and love I find there.

'You already know.'

'And now I want to hear it from you.'

Manoeuvring himself on the bed, he lies on his side and pulls me into his arms, holding me close while I tell him everything about the mysterious rose in Liberty and the disastrous trip to the corner shop.

'He asked me if I enjoyed New York. I think he knows.'

'He suspects. That's all.'

Something flits back into my head, a detail I need to sort out.

'You've got one of his men.'

He nods.

'Don't worry. We won't stoop to Boyd's level.'

'Really?'

'You have my word.' He holds my gaze, completely serious. 'There are two ways of getting information out of low-life. One's a good beating. The other's a fistful of cash. Which one do you think we're going for?'

'The fistful of cash?' I offer, hoping to God I've picked the right answer.

'Bingo.'

Snuggling closer into his embrace, I trace a finger across his shoulder.

'We'll find Boyd,' he whispers.

'And then what?'

Despite of the closeness of our bodies, I can see the distance in his eyes.

'I couldn't live with that on my conscience, Dan,' I tell him, determined to clear this up. 'And neither could you. You're not that type of man ... not deep down.'

His eyes flicker.

'And what if ...'

'What if what?' He frowns.

'If you do have him ... you know ... what if you get caught? What if the police trace it all back to you? You'll go to prison, and I can't lose you, not again.'

He nods.

171

'I made a promise. I'll stick to it.'

'So, what will they do?'

He stares into my eyes, evidently searching for the right words.

'Maya,' he says eventually, 'a fistful of cash isn't going to work with Boyd.'

'So, it's a good beating?'

He nods.

'Enough to scare him off ... for good.' His arms tighten around me. 'There's no other way. The man won't listen to reasoning. Believe me, I never wanted to be in this situation, but now I am ... I can't see any other way out of it.'

And I get it. He doesn't have a choice. For once in my life, I'll need to turn a blind eye, leaving morality to take a back seat; I know Boyd well enough to understand that. I give him a nod, deciding we've talked enough about Boyd. Our time together is precious.

I pull him in for another perfect kiss.

'Talking of trust ...' he smiles against my mouth. 'I once promised you more kink than you can shake a stick at.' In an instant, the shadows are knocked right out of the room. With a playful glimmer in his eyes, he gets up, walks over to the suitcase and unzips it. 'And just for the record, I'm more than willing to cater for my future wife's every wish.' He pauses, fixing his attention back on me. 'Shut your eyes.'

A delectable shiver of anticipation courses through me, and I do as I'm told.

'What is it?' I demand impatiently. 'Tell me.'

'I'd rather show you. Look at me.'

I open my eyes. He's back at the side of the bed now, both arms behind his back. Slowly, he brings his right arm to the front, revealing a single length of rope. The other hand follows, and two more lengths along with it. Taking a sharp breath, I stare at them.

'I had these delivered to me at the airport ... from a reliable source. A little present.' He comes closer, offering the rope to me. 'So, if you're in the mood for it, you're going to be a little tied up for a while.'

I reach up and accept my gift. Dropping two of the lengths onto the bed, I examine the third, running it through my fingers, surprised at how smooth it feels, almost silky, totally pleasant to the touch.

'Too much?' he asks.

'Probably not. I don't know. I've never tried it. What do you do with it?'

'Skipping.' He laughs. 'What do you think? Stand up.'

Leaving the rope, I follow his order. Immediately, I'm pulled in close and turned. I'm standing in front of him now, my back to his chest.

'I'm thinking of a simple crotch rope for a start with an added extra... just here.'

He reaches round and touches my crotch, pressing a finger against my clit. Instantly, I'm on fire.

'If you're good to go, we'll take it step by step.'

I'm already breathing fast, my heart racing. He presses at my clit again, dispatching another rush of heat to my core.

'I'm good to go.'

'Fair enough.'

Shifting my hair to one side, he skims a finger down the back of my neck, and I shiver, wondering what on Earth I'm letting myself in for. The finger glides across my shoulders, from left to right and back again, leaving a warm imprint on my skin wherever it goes. And then those big hands close around my waist, holding me tight, drawing me back into his chest.

'Trust,' he breathes against my ear.

He snuggles his head against my neck, draws the tip of his nose down to my shoulder, smelling me. And then, out of nowhere, he nips at my ear lobe, just hard enough to make me jolt. The thrill of the unexpected.

'Turn around.'

The hands are removed.

I face him again, completely aroused by the sight of him, the love and longing overflowing in his eyes.

'Legs apart,' he says. 'And no slouching, if you don't mind.'

Parting my legs, I wait while he returns to the bed, retrieves the first length of rope and comes back to me.

'Hands up.'

I comply, watching as he gets down to work.

'You know, I've fantasised about this ... right from the start.'

'I bet you have.'

I'm mesmerised by how deftly he moves. I always imagined rope play would be brutal, but this is something else. With the utmost gentleness and care, he wraps the doubled length around my waist, looping it at the front and coiling it around me a second time. Tucking his fingers under the waistband, he threads the end back through the loop and draws it downward.

'And now for the happy knot.' He gives me a roguish grin, twists the rope over on itself, checks the position, and creates a figure of eight. 'That should do it.'

Tightening the rope, he brings the knot right against my clit. It's firm, yet soft, and I gasp at the contact.

'You like it, then?'

He threads the rope between my legs, then moves behind me and draws it up between my buttocks, attaching it at the rear. Before I know it, he's in front of me again, slipping a finger under the rope and tugging at it lightly, over and over. The knot rubs against my clit, working me up into a super-sensitive, chaotic mess. I close my eyes and let out a good, long groan.

'Oh God.'

He tuts.

'If you want to get kinkier, you'll need to learn to control yourself.'

'I can't.'

Releasing the rope, he takes my chin in his hand.

'There's no such word as can't.'

I'm about to tell him there is, but there's a flash of something in his eyes, a promise, a delicious threat. And I'm left mute. He lets go of my chin, and collects a second length of rope.

'Give me your hands.'

Again, I follow orders. Immediately, he binds my wrists, attaching them to the top of the crotch rope and checking that the bindings aren't too tight.

'Where did you learn to tie a knot?' I ask. 'Scouts?'

He laughs.

'I never joined the Scouts. This is self-taught. Perfectly safe. Are you comfortable?'

'Yes, thank you.'

He takes my hands, easing them upwards and forcing the knot back against my clit. I groan again.

'Oh, we do like that, don't we?'

Already on the verge of coming, I just about manage to answer.

'Yes. But how are you going to ...'

'Fuck you?' he intervenes, raising my hands again. 'That comes later.' He lets go, releasing the pressure against my clit.

Feeling dizzy, I struggle to steady my lungs.

'Now,' he goes on, completely business-like. 'I like to take the standard crotch rope and add a little twist.'

Without warning, he lifts me in his arms, carries me back to the bed and lays me on the sheets. I lie immobile with my hands on my stomach. But I can't resist for long. Moving them toward my chin, I feel the knot tighten again. A spasm shoots through my groin.

'Ah, ah. Naughty.'

He waves a finger at me, taking a moment to admire his handiwork before he retrieves the final length of rope.

'Where's that going?'

'You'll find out.'

He throws it onto the bed, pulls off his T-shirt and drops it to the floor. Ignoring the scar, I focus on the rest of his torso, marvelling at the power of his muscles, tingling with excitement at the dark look in his eyes.

'It's a little hot in here,' he comments. 'I need to get comfortable.'

Resisting the urge to pull at the damn rope, I take in one deep breath after another as he sets about unfastening his jeans, easing them down and stepping out of them. Slowly, the underpants follow suit. Totally naked, he stands up straight, showing off his cock.

'That's better,' he announces.

Climbing back onto the bed, he lies next to me, drawing his fingers across my chest and circling my nipples, watching my face for every reaction. And he must like what he sees, because he's smiling now.

'So, your hands are here.' He presses them against my stomach. 'And here they'll stay. If they stray further north, then this happens.' Taking hold of my bound wrists, he moves them upwards, slightly. The knot rubs against my clit, causing another spike of pleasure. 'And once I've got you worked up, Maya, that's only going to get worse.'

A warning, eh? So, he thinks I can't take it. Well, in the unlikely event that I can't, I've already worked out the escape route.

'So, I'll move my hands south.'

'Not if I do this.' He picks up the final length of rope and dangles it above my stomach, skimming it across my skin. 'Now, this is where you really have to trust me.'

'Why?'

'Because I'm going to tie it around your neck.'

The world slams to a halt. Excuse me? Around my neck. Have I really just heard what I thought I heard?

'You're not strangling me.'

'Wouldn't dream of it.' He laughs. 'I'm not into asphyxiation. I'm just limiting your choices. And if you don't want to try it, we don't go there.'

He tips his head to one side, waiting for my answer. And I can't help myself. After all, I crossed to the dark side a long time ago. I'm a kinky weirdo now, and there's simply no turning back.

'I want to try it.'

175

He nods.

'If you start to panic, tell me straight away. I'll take it off.'

Getting to his knees, he leans over me, encouraging my head up. Taking his time, making sure everything's perfect, he wraps the rope around my neck, tying it beneath my chin with a knot I can't see. Finally, he takes the other end, attaching it to a loop at my wrists. Evidently satisfied, he sits back on his haunches.

'Now,' he says. 'How does that feel?'

'Absolutely fine, thank you very much.'

'Don't try to get one over on me. It's not a battle of wits. You're in my hands. I want you to feel safe.'

I gaze at him defiantly. 'And I do.'

'Good. Now, this is what happens if you go south.'

He nudges my hands towards my crotch. The rope tightens around my throat, just a little. It's slightly uncomfortable, but I can still breathe.

'See what I mean?' he asks, releasing the pressure.

'Oh.'

'You don't want to do that, do you?'

'Not really.'

'So, there's only one way to go.'

Up.

'You're a devious bastard.'

'You're too kind. Blindfold?'

I shake my head. 'I want to see you.'

He leans down, sealing his lips around my right nipple, sucking lightly at first. A flurry of tingles flutter through my breast, travelling quickly down to my crotch. Automatically, my hands rise and the rope tightens, rubbing deliciously against my clit. I let off a moan. And, oh Lord, despite all my bluster, it's completely obvious. There's no way I'm going to get through this in one piece. Releasing my nipple, he gives me a mischievous smile before moving to my left breast. Latching on, he repeats the process. Again, my hands move involuntarily, tightening the rope and rubbing the knot against the bundle of nerves, sending me into a whirl of lust.

'Oh God.'

'Stay still.'

'I can't.'

'Your problem.'

I return my hands to my stomach, determined to leave them there for the time being. I won't last long if I don't. But then he runs his mouth between my breasts, licking here, skimming his lips across my skin there, setting light to a thousand sparks. And now I just want to touch him. Without thinking, I raise my hands again. The knot presses against me. Shimmers of electricity erupt from my clitoris, reverberate across the walls of my vagina, and threaten to cause an implosion.

'Shit.' I lower my hands, too far.

The rope tightens around my neck. And that's not the way to go. I move my hands back into neutral, just above my belly button, and at the same time, he adjusts his position, trailing the heat of his breath across my stomach, down to my hips. Moving further, he works at my thighs, licking, kissing, nibbling playfully at my flesh, occasionally catching a ticklish spot. I shift my hands to stop him. Immediately, the binding around my neck tightens. I shift them up again, sensing the knot against my clit.

'Fuck,' I half shout, my brain fuddled.

His face appears in front of mine. He checks my makeshift necklace, giving me a little time to recover.

'How are we feeling?'

'A little ropey.'

With a laugh, he lies back by my side.

'How much more can you take?'

'Plenty,' I lie.

'Well, in that case, I might keep you here all day.'

Propping his head on one hand, he traces a finger across my breasts, over the rope, back onto my flesh, watching its slow progress in a lazy dream-like state. Vibrations permeate every part of me, muscles, nerves, sinews – and I wriggle under his touch. He stops at my right nipple, circling it for an age before leaning over again to suck. I buck, raise my hands, whimper at the flood of warmth between my legs. He sucks harder. I tug again. Whirlpools of pleasure spring into life, congregating into one, and I come, crying out, rolling onto my side and curling into a ball. Gently, very gently, he urges me back into position.

'Think how much more intense this can get,' he smooths my hair, 'if I bind your legs to the bed.'

Again, I can't answer. I'm focussing too hard on bringing myself back under control. Before I know it, he's straddling me, kissing my stomach, this time moving further out to the sides, tracing his lips up my flanks, one at a time. And I'm back to struggling with my hands.

'How do you feel?'

Seriously? He expects me to speak? While I'm flapping about in a delirious lather, floundering under a tide of coital ecstasy, losing myself in a full-on surge of sexual oblivion? I open my mouth, but nothing comes out of it, apart from yet another groan. I've broken into a sweat, and completely forgotten where I am ... let alone how I got here. I'm stranded in the moment, in my own little universe, with Dan. He's back at my legs now, sucking, kissing, nibbling, moving further down. Finally, arching himself above me, he takes the rope and pulls at it, over and over again, propelling me into another spin, a second orgasm.

'Jesus,' I scream. 'No.' I need to stop this. Because if I don't, I'll end up a husk of a woman. 'Coffee, coffee, coffee, coffee ...'

The words spin into darkness, and everything stops. I curl back into a ball, shivering, shaking, riding through the spasms inside. And somehow, I'm aware of him, stroking my brow, raining soft kisses onto my forehead. When I finally manage to open my eyes, he's smiling at me.

'So, I take it we're a fan of rope?'

'God, yes.'

'Jolly good.'

He sets about untying the knots, carefully loosening the rope and pulling it away. It doesn't take long and as soon as I'm freed, I stretch out, completely satisfied.

'I'm a wreck.'

'Pull yourself together, woman.' He moves between my legs. 'Don't get too comfortable. I'm only just warming up.'

Some tiny, half-forgotten voice of reason calls out from the back of my head. 'Excuse me, but shouldn't you tell him about the period thing, and the totally fucking up with the pill thing, and the possibly being with child thing?' Lost in the mother of all sex fugs, I flick it to one side, deciding I just don't need my conscience interfering right now. And I really don't need reminding I'm a top-notch prat. If this all ends in prams and bottles and baby wipes, I've only got myself to blame.

He enters me slowly, his cock smoothing against the inside of my vagina. I can barely believe it when a wave of energy unfurls inside. I writhe in his arms, raise my backside off the bed and cry out in surprise when he thrusts suddenly, lunging all the way in, immediately triggering a third orgasm.

He doesn't admonish me for my lack of control. Instead, he carries on, withdrawing and thrusting repeatedly, at full force. I reach up, grab hold of his biceps and dig my fingernails into his flesh, firing him up further. With his eyes fixed on mine, his lips clamped together, he keeps up the tempo, pounding through every single one of my convulsions.

'God, no,' I cry out.

'God, yes.'

I thrust a hand into his hair, tugging at it with all my might, but not for long. He grabs my hand and pins it down with a vice-like grip, reminding me who's in charge while he continues to drive into me at full force. The convulsions keep coming, along with a whole selection of strange noises from my mouth. A stifled moan, a squeak and a gurgle, and finally another of those long, ridiculous howls.

Fighting back a smile, he rams harder until at last, his lips part and I know he's on the edge.

'Fuck,' he grates. 'Fuck.' His muscles tense and he thrusts a few last times, filling me with heat as he judders through an orgasm of his own. 'Shit, Maya. That's so fucking good.'

He collapses on top of me.

'But I howled again.' I gulp for air. 'That's not good. You're turning me into a dog.'

He laughs into my neck.

'Make any noises you like. I love them all.'

We lie together, sweaty and spent, totally entwined. Gradually, our heartbeats return to normal. Breathing takes on its usual rhythm. Minutes pass in contented silence before he raises himself on his elbows and kisses me, long and hard.

'Do you know how much I love you?' I ask.

'If it's as much as I love you, you're in deep trouble.'

He's right, you know, my conscience pipes up. You probably are, you mad bint. The sort of trouble that takes nine months to make an appearance and then soils itself, repeatedly.

'I'm not in trouble,' I murmur, shoving the issue back in its box. 'I'm in paradise.'

The hours pass by in bliss, making love, sometimes with the rope, sometimes without. At some point, we pause for lunch. And then we're straight back down to the nitty-gritty. By the time we curl up in each other's arms, too exhausted to carry on any more, I've no idea what time it is. I'm drifting off to sleep when there's a knock at the door. I jolt awake.

'Yes?' Dan calls out.

Gordon pokes his head into the room.

'Wakey-wakey, sleepy heads. It's time.'

As quickly as he appears, he's gone again, leaving me to wince with embarrassment at the sudden realisation that he's been with us in the suite all along. I can only hope he hasn't heard any of my frenzied howls, or squeaks of delight.

'Time for what?' I ask.

'You'll find out.'

Dan's already up, tugging on his jeans. He pulls back the curtain and draws it again, giving me just enough time to realise it's already dark outside. I watch as he takes a couple of pills and slips on his T-shirt.

'A word of advice.' He gives me a peck on the lips. 'You'll need clothes for this.'

Leaving me no clearer on the matter, he disappears from the room. I haul myself out of bed, locate yesterday's dress and tidy my hair. As soon as I've transformed myself into something vaguely presentable, I venture out of the bedroom and wander through to the drawing room … straight into a gathering of the Maya Scotton Protection Society.

They've both got their backs to me, but Bill and Clive are unmistakable. Seated together on one of the plush gold sofas, they're busy talking to each other while Gordon's over at the far side of the room, methodically working his way through the drawers of a writing bureau. And then there's Dan, standing in a corner, deep in conversation with a stranger, the only man in a suit. Everyone else is dressed casually. I home in on my fiancé, sidling up and earwigging the conversation, picking up an occasional word or phrase: 'increased presence', 'round the clock', 'no expense spared'.

I'd ask them what's going on, but Clive's in front of me now. Somehow, in spite of my silent entrance, he's noticed. And somehow, in spite of his fight with Boyd, there's not a mark on him.

'Are you okay?' He touches my elbow.

'Of course.'

'And Lucy?'

'A bit of a wreck, to be honest. She's missing you.'

He looks at Dan.

'Soon,' Dan warns him, breaking off the conversation and holding out a hand to me. 'A few more days, Clive. Be patient.'

I'm guided over to the vacant sofa and take my place next to Dan. And while Gordon continues to open and close drawers, sometimes pausing to examine the contents, Clive sits back down next to Bill.

'Good to see you,' Bill smiles.

'Good to see you too,' I smile back. 'I didn't think you'd be here.'

'I came back over with Danny Boy. Getting used to that flight now. I came over before, to see him in hospital. My God, he was the worst patient you could imagine.'

He winks at me.

'Isn't this dangerous?' I ask. 'Everyone meeting here?'

'A little.' Dan nods at the stranger. 'Foultons fixed it up. They've gone out of their way for this.'

'But how did you get in?'

'The same way Dan did.' Clive's eyebrows twitch. 'Let's just say I feel like I'm in a Bond film right now.'

Dan slides a hand onto my lap, addressing me, and only me. 'Meeting in person is the quickest way, the safest way at the minute. Boyd's got our numbers and I wouldn't put it past him to have a lead on Bill.' He pauses. 'We're getting to the end game, Maya. Things are going to happen, but I've planned for this. There's increased security in Camden, down at the house in Surrey, in Limmingham too.'

'This must be costing a bomb.'

'It's a temporary measure.'

'Man, would you look at that!' Gordon slams a drawer, distracting everyone for a second. 'Letters. In these drawers ... letters from Royal dudes. This place is crazy.'

'You should bring Maya in,' Bill suggests, ignoring Gordon's outburst.

'No.' Dan slips a hand on my knee. 'We need to carry on as we are. Business as usual. Boyd suspects, but that's all. If we bring Maya in, he'll know for sure and then God knows what he'll do.'

'But you have protection in place,' Bill pushes. 'What does it matter if he knows? He can't harm anyone.'

Dan shakes his head. 'I'm not taking any chances. Did your men get anything?'

'Yes.' Any sign of the kindly old man disappears, revealing the darkness beneath. 'Our guest was perfectly willing to speak. He's been working for a character named Richard Dean, a well-known villain.' He studies Dan, picking up on something in his reaction. 'You know him?'

'An acquaintance,' Dan confirms. 'I met him a few times at Isaac's club.'

He doesn't explain any further. He doesn't need to. From the way Bill nods, it's perfectly obvious he already knows about the fat walrus and his sex den.

'We've had Isaac followed for weeks,' Dan explains to me. 'He's had no contact with Boyd, none that we could see. Isaac's obviously hooked him up with Dean and stepped back.'

'Well ...' Bill leans back, crossing his legs. 'I've asked around, and

I can tell you Dean's a nasty piece of work. He makes his money out of drugs, prostitution, gambling, that sort of thing.' He waves a hand, as if that sort of thing's nothing to get particularly hung up about. 'He'll do anything for money. And he's probably no friend of Boyd's, just happy to have his pockets lined in return for a little manpower and a place to hide.'

Immediately, Dan makes a decision.

'Then we'll line his pockets even more.'

'Be careful,' Bill warns. 'Dean knows you took one of his men. He also knows you won't be giving him back.'

I'm about to ask what on Earth he means by that, but I'm cut off, sternly.

'Relax. He's alive and well, and he wants to stay that way; Dean's not the type to forgive a Judas. We're helping our guest to disappear.' He looks back at Dan, his eyes hard. 'But that means your Mr Dean's a man down. I need to fix that before you do anything else.'

'Then get it done.' Dan sits forward, clasping his hands together. 'Quickly. Whatever Boyd's paying him, I'll go further ... just enough to encourage him to spit the bastard out.'

'It needs to be a significant amount of money.'

'I'll do whatever's necessary. I assume you can arrange a meeting?'

'Of course, but I wouldn't get involved, not personally. He's bad news.'

'I've met him before.'

'On different terms. Remember where you met him.'

'What of it?' Dan scowls, impatience getting the better of him. He's beginning to lose his temper.

'He knows about the club.' Bill glances at me, evidently uncomfortable now. 'He knows about your past. Who's to say he won't use that knowledge? If you pay Dean to give up Boyd, I'm willing to bet he'll come back for more. I'm talking blackmail, because that's the kind of man he is. Once he's got his claws into you, once he's smelt your money, he won't give up.'

'Oh, come on.'

'I'll say it again,' Bill growls, 'you don't want personal contact.'

'Then how do you suggest we do this?'

'Allow me.' Slamming a final drawer, Gordon perches himself on the arm of a sofa. 'Seriously, you need to look in those drawers. This place is full of secrets.'

The room dips into silence, everyone staring at Gordon, waiting for the first scrap of sense to dribble from his mouth.

'Fitting, really,' he beams at Dan. 'Seeing as we're being all, you know ... secretive.'

'If you've got something to say,' Dan admonishes him, 'get on with it.'

'Okay.' Unaffected by his friend's irritation, Gordon shrugs. 'I'm not scared of the big bad wolf, believe me. Nobody gets to Gordon Finn. I'll meet with Dean.'

'I can't let you do that,' Dan protests.

'And I can't let you stop me. You don't need any connections with this piece of crap. No more threats ... from anywhere. If we're still play-acting, Maya's my girlfriend.' He me blows an ironic kiss. 'So, logically speaking, I should be the one to sort this out, money and all.'

I check on Dan, catching the first signs of another objection.

'Do it,' I tell him before he can open his mouth. 'They're right. You don't need any more complications. You've got good friends here. Let them help you.'

'But ...'

'If you're really willing to do anything to make your future wife happy, then do this.'

He chews at his bottom lip.

'Fine, but I'm paying him back.'

'And that's the extent of your involvement,' I warn him.

'And that's you told,' Clive adds. 'I have to say, as your accountant, I concur with your future wife. Let Gordon deal with Richard Dean – I'm sure he has some twisted ways to account for cash transactions – and I'll find a way to pay him back, non-traceable.'

'Let's do this thing.' Like an over-enthusiastic inspirational speaker, Gordon springs up from the sofa, eager for action. 'And you two lovebirds?'

We look up at him in unison.

'If you want to thank me for this ... just remember to invite me to the wedding.'

Chapter Seventeen

'Yuk.'

I put down the mug.

My tea tastes strange ... metallic.

And something stirs at the back of my mind. Another week's passed in wilful oblivion. I still haven't come on, or worked out when I'm due, or even got round to using that bloody test.

'Later.'

I turn back to the current work in progress. It's almost finished. The wall sets off the vibrant white of the dress, the richly textured cotton, embroidered with tiny, delicate floral patterns. A host of multi-coloured sweet peas frame the scene. All I need to do now is finish off the details of my face, arms and hands, adding the engagement ring. I lean back, thoroughly satisfied with the week's work. This is my most personal painting yet, a message of my commitment to Dan. I swallow back a tiny wave of nausea, not for the first time today, and focus on the painted version of me, the flat stomach I've created.

'You should work on that bit,' a mischievous voice niggles in my head. 'Maybe a bump's in order. A massive bump, about the size of a bus. And huge bazookas too.'

'Shit.'

I can't put it off any longer. There are no more 'laters' to be had. It's time to confirm what I already seem to know. In a trance, I clean up, change into jeans and a blouse, grab my handbag and take it downstairs to the basement toilet. A silent cubby-hole buried away in the bowels of Soho, it's freezing cold in here, the air tinged with damp. Under the harsh light of a bare bulb, grey paint flakes away from the walls while up in the corner above the toilet, a desiccated fly, long since dead, lies suspended in an abandoned web. It's not the most salubrious place to welcome a new little person into my life; but it'll have to do.

On automatic pilot, I lift the cracked toilet lid, noting the tiny ceramic camper van resting on the cistern, and begin to follow the instructions. When I'm done, I lower the lid again and risk sitting on the crack. Clutching the plastic stick and gazing into space, I busy myself with thoughts of the other pressing issue in my life. Just as Dan promised, we seem to have moved into the end game. After spending the rest of Friday holed up at The Goring, I returned to Camden, digging in for the last few days of frustration – a quiet weekend at home followed by a working week at Slaters. I've been ferried everywhere by Carl, visited on a daily basis by Gordon, and quietly, in the background, Bill's played his shady part. And today, if everything's gone to plan, Mr Finn's finally met with the hideous Mr Dean.

I look down, releasing an involuntary 'Oh.'

There's a blue line in the indicator window, strong and unmistakable.

'Shit.' I've done it now. 'Fuck.'

I should be happy. I should be dancing with joy. But instead, I stay exactly where I am, perched on a cracked toilet seat and staring in dismay at a plastic stick. My brain descends into abject confusion. Pregnancy. Birth. Motherhood. Teeny-tiny clothes filled with a teeny-tiny wriggling baby. I shake my head. This can't be real. But in some disconnected, logical part of my brain, I know it is. I can't ignore the facts any longer, because the facts are lining up, one after the other, relentlessly. My period's gone AWOL, and I've got tender boobs, and tea tastes weird, and there's this little blue line …

'I'm not ready,' I breathe.

And neither, in all likelihood, is Dan.

'Shit.'

After all my complaints about being kept out of the loop, I've gone and made the mother of all decisions behind his back, and I can't imagine that going down too well.

'Shit, shit, shit.'

How do I tell him? What do I say? And when do I break the news?

I'm tugged from my thoughts by a ping of my phone. Hastily, I wrap the stick in the plastic bag and bury it back at the bottom of my handbag. Digging out my mobile, I'm thoroughly surprised to be greeted by a text from Lily.

Hope you're ok. Can we meet up? I want to talk.

I stare in disbelief at the words, bristling at the memory of her

185

tone the last time we spoke, dismissive and cold. But I hardly blame her. In her mind, I was the deranged ex-girlfriend. She had no choice but to keep her distance and protect her friend. But why is she contacting me now? With everything else that's going on, I should simply ignore the text. But I can't. I'm intrigued by this apparent change of heart. Overwhelmed by temptation, I tap in my reply and fire it off.

What do you want to talk about?

The reply comes immediately. One word.

Dan.

My interest's thoroughly piqued, my brain whirring with possibilities. Has she finally realised she misjudged me? Or is there something else I don't know about the father of my child? Going on past form, that's exactly the sort of blow fate would love to chuck in my direction. Unable to resist, I probe further, asking her what's going on. Giving nothing away, she insists on talking to me, face to face. And nobody's to know. Finally, I cave in.

When and where?

The reply shocks me.

Tonight? It's urgent. Please. I'll be at my new place until late. The Concordia on the north bank. Problems to sort out. Can you come over?

It doesn't take long to reach a decision. I've got the Steves' retirement do tonight and I'm hardly in the mood for it. At least this is an excuse to leave early. And if Lily's changed her mind about me, if Dan's told her the truth, then I can get a little advice on how to break my news to him.

I'll see what I can do. Need to show my face at a party first.

Almost as soon as I hit the send icon, I receive her reply.

That's fine. See you later. X

'Where have you been?' Lucy demands.

I take the last step up to the ground floor of the gallery, and say the first thing that comes to mind.

'On the loo.'

She watches me from the sofa.

'Bloody hell, you must have the shits.'

'Yeah,' I answer half-heartedly.

'The poshmobile's waiting outside.' She waves a hand at the window. 'Time to go home and get ready for the shindig.'

I look outside, to where the Bentley's waiting for me, Carl standing by the rear door, checking the street. He's even more anxious than this morning, and that's saying something.

'Aren't you coming?' I ask.

She shakes her head.

'I'm closing up here, going straight over to Covent Garden. Tweedledum and Tweedledee need help. They're flapping, as usual. I'll see you there later.' She frowns. 'Are you okay?'

'Yes.'

But I'm not. Of course I'm not. All I want to do is tell Lucy I'm pregnant, get the truth out into the open, collapse in a heap and cry. Because then I might just begin to process the fact. But as it is, with no release, my brain's had enough, gone on holiday, cleared itself out and hung up a sign saying 'back in a while'.

'I'd better go.'

Without another word, I leave the gallery, nod a greeting to Carl and slide into the back of the Bentley, where I find Gordon waiting for me.

'Hey.'

'I didn't expect you.'

'An added bonus.'

And a much-needed source of news.

'How did lunch go?'

'Well, that's why I'm here. Carl? Camden if you please.'

With an uneasy glance in the rear-view mirror, Carl starts up the engine and the Bentley pulls away. As we thread our way through Soho, Gordon starts on his story.

'So, Dean comes over to The Goring for lunch, and Bill was right, by the way. He is a seriously nasty individual. Dean's still pissed off about losing one of his workforce, even though he's been royally recompensed, so I let him vent his anger a little. And then, when he's finished, I make my proposition.' He leans over to me, lowering his voice. 'I tell him I want him to hand over Boyd. Money no object.'

Shifting uncomfortably, I peer out of the window. It's already dark, and the shoppers are out in force. Christmas madness, everywhere.

'And?' I ask.

'Dean says he doesn't know anyone called Boyd, so I remind him about Isaac's club, suggest Isaac's put them in touch. Dean starts to twitch, realises I've done my homework. I remind Dean of who I am, as if he doesn't already know. And he's interested. Oh yes.'

Straightening the collar of his coat, Gordon gives out a quiet, satisfied laugh.

'And then?' I ask wearily.

'He wants to know why I'm interested in this creature. I explain that you're the love of my life. I tell him about Boyd's fixation on you, his vendetta against your ex-boyfriend.' He does that thing with his fingers, making imaginary quote marks in the air. 'And then I tell him about the history of abuse. I suggest Boyd might not have been entirely truthful. Dean twitches even more, and I know I'm onto something. Seems he doesn't like dishonesty.'

'But he's a villain.'

'With a strange sense of morality. Honour amongst thieves and all that. Anyway, that does it. Dean suggests a price, and I agree.'

'That's it?'

'Yup. He'll cough up the goods tomorrow, in return for cash. Foultons oversee the handover. Bill's contacts take off with Boyd.'

'As simple as that?'

'All we needed was the link. And now we've got it.'

I can barely believe what I'm hearing. After all this time, we're finally down to business. This time tomorrow, Boyd will be out of our lives. I swallow back my own sense of morality. Whatever happens to him, he deserves it.

'How much?' I ask.

'None of your business.'

'Dan's going to pay you back.'

'Yeah, yeah.'

'And he's not to be involved.'

'Understood.'

Half an hour later, we pull up outside the flat. Just in time. Nausea's been building again. Any longer in the Bentley, and I would have been throwing up all over its expensive upholstery. Practically staggering across the pavement, I slam to a halt in front of the door. Roses. Everywhere. Scattered over the steps, stems broken, buds ripped apart, blackened petals, colourless in the dark. My heart beat triples in pace. I freeze and survey the road, wondering if he's here, watching me, waiting ...

I feel a hand on my back.

'One minute.' Gordon returns to the car, opens the front passenger door and stoops to speak to Carl.

'Do you know about this?'

'It's only just happened.' Leaning over, Carl touches his earpiece. 'Unmarked van. We're tailing it.'

'Call them off. There's no point now. How many have we got over the road?'

'Four.'

'Good. I'm staying with Maya. Come back at seven.' Gordon straightens up and slams the door. 'In you go. I'll clear up this shit.'

'But you need to get ready.'

'I'm always ready.'

While Gordon tidies up the ruined flowers, I busy myself with making him a coffee. A good five minutes later, he joins me. I guide him into the living room, leaving him to watch the early evening news, occasionally sipping at his drink, complaining that the English have no idea about decent caffeine.

After a quick shower, I sort out my hair and choose a dress: a short, smart red number from Harrods. With a flourish, I take it off the hanger and put it on, deciding it's the perfect antidote to Boyd's latest antics. Drawing every last bit of attention to myself, I'm about to let him know, loud and clear, that I'm anything but intimidated. The usual make-up and a pair of high heels complete the job. And then I spend a moment examining myself in the mirror, eyes drawn inevitably to my stomach, thoughts dragged unwillingly in their wake ... to the tiny speck of life hidden away behind the scarlet fabric. Tears blur my vision and suddenly, out of nowhere, I'm certain that raging hormones have nothing to do with the fact that I'm crying; and neither do shock or exhaustion. No. It's all down some strange, indescribable, instinctive form of love that's just made a surprise debut in my head. 'Ta daa!' it squeals in excitement. 'I know I've never been here before, but I like it, and guess what. I'm never going to leave!'

The Bentley returns at seven, taking us back down to central London and dropping us off at the edge of Covent Garden. With Gordon's help, I stumble across the cobbles, navigating a path through the evening crowds to the relative warmth of the market halls. I've had just enough time to register the wrought iron archways, a piazza overflowing with stalls and shoppers, when I'm guided into the gloom of a pub, through to a function room at the back.

'Look at you!' Lucy screeches as soon as I enter. 'Power-dressing now, are we?'

I smile in satisfaction. My choice of outfit has definitely hit the mark.

'Flipping heck. Billionaire's girlfriend.' Already several sheets to the wind, she smiles at Gordon and punches him in the stomach. 'How are you doing, big fella?'

'Fine and dandy.'

It's a bloody good job he's not about to become her real boss. If that were the case, I'm pretty sure she'd be searching for a new job come Monday. Dumping my handbag on the floor, I park myself on a stool and scrutinize the room. It's already filling up with bodies, and the thrum of conversation.

'This lot have been going for an hour already,' Lucy informs me. 'There'll be carnage later, especially when that thing gets going.'

She motions toward the far end of the room where, in the gloom, a DJ's busy setting up a disco. Without warning, Little Steve erupts out of the gathering and heads straight for us.

'Darlings, you made it,' he gushes. 'Guests of honour. The new owner and his lady love. Lucy, get these people a drink. On my tab. Get them pissed.'

'No,' I hold up a hand. 'Orange juice.'

'I beg your pardon?' Little Steve gasps, eyeing me suspiciously. 'What's going on here?' He puts an arm around my back. 'You're not preggers, are you?' He winks at Gordon.

'No,' I laugh, far too quickly for my own liking. 'Don't be daft. I'm just not in the mood.'

'But orange juice?' Lucy demands. 'Not wine?'

'Not wine,' I insist, levelling her with an 'I absolutely mean this' kind of a look. 'Orange juice. And don't lace it with anything.'

'And I'll take a pint of your lovely warm beer,' Gordon adds, leaning over to whisper in my ear. 'Actually, I'd love a piña colada.'

'Then have one,' I whisper back.

He shakes his head.

'And give myself away? Tonight, I'm as macho as they come.'

And so, the evening begins ...

Playing the part of the dutiful girlfriend, I spend an age circulating at Gordon's side, making endless small talk with Slaters' clients, past, present and possibly future. Soon enough, I'm worn out and feeling distinctly sick, but it's still too soon to make an exit. After managing to extricate myself from the public relations exercise with the excuse that my feet are killing me, I'm heading back to my stool when music blasts into life. The Weather Girls. 'It's Raining Men'.

Before it even happens, I know what's coming.

'Dance!' Lucy barks, grabbing me by the arm.

'No, not now!'

'Yes! Now!'

Ignoring my pleas, she drags me onto the dance floor and begins to gyrate, swiping her hands through the air and singing along like a woman possessed. Within seconds, we're surrounded by others, and

I have no option but to join in. Feeling distinctly awkward, I begin to move, doing my best to seem like I'm having a ball, but it's nothing short of torture. When the song finally draws to an end, I decide I've had enough. As Gloria Gaynor launches into 'I Will Survive' and Lucy twizzles round on the spot, I take my chance and make a hasty escape. I head back to the bar, dead set on returning to my stool, more than slightly triumphant when I reach my target.

I'm quickly joined by Gordon.

'Well, this is painful. A gay man, at a gay party, pretending to be straight.'

'Is it that bad?'

'It's worse than bad,' he grimaces. 'I'm like a child in a sweetshop, only I've been told I can't have any sweets because I'm off to the dentist.'

I laugh.

'Well, I'm at a gay party, pretending to be attracted to a gay man.'

'Then I'd say we're both in a pickle.' A glass of wine is thrust at him by an unknown admirer. He grabs it and slugs it back in one go. 'We'd better dance ... together.'

'Why?'

'Because that's what couples do.'

Utterly fed up, I follow him back onto the dance floor and do my duty. After three songs with Gordon, I'm temporarily back with Lucy before being passed from one Steve to the other. Before long, I'm exhausted, on the verge of throwing up over everyone, and maybe passing out.

'I need a wee,' I shout at no one in particular, making a second escape and slumping back onto the stool. Relieved to be left alone, at least for now, I close my eyes and steady my breathing. All I want is to go home and dive into bed, to brood over the whole pregnancy thing, and then sleep away my last night without Dan. When I open my eyes again, the crowd seems to have parted, and I can barely believe what I'm seeing: Gordon, right in the middle of the dance floor, getting into the groove with the Steves, singing along to Queen's 'I Want to Break Free'.

'Anybody would think he's gay,' Lucy grumbles, leaning against the bar next to me.

'Having fun?' I ask.

'Hardly.'

Which is obvious, seeing as she's on the verge of tears.

'I miss Clive.'

I slip my arm around her and draw her in tight. What on Earth do

I say? Don't worry, he'll be back soon. Tomorrow, perhaps. And he's missing you just as much as you're missing him. Just go and dance with a few gay men to pass the time, and that includes Gordon, by the way. I say nothing, of course. As it turns out, there's no need. She's distracted by something at the far end of the room.

'Oh, no.' She points at the stage. 'This isn't good. He's had at least eight margaritas.'

I follow the direction of her finger. Little Steve's tottering at the centre of the stage, a microphone clutched in his hands.

'Thank you, thank you, thank you,' he begins as the music dies down. 'Silence, please. I need to speak.'

'Oh God,' Lucy groans. 'I'd better sort this shit out.'

She's not quick enough. Before she can make it to the stage, Little Steve's already slurring through a clearly heartfelt but largely unintelligible speech. Finally, I begin to make some sense of it.

'So, as you know, me and my darling have been wanting to sell up for a while, and now we've got a camper van. Or should that be a camp van. Ooh er, missus!' He titters. 'Anyway, we're here tonight to celebrate the end of twenty … oh, I don't know, quite a few years in the business, selling paintings and all that …'

Lucy climbs onto the stage, almost loses her balance and manages to grab the microphone. Little Steve glares at her, and grabs it back.

'Our new owner is here,' he ploughs on. 'Where is he? Gordon? Gordon? Cooeee!' Shielding his eyes with his free hand, he finally spots Gordon waving from the crowd. 'There he is. Dances like one of us. In fact, I wonder if he is one of us.'

While Gordon makes a point of fighting his way off the dance floor and joining me at the bar, Little Steve staggers over to the DJ, issues an instruction and staggers back.

'Let's test it out. Where's Maya?' He hiccoughs, and seems to retch. 'Millionaires. Flies round a cow pat with that one.' He snorts like a demented pig. 'Ah, there you are.' He points directly at us.

My body tenses.

'Now then, you two haven't had a kiss all night and he dances like a queen, so. Time for the test! Take it away, maestro!'

The song begins. Cher, 'It's in his Kiss'. And I can't stop the horror from spreading across my face.

'What do they want?' I shout.

'Isn't it obvious?' Gordon points at his mouth.

'No. I can't do it.'

'I think we'd better.'

He nods at the crowd on the dance floor. Without exception,

they're all staring at us, clapping maniacally, urging us to get on with it.

'This is a complete fucking nightmare,' I complain.

'Tell me about it.'

'Now!' Little Steve screeches into microphone. 'Do it!'

I know it's a drunken joke, but this really is pushing things too far. Hopping off the stool, I plant a quick kiss on Gordon's lips and grab my handbag.

'Get Carl to pick me up.'

And with that, I march towards the door. It's time to get out of here. I've made it through the bar and out into the market hall when Lucy catches up with me.

'Where are you going?' she demands.

'Home.'

'But I can't go yet. I promised I'd stay until the end.'

'Then stay. It's not a problem.'

'Wait,' Gordon calls, pushing through the door and joining us. 'What's going on?'

I should tell him the truth, that I'm off to see Lily. Because I need to talk. I really, bloody need to talk. And right now, if she's come to her senses, Lily's about the only person I can confide in.

'I want to go home. I've had enough.'

'Don't blame you.' He pulls out his mobile. 'I'll get my jacket.'

'No. Stay for a while. You're having fun.'

'Evidently, too much fun. I'm coming back with you.'

I hold up a hand.

'I'll be fine ... on my own.'

He shakes his head.

'I don't know.'

'Gordon, I've been fine all week. You know I'll be safe. I've got Carl. Please. I need some space and you need to butter up the clients. Just take me to the car, come back here and tell them I'm not well.'

He thinks for a moment or two, glances back at the door to the pub, and finally nods.

Chapter Eighteen

'I need to see someone before I go home.'

I look at the rear-view mirror, a lozenge of darkness against the kaleidoscope of Tottenham Court Road. Carl's eyes flash back at me.

'Who?'

'Lily Babbage. A friend of Dan's. She's waiting for me at the Concordia ... on the north bank.'

Saying nothing, he focusses back on the road, and I begin to feel distinctly uneasy. Maybe he's under orders to ignore my requests, or perhaps he just feels the need to check with his bosses. Whatever's going on, I should explain a little more.

'I didn't tell Gordon. I'll go back to Camden afterwards. It won't take long, but I really need to see her. Please.' Still no answer. 'Perhaps you should radio in, let them know I'm taking a detour.'

His eyes are back on me.

'I'll do that,' he says crisply. 'What's the address for the Concordia?'

I give him what he needs, watching as he enters the details into the Satnav. As soon as the car pulls up at a set of traffic lights, he takes his mobile from the dashboard, taps in a contact and begins to speak. 'I have Miss Scotton with me. She's making a brief stop off before she goes home. She needs to see a friend.' He confirms he'll stay with me for the duration before listening to a voice at the other end of the line. 'I'd say half an hour.' He hangs up.

'Is that okay?' I ask.

He nods. His eyes flash again, this time catching the red glow of the traffic lights. As the colour changes to green, he looks away and we begin to move. Relieved to be getting what I want, I slump back into the leather seat and watch the ever-changing slideshow of Central London: pavements heaving with bodies, brightly-lit shops, pubs, theatres, restaurants, all busy. A hive of humanity on the other side of the glass, a world apart from mine.

I can barely remember what it feels like to be normal. I can only hope that speaking to Lily will help bring me back to reality. Realising I'd better let her know I'm on my way, I riffle through my handbag, managing to locate my purse, a hair brush, the pregnancy test wrapped tightly in its plastic shroud ... but no phone. In a fluster, I dig through the contents again. Finding nothing, I give up and stare out of the window.

'I think my phone's been nicked.'

'When did you last have it?'

'I don't know. I might have left it at Slaters.' I think again, shake my head. 'No. I'm sure I brought it out with me.'

'Don't worry. I'll contact Foultons.'

'But Dan uses it. He tracks me. He'll wonder where I am.'

The answer's terse.

'Don't worry.'

We circle Trafalgar Square, the hubbub of Friday night giving way to a quieter, more sober environment: Whitehall, Westminster, the Houses of Parliament. Veering right at the Thames and staying on the north side, we head west, probing deeper into territory I've never explored before, cold Government buildings, bland office blocks, empty-windowed, abandoned for the night. At last the Bentley slows, pulling in to what looks like a building site. Surrounded by the beginnings of a driveway, a circular apartment block sits at the centre, a brooding megalith reaching up into the dark, lit only on the ground and top floors. It's kept company by a single crane looming up behind the building, a red light winking intermittently at the top.

'Well, this is it,' Carl mutters.

He gets out, opens the rear door, and helps me into the night air. Immediately, my heels sink into sludge, the cold envelops me and I'm beginning to wish I'd brought a coat.

'Are you sure?' I ask.

'The Concordia.'

He points at a sign beside the door.

'But it's not finished.'

He shrugs.

'Let's go inside, see what's going on.'

Reluctantly, I follow him, stumbling through mud and cursing my choice of footwear. We're greeted by a security guard. Installed behind a marble counter, he looks up from a crossword.

195

'Maya Scotton,' I announce. 'To see Lily Babbage.'

'Top floor. She's still here.'

'Doing what?'

'Planning the décor, probably.' The guard twiddles a pen in his fingers. 'Or finding more problems. She comes over a lot. Regular visitor. Knows the boss. Gets away with murder.'

I peer back out of the glass frontage at the wilderness of mud and concrete and iron spikes.

'I know it doesn't look much at the minute,' the guard assures me. 'They're starting on the landscaping next week. It's not so bad inside, perfectly safe. The lifts are in full working order.' He points the pen at a metallic door. 'Help yourself.'

'I'll come up with you.' Carl leads me to the lift and presses a button.

About thirty seconds. That's all it takes for us to reach the penthouse. And by the time we arrive, my skin's prickling with anxiety. I edge my way out into a huge, gloomy space, taking in the fact that it's lined with the obligatory wall-to-ceiling windows. I count four panels of glass; the fifth is missing, a sheet of plastic fluttering in its place. For a few seconds the clouds give way in the sky and a full moon appears, casting a watery light across the room, urging shapes out of the shadows and revealing a mess that's anything but safe. Wires hang from walls. Buckets, tools and piles of plasterboard litter the place. Directly in front of me, on top of a workman's bench, two mobiles sit next to a drill and a length of rope. I'm about to examine them in more detail when the moon disappears again, leaving obscurity in its wake. The only illumination now is from part way down a corridor leading off to the right, where a door's been left open, allowing a shaft of light to cut across the floor.

'Lily?' I call. 'Are you here?'

No answer.

I move toward the light, listening to the constant flapping of the plastic sheet. An icy gust of air lifts it momentarily, and I halt. We're ten floors up and there's no protection against the drop. It's incredibly dangerous. Surely, Lily shouldn't be up here alone.

'Hello?' I call, becoming more uncertain by the second. 'Is anybody here?'

I sense a movement, turn back to the corridor. There's a figure silhouetted against the light.

'Glad you could make it.'

Immediately, I'm turned to stone, not thinking, not breathing. I'm not even sure my heart's beating, because I know that voice, its familiar Scottish lilt. As he moves forward, my eyes adjust to the gloom and his features emerge, like something out of a nightmare: ebony eyes, glassy with drink, moist lips, parted in a strange, unnatural smile.

'What's the matter?' Boyd asks, amusement clear in his voice. 'Confused?'

He waits for a reply, but my mouth won't function.

'Oh no.' He clasps a hand to his chest. Doing his best to mimic a woman, his voice takes on a falsetto quality. 'But Carl's a goody. How come he brought me here? I don't understand.' The hand slaps against his forehead, palm outwards. And as quickly as it sprang into life, the pantomime ends. Lips crack into a snarl. The eyes glint. 'Anyone can be bought for the right price, Maya. Or with the right threats.'

He brushes past me, jolting my senses back to life. Shock gives way to panic. Adrenalin surges. My heart thunders, causing a rush of blood through my veins. Lungs draw in a quick succession of breaths. I manage to turn, watching through bleary vision as Boyd heads straight towards Carl, and pats him on the back.

'Daniel's little crew took one of ours, so I took one of theirs. Didn't I, Carl?' He ruffles his hair. 'Just a little chat, that's all we needed. Turns out Carl's got things of his own he'd like to keep safe, pretty girlfriend, lovely mummy. He's a good lad at heart, so don't get annoyed with him, Maya. He didn't have much choice.'

Avoiding all eye contact, Carl stares at the floor. And suddenly it's clear to me, why he's been so uncomfortable all day.

'You don't have to do this,' I tell him, my voice unsteady with nerves. 'And you don't want to do this. I can see that. Whatever threats he's made,' I raise a shaking hand at Boyd, 'he won't carry them out. He can't. He's got no one behind him, not any more.'

Boyd laughs.

'I take it you're referring to Mr Dean's agreement with Mr Finn?'

I falter.

'How do you know about that?'

'D'uh. Carl told me, of course. Good God, you're slow.' He leaves Carl with another pat and saunters back to me, eyebrows raised. 'It's a good job I never put all my trust in Richard Dean, kept my options open. I've got a few people of my own, Maya. Well, I call them people. They're more like animals, really.' He sniggers. 'Animals, aren't they, Carl?' Keeping his eyes fixed on mine, he raises his voice. 'They belong in a zoo. And Carl knows what they'll do if he upsets me.' He claps his hands. 'So, there's nobody to help you, Maya.

Nobody to come to your rescue, because nobody knows you're here.'

I swallow hard, wondering if I should appeal to his better nature and tell him I'm pregnant. I open my mouth, stopping just in time, because there's no point in trying that. Boyd's got no better nature. If he finds out I'm carrying Dan's baby, I dread to think what he might do. It's best to stay silent.

'We took your phone, lifted it at the party. You're currently on your way to Camden, but you're stuck in traffic. Carl's looking after you. At least that's what his employers think ... and your Mr Foster.' With a dismissive wave of a hand, he turns his back on me. 'You'd better go and update Foultons. Let them know everything's fine.'

Without a word, Carl steps back into the lift.

I watch the door close and begin to shake. I'm on the brink, staring into a chasm, and once I topple over the edge, there'll be no escape. Tear ducts sting. My throat constricts. It's the last thing I want to do, show him any sign of weakness, but my body's got other ideas. The first tears well in my eyes.

'Worth his weight in gold, that one,' Boyd goes on breezily.

He sidles over to me, standing so close I can smell his whisky breath.

'Please,' I manage to beg. 'Please let me go.'

He shakes his head, moves a strand of hair away from my face.

'I can't do that. If I do that, I'll have no meaning. I was born to make you happy, born to take care of you.'

The clouds part again. Moonlight floods the room, and I can see him clearly, the expression on his face that's meant to be tenderness. But it's all pretence, a brittle outer shell that's easily cracked. I look into his eyes, at his pupils: two contracted dots, each one a full stop. This is the end.

Lowering my head, I let the tears flow.

'Oh no, don't cry. There's no need to cry. I'm going to whisk you away and make you the happiest woman in the world. I'm going to give you everything you want.'

And control me with fear.

'It's been a good game. Such a shame it's over.' Placing a finger under my chin, he forces my head back up. I meet an unreadable face, shrouded in shadow now the moonlight's gone again. 'But now I have to act, because you've backed me into a corner. You need to understand that. It's not my fault.' He picks up the length of rope. 'Turn around.'

I stare at the rope.

'I said turn.'

'No.'

He's so quick, I don't have time to react. He might be drunk, but he's still too much for me. I'm grabbed, swung round, and clamped tight in his arms. I'd go for a knee in the balls again but he's already pre-empted that, angling his body sideways against mine. I cry out, incoherently.

'And what's the point of that?' he demands, slapping a hand over my mouth. 'Who do you think's going to hear you? Now be a good girl and stop struggling.'

His grip tightens to the point of pain. Suddenly, the arms release me and he grabs my wrists, tugging them behind me with such force it takes the air clean out of my lungs. Before I can steady myself, he's already binding my wrists. The rope's coarse and hard against my skin, far too tight, threatening to cut off the blood flow, but Boyd doesn't care. When he's done, he pushes me away. I stagger toward a pile of plasterboard, and manage to straighten up.

'Sit. On the floor.'

Bewildered, I do as I'm told, sitting in the filth with my back against the boards. As the clouds part again and the darkness thins, I watch him reach into his pocket. He pulls out a rose, just the bud, the stem already torn off. He holds it out, bringing it right in front of my face, and I flinch.

'They say romance is dead. And do you know what? I think they might be right.' With a sneer, he crushes the rose in his fist. 'At least yours is.'

The crumpled petals drop to the floor. The clouds return. Shapes lose their form, disintegrating into the murk.

I close my eyes, all too aware of the cold air, the rough surface of the concrete floor, the hard boards digging at my back.

'I know the truth, Maya. I know he played songs for you in that bar. I know he didn't mean a word of it when he knocked you back in the nightclub. I know you met in New York ... and I know you've seen him since.'

I open my eyes. Boyd takes a hip flask out of his jacket pocket.

'Carl's only confirmed what I already knew. You and Mr Foster were trying to pull the wool over my eyes.'

'You didn't know anything.'

I have no idea why I'm arguing.

'Oh, yes I did.' He swigs from the flask. 'Even before my little helper came along. But how? That's the question.' He screws the top back on the flask and places it on the workbench. 'Phone tapping? Spies in the woodwork? Top of the range surveillance? No.

None of the above. There's no need for all that malarkey.' He pauses, his lips rising into a smirk. 'Not when you've got your very own Lily Babbage.'

He watches me, satisfied with the shock that's taking hold of my face.

'Lily Babbage,' he repeats, slowly this time, emphasising every consonant, every vowel. 'Strange name that. Do you think she's related to that guy who invented the computer? I never asked. Too busy banging her ... for weeks on end ... so I could have access to this.'

With a flourish, he picks up one of the phones.

'Oh no, wrong one.' He squints at it. 'That's the one Carl called me on.' He chucks it into the gloom. I hear it skid across the floor. 'Don't need that any more. No, no, no. This one.' He picks up the second mobile. 'The Babbage phone.'

In disbelief, I stare at my undoing, raking back through every single thing Lily told me. She'd gone back to men. She'd met someone. Hot in bed. Don't tell Dan. Shit. After the fiasco with Sara, I should have known Boyd was the mystery man, that there was never any high-tech magic at his fingertips. All the time, he was simply tapping Lily for information. And like a complete idiot, I gave him everything.

'Where is she?' I ask.

'At her other place ... asleep.'

'What do you mean?'

'A few sleeping pills.'

'Have you hurt her?'

'No, no, no, no. Honestly, I'm not that bad.'

Jesus. Not that bad?

'You tried to kill Dan,' I remind him.

He pulls a face, as if I'm splitting hairs.

'And you threatened everyone. Everyone I know.'

'Aye, well. I never meant it. Well, I meant to have him killed. Obviously. The man's a prat, swanning around like he's God's gift to the vagina. And okay, I poisoned his dog, but we've been over that. I don't go around killing everybody. It's not like I'm unreasonable. I didn't kill the teenage pothead, did I?' He straightens his suit. 'Miss Babbage is perfectly fine, don't you worry. She could do with a rest after all that sex. I tell you what, it's nearly worn me out. She's got a big appetite on her for a skinny madam.' He tosses the phone back onto the workbench. 'I don't know how she does it. Barely eats a thing. Fucks like a randy demon. Anyhow, in between all that she fills me in on her life, her friends, their little problems ... including your Mr Foster.' He clutches both hands to his chest this time, acting out the scenes for me. 'Oh no, he's had an accident and he's going to die. He's in a coma. A coma, I tell you!' He rubs his hands together gleefully, then shakes his head, pouting like a clown. 'Oh, but thank God, he's woken up. He's going to live! He's going to live! Oh, oh, he's split up with his girlfriend. What am I to do?' He changes to an overly deep voice. 'Go and see her, Lily. Make sure she's alright. Get them back together.' And now he's Lily again. 'Oh, I've done it, and it didn't work.' He catches his breath, evidently done with the play-acting. 'She wasn't convinced, by the way. That meeting in the coffee shop.' He waves a hand. 'And neither was I. But when Mr Swanky Pants got his marbles back, he did a better job than you. He managed to convince Lily he'd had enough. And I almost believed it too ... until Gordon the moron turned up. So I sent in that other one. What's her name? Clarissa?'

'Claudine.'

'Whatever. That did the trick.'

Because I called Lily.

'I was with her, Maya. Right by Miss Babbage's skinny little side, all sweaty and naked and post-coital, listening in on your blathering.'

He raises his head, pinning me down with those flint-like eyes. Serious now, he lowers his voice.

'Now, I've asked you before ... and I'm asking you again ... did you enjoy New York?'

I won't give him the pleasure of a response. Seeing as he already knows the answer, I don't see any point.

'Lost for words, eh?' He leans back. 'You should have told me the truth. I don't like it when you lie to me. It's very hurtful.'

'What are you going to do?'

'I'm going to wait, of course.' He frowns at me. 'For Mr Swanky Pants.'

'What?'

'He'll be here soon.' He points at Lily's phone. 'I didn't just trick you with that thing.'

He wanders off, checking the plastic sheeting, eyeing up the contents of the room, leaving me to deal with another bout of shock and tears. I should have known it. I'm in his grasp again, but that was never going to be enough. No. Boyd won't rest easy until he's eliminated the threat, and he's clearly determined to do it in front of me. In a split second, the life I should have had disintegrates into dust, shock gives way to grief, and my heart breaks for Dan, for his unborn child, for everything that's good in this world.

'I've had this place in mind for a while.' Boyd returns to me, kicking at my foot and demanding my attention. 'Perfect location for a showdown. Lily Babbage, she's got more money than sense, that girl, and she's picky too. I thought I'd never hear the end of it, all those plans.' Ignoring my tears, he goes on as if he's chatting to his best mate. 'She's always over here, you know, demanding personal attention from the boss. Oh, I'm not sure about the lighting. Maybe I should change the bathroom. No, no, no, that kitchen's never going to do. And that window's not right.' He points at the plastic sheeting. 'How can a window not be right? I ask you.' He shrugs. 'Anyhow, she wants to see him again ... tonight. She's sent him a text, as usual, and she won't take no for an answer, as usual. Well, I say she sent him a text. I mean me, of course.'

He checks his watch.

'So, here's what happens next. Mr Foster arrives downstairs, probably with that big chunky bodyguard. He's greeted by the night watchman, who's actually my night watchman, your driver ... and a gun. The bodyguard's held at gun point, Swanky Pants takes the lift to the top floor, otherwise, bang, the chunky fella's dead. And then that door opens ... and then, well ...'

He pulls a black handgun out of his pocket.

'Browning 9mm. I won't bore you with the finer details. I'm more of a shotgun man, really, but I've done a wee bit of target practice and I have to say, I'm not too bad.' He raises it, narrows his eyes and aims it at the lift door. 'I should have prepared a speech really. You know, the final bad-guy speech. Because I am the bad guy in all this, aren't I?' He sits next to me. 'Trouble is the bad guy always gets foiled, right at the last minute. He's so busy with his final speech, it gives the hero time to fight back. Big mistake. But I'm sorely tempted.' Clearly restless, he stands again. 'So, Mr Foster, you've annoyed me for long enough ...'

I hear the whir of the lift mechanism.

'Oh, here we go,' Boyd announces. 'Bob's your uncle, Fanny's your aunt ... and Daniel Foster's dead.'

Chapter Nineteen

He levels the gun at the lift door. The seconds lengthen, drawing out to breaking point, and I register sounds, disparate and unreal. Shallow breaths. The quiet thrum of the lift. A siren wailing. The rumble of London's traffic. The squeal of a train.

And then it's all gone, muffled by terror.

I watch from a distance, as if I'm really not here. I'm locked inside my head, in a nowhere land. The door opens. He's standing in full view, wary, scanning the room, taking in Boyd, the building debris, the open space where a window should be. And then his eyes lock onto mine.

'Oh come on out, Daniel,' Boyd calls, carelessly waving the gun. 'It's no use staying in there.'

Keeping his vision anchored on me, he advances out of the lift, slow and silent, coming to a halt about ten feet away from Boyd.

'Put your hands up,' Boyd orders.

'They've already frisked me.'

'I don't care. Hande hoch.'

Dan raises his arms. Breaking eye contact, he scours the room again, quickly searching for possibilities and probably finding none, before he focusses back on me. Lips part. Eyes soften. He's made up his mind. These could be our last few moments together, and he's not prepared to waste them on Boyd. Instead, he'll spend them with me.

'Nice to see you again.' Boyd's words grate against my ears. 'You're looking well. Isn't he looking well, Maya?'

I ignore him. I'm entirely with Dan, silent, defiant, denying Boyd's existence, not giving him the pleasure of a reaction. But like an irritating insect, his voice continues to buzz around my head.

'Not bad going. An excellent recovery. I'm impressed.'

Dan smiles, but not at Boyd's words ... at me. And in those few seconds, I see it all: a confirmation of his love, his admiration, his faith. Through the tears, I return it all, a hundredfold.

'I don't like being blanked,' Boyd growls. 'If you don't want Maya to suffer, look at me.'

With a flicker of the eyelids, Dan gives me the slightest of nods – a silent goodbye, perhaps. And then, he faces Boyd, full-on, utter contempt taking up residence on his face.

Satisfied he's finally the centre of attention, Boyd waves the gun.

'Well done on surviving the crash, but not so well done on trying to dupe me. Careless work. And don't bother trying to argue the toss. I know it all.'

'You don't know anything.'

'I warned you not to mess with me. You think you're so clever, but guess what? You're not as clever as me.' He moves forward, training the gun back on Dan's chest. 'Tell him, Maya,' he bleats. 'Tell him how I know. Tell him how I did this.'

I have no choice. It's clear from his face he expects me to answer.

'Lily,' I whisper. 'He's been seeing her. I called her ... a few weeks ago. I gave it all away. I'm sorry. And now he's got her phone. He used it to get us both here.'

Dan's lips twitch.

'Where is she?' he demands.

'Wouldn't you like to know?' Boyd snarls.

'If you've harmed her ...'

'You've only got yourself to blame, not that you can do anything about it now. You're about to die.'

My heart falters. My lungs flail. I want to scream, but I can't. My body's refusing to follow orders again.

'I knew. Right from the start. I knew.' The temptation's clearly too much for Boyd. He can't resist a little 'evil villain' gloating. 'Let's talk about Mr Finn, for example, the one who's apparently buying that shitty little gallery, the one you sent in on her birthday.' He waves the gun at me. 'Did you think I wouldn't investigate? Did you think I wouldn't find out he was at Cambridge with you? Stupid, fatal mistake, Mr Swanky Pants. And then New York.' He tuts and shakes his head. 'Dearie me. A brazen act of defiance.'

'I didn't see him in New York,' I tell him.

'Oh, shut the fuck up, Maya,' Boyd spits. 'Don't you get it? I had no proof of that, not until Carl sang like a canary.'

'Get on with it,' Dan interrupts. 'If you're going to shoot me, just get the fuck on with it. I'm sick of your voice.'

'What?' Boyd opens his mouth in pantomime disbelief. 'No bargaining?'

'What's the point?'

He cocks his head to one side, examining Dan, trying to work out if he means it or not.

'Look at that, Maya,' he says at last. 'When it comes to the crunch, Mr Wonderful just rolls over and gives up. I've got to ask, old boy. Do you actually want to die?'

'If I can't have Maya,' he says quietly, 'then I don't want to live.'

'Oh, come along now.'

'And as long as she lives, I don't care what happens to me.'

'But she'll be mine,' Boyd taunts him, clicking back the safety mechanism, his hand unsteady.

'Not for long.'

'Oh, those friends of yours.'

Bill, Gordon, Clive. Dodgy connections, money and a fierce loyalty. I don't doubt that retribution will come, and quickly too. But not soon enough.

'They won't stop until they've found you,' Dan smiles. 'And they won't stop until you're dead.' He looks at me, softening his voice. 'And they won't stop until you're safe. I promise. I love you, Maya. I'll always love you. Whatever happens, remember that.'

Short, sharp breaths catch against my throat. I don't want to remember. I want to experience it ... every single day of my life. And there's someone else who needs his love and protection. His child. If Boyd never faces retribution, there's no way he'll let me keep this baby. Another life damaged by hatred. History repeating itself.

'She'll forget you before the week's out,' Boyd crows.

'She'll never forget me,' Dan affirms, his attention secured on my face.

'No,' I rasp, fighting back a maelstrom of emotion. He can't die without knowing about our child. There's no way I'm letting it end like this. 'No.' I turn to Boyd, ready to beg one last time. 'I'll come with you. Just leave him. There's no need to do this.'

'Oh, there's every need to do this,' Boyd replies. 'My doctor once told me to remove all the negative influences in my life.'

'What made you like this?' I sob. 'What fucked you up so much?'

'I'm not fucked up. I had the perfect childhood, unlike this one.' He motions the gun at Dan. 'And yes, I do know about that. Lily told me everything. Very sad. But it's just the way the world works. Some of us take whatever we want, and some of us have everything taken away. If anyone around here's fucked up, Maya, then it's him.

He's covering it all up, but it'll come out in the end. I'm doing you a favour. I'm saving you.'

'Please.'

'Enough,' Boyd snaps. 'Shut … your … mouth.'

I look back at Dan. The clouds part again and I catch it in a few moments of moonlight: the slightest movement in his eyes, towards the workbench.

My heart begins to race. I get it. He's not giving up at all. In fact, at the very least, he's planning on going out with a fight, and I have my part to play. Determined to do everything in my power to help, I stretch out my legs, slowly, carefully, realising I can just about reach the bench. It's definitely a long shot, but when I kick, if I kick hard enough, I might be able to provide a second's worth of distraction. I just need to wait for my cue.

Dan raises his arms further into the air.

'Any last words?' Boyd asks with a smile.

'Just one.' Dan smiles back. 'Kick.'

Before I can make a move, a shot rips through the air. I give a start, realising it's distant, coming from outside. And then I notice Boyd's confusion. While he glances at the lift, I lash out, kicking at the bench with all my might.

A screech of metal against concrete.

The bench keels over, taking the drill with it.

On top of the gunshot, it diverts Boyd's attention for long enough. Springing into action, Dan hurls himself at Boyd's legs and brings him to the floor.

Almost immediately, I hear a second shot, deafening this time, leaving me stunned for a moment before I understand what's happened. Boyd's managed to fire the gun. Blinking back tears, I scramble to my knees, and peer into the shadows, breathing out with relief when I realise the bullet didn't find its mark.

Both men are still moving, wrestling each other, writhing on the floor, throwing punches whenever they can. I have no idea how it happens, but the gun's dislodged. Clattering past me, it skates to a halt next to the lift. I'm staring at it, wondering if there's enough time to get over there and grab hold of it when the lift mechanism kicks into life. Someone's on their way up.

Sixty seconds. That's all I've got. And I'll never make it. If that's one of Boyd's lackeys coming to lend a hand, we're finished.

Counting in my head, I look back, just in time to watch Dan stagger to his feet, closely followed by Boyd. Neither of them wastes any time, immediately hurling themselves into another struggle.

Ten seconds ...

Boyd's slammed against the wall, and while Dan rains a succession of vicious blows into his stomach, he raises his hands, obviously aiming for his opponent's eyes. The blows stop. Instinctively, Dan protects himself and Boyd takes his chance, throwing a punch at his chest, sending him backwards, staggering into buckets and falling on his back.

Twenty ...

Boyd's on top of him now, pounding a fist into his face, but somehow Dan manages to wrap a hand around his throat and push him back. Both men roll, stumbling to their feet in unison. Locking together again, they pitch towards the windows, and my heart hammers at my rib cage. Before I can make out who's got the upper hand, they wheel further towards the plastic sheeting. Either one, or both of them are about to go over the edge. I'm certain of it.

Thirty ...

I need to act. And I need to do it now.

Still on my knees, I shuffle to my handbag and nudge it over, spilling the contents across the floor. Straight away, I spot the rape alarm. Manoeuvring myself into position, I pick it up, fumbling blindly behind my back until, at last, I manage to press the button. Immediately, a screech rips through the air, continuing even when I drop the alarm. I look up ... and freeze.

There's only one body silhouetted against the moonlight now. Through the tears, I can barely make out who it is. Pulse racing, I do my best to focus.

The clouds part again.

'Oh, thank God.'

He's standing absolutely still, rigid, holding on to the window frame, bent forward slightly and staring down at the ground ten floors below.

'The lift!' I shout, eager to knock him back into action. 'Dan, there's somebody coming up!'

Gathering his senses, he checks on me, and then the lift. But it's too late. The door opens.

I hold my breath, then slump in relief at the sight of Beefy, holding a gun. I have no time to ask what's going on. Dan staggers towards me, crashing to his knees, silencing the alarm and pulling me into his arms. Folded in his warmth, held tight as if he'll never let me go again, I begin to shake and sob while he rocks me gently, soothing me back to life. At first, all I can hear is the thudding of his heart, the deep gasping of his lungs. And then, as the tears die away and we both steady ourselves, the sounds of the city return: a passenger jet soaring overhead; a train scraping along tracks; the distant roar of traffic.

At last, I hear Dan's voice.

'It's over. He's gone.' He pulls away and checks my face, my throat, my arms. 'Are you okay?'

I nod.

'It's over,' he repeats. 'It's over.'

'Untie me.'

I turn slightly, allowing him access to my hands. As soon as I'm freed, I run a hand through his hair and inspect the damage. A bloody nose, a bruise emerging on his left cheek, an eye that seems to be swelling.

'You need to get checked out.'

'I'm fine.'

'You don't look it,' Beefy intervenes.

I glance up at him, realising for the first time that Carl's by his side.

'What's he doing here?' Dan spits.

'He came to his senses,' Beefy explains.

'Came to his senses? He brought Maya down here. I should rip his fucking throat out.'

'Calm down. Once he realised what Boyd was going to do, he swapped sides. If it weren't for him, we wouldn't have Boyd's minion handcuffed to a gate downstairs.'

Dan's body grows tense. Certain he's about to carry out his threat, I grab him by the arm and somehow manage to hold him in place.

'Leave it,' I plead. 'He had no choice.'

Tightening my grip, I give him a determined glare. There's been enough violence and I'll be damned if there's any more. While Beefy and Carl go to the window, I wait for Dan to relax, only letting go of him when I'm satisfied.

'What happened? I didn't see.'

He stares at me, breathing deeply, his face taut.

'I killed him.'

'You fought. It was self-defence, an accident.'

'No.' He wipes blood from his nose with the back of his hand, and stares at the floor.

'The alarm went off, he looked away and I saw an opportunity ... I pushed him out of that window.' He pauses, just long enough for me to process the information. 'I killed him, Maya.'

I put a palm to his cheek.

'You're confused. You did what you needed to do.'

'I did what I wanted to do.' His eyes search mine for understanding. 'I hated him and I wanted him dead. That's the truth.'

I frown.

'But you didn't plan it?'

His breathing quickens again.

'No.'

'It was a split-second thing?'

'But I made a choice.' He bites at his bottom lip, a fruitless attempt to maintain control. It doesn't work. A tear betrays him, sliding down his cheek, and then another. 'I couldn't have him tormenting you, not any more. I couldn't ...'

I pull him into my arms, letting him dig his head into my neck, immediately giving him the words he needs to hear.

'I understand, completely.'

It's the only thing to say. Because I made him promise not to go down that route, but in heat of the moment, he took his chance and put an end to a life – a fact he could have kept from me – but he's chosen to tell me the truth. And he thinks I'll hate him for it. But it's not that simple any more, because I have this new life inside me, a new urge to protect, a deeper, unshakable love for the man kneeling in front of me. Boyd threatened to destroy it all, and I'm glad he's gone. In the last few hours, my world's shifted on its axis, a move so slight it's barely noticeable ... and it's taken my moral compass with it.

'Sometimes, it's just not black and white,' I whisper.

He lifts his head.

'If you hadn't pushed him, he might have pushed you. If he'd had a chance, he wouldn't have hesitated. As far as I'm concerned, that's still self-defence. You have nothing to feel guilty about.'

'I agree.' Beefy's voice cuts across us.

We both look up.

'Maya's speaking sense.'

'I need you to check on Lily,' Dan tells him.

'I'll get somebody else to do that.' He pulls out a mobile. 'I'm staying here.'

'There's no need ...'

'Yeah, there is. The police are on their way, I'm a witness, and I need to make sure you tell the truth.' He kneels in front of Dan. 'And I mean this truth. Listen to me. He came at you, you punched him, he lost his footing, and fell. That's what I saw, and him too.' He motions to Carl. 'Now, you don't want to land us in trouble, do you?'

Dan shakes his head, half-heartedly, and stares into the shadows. In spite of Beefy's words, I'm not entirely sure he's about to toe the line. Maybe, a little more persuasion's in order. For a moment, I toy with the idea of telling him the baby news, but it doesn't seem the right time or place to do it, not with Boyd's shadow still lingering in the room. I'll just have to try something else.

'You'll go with Beefy's story. Don't give them the slightest excuse to put you away.' I take his hand in mine. 'We've spent enough time apart, Dan. Boyd's not going to win.'

Chapter Twenty

I roll my head and flex my shoulders. I have no idea what time it is. I've been here for hours, curled up on this sofa, staring out at the black slick of the river. But now, the first signs of dawn are showing in the sky, a weak grey glow, diluting the darkness and gently nudging the city back to its senses. Determined to stay awake, I yawn, blink, rub my eyes, decide it's time, yet again, to sort through last night's events in my head ... but exhaustion's finally clouding memory. The sequence has begun to fray and merge.

I'm held in his arms, aware of more bodies in the desolate space around us. They're asking questions. So many questions. I hear the crackle of a radio, see the flash of a police uniform. And now he's gone. I'm in a car with a stranger; I'm sitting at a table in a tiny room, struggling to answer more questions; I'm crying, sobbing, letting out all the pent-up anger and frustration and loneliness. Another car. This time, with Beefy. He brings me back home, to Lambeth.

And Dan's still not here ...

'There you go.' Beefy holds out a mug. 'How are you feeling?'

'Tired.' I take the mug from him. 'Scared,' I add. 'I'd feel better if Dan was home.'

'He won't be long.'

Somehow, I can't believe that, because nothing ever seems to go right in our world.

'Will they charge him?'

His eyes flicker.

'Only if the silly bugger says the wrong thing.' He sits next to me. The cushions dip beneath his weight.

'Is he on his own?'

'Clive's down at the station.' He sips at his tea. 'There's nothing to worry about, believe me. Foultons are helping with enquiries. I've

211

told the police what I saw. Carl's been arrested ...'

'What?'

'He did what he did, Maya. There's no ignoring that. But he'll be fine. As long as he sticks to the official story, we'll make sure he's treated with leniency. We'll look after him.' Another sip of tea. 'The evidence stacks up against Boyd. The stalking, the attacks, the threats, what happened last night. Plenty of witnesses too.' He sucks in a breath. 'There's only one possible glitch. And that's all down to Dan.'

And I can only hope he doesn't let his conscience get the better of him.

'You know,' Beefy muses. 'I've been with him ever since the accident, spent a lot of time with the man, one way or the other. I've worked in protection for a while now, met a lot of rich types, and most of them have got their heads up their arses. But he's alright. I like him.' He lifts his mug in the air, as if he's making a toast. 'He's got morals.'

'That's what I'm scared of.'

'He's also got you. He's not an idiot. He won't jeopardise his future. He'll be home.'

We sink into a calm silence, both of us gazing out of the windows. The sun's risen now, bringing with it the beginnings of a harsh, blue winter sky, scratched by a few lonely wisps of cloud.

'Sorry for being a prick the other week,' Beefy says. 'In the nightclub. I didn't like doing that.'

'You knew what was going on?'

'Of course, but I was under strict orders to play along.'

'You did pretty well.'

He raises the mug again.

'Don't know what I'm doing in protection. I should be an actor.'

We laugh quietly, and suddenly I'm overwhelmed by the urge to say something personal.

'I'll miss you.' Those words feel strange on my tongue. After all, the first time I ever set eyes on Beefy, he gave me a serious case of the willies. 'Now Boyd's gone, I suppose you'll be moving on.'

He shakes his head.

'Actually ...' His thick lips curl upwards. 'You'll be seeing a lot more of me. I'm coming to work for Dan.'

'You are? Doing what?'

'Security, of course. I'll be heading up a small team.'

'Team?'

'He's a rich man and once he's sold the company, he'll be a

stinking rich man. It's prudent to have a little protection on hand.' He notices my unease. 'You'll get used to it. You'll have your freedom. I won't be shadowing your every move.' He pauses, a mischievous glint in his eyes. 'I heard what you did to my colleague.'

'Oh?'

'You know?' He mimes a throwing action. 'I'm quite attached to my mobile. Don't fancy having it chucked in the river.' He laughs again. 'To be honest, I need something a bit more relaxed, a bit more local now we've got the baby … and a second one on the way.'

Bloody hell, he's been busy. I gawp at him for a few seconds, trying to imagine this mountain of muscles gently rocking a baby to sleep. And then, out of the blue, my brain's ambushed by visions of Dan doing exactly the same.

'Babies.'

'What about them?'

'Well …'

It's no good. I can't keep it to myself any longer. I need to tell someone and at this particular point in time, Beefy seems to be the perfect sounding board.

'I'm pregnant.'

I catch him part way through a gulp of tea. He swallows, chokes and coughs.

'Congratulations,' he splutters, wiping dribble from his chin. 'Does Dan know?'

'Not yet.' I wince. 'It wasn't planned. I cocked up with my pill … and everything else.'

'You should have told him last night.'

'It didn't seem like the right time.'

He nods.

'I take your point. Are you happy about it?'

I nod back.

'It was a shock at first, but I want it. I'm just scared Dan's not ready.'

He chuckles.

'Nobody's ever ready for parenthood. Wham! It's like being hit by a hurricane. Suddenly, your entire life's a mess and right at the centre of it, there's this tiny little thing, drinking milk and filling its nappy and crying.'

'You're not exactly selling it to me.'

'But then it smiles at you,' he goes on, ignoring my complaint. 'And that first smile. Well, it's worth a million quid. Have no fear. That man loves your bones. He'd do anything for you. He'll be made

213

up.'
  'Really?'
  'Really.'
  'Still ...'
  'Just tell him, Maya. And do it soon.'

Leaving Beefy to finish his tea, I head upstairs for a shower, stopping in my tracks when I'm confronted by a huge, freestanding bath, freshly installed at the far end of the en suite. I can't help smiling at the fact that Dan's been busy preparing for my return, and I'm sorely tempted to break it in, but there's no time. Leaving the bath for now, I take a quick shower instead. Back in the bedroom, I discover a pair of combats hanging in Dan's wardrobe, nestling up against one of his suits. I pull them on, along with a shirt, and go back down to the living room to settle in for the wait. Just after seven, Clive calls with new information. Dan's still at the station. No charges, but he's helping with enquiries.

'There's nothing more I can do here,' he says. 'I'll come and join you.' He pauses, and I know what's coming next. 'Any chance you could get Lucy over there?'

'Of course,' I smile.

At the end of the day, after everything Clive's done for us, he deserves plenty in return. As soon as he's gone, I wake Lucy with an early morning call. Silencing her questions, I tell her to get a cab over to the penthouse.

'What the fuck are you doing here?' she barks, marching through the door and surveying the kitchen. 'Don't tell me you're back with that piece of shit.'

'Sit down, Lucy.'

'What the fuck's going on?' She comes to a halt next to the counter, sways a little and clamps her hands on her head. 'Jesus, I've got the hangover from Hell.'

'I said sit down.'

While Beefy beats a hasty retreat to the lobby, closing the door behind him, I set about filling the kettle.

'What are you doing?' Lucy demands.

'Making tea. Sit down.'

'I don't want tea.' She eyes me warily. 'Well, actually I do. My mouth's like sandpaper. I'm never drinking again.'

'That might be a good idea.'

'So, what's going on?'

214

'Sit.' I point at a stool. 'You're getting tea and the truth. It'll sort out your hangover, trust me.'

Slowly, uneasily, never once taking her blurry eyes off me, she lowers herself onto the stool. And then I begin. Busying myself with the usual tea rigmarole, I fill her in on everything that's happened since the accident, leaving out Clive's involvement for the time being. She needs to take in the facts before she takes off like a firework.

'This is fucking mad,' she breathes when I'm done. 'No. It's beyond fucking mad.'

'Tell me about it.'

'This sort of shit happens in films ... or on EastEnders. This isn't real.'

'Well, it is real. It all happened.'

She stares at me, goggle-eyed, opens her mouth as if she's on the verge of saying something, and then closes it again, several times. Good grief, this is painful. I knew it would be difficult, but the alcohol-induced fug isn't helping matters.

'So, you didn't shag Gordon?' she asks at last.

Incredible. After everything that's happened, this is what her brain decides to obsess over?

'Absolutely not. He's Dan's friend. And he's gay, by the way.'

'You are kidding me.'

'No, I'm not. Come off it, Luce. You saw the way he danced last night.'

She shakes her head.

'Gay?'

'And he's in the closet, so keep shtum.'

'But, he's gay?'

I'm about to remind her that Gordon's sexuality is possibly the least important thing in all of this, but I get no chance.

'You've been lying to me for months.' She scowls at me.

'Yes.' I yawn. 'But I had no choice. And you can't complain. You lied to me.'

'When?'

'When you and Clive lured me over here.'

'Yes ... but ... I didn't lie to you for three sodding months.' She sinks into a temporary silence, her face gurning its way through several unpleasant emotions: anger, disbelief, annoyance, confusion. 'I can't get over it,' she murmurs at last. 'Gordon's gay.' Her eyes seem to lose focus. 'But what about Clive?'

Ah, so we've finally got to the inevitable crux of the matter.

'He's not gay.'

215

'You know what I mean.'

'Of course, I do.'

And now, after all this time, I finally get to put an end to the torture. I can barely contain myself. The words bubble up from my lungs, bursting from my mouth with a good helping of childish excitement.

'He didn't want to split up with you.'

I'm half expecting a tirade of abuse. Instead, a small smile jitters across her lips ... and I'm thoroughly relieved.

'What?'

'He couldn't see you. He had to keep his distance. We couldn't have any links between me and Dan.'

'And you knew this all along?'

'Yes. I wasn't supposed to know, but I forced it out of them. They made me promise not to say a word. I'm so sorry, Lucy.'

With a dismissive wave, she springs up from the stool, sways again, and then circles the kitchen, deep in thought.

'The fewer people who knew, the better,' I press on. 'I wanted to tell you. Honestly, I did. And I nearly told you, more than once. You were a complete nightmare ...'

'He still wants me?' she cuts in.

'Yes.'

'He does?'

'Yes,' I repeat with all the patience I can muster.

'He still wants me,' she cries jubilantly, throwing her hands in the air. Without any warning whatsoever, she dances off round the living room, almost falling over the coffee table in the process.

'And you clearly still want him,' I shout. 'I thought he was a cu ...'

'Don't you dare!' Swinging to a halt, she aims a finger at me. 'That's foul language, Maya Scotton. You're talking about the man I love.'

'Fair enough,' I laugh.

Lowering her arm, she surveys the apartment.

'So where are they now?' she asks.

'Down at the police station. Clive says he'll be here soon. He wants to see you.'

I watch as joy flits across her face, only to be replaced by a shadow.

'And what about Dan?'

'I don't know yet.'

Right on cue, I hear a key in the latch. Facing the door, I hold my breath, and then sigh in disappointment as Clive appears on his own.

'He's still there?' I ask.

Casting a nervous glance at Lucy, he nods.

'So, what's going on?'

'Like I said, he's helping with enquiries.' He advances slowly, his eyes flitting in Lucy's direction, and then back to me. 'They've got the gun. Boyd's prints are all over it. They found Lily at her house. She's in a state, but she confirmed she'd been seeing Boyd for weeks, only she didn't know him as Ian Boyd. They found the site manager too, tied up in a cleaning cupboard. He's okay. The picture's coming together.'

'I should be with him.'

He shakes his head.

'He'll be here soon enough. Just have patience.' He swallows. 'Everything's going to be fine.' And now, finally, he turns to the hung-over elephant in the room. 'Hello, Lucy,' he ventures.

While the seconds drag their feet, I watch as Clive attempts a hopeful smile, and Lucy glowers back at him.

'You shit.' She sidles forward. 'You put me through hell.'

'I didn't have much choice.' He holds up his hands.

'I should deck you right now.' And she wouldn't get very far. 'You're a lying git,' she growls.

So, just like me, she's putting up a fight before the inevitable reunion. Trouble is, I'm too tired to let it go on. In fact, I'm in the mood for a little fast-tracking.

'Clive, can you take her away please?'

'We're staying here until Dan gets home.'

'I'm perfectly capable of dealing with this on my own.' I give him a cold stare. 'Take her to your place. You're only down the road. You can come back later and check on Dan.'

'But ...'

'I've got Beefy.'

I'm determined to stand my ground, and Clive knows it. With a nod, he holds out a hand to Lucy. And as if it's covered in something distinctly disgusting, she simply stares at it.

'Lucy,' I snap. 'Drop the act. You already know what's been going on. Just get to the bit where you fall into his arms and sod off, will you?'

She opens her mouth to protest.

'I mean it. I've got enough to deal with.'

'She has,' Clive confirms. 'We should leave her in peace.' And then he opens his arms. 'Ready?'

Thankfully, she can't fight it any longer. The smile reappears.

Broadening quickly, it threatens to explode right off her face.

'Oh, okay,' she squeals. 'Go on then!'

With a half-demented laugh, she flings herself into his arms, letting him embrace her with all his might. I should really look away, give them a bit of privacy, but I can't help watching as he kisses the top of her head, and then her cheek. My heart's flooding with warmth for my friend, but as soon as they launch into a full-on snog, I decide enough is enough.

I cough, loudly.

They break the kiss.

'I'll just ...' Clive motions to the door.

'Yes, you do that,' I smile.

And with no further ado, he leads Lucy out of the apartment.

Finally left alone, I lie on the sofa and go back to waiting. At some point I must have fallen asleep because the next thing I know, there's a finger lightly tracing a path down my cheek. I open my eyes, slowly focussing on Dan's face.

'You're back.'

'I am.'

I sit up, taking in the fact that he's kneeling next to me, still wearing yesterday's work suit. There's dried blood on his collar, smeared across his sleeves and down the front of his shirt. And the bruises on his face are deepening now, contrasting with the pale grey of his skin.

'You're a state.' I brush the stubble on his chin. 'How's Lily?'

'She's okay. She's been checked by a doctor. She's at home. Her parents are with her.'

'Don't you want to see her?'

'Tomorrow. I'm too tired right now.'

He readjusts his position, and I catch the slightest hint of discomfort in his expression.

'Your leg's hurting.'

'It's fine.'

He's lying, and I know it.

'You need your pills.'

'Later.'

We stare at each other for a while. On my part, I'm just trying to enjoy the calm after the storm, but there's something strange in his eyes, something that sets me on edge.

'You stuck to the story then?'

He nods. 'Self-defence. They're satisfied.'

'So, that's it?'

He looks away.

'What's the matter?'

I'm answered with silence.

'It's over, Dan. Don't let it get to you.'

'It's not over yet.'

Suddenly, he buries his head into my lap, clamping his hands tight against my thighs. Perhaps it's the shock and exhaustion catching up with him. The truth is I have no idea what's going on inside his head, but whatever it is, I need to give him time. Smoothing his hair, I do my best to reassure him. A few minutes pass like this before he finally looks up, gazing at me as if I'm an object of worship, something he shouldn't really touch.

'I need to tell you something,' he says.

Flickers of uncertainty appear. Again and again, his lips seem to form a word, and then reject it.

'Just say it,' I prompt him.

He nods and swallows, eventually making a start, his voice uneven, threatening to crack at any minute.

'If you knew I'd done something wrong ... could you still love me?'

'If this is about Boyd, you didn't do anything wrong. You had no choice. It was either you or him.'

'I'm not talking about Boyd.'

Suddenly, I'm cold.

'Then who?'

He closes his eyes, lowering his head back into my lap, clearly working up to an admission. Another bombshell ... after all the promises that there'd be no more. I steel myself for the task ahead. Whatever it is, I'm simply going to hold my ground and hear him out.

'Talk to me.'

'I don't want to lose you. I can't lose you.'

My stomach churns. Willing my body to behave, I take in a deep breath. If this is morning sickness, then it's just about the worst time it can kick in.

'That's not going to happen.'

He lifts his head again.

'I tried to forget, tried to block it all out, but I can't. It's eating away at me, Maya. It's been eating away at me for years.'

'No more secrets,' I remind him.

'No. No more secrets.' He hesitates, and then he tells me something I already know. 'I killed Boyd.'

'We've been through that.' I cup his cheek, wondering why on

219

Earth he feels the need to plough through this again.

'It's not the first time.' Keeping his eyes fixed on mine, he watches my reaction. 'It's not the first time I've killed a man.' Finally, he gives me the beginnings of the truth. 'She looks like him,' he says quietly. 'Layla.'

And that explains it all. I hardly need him to go on. Outside, the clouds shift, parting slightly, revealing a patch of blue, a glimmer of sunlight. And I already know what he's about to admit.

Chapter Twenty-One

A shaft of sunlight falls across the apartment, breathing life into the picture of Limmingham. I urge him up from the floor, onto the sofa next to me.

'I need a coffee,' I lie.

Because I don't need a coffee at all. I just need a few minutes to sort this out in my head. Leaving him in silence, I go to the kitchen and set about fiddling with the coffee machine. I have no idea what I'm doing – pouring water in here, coffee there, flicking switches, pressing knobs – but something gurgles and hisses, and by some miracle, dark brown liquid begins to appear in the jug. As I watch it dribble out, the facts congregate from two separate directions, linking together, one by one: the beating, the brain haemorrhage, an ambulance over the road; an emptied bank account, a life abandoned, a two-year disappearance. So now I know why he ran, and why he came back a changed man. He was the stranger in that alleyway. I should be shocked, but I'm not. I can barely believe I never saw this coming.

The hissing and gurgling come to an end. I pour out two mugs of coffee, and silently resolve to understand. He's expecting me to take the moral high ground, but it's a simplistic place, and for the second time in twenty-four hours I'm determined to steer clear. After all, we've come too far to jeopardise this, and he's changing again, gradually reverting to his true self: very sweet, very kind, a little lost. Those were Lily's words, and that's the real Dan, the father of my child. Whoever he was when he turned up in Limmingham, he's not that man any more.

I carry the drinks over, and hand him a mug. Curling his fingers around it, he stares at the floor.

'It all makes sense now,' I begin, staying on my feet. 'How you

221

reacted with Layla.'

He looks at me. I say nothing. Holding his gaze, I show no surprise, no judgement. I need to let him speak before I say my piece.

Finally, he nods.

'Every time I look at her, I see him, his face, his eyes.'

'I've seen a picture of him.'

'Then you know.'

'I thought she reminded you of what he'd done to you.'

'No.' The mug shakes in his hands. 'It was after I left Cambridge, the first thing I did ... I went back to Limmingham. I didn't know how I'd got there. I didn't know why I was there. I had no idea what I was going to do. It was like someone else had taken over.' He closes his eyes against the memory. 'I was angry, confused ...'

'Grieving,' I add.

'I suppose so. I'd lost my mother, my family, my adoptive parents ... myself. I suppose I was looking for someone to blame.' Eyes open now, he focusses back on me, uncertainty clouding his features. 'He was the obvious target, the first link in the chain. If he'd never existed, then none of this would have happened. I suppose that was the logic.'

Leaning forward, he places the mug on the table, spilling a little coffee in the process. And then he clasps his hands, gazing at the floor again.

I wait for his explanation. It's not long before it begins.

'I rented a room, hung about town for a few days, went to the same pub, watched him getting pissed, mouthing off, full of himself, oblivious to all the damage he'd done.' He pauses. 'He looked at me, once or twice, but I don't think he recognised me. I'm not surprised. I was a mess. No one would have recognised me.' A frown creases his forehead. 'I saw her one day, walking through town, doing the shopping, getting on with her life. It was as if I'd never existed.'

'So that upset you?'

'No.' He shakes his head. 'I felt nothing. I had no feelings for my own mother. He'd taken those too.' He blinks back a tear. 'And then one night, I followed him home. I'd been drinking all day, trying to blot it out. He turned up in the pub. I watched him laughing, cracking shit jokes, acting like the big I Am. And then something broke.' He stares at me, lips trembling with nerves and half-forgotten emotions. 'I followed him home, and jumped him, and beat the shit out of him. He begged me to stop. He looked up at me ... with those eyes, begging. But I just carried on, because I couldn't stop, because I'd never felt anything like that before. Rage. Pure rage. I was out of control.' He glances out of the window, slowing down. 'And then the begging stopped. I thought I'd killed him. I panicked, ran away, left the country.'

Something jars in my head. Rummaging through the mass of details, I grasp for the relevant facts.

'But he died of a brain haemorrhage,' I say. 'Two weeks later.'

'I know. And it's no coincidence.'

'It might be.'

'It's not,' he says emphatically. 'I caused his death, and that's three people, Maya. Three.'

I put down my mug.

'You didn't kill your wife,' I remind him. 'That wasn't your fault. And if you hadn't pushed Boyd, he would have come back ... time and time again. And what you did to your stepfather ...'

'Was murder.'

'No. It's just like what happened with Boyd, you didn't plan it. That's not murder.'

'Then what is it?'

'Legally speaking? Manslaughter, at the very worst ...'

He cuts me off, his temper on the rise.

'Call it what you want, but I killed him. So, if you want to walk out of here, if you never want to see me again, I understand.'

'What?' Where the hell did that come from? He seriously believes I'd dump him over this? I begin to laugh, a quiet laugh of disbelief. He must be exhausted, utterly fuddled by the last few hours, because that's the only decent reason I can think of for the rubbish that's just spilled out of his mouth. 'You'd give up that easily?'

He narrows his eyes.

'I love you. You're the only woman I've ever loved, but I never want to see you miserable, and if staying with me makes you miserable, knowing what you know ... I don't want it.'

Oh boy, he's just said the wrong thing. Disbelief's right out of the window. There's no room for it, not with my own anger bubbling up like a pan of milk. When it gets to boiling point, there'll be no stopping it.

'I know what this is. You're as masochistic as me.'

'How do you work that one out?'

'You thought you'd killed your stepfather, you thought you'd caused your wife's death, so you shut yourself off from everyone ... for years.'

'I told you,' he growls. 'I'd caused enough hurt. I didn't want to cause any more. That's why I shut myself off.'

'No,' I growl back. 'You were punishing yourself because deep down, you think you're worthless. Deep down, you think you don't deserve happiness. And you'd love to go on punishing yourself. You'd love me to walk out of here so you can wallow in your guilt. But guess what? That's not going to happen. I'm going nowhere.' Realising I've begun to shout, I raise an unsteady finger at him. 'So, you'll just have to deal with the guilt some other way.'

'How?' he demands. 'How do I do that? I hurt my sisters. I killed their father. I destroyed their lives.'

'Their lives were already destroyed. Layla told me she was glad he died.'

'So, does that make it acceptable? Does it? Our mother drank herself to death because of what I'd done. Was Layla glad about that?'

'Your mother drank herself to death because of guilt.'

'Oh, come off it.'

'Guilt, Dan.' I glare at him, determined to get my point across, even though I haven't got a shred of proof. 'Guilt that she'd been such a shit mum. Guilt that she'd ruined your life. Jesus. It must be fucking genetic.'

He bites his lip, obviously wrestling the urge to sling something back in my direction. But this has gone far enough. We're sniping at each other, sliding into a full-blown argument. And this isn't the time.

'What you did,' I say, 'I understand.'

He shakes his head.

'After everything you'd been through, I understand why you lost it. I understand why you lashed out. I don't condone it, but I understand. Get that into your thick head.'

In a huff, I walk off to the window, cross my arms and stare at the blue sky. I need to calm down. I need to get this back on track. And I need to banish anger, because true to form, it's achieving nothing. As the seconds tick by, I'm aware of a movement behind me. He's getting up, coming to join me.

'I'll find a way to deal with it. I'm sorry.'

'I don't know why you're apologising. Life dealt you a shit hand. You made mistakes – we all make mistakes – but you've got a conscience, Dan. You regret what you did, and that's why I'll never walk away.' I look at him. 'Tell me this is the last bombshell … and mean it.'

'This is the last,' he confirms, his eyes softened. 'I swear. I wanted to tell you, but there was never a right time.'

'Never is.'

'How do you slip something like that into conversation?' He touches my arm. 'It's the last layer. You've peeled them all back, every one of them. You've got right to the heart of me.' He pauses, watching my every reaction. 'I just hope you can still love me.'

'How could I ever stop?'

Slowly, tentatively, he takes me into his arms.

'So, how are we going to deal with this?' I ask.

He shakes his head. He clearly has no idea.

'You need to tell Layla.'

'She'll never forgive me.'

'Complete honesty. No secrets. You own up to what you did. That's the only way you're ever going to be able to face her.'

'And what if she goes to the police?'

'She won't.'

'People change when they find out the truth.'

'Not always. I've just found out the truth, and I'm still not giving up on you. She deserves the facts.'

'I can't ...'

I place an index finger on his mouth.

'No more arguing. I'm taking the lead on this, and you don't have a choice.'

He gazes at me. Despair and confusion take a bow, leaving admiration and love to step into their place.

'The tables are turning.'

'You'd better believe it, Mr Foster.'

He pulls me in for a kiss. It's long and patient and tender, and it does the job. Before long, we're together again, completely together, two halves of a whole. So, is this the moment, I wonder? Should I reveal my own little secret? After all, I've just demanded honesty. It would be wrong of me to hold it back any longer. As soon as the kiss comes to an end, I study his face, deciding that today's not the day. He's dealt with enough over the past few hours. I'll tell him tomorrow, when things have settled down a little.

Or maybe ...

'Are you okay?' he asks, dipping his head.

'Fine. But you're not. I'm giving you three hours.'

'For what?'

'To clean yourself up and get some sleep. And then I want you in the bedroom.'

That does it. He's close to keeling over with fatigue, but the light returns to his eyes.

'That's my territory,' he reminds me.

'Not today.' I glance out of the window. 'Look at that sky. Bright blue. Have you noticed?'

His arms tighten around me.

'Every day's a new beginning,' he murmurs.

I brush my lips against his. 'And this is yours.'

I wait until Dan's in the shower, before I make a move. Opening the front door, I join Beefy in the lobby.

'How is he?' he asks.

'Fine. Just cleaning up. Listen. I need your help. Can you find out his sister's number?'

'Which one?'

'Layla.'

'Probably.' He pulls his mobile out of his pocket. 'I'll get onto Foultons.'

'Get me the number, and then lend me your phone.'

He clutches it protectively to his chest.

'I'm not sure about that.'

'I need it, Beefy. Mine was nicked.' I give him a reassuring smile. 'Don't worry, it's not going in the river. I just need to speak to her.'

He stares at me, and I know exactly what's going through his mind. The last time he colluded with me, it ended in disaster.

'Look,' I explain, 'we both know what happened last time she visited. I'm not an idiot. I'm not risking that again.'

His lips part.

'It's about the baby,' I lie for good measure. 'I need some advice. I need to talk to someone who's been through it.'

'You've not told him yet?'

'No. Just trust me, it's not the right time. But I do need to speak to Layla.'

He grimaces.

'Oh, come on, Beefy. I'm desperate.'

He stares at me a little longer. Finally, his features soften. He taps in a contact.

'And Beefy?'

'Yes?'

'Don't say a word to Dan.'

With surprising swiftness, Foultons provide the number. And with totally expected reluctance, Beefy hands over his mobile. Borrowing his jacket and taking my handbag, I leave the apartment and walk down the Embankment. Layla answers before I even make it to Lambeth Bridge.

It's a long conversation. After updating her on the latest events, including the fact that I'm pregnant, I take my time, passing on the facts of Dan's involvement in her father's death. A long silence follows, and then she confirms what I predicted: she's not interested in contacting the police, and she doesn't blame him either. She just wants her brother back. And there's more to the story, she tells me. A few extra facts come my way, leaving me jittering with excitement. I want to run straight back to the apartment and blurt them out to Dan, but I promise to hold my tongue. She wants to tell him herself. We quickly firm up a plan, and decide to waste no time. She'll visit on Monday. I just need to find a suitable location.

By the time I end the call, I've reached the London Eye. Standing beneath the vast metal stays, I watch the crowds, look up at the pods, and a mad idea enters my head. It's a long shot, maybe too short notice. But I'm going to give it a try.

'Wakey, wakey, sleepy head.'

Still dressed but under the covers with him, I brush my lips across his cheek. He stirs.

'Mmm.' His arms come around me, drawing me in against his warmth. 'What time is it?'

'Just after four.'

He opens his eyes. They're half-focussed but brighter than before. 'You said three hours.'

'I gave you a little more. You were shattered.'

'What have you been up to?'

'Nothing much.'

'Try out your new bath?'

'Not yet. But thank you very much for the present.'

'My pleasure. So, what have you been up to?'

'I went for a walk.'

'A walk?'

Although I'm trying out my best poker face, it's clearly malfunctioning. He picks up on something, maybe the remnants of excitement.

'We don't have secrets any more,' he reminds me.

'I know.' And it's not a secret, I assure myself. It's a surprise. 'I just went for a walk, and enjoyed being free.'

Satisfied with my answer, he squeezes me in closer for a long, dreamy kiss. Slowly coming back to consciousness, he tightens his left arm, restricting my movement, and bunches his fingers into my hair, manoeuvring my head back, giving him access to my neck. It's his usual dominant way, casting off the baggage and becoming someone else. And I love it. Already, as his mouth traces a line from my ear to my neck, I'm on the verge of melting. But I mustn't, because today I'm determined to go down a different path.

'No.'

He carries on regardless.

'Coffee.'

He stops immediately. 'What's the matter?'

'Nothing.'

Questioning me with a look, he brings his left hand to my chest, rubbing a thumb lightly over my right nipple. Even through the bra and shirt, it has the desired effect. I let off a groan.

'I'm the one in charge, remember?' I push his hand away and pull myself together.

'I thought you were joking.'

'No, I wasn't. And you're just going to have to go with it.'

'Go with what, exactly?'

Oh boy, is he in for a surprise. I smile, mischievously.

'Have you ever been submissive?'

His eyes widen.

'Not my style.'

'Well, you know what they say: a change is as good as a rest.'

'Maya, you know what I like.'

'I know what you think you like. How do you know if you've never tried it?'

I think that might be fear creeping across his features. A spot reassurance is in order.

'I'm not going to tie you up or gag you, or make you pretend to be my dog. But you are going to do everything I say.'

Clearly weighing up the pros and cons of the situation, he watches me.

'Okay,' he says at last. 'Your call.'

And thank God for that because without Dan's agreement, I'd stand no chance. I'm under no illusions. He's giving me control; I'm not taking it. And now I have the upper hand, it's time to issue the first order. This is going to feel distinctly weird.

'Sit up.'

He does as he's told, checking back on the slats before eyeing me suspiciously. He thinks I'm about to go for the cuffs, but the last thing I want is to restrain him. I want to drive him mad ... and then I want to feel his hands on me.

'Hold the headboard.'

Again, he complies.

I slip back out of bed, pulling the covers away and revealing him in all his naked glory. He smiles down at his cock, evidently proud that it's already erect. And then he stares at me, totally unabashed.

'So, what now?' he asks.

'Shush. You'll find out.'

I start by giving him exactly what he likes. Very slowly, I unbutton the shirt and let it slide it from my shoulders. Reaching behind, I unhook my bra, gradually pulling it away from my breasts, and drop it to the floor. His lips curve into a smile. He raises a knee, a sure sign his cock's beginning to act up.

'Stay exactly where you are,' I order him, because I'm about to work him up even further.

I begin to play with my nipples, circling them with my fingers, watching as his chest rises and falls, with increasing speed.

'Oh fuck, Maya.'

'Shush,' I admonish him, giving him my best evil stare. 'I'm having some 'me' time. Don't ruin it.'

Moving downwards, I brush my fingertips across my sternum, my belly, and come to rest at my combats. Unfastening the buttons, I lower them gradually. I'm almost down to my ankles when I hear him groan. I check on him, just in time to see the hands come away from the headboard. If I let him go any further, he'll pounce and have me on that bed in a nanosecond. I wave a finger at him and tut, waiting for the hands to return to the headboard before I go on with the show, kicking off the combats and removing my knickers.

He gazes at my crotch, his eyes brightening with pleasure. His breathing quickly becomes shallow.

'You're not having me yet,' I tease him. 'I'd like a decent orgasm before you get going.'

'I beg your pardon?' His mouth falls open in mock disbelief.

'If a job's worth doing, it's worth doing yourself.'

With a quick jiggle of the eyebrows, I part my legs and begin to rub an index finger lightly at my clit. Slow circular movements quickly bring warmth to my crotch. Spreading inwards to the back of my vagina, it balls and burgeons, causing gentle waves of pleasure to ebb and flow inside me.

'Oh God, that's good.'

'I should fuck you right now.'

In an instant, I come, tipped over the edge by the delicious threat in his voice, the wicked determination in his eyes. I'd intended to drive him wild for a good ten minutes before I got to this point, but never mind. Go with the flow, I tell myself as I contract and buckle and moan.

'You stay where you are,' I warn him breathlessly, vaguely aware he's moving again. 'Stay on the bed. Hands up.'

'I'm warning you, Maya. You're going to get it hard.'

'And I'm warning you too.'

Still pulsating inside, I climb onto the bed and straddle him, rubbing my crotch against his balls.

'Feel that?' I ask. 'I'm wet.'

'You carry on like this, and I'll have no marbles left.'

'That's the general idea. Shut your eyes.'

'What?'

I place a palm on either cheek.

'I said shut your eyes. Remember the song? New York? Whenever things get bad, just shut your eyes and think of our place together. It's in here.' I touch his forehead. 'And here.' I touch his chest. 'Don't think about the world outside. Don't think about the future or the past. Just think about this, right here, right now.'

'Oh, I get it.' With a smile, he complies, lowering his eyelids.

Taking hold of his shoulders and covering his face with light kisses, I grind against him down below. Before long, I've managed to work him up into a frustrated mess. He's breathing quickly, letting out the occasional quiet groan.

'Where's the gel?' I ask, coming to a halt.

'What gel?' He opens his eyes.

'Well, not hair gel, you idiot. That stuff you use for the tradesmen's entrance.'

Suddenly, he seems almost terrified.

'Don't worry,' I add quickly. 'I'm not going in your back door. Not today. I just need some lubrication.'

I'm given a 'thank fuck for that' kind of look.

'In the drawer,' he smiles, blinking lazily. 'The special drawer.'

Within seconds, I've launched myself off the bed, fetched the tube of lubricant, and I'm straddling him again.

He tuts. 'Fail to prepare, Maya, and you prepare to fail.'

I grab his chin.

'Bollocks,' I breathe into his face. 'Smarty had a party and nobody came.'

'What's that supposed to mean?'

'No idea. Shut up. And close your eyes again.'

Squeezing out a little gel, I lubricate my hands, clasping them both around his cock, right next to his balls. Interlocking my fingers and holding him just tight enough, I twist my fingers around his shaft, moving them upwards in one long motion towards the end of his penis, and then back down again.

In silence, I repeat the action, taking my time, sometimes twisting, sometimes not. It's not long before he's totally hard. Eyes still closed, a smile plays on his lips while he drinks it all in, giving in to me completely.

And now, it's time to move on to the second phase. I squeeze, contracting and releasing my grip right from his balls up to the head, over and over, slowly and patiently, watching in satisfaction as his lips part and tiny beads of sweat appear on his forehead. Swallowing a growl, he knocks his head against the headboard, tightens his grip around the wooden slats and arches away from the bed, lifting me up in the process.

'Fucking hell, Maya.'

'Shush.'

For a moment, I toy with the idea of delaying his orgasm, quickly deciding it's best not to play with fire. Instead, I carry on, relentlessly squeezing, releasing, and twisting again.

A minute or so later, he grimaces, groans and comes. I squeeze again as he ejaculates, sending him into a spin.

'Shit!' he cries out, spurting semen all over his stomach and my hands. 'Shit!'

'Did I say you could talk?'

Biting back a smile, he shakes his head and then, while he shivers and quakes beneath me, I run my thumb up the underside of his penis, again and again. When he finally seems to have come down from his orgasm, I order him to look at me. He complies, watching as I swipe a finger through the semen and take a taste.

'Salty. Oh, hang on a minute. Is that garlic?'

'Possibly.'

I take more on my fingers, rubbing it across my chest, my nipples.

'What are you doing?'

'Moisturising.'

With a laugh, he can't help himself any longer. Letting go of the headboard, he grabs hold of me, one hand at the base of my spine, the other smoothing over my breasts.

'Jesus, Maya. Where did you learn to do that?'

'Trade secrets.' I wink. 'And I've got a few more tricks up my sleeve. I've been dying to try them out. The internet's a wonderful thing. Hands up.'

Again, he obeys, allowing me to run my hands across his warm chest, loving the softness of his skin, the hardness of his pecs, his biceps, his shoulders. Moving between his legs, I skim my palms across his shins, over his scars, further up, taking in the tautness of his thighs. And while I do, he simply gazes at me.

'That's the first time I've let a woman take the lead in years.'

'You didn't enjoy it?'

'On the contrary.'

He moves suddenly. I'm grabbed, manoeuvred up the bed and rolled onto my back. He pins my arms above my head. 'Looks like we're going to have mix things up around here.'

'Letting go,' I whisper. 'Just soaking it up. It's a liberation.' I pause, giving him a cheeky grin. 'And it works both ways.'

Chapter Twenty-two

The next morning I'm sitting in the Mercedes on a quiet Chelsea street. Waiting for Dan to make a move, I stare out of the windscreen, watching as leaves squall in the air. Spiralling upwards, they're quickly lost against the grey stone of the townhouses, and the heavy layers of grizzled cloud above. Snatched away by winter's capricious moods, yesterday's blue skies have already disappeared.

'Lily's house.'

He slips a warm hand across my thigh, leans over and glances up at the Georgian façade: four storeys in all, the windows growing smaller with each floor.

'It's beautiful. Why did she want the apartment?'

'Because she fancied it.'

'Rich people are weird.'

He plants a tender kiss on my lips.

'Some of us are alright,' he smiles, his eyes sparkling.

I touch his cheek, relieved that an evening of relentless sex topped off by a decent night's sleep seems to have improved his mood. The bruises are deeper this morning; but his features are softer, more relaxed. So far, the day's been calm, quiet, spent doing nothing in particular, just enjoying each other's company ... with no mention of the past.

But all that's about to change.

'This isn't going to be easy.'

'I know.' He blows out a breath. 'Let's get it done.'

He gets out of the car, circles round to my side and opens the door, offering me a hand. Happy the good old-fashioned romantic gestures haven't disappeared, I put my fingers into his and allow him to help me to my feet. He leads me to a glossy black door, and rings the bell. Within seconds, the door opens, revealing a petite, stylish woman in her fifties.

'Mrs Babbage,' Dan greets her.

'Daniel,' she answers coldly.

'This is Maya.' He motions back to me.

Lily's mother nods. 'We were wondering when you'd turn up.'

'I'm sorry. I would have come yesterday, but ...' He lowers his head. 'I'm sorry. I wasn't thinking straight. Can I see her? I need to know she's alright.'

'She's anything but alright,' Mrs Babbage frowns. 'Far from it.' She stands back. 'But she wants to see you. She's in the drawing room.'

I'm guided through a hallway, given just enough time to register the black and white tiled floor, the pale cream walls adorned with watercolours, before we're quickly ushered into a vast, richly furnished drawing room. There's a fire burning in the hearth and even though it's daytime, every single antique lamp and light has been switched on, blazing out illumination: a desperate attempt, I'm sure, to keep the shadows at bay. Still in her dressing gown, Lily's curled up in one corner of a huge, overstuffed modern sofa. She raises her head, stunning me with her appearance. Her hair's a mess and yesterday's make-up hasn't yet been removed. Stripped bare of her usual armour, she seems strangely vulnerable. I take a seat next to her, and hold her hand.

'How are you?' Dan asks.

He stands by the fireplace, observing his friend. She wipes her nose on the sleeve of her dressing gown and shakes her head.

'I don't know.'

'I'm sorry you got dragged into this.'

Fighting back tears, she gives him a contemptuous smile.

'Well, maybe if I'd known what was really going on, I might have been more careful.'

'Maybe.'

'I might have told you about him. I might have checked him out. I might have put two and two together, but I didn't. I couldn't, because you told me nothing. And I told him everything. I thought I could trust him.'

Silence ensues. While Lily gives in to the tears, Dan chews at his bottom lip, trying to come up with the right words. At last, he speaks again.

'I know you're angry with me, Lil, but I couldn't tell you the truth. There was too much at stake. I'm sorry I didn't protect you. I should have ...'

'I'm not angry with you,' she interrupts, wiping her nose again. 'Not really. I'm more angry with myself.'

'Don't be. You're not the only one he conned. He tried it on with Maya's sister.'

She looks at me.

'He did?'

'Yes,' I confirm. 'A while ago. It didn't last long.'

Her eyes flicker.

'But this went on for months,' she murmurs. 'Months. I let him in and he lied to me. He wasn't who I thought he was.'

I squeeze her hand.

'Did he hurt you?' I ask.

'Only in here.' She places a shaky index finger on her forehead. Pulling her hand out of mine, she wraps her arms around herself. 'I've been so stupid. He tried to kill Dan, he tried to take you, and it was all my fault. I let him sweet-talk me, and all along he was using me. Do you know how that makes you feel?' She draws in a breath. 'I feel ...'

She silences herself, but I know she's got more to say.

I turn to Dan.

'Can you leave us alone for a few minutes?'

He seems confused.

'Please. Just a few minutes.'

He looks from me to Lily, then nods and leaves the room.

'That word, Lily. You can say it now.'

She gazes at me, slowly working up to the moment.

'Violated,' she says at last, barely audible now. 'I feel violated.' She swallows, and it's a few seconds before she can go on. 'I feel like he's taken a piece of me, just taken it, because he lied and used me, and because ...'

She stifles a sob and stares into space. I reach up, moving a strand of hair away from her face, and wait. When the next words finally arrive, quietly laying out her confession, they floor me.

'He had this thing. He wanted to play games. Role-play. Him forcing himself on me. At least I thought they were games. Now, I'm not so sure. I feel ...' she hesitates, 'as if he did it for real. Is that stupid?'

'No.'

'Was he like that with you?'

'No. Just controlling. But when I finished with him ...'

She makes eye contact, and I know I don't have to go on. She understands.

235

'He didn't get the chance,' I explain. 'But I felt the same. He'd taken a piece of me too.' I hold her hand again. 'When I look at you now, I see me a few years back. Empty, hopeless, scared. I ran away and hid, went into self-destruct mode, and he did that to me. Boyd did that. Whatever self-esteem I had left, he crushed it, sapped every last bit of strength I had. But you know what? It didn't need to be that way.'

'It didn't?'

I shake my head.

'I could have chosen to come out fighting, but I didn't, and I lost three years of my life because of it. I don't want to see you destroyed. No woman should ever be destroyed by a man. I want to see you fight your way out of it because you owe it to yourself.'

'I need to fight?' It's partly a question, partly a half-hearted statement. She doesn't seem entirely convinced by my speech. Perhaps I should add on a little extra.

'I'm going to need you, Lily.'

'Why?'

'Because we're getting married next summer.'

She nods, plays with the cord on her dressing gown.

'And I'm having a baby.'

The fingers come to a halt. Her lips twitch, threatening to break into a smile.

'He doesn't know yet.' I glance at the door. 'So, don't say a word. It's early days. I've only just found out. This is between you and me for now. I'm only telling you because I want you to be godmother.' I give her a moment to take in the news. 'So, do whatever you need to do. Fight back, and don't lose any of your life to this.'

'But I don't know where to start.'

And I'm the last person who should be giving advice.

'Get some counselling,' I suggest, rummaging around for anything vaguely sensible. 'Put on your glad rags. See your friends. Do your charity stuff. Be Lily Babbage again.'

'Is it that simple?'

'Probably not.' I smile wryly. 'But it's a start. And I'll be with you every step of the way.'

This time, she squeezes my hand.

'And I'll tell you what else is a start,' she smiles back. 'I'm pulling out of that fucking apartment. I can't live there, not after what happened.'

'There you go. Fists up.'

'Fists up,' she echoes.

There's a quiet knock at the door. Dan reappears.

'Can I come back in?' he asks. 'Your parents are giving me an earful.'

Lily nods. While Dan takes his place back by the fire, I give her a raised eyebrow, reminding her to keep a lid on our secret.

'So, are we okay?' he asks.

'We will be,' Lily confirms. 'Congratulations.'

'On what?'

'Getting married. Maya told me.'

'Oh. Well, thank you.' He smiles briefly, before fixing Lily with a super-serious gaze. 'Listen, I know this is painful for you, but I need to know something.' He pauses. 'How did you meet Boyd?'

'Is it important?'

'It could be.' He rubs his chin. 'It's been playing on my mind. You're not exactly easy to bump into, Lil. You get driven everywhere, your shopping's done for you, you move in pretty elite circles. Where did you meet him?'

'At a party.' She shakes her head. 'A friend introduced us. Well, I say a friend. She's an acquaintance really. I haven't known her that long.'

'What's her name?'

I know the answer before it's even escaped from her mouth.

'Claudine.'

I look at Dan. The mask's in place. No trace of shock.

'How long have you known her?' he asks.

'I met her last autumn, I think.'

His eyes flit to me.

'So, she's been scheming all along, even before she got hold of Boyd. God knows what she'll do now he's gone.'

'She'll stop,' I tell him.

'Will she?'

'She's got nothing more on you.'

'What's going on?' Lily demands. 'Do you know her?'

'A woman with a grudge,' Dan explains. 'But why weren't you suspicious? She's the one who caused all the trouble at The Savoy.'

She shakes her head, confused.

'She was there with Isaac,' he presses.

'I sold her tickets, but I don't know anyone called Isaac.'

'The one I ...' He waves a hand.

'The one you duffed up? I didn't see. I followed Maya out. By the time I got back, it had all blown over. I didn't see Claudine. Nobody mentioned her name. I didn't know she had anything to do with it.'

'She took off. Isaac was close behind.' He runs his fingers through his hair. 'Stay away from her. She's poison.'

'So, you'll tell the police? You'll tell them she was involved?'

'No,' Dan smiles. 'She's not broken the law and she'll give them nothing. Besides, I don't need the police. I'll deal with this my own way. We'll see you again later in the week, Lil. Look after yourself.' He steps forward and holds out a hand to me. 'We need to go.'

It's almost an hour later, after a near-silent drive through mid-morning traffic chaos, and I'm standing in front of yet another Georgian townhouse, this time in Belgravia, and it's one I've visited before. Guarding me from view on a higher step, Dan stands in front of me.

'Sure about this?' he asks.

'Of course I am. Partners, remember?'

The truth is I don't want Dan ending up in trouble. Over the next few minutes, it's highly likely he'll lose sight of his temper, and I need to be on hand to keep him under control. He nods uncertainly, and presses the bell. It doesn't take long for the call to be answered.

'Goodness me. Look what's crawled out from under a stone.'

I can't see him, but the sound of his voice sends a prickle down my neck.

'Got a few minutes, Isaac?' Dan asks. 'For old times' sake?'

'What's the matter? Come to your senses?'

'Yes.'

A sickening belly laugh.

'I'm not surprised.' Warmth slips into the walrus's tone. 'It's been all over the news. Man falls to his death at the Concordia. For a while, I thought it was you, but they confirmed the name this morning. Apparently, there was some sort of a fracas. Nice bruises. I'm assuming you were involved.'

'Correct.'

'That's two near-death experiences now. They say it changes a man.'

'It certainly does.'

'Well, you'd better come in.'

Without warning, Dan stands back, revealing my presence. I look up at the drooping features, the grey eyes that miss nothing, and I feel distinctly nauseous.

'Oh,' he sighs, pursing his slobbery lips in dismay. 'On second thoughts, I don't really have time.' He shakes his head. Rolls of flab wobble under his chin.

'Then I suggest you make time,' Dan replies coldly. 'After all, it's in your interest.'

The grey eyes examine me, and then return to Dan. Without another word, he stands back, allowing us into the hallway before closing the door and leading us through to his gloomy study. Eyeing up the erotic paintings, the manacles and whips hanging on the walls, I inch my way into the room, coming to a halt at the edge of the worn rug, just behind Dan.

'You're in luck. My little chick's here.' Isaac motions to one of the two Chesterfields where, draped in a crimson silk dressing gown, Claudine's currently sipping on a glass of red wine. Without offering a seat, Isaac lowers himself onto the second chair and picks up his whisky. 'We were just having a chat. Claudine's very upset.'

'Really?' Dan asks. 'What's the matter? Did she break a nail?'

'You got away with murder,' Claudine purrs, crossing her legs and making absolutely sure the dressing gown falls away from her crotch.

'Self-defence.'

'You killed my friend.'

I try to move forward, but I'm held back by a strong arm.

'He wasn't your friend and I didn't kill him: two facts you need to understand.'

'Murder,' she breathes.

'Oh for fuck's sake,' Dan complains. 'What is this? Some pathetic vendetta for a man you hardly knew?'

'Justice.' Her green eyes flash at me, cat-like.

'Justice,' Isaac repeats, taking a sip of whisky. 'The backbone of civilisation. Wherever there's crime, there must be justice.' He examines his glass. 'Now, whatever you say, Daniel, we all know you were responsible for poor Mr Boyd's demise.'

'You weren't there.'

'But I know what sort of a man you are.' Eyes charged with vitriol, he glares at Dan. 'You might have fooled the police, but you don't fool me. You've clearly escaped the justice you deserve, but I can still make sure you're punished.'

I take a peek at Claudine. A twisted, self-satisfied grin's just landed on her face.

'If I remember rightly,' Isaac drawls, 'you attacked me at The Savoy, and then ransacked my lovely gentlemen's club. Plenty of witnesses all round. I could always press charges.' He lowers his voice. 'I gave him a chance, m'lud. That's why I delayed. But he wouldn't leave me alone. Harassment, m'lud. Pure and simple.'

239

I brace myself, ready to hold him back, but Dan's unbothered.

'You can try it,' he says. 'And I guessed you might. But before you do, let's get a couple of things straight here.'

'Go ahead.'

'Lily Babbage.'

Claudine stirs.

'You put her in touch with Boyd. You endangered her life. Not to mention what you did to Maya. The pair of you set up that ambush at The Savoy. You put her in serious danger, more than once.'

Isaac raises his glass. 'All part of the service.'

'You're a sick fuck, Isaac. I'll never forget what you've done.'

'No skin off my nose.'

'And now Boyd's gone, I'm not stupid enough to think that's the end of it.'

Claudine's grin deepens, twisting further, transforming her into a grotesque caricature.

'You're obsessed with me, Claudine. I've no idea why, but I know this. When you realised you couldn't have me, you decided to destroy everything I had, and that's just plain nasty.' As if he's reprimanding a small child, he shakes his head. 'So, go to the police and press charges. Do what you like, but remember this. You're getting nothing out of me. Neither of you.' He pauses again, holding a finger in the air. 'Not unless we're talking about evidence of tax avoidance.'

'What are you going on about?' Claudine demands, scowling now.

'Tax avoidance,' Dan repeats. 'Not yours, of course. You don't pay tax.' He levels the finger, aiming it straight at Isaac's head. 'His. Little scams here and there. Creative accountancy.'

I gaze in admiration at my fiancé. In amongst everything else, he's obviously found time to think about the future, putting together back-up plans for every single possibility. Some things about Dan are never going to change, and right now, I'm pretty glad about it.

'You have no proof,' Isaac growls.

'You want to try me?'

'I have friends.'

'If you mean Richard Dean, he's no longer interested in your friendship.'

'You need to go.'

'But I'm not finished yet,' Dan announces, suddenly breezy. 'I thought we could talk about Claudine and that illustrious Member of Parliament. Isn't he Foreign Secretary now? I've got some photos. Pretty sordid stuff, to be honest. I'd rather look at paint drying, but

I've got them locked away safely for a rainy day.'

'You wouldn't …' Claudine gets to her feet.

'Ruin you publicly?' Dan cuts in. 'Let your poor mother know what you really get up to behind closed doors?' He laughs. 'She wouldn't be welcome back at the WI after that.'

I watch as Claudine's lips part in shock, and I can't help myself. I begin to snigger.

'So,' Dan goes on, 'if I ever hear from either of you again, if you ever try to worm your way back into our lives, I'll bring you down, both of you. Don't doubt it.'

Goggle-eyed, Claudine stares at Dan, and then she turns to me.

'Oh, it's funny, is it?' she sneers. 'Haven't you got anything to say for yourself, sewage mouth?'

'Actually, yes.' I bite back the laughter and hold up the middle finger of my left hand, making sure she sees the engagement ring in the process. 'Fuck you, Claudine. Fuck you, you sad piece of shit.' I lower my hand and smile at Dan. 'I think that should do it.'

'Hear, hear, sewage mouth,' he looks at me, proudly. 'Couldn't have put it better myself.'

Chapter Twenty-Three

I flush the toilet and lower the lid. Today's a bad day. I've felt sick ever since I woke up this morning. I don't know whether it's pregnancy-related, or the thought of what's going to happen later. Whatever it is, my stomach's churning and curdling and generally refusing to keep anything down. I gaze at the pale face in the mirror, reassuring myself with the thought that maybe later a little sympathy and support might come my way. But for now, I need to go it alone. I wash my hands, rinse my face, and make my way back out into the office.

'Are you okay?' Dan asks. Dressed in jeans and a shirt, sitting back in an office chair with his feet up on a box, he's already made himself at home.

'Yeah, fine.'

'Were you just sick?'

'Er ... a little bit.'

While I perch myself on his new desk, he studies me suspiciously.

'I think it was the bagel I had for breakfast.'

'A plain bagel?'

'It didn't taste right.'

He's about to probe further when I'm saved by Lucy's appearance.

'The Steves are here,' she announces, waving a pile of papers about. 'They're waiting upstairs. And these are all the sales from the past six months.' She hands the pile to Dan. 'I've put them in order. They're logged on the computer.'

'I want you to write to all the regulars.' He begins to rifle through the sheets. 'Explain the gallery's closing for a couple of months for renovations. We're looking at February and March. And get in touch with the press while you're at it. I want them here for a shindig. I want to reveal the plans. And contact all the artists on the books.

Explain everything to them.' He picks up a card and waves it at Lucy. 'There's an exhibition at The Slade. We've been invited. Confirm my attendance, and Maya's.'

'Would you like me to wipe your arse while I'm at it?' Lucy grins.

Well, I'm willing to bet Carla's never spoken to him like that. I'm half-expecting him to sack her on the spot. Instead, his lips curl upwards.

'No, thank you,' he grins back. 'I've got Maya to do that.'

'Dan!' I snap.

'Sorry, darling.'

He goes back to searching through the paperwork.

'Why are you in such a rush?' I demand. 'You don't even own this place yet.'

'As of next week, I do. Can't rest on my laurels. And I need to go back into Fosters tomorrow.'

'Already? One day off?'

'It's all I need.'

'After what you've been through ...'

'There's a lot to do, going public with the sale, negotiations, that sort of shit.'

I settle into a grump, wondering if he's really changed at all. After everything that's happened, after all the promises, it's only Monday and he's straight back into taking on the world at top speed. As soon as he woke up this morning, he was itching to get into Slaters.

'What happened to smelling the roses?' I ask.

He gazes up at me.

'I meant it, every word of it. But I need to get things rolling.' He takes hold of my hand. 'And then I'll slow down.'

'And what about the operation?'

He shrugs. 'I'll slip it in.'

'You promised.'

'After Christmas.' His eyes glimmer. 'I want to enjoy some time with you first.'

'How can you do that while you're in pain?'

'Pain?' Lucy interrupts. 'What pain?'

'His leg,' I explain. 'Constant pain. He needs another operation ...'

Before I can go any further, Dan's speaking again.

'I can deal with it. I don't fancy another few weeks in plaster, not yet. There's too much to do ...'

'January,' I insist.

'You can still work in a wheelchair,' Lucy chirps.

Dan glares at her. 'That's not going to happen.'

'Well, whatever,' she glares back. 'You're getting it done. In January.'

Open-mouthed, he looks from Lucy to me, then back again.

'Am I being ganged up on?'

'You most definitely are,' Lucy confirms. 'And I'll get Clive in on it too, if you're not careful.'

'Seems like you've got no choice,' I add.

He slides the paperwork onto the desk and holds up his hands in defeat.

'Fair enough. January.'

'So.' Lucy switches her attention to me. 'Did you show him the studio?'

'Yes.'

She claps her hands. 'What did he think of the portraits?'

'Fucking wonderful.' Taking his feet off the desk, he sits up straight. 'I want to show them.'

'What?' I gasp. 'Where?'

'Well, here of course. Before the renovation. On the press night.'

'But ...'

'We do landscapes and seascapes,' Lucy reminds him.

'And now we do portraits. We're branching out a little. Not too much.' He stands up. 'This is a new era, Lucy, and that means a few changes ... and maybe a second gallery.'

'What?' I gasp again.

'Don't worry, sweet pea.' He touches the end of my nose. 'I'll run it by you before I make any decisions. Now, shall we go upstairs?'

We find the Steves lounging together on a sofa. Without a care in the world, they're busy studying an atlas.

'Oh, here he is,' Little Steve calls out. 'He who shall not be named.'

'Nice to see you too.' Dan takes a seat opposite, motioning me into place next to him.

'Good news. We've decided to forgive you. For everything.'

'Glad to hear it.'

'And your American friend.'

'He'll be pleased.'

Big Steve closes the atlas, shuffles over to let Lucy join him, and nudges Little Steve in the side.

'Oh yes,' Little Steve goes on, prompted by the nudge. 'Don't take this the wrong way, Dan, but I need to ask you something. Are you sure he's not gay?'

'Absolutely,' Dan shoots back quickly.

'It's just that he dances like a queen.'

'He's not gay. Shall we change the subject?'

'Mmm.' Big Steve studies Dan's face, evidently searching for signs of lying. 'So, you two are getting married?' he asks, evidently giving up.

'Yes, we are. You're invited, of course.'

'We'll be on the road.' He taps the atlas. 'But we'll make the effort to come home for that. Wouldn't miss it for the world. I'm just glad our two favourite ladies are happy again. And we know Slaters is going to be safe in your hands, Daniel.'

Lucy coughs.

'What's up?' Little Steve bristles.

'He's branching out ... into portraits,' she explains.

'And?' He turns to Dan. 'I'm guessing you'll be starting with Maya's work.'

'Correct.'

'Well, I'm not surprised.' He winks at me. 'They're incredible, darling.'

'Thank you.'

'I must say, I never thought you'd go in that direction, but maybe people are more your thing now. Feelings, experiences, humanity. It must be the Daniel Foster effect. You'll be getting commissions,' he states matter-of-factly.

'Oh, I don't know.'

'Trust me. I can smell success. And we ought to celebrate.' He claps his hands and leans forward. 'How about we close early and take a long liquid lunch?'

'Can't,' Lucy answers. 'Clivey's taking me out for dinner.'

'And neither can we,' Dan adds. 'Maya wants to go for a walk.'

'A walk?' Little Steve stares at me, aghast. 'What's that all about?'

'Putting one foot in front of the other.' I give him a sarcastic smile. 'Fresh air and freedom.'

And a couple of bloody big surprises.

'I don't get it, darling. Do you?' Little Steve pouts at Big Steve, and Big Steve shakes his head. 'The weather's a bitch today. Who'd want to walk in that crap?' He waves a hand at the window, and then he begins to bounce around on the sofa, clapping again like an over-excited sealion. 'Good God, I've just realised something. This is the first time you two have been here together since ... well, just after you met.'

I think back to that first time, and Dan's unexpected appearance.

'Do you remember what you said?' Little Steve asks Dan.

'Of course I do,' he answers quickly, sliding a hand around my back. 'I always get what I want in the end.'

Oh yes, you do, I muse silently, planting a kiss on his lips.

And maybe a little extra on the side ...

A taxi drops us off outside Lambeth House.

'Are you sure about this?' Dan asks. 'It's about to piss down.'

'I want a walk.'

And we need to be at our destination within the next half an hour.

'I'll get an umbrella.'

'No.' I grab hold of his arm. There's no time for that. We're cutting it fine as it is. 'We'll be okay.'

'We'll be wet.'

'I don't care.'

He shakes his head at me.

'Your future wife gets what your future wife wants,' I remind him. 'And right now, she wants a walk.'

With a sigh of resignation, he holds out a hand, palm upwards. 'Come on then. A walk, it is.'

Beneath a leaden sky, we make our way down the South Bank, passing the first bridge and skirting along the side of Lambeth Palace. It's not until we've crossed the road at Westminster Bridge that the crowds really show up in force. The Eye's looming in front of us now, a circle of steel, turning relentlessly, swallowing up a seemingly endless supply of eager tourists. Still holding Dan's hand, I pull to a halt and look up, involuntarily putting my free hand to my stomach, sensing that its contents are already beginning to swirl. It's okay, I tell myself silently. I can do this. And besides, it's all planned. There's no turning back.

'What's the matter?' he asks.

I nod up at The Eye.

'Big round thing,' I stammer. 'Fancy a ride?'

'In that? You'll have a meltdown.'

'No, I won't.' I swallow hard, determined to stand my ground. 'I want to go on it.'

'Maya.' He's trying to be understanding. I know he is. But there's a hint of exasperation in his voice. 'Gibb's lighthouse was one thing. This is another. You'll be trapped in there for at least an hour.'

'Actually, it's half an hour,' I reply, my knees already threatening to give way. 'I can deal with it. I want to do this, Dan. In fact ...' I pull a piece of paper out of my coat pocket. 'I've booked us a private capsule.'

He frowns.

'Are you mad?'

'Possibly.' I wave the paper about. 'I got lucky. There was a cancellation. It cost an arm and a leg.'

'Maya ...'

'I want to face my fears, Dan, and I want to do it in style. No arguments.'

He squeezes my hand.

'Fruitcake.'

'You're one to talk.'

I lead him through the crowds, up a set of steps to the VIP entrance. With the ticket checked, we're scanned by security guards, Dan grumping when he sets off an alarm, and he's forced to show the scars on his leg. Finally, we're guided to a short queue. Listening to the hubbub of voices around me, I shuffle nervously from one foot to the other. I've fulfilled my part of the plan, and now I need to know my accomplice has followed suit.

'Just a minute,' I mutter. 'Wait here.'

'What?'

'Wait.'

Leaving him in the queue, I head back to the VIP gate, scanning the crowds for one face in particular, and thankfully finding it. I issue a particular set of orders to the security guard before returning to Dan's side.

'What was that all about?' he asks, perplexed.

'I just wanted to know how fast it goes.'

'Isn't it obvious?'

I shrug and slip into silence. Before long, we've reached the front of the queue. Our capsule arrives, the door slides open, disgorging its previous occupants, and I stare straight ahead into what's to all intents and purposes, an egg. I swallow, realise my mouth has dried up, and look at Dan. Ignoring everything else, he's fixed on me.

'You don't have to do this.'

'I want to.'

There's a woman in front of us now. She's motioning towards the egg, urging us in, and it's clear we need to be quick about it.

Breathe, I urge myself. Just bloody well breathe.

'Get behind me. Put your arms around me, like you did at the lighthouse.'

He nods, and does as he's told.

'Now, get me in that pod.'

Quickly, he manoeuvres me forward, across the threshold, into the capsule, and then down to the far end. Suddenly, I'm surrounded by glass. I'm about to be totally exposed to the height. My heart rate's already on the rise, and there's a distinct possibility I might just vomit, but I'll keep this under control if it kills me. Unsteady on my feet, I pivot round in his arms and clamp my hands to his back.

'Just stay like this.'

His eyes settle on mine. I hear a soft thud, the door closing, and then it's quiet, the sound of the crowd muted. I'm sorely tempted to glance over his shoulder, but I can't. I need to keep his attention fixed on my face.

'Okay.' I swallow again. 'Keep holding me. Don't let go. Keep looking at me. Stay right where you are.'

Because I've been the queen of sneaky, and the last thing I want right now is for you to see what's going on behind you. I wait a minute or so, until we've risen past the point of no return, and then I make a start.

'Okay, so, you know I'm shitting myself?'

'Of course.'

'I'm facing my fears head-on.'

'I know that.'

Three short, sharp breaths.

'And you're about to do the same.'

His body becomes tense.

'What do you mean?'

My heart jitters. It's crunch time.

'The first thing you need to know is this ...' Oh shit, it's gone. Now it's time for the grand performance, I seem to have forgotten every last bit of my rehearsed speech. In the absence of anything else, I opt for the usual incoherent babbling. 'I've messed up. When I thought we were over, I stopped taking the pill, and then in New York I got carried away, and then I was going to sort it out, but I never got round to it in time, and I didn't sort it out, and well, your Gentleman's Relish, it's taken effect.'

'Relish?'

'There's a bun in my oven.' I smile uneasily. 'And you put it there.' Oh, just say the words ... 'I'm pregnant.'

His lips part. His forehead furrows. I watch the blue irises harden. He shakes his head and suddenly my pulse is racing. Is he annoyed? Angry? Pissed off that I've gone and done this behind his back? I reach up and close his mouth.

'You're going to be a dad.'

'Pregnant?'

'Sorry.'

He blinks a few times, shakes his head again, and then goes back to staring at me.

'Are you angry?'

'No,' he answers quickly. 'You're pregnant?'

'Yes.'

'A baby?'

'Yes.'

'You're going to have a baby?'

'Yes.'

His eyes lose focus.

'Dan, are you alright?'

'A baby ...'

'This is shock, isn't it?'

'Yes.'

'Good shock?'

'Probably.'

'So ... you're okay with it?'

'Okay with it?' He takes a few, deep breaths. 'Of course I'm okay with it. A baby ... it's ... yeah ... a baby.' The ghost of a smile flits across his face. It's quickly banished by disbelief. 'But fucking hell, Maya, you're pregnant, scared of heights and we're on the fucking London Eye?'

'I'm fine.'

'Oh yeah, right.'

'Yeah, right. Now let go of me.'

His arms tighten.

'No. You'll go into meltdown.'

'Let. Go. Of. Me.'

'No.'

'I'm going to be sick,' I lie.

And that does it.

'For fuck's sake.'

As soon as his grip loosens, I pull away and try to compose myself. It's not easy. We're already ascending above the trees in Jubilee Gardens, and worse than that, I'm being subjected to a Daniel Foster glare.

'Of all the mad things you've ever done,' he growls, raising a finger at me, 'this takes the fucking biscuit. You're putting our baby at risk ...'

'Oh, calm the fuck down,' I growl back. 'As long as you stay calm, I'll be fine. And stop pointing at me.'

249

Still glaring, he lowers his hand.

'Now ... I want you to turn around.'

'What?'

He cocks his head. The glare disappears. It's replaced by confusion.

'And I want you to listen.'

Slowly, the realisation dawns on him. He knows exactly why I've lured him onto the Eye, landing him with the pregnancy bombshell as we rise into the air. And what's more, he already knows who's standing behind him, who sneaked in, unnoticed, while he was dealing with an anxious fruitcake of a fiancée. He looks out of the pod, his eyes flitting sightlessly across London's rooftops.

'Well done,' he whispers.

'I'm sorry, but this was all I could think of. And it's done now, so you'd better get on with it.'

He nods at me, and turns. I stumble over to the bench at the centre of the carriage, plant myself on it, grip the edge and stare at my shoes. As Layla's voice wafts through my head, I can only imagine the expressions flitting across his face.

'Hi, Dan.'

Well, at least she's calm. And considering what happened the last two times she tried to make contact, that's a bloody miracle. I sit and wait, every muscle clenched in preparation for a nasty scene. I'm shocked when he simply says her name.

'Layla.'

'Please don't panic.'

No answer.

'I know you want to kick and scream and get out of here, but so does Maya.'

'You knew she was pregnant?' he asks.

I'm assuming she nods.

'But I didn't know she was scared of heights.'

I manage to look up, and find her shaking her head at me. I'm getting a silent telling-off from my future sister-in-law. But that doesn't bother me. I'm more concerned about the man who's standing between us, currently fixated on the floor. The desperation's clear to see, in the quick rise and fall of his chest, the blank expression in his eyes, the twitching fingers. I just want to throw my arms around him and tell him everything's going to be fine.

'Pregnancy aside,' Layla goes on. 'If Maya can take it, so can you.'

'I don't exactly have much choice, but I suppose that was all part of the plan.'

'Sure was,' I tell him, blithely. 'Let's call it revenge for all those times you trapped me. There's no getting out of this, Dan. You can't run. And you need to stay calm for my sake.'

He nods, returning his attention to the floor.

Well, I reassure myself, at least he's not whirling about like an octopus on acid... not yet at any rate.

'Let's just get this out in the open,' Layla begins. 'Maya told me what happened. You were the one. You beat him up.' She's talking quickly, clearly determined to reach the end point before he implodes. 'And first of all, I want you to know this. I don't blame you. I saw what he did to you, I saw how he behaved, and I don't blame you at all.'

She pauses, giving him time to reply, but nothing comes.

'He turned on me after you went. I want you to know that. I didn't have to put up with anything like you did, but he was a bastard to me. I lost count of the times I wished he was dead.'

I hear a tiny groan, and realise it's mine.

Snapping into action, Dan comes toward me.

'Are you okay?'

'I'm fine.' Out of nowhere, irritation's taken hold. It's probably something to do with the fact I've just spotted Big Ben. It's already below us, and now I really do feel sick. 'Get on with it...'

'But ...'

He reaches out, and I bat him off.

'I'm three miles high in a stupid glass egg,' I snarl, locking eyes with him, 'and I want to puke. I'm not exactly enjoying this, Dan, so just fucking get on with it. You're going to be a dad and I don't want any twisted shit left in your head. I want you happy and sorted. Capiche?'

He blinks a few times. 'Capiche,' he murmurs before turning back to his sister.

'Layla,' I breathe. 'Tell him what you told me.'

'I can do better than that.' She reaches into her handbag and pulls out a sheet of paper, nervously offering it to Dan. 'A post-mortem report.'

As if he's scared it might burn a hole in his hand, he stares at it.

'You never checked it out?' she asks.

He shakes his head.

'Just ran away and buried your head in the sand? Well, that's a shame. The coroner said there was no definitive link between the assault and his death.'

'But it's possible ...'

'No, it's not,' she cuts in. 'He had a scan, just after you beat him up. There was no bleeding at the time, nothing ... but they did find a tumour. Malign. Inoperable. It ruptured later, caused the haemorrhage. Even if you'd never touched him, he would have died. That's what killed him, Dan. The tumour. Not you.'

She offers him the sheet again and this time, he takes it.

While he begins to read, I force myself to look out over London, taking in as much as I can: The Houses of Parliament in the distance; toy cars streaming across Westminster Bridge; bathtub boats skimming along the Thames. That's all I manage before panic kicks in. We're heading towards the top of the Eye's rotation now, high above the city, and that's more than enough for me. I shut my eyes again.

'I didn't?' he asks at last.

'You didn't,' Layla confirms. 'One hundred percent. You didn't kill him.'

For the next few seconds, I hear nothing apart from the soft rush of air through the pod's vents.

'And there's something else,' she says at last, her voice almost breaking. 'He didn't want a police investigation.'

'Maybe he'd just given up. I presume he knew he was dying.'

'I think it was more than that.'

Another pause, and I know what's coming next.

'After it happened, he wasn't himself. Mum found him one night, in the outhouse, sitting on the floor, staring into space. I never understood why he did that, but now I do. He knew it was you. He could have had you charged for it, but he didn't.'

More silence.

'So, he found a scrap of humanity? It doesn't let me off the hook. I still did what I did.'

'The fact is, you lost control and beat him up, and he understood. That's it, Dan. You didn't kill him. And before you go on about Mum, she was already knocking it back, even before he died. She was always going to drink herself to death. That's her fault, not yours.'

The seconds drag by.

'There's a hole in my life, Dan. And it's not because my parents are dead. It's because I lost my brother. If you want to make amends for what happened, there's only one thing you need to do ... come back to me.'

'Do it,' I urge him.

I'd love to watch what happens next, but until we've passed the top, there's no way I'm opening my eyes again. There's no more talking. That's all I know. They could be staring at each other. They could be hugging. I have no idea. In darkness, I count the seconds, making it to just over a minute when I'm stopped by a hand on my shoulder, an arm sliding around my back, strong and protective.

'Keep breathing.' He pulls me in to his chest, and holds me tight. 'You're doing brilliantly.'

I dig my head into his neck, drinking in his scent, aware that his heart's thumping.

'You, too.'

As the minutes pass, his heart rate slows, and I sense the tension ebbing away from his body.

'How's Sophie?' he asks at last.

One little question, a tiny step towards normality.

'You know about the cancer?' Layla's voice now.

'Yes.'

'The chemo's going well.'

'Good.'

'She's coming round, gradually, accepting what he was really like. She wants to see you.'

I wait, silently urging him to accept the offer. Finally, it comes.

'And I want to see her too.'

'Oh, thank fuck for that,' I sigh.

Half-opening an eye, I squint out of the glass. We've passed the highest point. I straighten up a little, realising that Dan's sitting to my right, and Layla's on my left. Reassured by their presence, I keep my eyes open, watching as we descend back towards the water. Before long, we're engulfed by a mesh of steel. The nightmare's nearly at an end.

'It's good to have you back, Layla,' Dan says. And then he squeezes me. 'We're nearly there, sweet pea.'

He's not just talking about the ride. He's talking about us.

'I know,' I smile. 'We are.'

Chapter Twenty-Four

'This isn't fair.' The paper hat slides down Sara's head one more time. She rearranges it. 'You two are totally sober.'

'I'm driving,' Dan reminds her.

'Yeah, but what about Maya?' She takes a glug of wine and glares at me. 'Why aren't you drinking?'

'I'm not in the mood.'

My sister eyes me with curiosity, obviously finding it hard to believe my statement. I could always tell her the truth, I suppose, but I'm only six weeks' pregnant. It's too soon. Instead, I lean back in my chair and wish I hadn't eaten that last mince pie. On top of a pile of turkey, sprouts and roast potatoes, not to mention the huge mound of Christmas pudding, it was definitely a step too far. I'm stuffed – fit to burst – and ready for a good lie-down. But there's no chance of that because I'm stuck in the middle of Christmas Day, wedged at the dining table with Dan and Sara, enduring the traditional after-dinner game of Scrabble. And even when this yearly torture comes to an end, it won't be over, not by a long shot.

'I expect you'll be going early,' she grumps. 'Leaving me with this lot. You'll want to go back to your posh cottage.'

'It's not posh.'

In fact, it's a tiny, cosy little place a few miles down the coast, complete with open fire and sea views – all we could manage to rent for a few days at short notice, but it's perfect. We've already spent three days on our own, making love, taking walks, cuddling up in front of the fire. And right now, I'd love nothing more than to return to our hide-away, as compact and bijou as it is, and simply relax.

'We've got to go over to Layla's,' I explain. 'So take your turn. We can't stay here all night.'

'But I'm pissed. I can't spell any more.' Her head slumps to the table.

'Then stop drinking. Come on.'

Raising her head again, she struggles to focus, examines her selection of letters and finally, with extremely wobbly hands, places out the pieces. My eyes expand as the word appears. I'm just glad Dad's slipped upstairs for a while. When she's done, she sits back, distinctly pleased with herself.

'You can't have that.' I can barely believe what I'm seeing. 'It's filthy.'

'I bet it's in the dictionary.'

'I don't care if it is. What if those two see it?'

I nod towards the two boys. They're busy arguing over the instructions to a Lego castle.

'They're not interested in Scrabble,' Sara muses, slugging back more wine and helping herself to an after-dinner mint. 'All they're interested in is sodding presents and sodding arguments. Thank God they're going to their dad's tomorrow. At least I'll get some peace.'

I look at her in astonishment. I might only be six weeks pregnant, but I can't imagine ever feeling that way about my own child.

'You need to cheer up. Get a bit of the festive spirit into you.'

'Festive spirit?' She raises her glass. 'This spirit is good enough for me.'

Typical. She's having a bad time and she wants the whole world to dance to her miserable tune.

'You're ruining Christmas Day.'

'It's already ruined. My marriage is a wreck. I'm living in a poky shithole down the road. My kids barely notice I'm alive.' She takes another swig of wine before she delivers her final point with all the vitriol she can muster. 'And I work in a chip shop.'

I roll my eyes.

'There's nothing wrong with working in a chip shop.'

The truth is Sara's just not used to working at all. Reality's hit her hard.

'You must be getting maintenance from Geoff.'

She laughs. 'Not much.'

'Well, you should take him to court. What's your new place like?'

'Small and smelly. I suppose it's karma. If you act like a shit, you end up in the shit.'

And now we're truly descending into the realms of self-pity.

'Bollocks,' Dan interrupts. As the only sober person at the table with any grasp of maths, he's been busy totting up the latest score. 'Plenty of people act like shits and get away with it. There's no such thing as karma. You've had a run of bad luck, that's all.'

'So when's it going to end?'

'Probably sooner than you think.'

'What do you mean?'

He shakes his head.

'Eleven,' he says, scribbling down the score. 'You got eleven for that.'

'And you need to take it off before Dad gets back.' I tap the board.

'Can't.'

'Well, haven't you got an A?'

'No.'

'What's going on?' Mum demands from the sofa. Graciously giving up her Scrabble place for Dan, she settled down with her Christmas crossword a good half an hour ago.

'Nothing.' I wave a hand dismissively.

'It's staying,' Sara insists. 'It's all I've got.'

'Dan, she can't have it, can she?'

'Well ...' He rubs his chin, speaking quietly. 'It probably is in the dictionary.'

'Do you fancy explaining it to my dad?'

He pulls a face, as if I'm asking him to lick a gutter.

'Because I'm not going to.'

'Surely he knows what it means.'

'It's staying,' Sara grunts, pushing herself up from the table, nearly upsetting the Scrabble board in the process. 'I need more wine.'

I watch as she staggers over to the sideboard.

'I'm sorry about this,' I whisper to Dan.

'Sorry about what?'

'Christmas Day, Scotton style.'

'I wouldn't want it any other way.' He twirls the biro in his fingers. 'Hat included.'

Smiling like an idiot, I toy with the idea of smuggling the paper hat back to the cottage and forcing him to wear it ... and nothing else.

'Well, Sara's getting on my nerves.' And that's only bound to get worse. She's currently pouring herself yet another huge glass of Pinot Grigio. I turn to Dan. 'Are you alright?'

'Why wouldn't I be?'

'The last time you were here, it wasn't exactly easy. Are you okay with her?'

'The wine demon? Of course.' He lowers his voice. 'It's ironic.'

'What?'

'When we were kids, she made both of us miserable, and now look at her. Who's the most miserable person in this room?'

She is, of course. Slugging back more wine, she's currently busy scowling at her sons.

'She hates everyone and everything at the minute,' I observe.

'She hates herself. And maybe she always has.' He puts down the pen, rearranges his Scrabble tiles and looks back up at me. 'Does it worry you?'

'Of course it does.' Because when all's said and done, she's still my sister. 'I'd like to help her ... I think. Even though she's never helped me ... or anyone for that matter.'

'I have an idea.'

'Which is?'

'We can buy her a house.'

Well, that's a bolt out of the blue. I stare at him, stunned.

'A house?' Probably sooner than you think. So that's what he meant.

He nods.

Oblivious to our conversation, Sara's already given up on her boys. She's now examining the soap I gave her, failing completely to hide her disdain. At least Mum managed to feign satisfaction with her own slab of congealed oil. Dad, on the other hand, instantly fell in love with his new biscuit tin, and my two nephews were more than happy with a twenty pound note each. 'Universal gift vouchers,' I informed them. 'Redeemable at any store.' It seemed to do the trick, but I need to do better. Silently, I resolve to be far more organised about the whole gift thing in future.

'It won't solve everything.' Dan's voice nudges me out of my Christmas present debrief. 'But it's a start.'

I turn back to him, overwhelmed by the idea of what he's proposing.

'You'd do that for her?'

Because after everything she did to him, he owes her nothing.

'If everyone around us is happy, then you're happy.' He surveys his Scrabble tiles one more time. 'That's all I care about.'

'Can I tell her? It's a better Christmas present than soap.'

'Not yet. She's three sheets to the wind. She'll be overcome by righteous indignation and tell me to fuck off. Leave it for a few days.'

I spend a few seconds admiring my perfect fiancé: the tufts of blond hair sticking out from under his paper hat, the bright blue eyes, warmed by the copper specks. All in all, his ruddy gorgeous face still turns me on big time, and I'm sure it always will.

'You've really have got a soft centre, Mr Foster.'

'Drop it,' he mouths, glancing towards the hall. 'Your dad's coming back.'

'Oh, those sprouts have gone right through me!' Still buckling his belt, Dad appears in the doorway. 'Is it my go?'

'Yes,' Sara calls out, mischievously. 'I've just got eleven. See if you can do better than that.'

'Sherry?' Staggering across the living room, and just missing my two nephews along the way, Dad retrieves a bottle from the sideboard. 'Come on. It's Christmas.' He stumbles back towards us, pausing at Mum's side and waving the bottle in front of her face.

'Not much for me, Roger.' She fills in another clue on her crossword. Despite all her efforts to appear normal, it's obvious she's already half cut. Her eyes lost focus just after dinner.

Dad tops up her glass and returns to the table.

'Dan?' He offers the bottle.

'I'll stick with coffee.' Dan taps the side of his mug with the biro. 'Driving.'

'You should have stayed over.' Dad lowers himself back onto his chair. 'You two could have slept on the settee. Maya. Come on. You always slug back the sherry with me.'

'Not this year, Dad.'

'Why not?'

I watch as Dan's fingers hover over his pieces, as he picks one up, deep in thought about his next move.

'I'm just not in the mood.'

'You're always in the mood,' Dad laughs.

And then, Sara's words cut across us, like a knife.

'Are you pregnant?'

Dan drops the Scrabble tile.

She's done it again. There must be something about this living room that transforms Sara into a deadly truth-seeking missile.

'You are pregnant,' she insists, joining us. 'Bloody hell, you're pregnant.'

'Yes,' my mouth shoots out.

Sara's face descends into chaos. Clearly, she doesn't know whether to be pleased or shocked, or just plain jealous.

'Are you?' Dad falters. 'Well, bugger me. Audrey, did you hear that?'

'Uh?'

'You're going to be a grandma ... again.'

'Eh?' Mum drops her pen and frowns at Sara over the top of her glasses. 'Oh, don't tell me you're back with Geoff.'

'Not me,' Sara hisses. 'Maya.' Finishing off her wine, she refills the glass with sherry.

'Maya?' Rising to her feet, Mum's unaware of the fact that her crossword book tumbles to the floor. 'Maya's pregnant?'

I let my head fall into my hands. And then I feel Dan's hand on mine.

'Yes, she's pregnant,' I hear him confirm. 'We didn't want to tell anyone yet. It's early days.'

'And it's yours?' Mum demands.

I hear him confirm that too, with the patience of a saint, before he goes on to field a tide of questions. It's due in August. No, we don't know the sex, and we want it to be a surprise. Jack for a boy, Ruby for a girl. And yes, we're getting married. In the summer. No date set, as yet. At the house in Surrey.

'Oh my good God,' Mum squeals. 'Come here and give us a hug.'

I'm urged to my feet and before I know it, I'm being squeezed and kissed and squeezed again. And then it's Dan's turn. I step back and watch, enjoying every second of it. There's something quite endearing about a multi-millionaire sex god being hugged half to death in a suburban living room ... while wearing a paper hat.

'Oh my goodness. This is wonderful news. Roger, this is wonderful news.'

'Mmm,' Dad murmurs. He leans forward, his attention waylaid by the Scrabble board.

'So where will you live?' Mum asks.

'In Surrey.'

When all the decorating's finished. For the past month, while the house has been undergoing renovations, we've been based in Lambeth. Under my supervision, the plans have been drawn up for my new studio and in the meantime, while I've gone back to painting, Dan's been pushing on with the future, setting up Slaters and overseeing the sale of Fosters. Our perfect life is coming together. And I couldn't be happier.

Dad squints a little, reaches out and touches a piece on the board.

'What's the matter?' Sara slurs mischievously.

'Is this in the dictionary?' He runs his finger across Sara's word. 'It's just I've never heard of it.'

'Yes, it's in the dictionary.'

'It is? So, what is it then? What is minge?'

'Well that was embarrassing.' I slip my hand into Dan's.

Hearing your mum explain the word 'minge' to your dad can

never be anything else. It was enough to signal the time for our departure.

'Priceless.' He laughs.

'It's not always that bad.'

He's staring down the road, breath clouding in front of his face.

'Are you okay?'

He nods towards the house where he spent the first ten years of his life. Tonight, it's swathed in Christmas lights, but back then it must have been a dark place.

'Bricks and mortar,' he mumbles. 'That's all it is. Bricks and mortar.'

I link my arm into his.

'This is hard for you. We didn't have to come.'

'It's not something we can avoid. I just need to get used to it.' He looks at me. 'Shall we get going?'

Leaving the Mercedes outside my parents' house, we walk through quiet streets, hand in hand, saying nothing. He needs time to compose himself, and I'm perfectly willing to let him have it. Within minutes, we reach Layla's house. Dan hesitates at the bottom of the drive.

'Ready?'

'Not really. I have no idea what to say.'

Staring at the curtained windows, he trails into silence, and I understand. He's about to meet Sophie for the first time in years, and even though the ice has been thoroughly broken with Layla, this is another huge step.

'The big talk can come later, if it ever comes at all.' I squeeze his hand. 'This is where small talk comes in handy. Exchange a few pleasantries, ask about the kids, that sort of thing. Just get comfortable.'

'Small talk,' he grimaces. 'Good job I've had some practice.'

We move to the front door. I ring the bell. Dan lets go of my hand and stands back. It's not long before Layla appears, her face expectant, bright with excitement.

'I've brought you a present.' I encourage Dan forwards.

'Happy Christmas,' she beams, welcoming us into the hall with a hug. 'We're all in there.'

We're quickly guided through to the lounge. With a Christmas tree dominating one corner, the room hardly seems big enough for all of us. Three children are squeezed together on the settee: Layla's two boys and a girl, obviously Sophie's daughter. They're too busy watching a film to notice anything else. A man hovers by a buffet laid out on the dining table. He helps himself to a slice of pork pie, and nods at us. Layla's husband, I decide. And sitting in an armchair, a woman in her early thirties, a little gaunt, wearing a headscarf, but the similarity is unmistakable. This must be Sophie. Her eyes light up as soon as Dan enters the room.

'So, children,' Layla announces. 'Here's your Uncle Dan. And he's brought Auntie Maya to see you.'

The children look up in unison, and then go back to the film.

'They're just watching Frozen,' she explains. 'You know what kids are like.'

'Not yet,' Dan smiles.

The youngest boy slides off the settee, fetches a piece of paper and hands it to him.

'I made this.'

Dan takes it, uncertainly.

'A Christmas card?' he asks. 'Thank you. It's lovely.'

'You're my mummy's brother.'

'I am.'

'And you're my uncle.'

'I am.'

He stares at Dan for a few seconds more, then takes his place back on the settee.

Sophie's on her feet now, inching her way towards us. She stops at me first, touching my arm.

'Thank you, Maya, for bringing him back.'

'It's my pleasure. Good to meet you, Sophie.'

'Good to meet you too. We're going to be great friends.'

With a smile, she turns to Dan and opens her arms. And without a word, he steps into them, leaning down and letting her kiss him on the cheek.

'I'm sorry,' he whispers. 'For taking so long.'

She pulls back, holding his face in her hands.

'Don't be daft.' There are tears in her eyes. 'I understand. Now ... let's get on with the job of building those bridges, shall we?'

Chapter Twenty-Five

I'm roused by a kiss. It invades my sleep and soon becomes real. Breaking it, he pulls back and says nothing. He doesn't need to. The look in his eyes says it all. Pure love, pure reverence, pure intimacy. Slowly, he manoeuvres himself on top of me, easing my legs apart. There's to be no foreplay this morning. We're getting straight into the action.

With another kiss, he presses his cock against me, entering without any resistance whatsoever. I'm already wet. With one hand under the small of my back and the other at my shoulder, he drives inwards, filling me completely before he withdraws. I run my hands over his broad shoulders, loving the power that's arching above me, moaning softly as he drives, withdraws, adjusts his position, and drives again. I'm super-sensitive down below, every single move keenly felt. Flutters quickly become ripples. Undulating through my muscles, they swell, transforming themselves into waves of sheer pleasure that ebb and flow through my vagina. Sometimes kissing me, sometimes holding eye contact, he keeps up the action, maintaining a gentle but relentless rhythm, and sending me to the edge of sanity. Every now and then, a squall of rain patters against the window. Apart from our ragged breathing, the occasional groan, it's the only sound in the world.

Finally, he's there. Twitching and jerking, he fills me with a few last thrusts, and I implode, muscles contracting in one delicious flood of heat that leaves me gasping and writhing beneath him. He collapses on top of me, still throbbing inside, waiting until we've both come down from the high before he speaks.

'Thank you,' he whispers against my mouth.

'What for?'

'The best Christmas ever.'

I gaze up at him in surprise.

'Overcooked sprouts, a pissed-up sister and nightmare Scrabble?' He laughs.

'Being with you.' He pecks me on the mouth and withdraws.

'Are we having a cheesy moment?'

'Yes,' he says proudly. 'And there's nothing wrong with cheese.'

He reaches over to a box of tissues on my bedside cabinet, and pulls out a handful. Concentrating fully, he sets about wiping his semen from me.

'Last Christmas was fucking miserable.' He tosses the tissue onto the floor. 'Spent it on my own.' He rolls over onto his back and I cuddle up to him. A warm arm closes round me. He rests his chin on the top of my head and pulls the duvet over us. 'I never thought in a year's time I'd be engaged to the most beautiful woman in the world.'

'Oh, come on.' I prod him. 'I am not the most beautiful woman in the world.'

'Oh yes, you are.' He runs a hand across my stomach, down to my crotch, urging my legs apart. I'm still tingling from my climax. If he goes on like this, I'll be cross-eyed with ecstasy before breakfast. 'I never thought I'd be a dad ... and I certainly never thought I'd be back in touch with my sisters. You've given me all that, Maya. You've given me happiness.' He presses a finger against my clit. An arrow of warmth shoots right through my groin. 'I'll never be able to pay you back.'

'Oh, I can think of a way.'

'Which is?'

'More kink.'

'Filthy woman. You've had plenty.'

And I have. Over the past month, we've used the cross more times than I can remember – only for pleasure – and experimented a little further with rope. But more often than not, we've returned to his favourite, the cuffs. Yesterday morning, he even presented me with my first ever Daniel Foster Christmas present: the Rolls-Royce of all vibrators. And he's already managed to send me mad with it. The only thing that's out of bounds is spanking. He's made that perfectly clear.

'I want more.'

He circles the finger.

'I bet you do. And you'll get it, believe me. But before that, I'm making you breakfast in bed.' The finger's removed.

'Oh,' I whine.

'No complaints. I need to feed the pregnant one. Tea and toast?'

'Perfect. Use the teapot.'

'Yes, boss.' Shuffling out from beneath me, he rolls out of bed. 'Jesus, it's fucking freezing. I'll put the heating on.'

He slips on his jeans, runs his fingers through his hair and goes over to the window, twitching back the curtains.

'It was a crap present, wasn't it?'

'The teapot?'

'I get a vibrator. You get a tea set.'

'It's the best present ever.'

'You don't even like tea.'

'I can always put coffee in it.' He winks. 'Now, stop complaining. It's our last day in Norfolk. I'm going to cook us a wonderful dinner. We'll have cuddles in front of the fire, maybe watch a slushy film and, oh yeah, and I'm going to fuck you senseless.'

'That's the day planned then.'

'Almost.' He retrieves his sweatshirt and puts it on. 'Before we go back to London, there's one other thing I'd like to do.'

The cemetery's at the top of the hill, overlooking the town. The Mercedes comes to a halt in the car park. He kills the engine and doesn't move. Sitting absolutely still, he stares ahead at a bench, a collection of wind-worn trees.

'Are you sure about this?'

'Yes,' he says curtly. 'You don't have to come.'

'I'd like to be with you, if you're okay with that.'

He seems to think, and then nods. He gets out of the car, circles to my side, opens the door and offers me the customary hand. As soon as I'm on my feet, the cold makes its move. A wall of wind rolls up the hill. I fasten my coat and look to the left: a handful of people lost among the gravestones, visiting the departed on a cold, grim Boxing Day morning. And then to the right: under a grey, colourless day, roof tops huddle at the centre of town, the squat tower of Limmingham church almost lost in the clouds.

'So, where is it?' I ask.

'At the top.' He points up the hill. 'Row twelve.'

Suddenly, he seems unsure of himself. I take his hand in mine and give it a squeeze.

'We can go back to the cottage.'

He shakes his head.

'I want to do this. I need to ...'

Slowly, we make our way along a path between the gravestones, some adorned with flowers, some too old to be remembered by the living. Here and there I spot an offering, a personal memento, a photo, a pint glass, an angel. At the top of the hill we come to the smaller memorial stones, the ones belonging to the cremated. Leading me by the hand, he takes a left, peering at the inscriptions, one after the other, caught up in the business of locating the right name. At last he comes to a halt, staring at one stone in particular.

'Miriam Eleanor Taylor,' he reads. "Much-loved wife and mother'. You couldn't get much further from the truth.' A smile touches his mouth, but steers clear of his eyes. 'Layla said she didn't know what to put.'

His attention strays to the next grave. Saying nothing, he pulls his hand away from mine and balls his fists, and I understand why. This is his stepfather's grave.

'You're here to see your mum.' I smooth my hand on his coat sleeve. 'Not him. He doesn't deserve to be remembered.'

'No.'

The word almost disappears on another gust of wind. Lost in thought, he stares at the block of granite, the empty flower holder.

'What made him do those things?' he asks at last, with all the innocence of a child. 'What makes a human being behave that way?'

He glances up at the sky, as if he's searching for answers, and rubs away a tear.

'You'll never know. Not for sure. Whatever the reason, it wasn't your fault. That's the only certainty.'

'I'm sorry. I didn't mean to cry.'

'There's no need to apologise.'

He chews at his lip, turns his attention back to his mother's grave.

'I'll give you some time on your own.'

His hand comes back to mine.

'No. Stay. I won't be long.'

For a few minutes, we stand in silence, braced against the wind. I have no idea what's going through his mind. Perhaps he's asking her why she let those things happen; perhaps he's trying to understand; maybe he's forgiving her. It's not my business to ask. Giving him the space he needs, I look back down at the town, and then the sea, trying to figure out where the horizon lies, but I can't. Everything's blurred. No clarity. No black and white.

Finally, his fingers tighten around my hand.

'Done?' I ask.

'Done,' he confirms. And then, out of nowhere: 'I'd like to go for a walk.'

'A walk?'

'Down by the sea ... I want to show you something.'

The drive into town doesn't take long. The roads are deserted. We park near the seafront. Dan produces an umbrella from the boot, and we walk through the winding streets of Old Limmingham, finally emerging onto the cliff-top. Sweeping in from the North Sea, the wind grips us immediately.

'On second thoughts.' He pulls up his collar. 'Perhaps we should just go back to the cottage, light the fire and have sex on the rug.'

'That rug's seen better days,' I complain. 'And besides, I'm intrigued. What is it you want to show me?'

He seems embarrassed.

'It's not really worth it.'

'I'm sure it is.'

'I don't know ...'

'Dan.'

Reluctant now, he takes me by the hand and leads me down to the promenade. A smattering of rain soon gathers force, threatening to soak us. He puts up the umbrella and aims it into the wind. Wrapping his free arm around me, he pulls me in to his side, making sure I'm protected from the worst of the elements.

'This is pure madness,' he says. 'You'll catch cold.'

I tut. 'We're not in a Jane Austen novel. People don't get ill because they get a bit wet, not in the real world.'

'Well ...' He nods at my stomach, and I understand immediately. He's worried about the baby.

'I'm pregnant. Not ill. Don't get over-protective.'

'I can't help it.' He shrugs. 'Come on. Let's get this over and done with.'

Leaving the pier behind, we walk along the promenade, past cafés and shops, all closed for the winter; buckets and spades and seaside tat piled up in the windows. We pass a lone dog-walker, a scattering of fishing boats that have definitely seen better days, a small Victorian pavilion. And then, the promenade gives way to a narrow, uneven path, a final stretch lined with beach huts – the southern tip of the town. We pick our way along the path, dodging puddles until we come to the very end, where any sign of civilisation has disappeared. Beyond this point, there's nothing but wild beaches and rugged cliffs: it's marked by a groyne, a wooden coastal defence that stretches out into the sea, protecting the cliffs from erosion.

'Can you see it?' he asks, coming to a halt.

'What?'

'There.' He points at a length of timber.

I snuggle up next to him, following the direction of his finger. At first, I see nothing, but then it emerges, faint, but still visible. Carved into the wood, a capital D.

'I was nine when I did that,' he smiles wryly. 'Making my mark on the world. I'm surprised it's still here. The woods were your sanctuary. This was mine. It took me a few days to finish.'

Moved beyond words that he's chosen to share this with me, I stare at the carving, one tiny remnant of his childhood. And I conjure up an image in my head: a solitary boy avoiding the world, perhaps on a day like this, losing himself in his task.

'Thank you.' I look up at him. 'For showing me.'

His eyes glint. His lips part, as if he's on the verge of telling me something else. And then he takes in a breath.

'We're about to get very wet.' He nods out to sea, to a curtain of rain sweeping in. 'I don't think this umbrella's going to be enough. Come on.'

Hastily he leads me back the way we came, guiding me under the cover of the pavilion just in time to avoid the downpour. There are benches here. Closing the umbrella, he takes a handkerchief out of his pocket, dries off a bench and motions for me to sit. Taking a seat next to me, he settles into silence for a few minutes, watching the maelstrom of raindrops as they churn up the sea.

'I always felt more at home here on days like this,' he says. Leaning forward, he clutches his hands together. 'Grey. Miserable. Wet. Cold. When the sun came out, when the holiday crowds arrived, I felt like an alien. I used to come here and watch them, all those happy families. Buckets and spades, deckchairs, sandcastles. I had no place here in the summer. But on days like this ... it was my kingdom.' He falters. 'I liked being alone. But now I never want to be alone again.' He pulls a penknife out of his pocket. 'I was going to carve an M next to the D.'

I laugh.

'You really are in a cheesy mood today. Maybe some other time.'

'Maybe.'

He puts the knife away and draws me in for a tender kiss. Protected from the cold and the rain, I'm enveloped in his arms, the warm perfection of his lips. After an age I'm released, and we sink back into silence, cuddled up against each other on the bench, watching the worst of the storm sweep past.

'I was proud of you at the cemetery. That took a lot of guts.'

He shrugs off my compliment.

'I said goodbye to her. Properly. I'd never done that before ... and

267

I forgave him.'

I look up at him. My expression asks the question. Why?

'Because I pity him. Just like I pity Boyd.'

'Pity? One of them abused you. The other tried to kill you.'

'And neither of them knew contentment or love, not like I do.' His gaze penetrates me, right to the core. 'Boyd was ill. And my stepfather? Well ... there must have been a reason.'

He's right. Those who torment are never happy. I think of Boyd and what he did to me, crushing any self-confidence I had left. And then I think of Sara, perhaps the root cause of all the weakness. Silently, I forgive them both ... and banish their misery from my life.

'Don't you ever wonder about your real dad?' I ask. It's a question that's been lurking at the back of my mind for a while now, and this seems to be the perfect time to ask it. 'Don't you ever want to contact him?'

He looks out to sea. Grey waves swell and surge, tumbling over each other in an endless race to reach the shore, each one crashing to pieces before it's dragged back into the mass.

'I did a bit of research,' he admits at last. 'When I was off work. The devil makes work for idle hands. He's still alive. Lives in Suffolk.'

I hold my breath, wondering what's coming next. A host of half-siblings?

'He's an alcoholic,' he informs me, 'with several broken relationships behind him. He's been in prison a few times.'

'You don't want to meet him?'

He shakes his head and pins his gaze on me.

'He walked out on us, Maya. He didn't care. He's never been there for me, never made the effort to find me. As far as I'm concerned, he has no right to be in my life. He might have other kids. I didn't bother finding out. And if there are any, I don't want to risk contacting them. I don't want any more heartache or trouble. I have Layla and Sophie. That's enough.'

'So, what do we tell this one?' I touch my stomach.

'The truth ... eventually. I've done what I can, but some ghosts just need to be left where they belong.'

I nod my agreement. He's made his decision. His real father – and everyone associated with him – is out of the picture for good, and I respect that.

'I understand.'

'What's the point of clinging to the past? What's the point of letting it crush you? I'm moving on. I'm through with it.'

I reach up and brush a finger down his cheek. I'd like to tell him we're never through with the past, that it's with us forever, sometimes out of sight, sometimes in full view, always unchangeable. We can only ever learn from it ... and manage the consequences.

'How about you?' he asks. 'I read that interview, the one you did in New York. This place had an effect on you too.'

Oh, the interview. I'd forgotten about that, and the truths I let out into the open.

'I'm dealing with it,' I tell him. 'I'm moving on, just like you. The person I was ... she didn't feel like she belonged, she didn't feel like she had any merit. But I'm not that person any more.'

'No you're not,' he answers quickly. 'And I'm the luckiest man in the world because you're going to be my wife, my partner.' He arches an eyebrow. 'And the mother of my children.'

'Children?'

'Are you really going to stop at one?'

I place a hand on my stomach. I've not even felt the baby move yet, but we've had the first scan and I'm already in love with this new little being. And so is Dan. More than once, I've caught him gazing in wonder at the picture.

'Probably not.'

'I didn't think so.' He smiles. 'The person you were ... leave her here. Leave her with that boy.' He nods towards the groyne.

I put my hand in his. His grip tightens and he stands. I stand too. He picks up the umbrella and flips it open.

'Ready to weather the storm together?' he asks.

'With you, I'm ready for anything.'

Chapter Twenty-Six

I stare at myself in disgust. It's not the hair that's the problem. That's fine. An elegant up-do, all curls and twists and things, crafted by a professional hairdresser. It's not the make-up either. I've done that myself. And it's definitely not the jewellery. The sweet-pea necklace and matching earrings were a no-brainer. From the neck up, everything's fine: simple, understated, and me. No. The real issues begin from the neck down. Twelve thousand five hundred pounds' worth of designer wedding dress, made to order at Dan's insistence. It looked glorious on the page, great on the rail and fine on me … when I last tried it on, two weeks ago. But now …

'Jesus.'

Twelve thousand five hundred pounds' worth of creamy silk balloon out from the waist down. And from the waist up, the bodice hangs loose, my boobs dangling precariously in a strapless bra that's barely doing its job. Maybe I shouldn't have wriggled out of that one last fitting. I just hope I can do it up.

'Shit.'

I've been determined to control every last bit of our wedding, banishing Dan from all preparations apart from the rings and the men's suits, investing in months of planning for it, hell-bent on organising something traditional, romantic and perfect. But the closer we've got to the special day, the more the nerves have played me up, taunting me that I've forgotten something important. And it seems I've fallen at the first hurdle. An expensive, disastrous joke of a wedding dress. I hear a peel of laughter from outside, sense a prickle of anxiety deep inside. There's a whole host of people waiting out there for me, including Dan. I check my mobile. Almost time to go. In less than an hour, I'll no longer be Maya Scotton. Looking like half a tonne of potatoes squeezed into a silk purse, I'll be

Maya Foster. And there's only one question now.

'What the fuck else can go wrong?'

The door to the en suite springs open and Lucy flies out, holding the ribbon from the back of her lilac dress.

'This has just gone down the toilet.'

'Lucy!'

'It's not my bloody fault. Why does it have to have a stupid ribbon at the back? I've washed it in the sink. It's soaking.'

'Never mind about that. It'll dry. Come and do me up.'

I watch in the mirror as Lucy sets about lacing the bodice.

'Oh ...' she murmurs.

'What?'

'It's going to be a bit tight.'

'Oooooh, fuck.'

'If you'd gone to that fitting ...'

'I know,' I squeak. 'But I couldn't face it. Shit, Lucy. It's awful.'

'Calm down. I'll fix it. You'll just have to have bigger gaps in the lacing. It'll look like it's supposed to be that way.'

I stare at the front. Somehow, with the lacing loosened, it doesn't look like it's supposed to be that way at all. I turn to inspect the back, and sense a lump in my throat.

'It's a mess.'

Suddenly engulfed by wedding madness, I burst into tears.

'Trust me, it's the best anyone can do.'

'I'm a stupid fat pregnant idiot,' I wail. 'And I've got tits like melons.'

'You're not fat, Maya. And you've always had tits like melons. You've just gone from cantaloupe to full-on watermelon. It's only temporary. Don't let the hormones get to you. Put a cardy over the top.'

'I am not getting married in a cardigan.'

For a split second, I think about stamping my feet and throwing myself onto the bed. But that wouldn't do. Instead, I carry on weeping, watching helplessly as Lucy rummages through my wardrobe.

'This,' she announces, presenting me with something I've never seen before: a dainty green cardigan that must have come from Harrods. 'Put it on. Don't do it up.'

I follow her instructions.

'It's green.'

'And it's all you've got.'

'But it doesn't go ...'

271

While I sob uncontrollably, she squeezes my arms into the cardigan and tugs it up over my shoulders.

'There. You look fine.' She pats my stomach, lightly. 'Trust you to be pregnant on your wedding day. You never do anything by halves. Who am I going to get drunk with?'

And trust Lucy's brain to fixate on booze.

'This isn't an excuse for a piss-up. Even if I wasn't pregnant, I'd be staying sober.'

With a shrug, she grabs a tissue from the dressing table and offers it to me.

'Clean up your face and give me a break. I've been a virtual saint since I got back with Clive.'

Which is completely true. Now that she's co-habiting with her pet accountant, she's happy enough to drink in moderation, apart from on the big occasions. She's reined it in for months, and I shouldn't resent her letting loose.

'Why don't you get pissed with Clive?' I suggest, dabbing my eyes and sniffing away the tears.

'No way. He's a nightmare when he's had a few.'

'Then how about Lily? She needs cheering up.'

It's not an entirely mad suggestion. For weeks now, we've all been trying to jolly her along. And as part of Operation Let's-Get-Lily-Back-On-Track, Lucy's met up with her on several occasions.

'Lily,' she muses. 'She can knock it back, you know.'

'Well then, there's your mission for the day, and there's your drinking partner. Make sure she enjoys herself.'

'Mission accepted.'

While Lucy looks out of the window to check the current situation, I inspect myself one more time. I'm calm again, almost. But that cardigan ...

'How's Dan's leg today?' she asks.

'I don't know. It was okay yesterday.'

And in actual fact, it's been okay for a while. Since the operation in January he's suffered nothing more than an occasional twinge.

'He'll be fine.'

'And how about you? Are you going to get through this in one piece?'

'Of course.' I place a hand on my stomach. 'Full of energy today.'

Because Mr Foster was banned from our bedroom last night, and although it was torture, I made the most of it with a full night's sleep.

'I mean with the weather.' She turns from the window.

'What about it?'

'Didn't you check the forecast?'

'Should I?'

'Storms.'

'Shit.' My bottom lip plummets. The second hurdle falls. 'You're shitting me.'

'No, I'm not. Perhaps we should move everything into the marquee.'

'But the marquee's set up for the meal.'

'We've got enough hired hands to sort it out.'

I'm sure we have, but seeing as I'm heavily pregnant and dangerously hormonal, and wearing a stupid green cardigan, I'm in no fit state to deal with complications. I took a quick look inside the marquee first thing this morning, and it's beautiful: each table adorned with a crisp white cloth, glimmering silver cutlery, an array of glasses and a floral centrepiece – a shower of sweet peas. If we move one single thing, it'll be completely ruined, and I'll have a monumental breakdown.

'It's too late,' I tell her. 'We'll get through the ceremony before anything happens.'

'With any luck.'

'And anyway, Norman's built that arch …'

'You and your sodding sweet peas.'

'It's romantic.'

'It's mad. That's what it is.'

It may well be mad, but it's what I want. With more tables and chairs laid out in the orchard for guests to relax with drinks, we'll be getting married on the lawn at the back of the kitchen garden, in the space reserved for my new studio. Norman's spent weeks building a wooden arch out there, planting the sweet peas and training them over it. The end result is pretty amazing, and Norman's rightly proud of his efforts.

'The sweet peas are important,' I remind her, as if it's needed.

'And you can bloody over-egg the pudding, you know. You could have had other flowers.'

She's on the verge of saying something else when we're interrupted by a knock at the door. Without waiting for an invitation to enter, Mum appears, looking decidedly strange in a flouncy, knee-length peach-coloured dress.

'Maya!'

She rushes at me, like a crazed fan. From the grin on her face I'd say she's already been helping herself to the champagne. She wraps me in her arms, squeezing the living daylights out of me before she finally remembers she's creasing the bride, and squashing the baby bump.

'Mum.'

'Oh, my girl. My little girl's getting married,' she gushes.

'No shit, Audrey,' Lucy says. 'Is that why she's wearing that big posh dress?'

'You look beautiful, Maya,' Mum gasps. 'But I'm not sure about this.' She re-arranges the cardigan.

'Leave it,' I snarl.

'He's a lucky man.'

'Is he?'

'And you're a very lucky woman.'

'Well, I know that.'

'Soon to be a very wet woman,' Lucy grumbles.

'He's offered to pay for a conservatory. Did you know that, Lucy?' Mum asks. 'An early Christmas present. How lovely is that?'

I tug on the sleeve of the peach-coloured dress and give her a bad-tempered 'shush.' On top of the conservatory, Dan's also made sure his sisters have enough money to buy their own places in Limmingham. And, in spite of the past, he's done exactly the same for Sara. Our respective families are safe and secure, and that's all we both want. No gushing thanks. No publicity.

'Is everyone here?' I ask, doing my best to deflect the conversation.

Mum gives an exaggerated sort of nod that threatens to dislodge her elaborate bun.

'Everyone. Oh, Ethan and Damian look so smart in their little suits.'

I bet they do. Like butter wouldn't melt in their mouths. But I know my nephews better than that.

'They're all taking their seats for the ceremony. And Dan's ready. Oh, he looks lovely, Maya. He's so nervous. I don't know why.' She stops abruptly and glares at me. 'You're not going to run out on him, are you?'

Whoa! Where did that come from?

'No chance,' I reassure her. 'I gave up running away a long time ago.'

'He's not worried about that, Audrey,' Lucy intervenes. 'He's nervous because he doesn't want to cock it up. Clive told me.'

'What's he got to cock up?' I demand, grabbing my flowers from the dressing table. Sweet peas again. More egg in the pudding. 'If there's any cocking-up to be done today, then it's all down to me.'

'Oh Maya,' Mum sighs, putting an arm around me. 'It'll be lovely, whatever happens. Now ... your dad's waiting for you downstairs and I'd better get seated.'

And with that, she skitters out of the room.

Lucy examines her ribbon.

'Still wet.'

'And I'm still wearing a cardigan.'

I push out the mother of all pregnant sighs and gaze at my friend. If I'm not much mistaken, those are tears in her eyes. And now I just want to push all the silly niggles to one side.

'I don't care if you don't,' I smile.

Letting go of the ribbon, she comes forward, opens her arms and hugs me.

'It's the end of an era,' she moans. 'It really is.'

I pull back and wipe away the tears, smudging her mascara in the process.

'It's not the end of anything, Luce. It's the start of something new.'

'A new beginning,' she agrees. 'We're finally growing up.'

'At last,' I laugh. 'And let's face it, it's about time.'

As soon as Dad sees me, he smiles proudly, takes my hand in his and kisses me on the cheek.

'Look at you. My beautiful daughter.'

I'm sorely tempted to tell him the truth. I am, in fact, a beached whale, wrapped in expensive silk and squeezed into unwanted knitwear. But it's my wedding day, and I'm going to rise above it all.

'Thanks, Dad.'

'You deserve the best, Maya. Love, respect and friendship.'

'And that's what I'm getting.'

'I know.'

With another smile, he leads me out over the lawn, through the orchard and past the gate to the kitchen garden, my first choice of location for the ceremony until I realised the destruction of Norman's vegetable patch was out of the question. Skirting round the wall, we come to the meadow at the rear. Putting plans for the studio on hold for a few weeks, it seemed a perfect second choice. I'm confronted by two rows of white chairs, the backs of various heads, the arch set up ready on a low platform, and to the left, a string quartet working their way through a medley of our favourite songs.

I pause, taking stock for a few seconds. The first time I ever came out here it was a warm summer's day but now, almost a year down the line, the sky's a brooding Prussian blue, the air too warm for comfort, the wind growing restless. I can only hope Lucy's prediction doesn't come true; that we manage to get through the ceremony without a downpour, or worse. Closing my eyes, I breathe deeply, focussing on the music, a string version of 'You Don't Know Me'. Stay calm, I tell myself. Remember what's important here. The incredible journey that began with this song; the man who's waiting patiently for you to join him.

I sense a flutter of nerves in my stomach. It's quickly followed by a bout of baby movement. Holding on to Dad's arm, I give the tiny arms and legs time to settle into place. That's a foot in my ribs, I'm sure of it, and I have no idea what's pressing against my bowels, but suddenly I need to visit the toilet.

'She's here!' Ethan squeals, leaping up and running down the aisle.

There's a rumble in the distance.

'Fucking brilliant,' I mutter.

The music changes to Pachelbel's Canon in D, the signal for me to move.

So this is it.

No time for the loo.

'Ready?' Dad asks.

I swallow, watching as Dan rises to his feet, taking his place in front of the arch, his broad shoulders gorgeously accentuated in a morning suit. Clive stands next to him, and they nod at each other. Finally, Dan turns, giving me a tender smile that's mine, and mine alone.

'Ready,' I reply, smiling back.

On automatic pilot, I begin to walk down the aisle, casting acknowledgements at various familiar faces. On the left: The Steves, Mum, Sara and her boys, along with a host of my extended family – aunties, uncles and cousins I haven't seen for years. On Dan's side: Jodie and her mum; Norman and Betty; Bill, Charles, Kathy and the rest of their family, flown over from Bermuda; Gordon sitting with a man I've never seen before; Layla and her husband, Sophie, Dan's niece and nephews. And then there's Lily, seated with her mother and a few other people I don't recognise, members of Lily's and Clive's families, people from Dan's past.

As I approach the arch, my eyes return to Dan, and I'm caught again, lost in the bright blue irises. My heart beat trembles and trips. Blood rushes through my veins. I don't know whether I'm about to pass out or vomit as I step up onto the platform. Luckily, Dan takes my hand and steadies me. And then he draws me in close, leaning down to whisper in my ear.

'You look fucking amazing.'

'You look fucking amazing,' I whisper back. 'I'm a disaster.'

'Not from here, you're not.' His arms tighten.

'I need a wee.'

'Jesus, now? Can't you wait?'

The baby stirs again, thankfully moving into a better position.

'Possibly.'

I hear another roll of thunder. It's still miles away, but it still makes me jump.

'We can postpone, you know.'

'No. We're doing it now.'

He shakes his head.

'You're completely mad ... but I love you.'

'I should bloody well hope so. You're about to marry me.'

'Don't get feisty.' He brushes his mouth against my ear, setting off a host of tingles. 'You'll give me a stonker.'

I hear a cough.

'Are you ready to start?' the registrar asks. 'Only I think we're running out of time.'

I simply nod.

And then it begins ...

In a dream world, I gaze into Dan's eyes, doing my best to keep hold of the registrar's words as the most important minutes of my life pass by.

'Ladies and gentlemen, we are gathered here today to witness the marriage of Daniel Foster and Maya Scotton ...'

I feel a rain drop, and then another.

Before I know it, Dan's reciting his vows, slipping a platinum ring onto my wedding finger.

'I give you this ring, as a sign of our love, trust and marriage. I promise to care for you above all others, to give you my love, friendship and support, and to respect and cherish you throughout our life together.'

It's my turn now. Stumbling through my vows, I'm feeling the raindrops gradually gathering momentum.

'You may now kiss the bride.'

'Oh, thank fuck,' I breathe.

Big, firm hands encircle my waist and draw me in. And then his lips are on mine, absolutely perfect, as soft and warm as ever. I'm thinking of that first kiss, wedged up against a counter in his kitchen, the incredible chemistry that started then and still hasn't waned. For a few long moments, I'm totally adrift, temporarily ignorant to the fact that the storm's closing in, that there's a foot in my ribs again, that I'm wearing a cardigan on my wedding day. And then I'm released, returned to reality. I'm aware of applause ... and more rain.

'You've got your happy ever after, Mrs Foster,' he murmurs against my mouth.

'Thank you, Mr Foster,' I murmur back. 'You do know it's raining?'

He smiles knowingly, turns and holds out a hand to Clive. I watch as a white umbrella sprouts into view. Clive hands it to Dan.

'Fail to prepare,' he raises it over our heads, 'and prepare to fail.'

I look around at our guests, all now sheltering under a forest of white umbrellas. And it's a good job too. The shower quickly morphs into a violent downpour.

'Sneaky git. What would I do without you?'

'Well, for a start,' he says proudly, 'you'd get very wet.'

A streak of lightning illuminates the sky in the distance. I give a start and crumble into Dan's embrace, counting the seconds. Nine of them pass before the thunder follows.

'To the marquee,' I hear him shout. 'Now!'

Under the umbrella, with Dan's arm clasped around my waist, I'm guided quickly back through the orchard and the garden. We stop by the opening to the marquee. As guests scurry past us into the shelter, someone takes the umbrella from Dan. He glances out at the rain.

'Just think of this as a big thunder tent,' he suggests.

'That might work.'

'We can always go inside the house for a while.'

'No. I want to stay here.'

'Are you sure?'

He looks down at my stomach.

'The baby's fine. I'm going to ride this one out.'

'Fair enough, but I'm not leaving your side.'

Taking my hand, he turns to our guests, beaming his happiness at them, and leads me into the throng. We're hugged and kissed and congratulated, one smiling face after another presenting itself in front of us while the rain gathers force outside, hammering against the tarpaulin until I'm struggling to hear what people say. Here and there, above the din, I catch a crack of thunder, and each time I hear it, it's louder. With no regard at all for my wedding day, the storm's about to pass right over our heads ... and I've begun to tremble. I'd love nothing more than to hide under a table, but I think that might

278

be a step too far. Instead, I tell myself I'm all grown up now. I can stay in control.

Clive approaches us.

'We're swapping the order,' he shouts over the noise of the rain. 'Official photos later when it's cleared up outside. And they can't serve dinner until it stops raining.'

'That's okay,' I shout back. 'Just keep everyone's glasses topped up.'

'Limitless champagne on empty stomachs,' he laughs. 'That should work well.'

With a mock salute, he marches off to liaise with the waiting staff.

He's quickly replaced by Lucy.

'We need to get you inside.'

'Why?' I demand.

'Weather. Baby.' She points at my stomach. 'Quivering, pregnant mess.'

'She's coping,' Dan reassures her.

But I'm not so sure about that. The trembles have already mutated into shakes.

'I'm perfectly alright,' I lie. 'Go and get drunk.'

She stares at me, and then at Dan.

'Suit yourselves. But don't come running to me when she starts swearing.' With a wave of the hand, she heads off to help Clive.

Another few minutes pass by in a whirlwind of chat. At some point, I thank Norman for the arch, and Betty for the cake. Jodie informs me she can spruce up my make-up. With a wink, Kathy tells us she's bought 'nice clean sheets' as a wedding present. Bill asks us what we think of his Bermuda shorts, and Charles introduces me properly to his family. I do my best to focus, but it's not easy. With my heart pounding and thumping, I'm half-listening to the storm, constantly gauging its movement, checking every now and then on the flapping marquee, the rain squalling in through the doorway.

'That was beautiful, darling,' Little Steve enthuses, clapping his hands together. 'Just perfect. I cried like a baby.'

'He did,' Big Steve confirms, looking dapper in a black suit. 'It was embarrassing.'

Thunder erupts nearby. Dan's arms close around me. The children are screaming now, all apart from Damian who's wheeling around like a maniac.

'I'm glad you made it,' I tell them, my voice cracking with anxiety. 'I thought you'd be too busy terrorising Europe.'

'Darling,' Little Steve breathes, 'we've been concentrating on

France, but we had to shoot back for this. Wouldn't miss it for the world.'

Another thunderclap. Closer this time. I jolt again, leaning into Dan's side. I hear the children screaming again. Through half-closed eyes, I watch as Damian jumps up and down on the spot, laughing at his brother.

'How's the painting going, Maya?'

'Portraits,' I gasp. 'I'm working on portraits. Commissions.'

'Big commissions,' Dan adds quickly. 'Don't undersell yourself, Maya.'

'We've popped into Slaters,' Big Steve adds. 'You're doing wonders.' He pats Dan on the arm. 'Three floors fully functioning. And what's this about a new gallery?'

'I've got some land on the North Bank. We're having plans drawn up.'

'But you're still running Fosters?'

'Not for much longer. There's a deal in the pipeline.'

'I don't know how you do it all.'

'Lucy virtually looks after Slaters on her own. I'm collaborating with Gordon on the new place. He's taking on a lot of the work for now.'

He nods over to where Gordon's sitting at a table with Clive, Lucy, Lily and the mystery man. I have no idea what they're discussing, but Lucy's in fits of giggles. Lily, meanwhile, is busy knocking back a glass of champagne. As soon as she finishes, Lucy slides a fresh glass towards her. She's clearly accepted her mission, and it looks like we'll have a legless Lily before dinner's served.

'Who's that chap with Gordon?' Little Steve enquires.

'Mark,' Dan answers. 'Gordon's boyfriend.'

Little Steve's mouth opens. 'No.'

'Yes,' Dan confirms. 'He is gay.' And before I can ask the obvious question, he's already answering it. 'He came out to his parents and risked everything.' He turns to me. 'Inspired by you, actually. Anyway, they've accepted it, albeit grudgingly. So it looks like ...'

Another clap of thunder cuts short Dan's explanation. It's deafening this time, causing virtually everyone in the marquee to jump. I whimper, press myself into Dan's chest and watch out of the corner of my eye as Damian pirouettes on the spot.

'We're all going to die!' he shouts.

And with that, Layla's boys begin to cry, Sophie's daughter rushes into her mother's arms and Ethan scoots under a table. Damian laughs at it all, and then shouts his warning one more time. My brain clicks into action. I may well be on the cusp of hyperventilating, but I'm not having that. Anger trumps terror, and before I know what's going on, I've unpeeled myself from Dan's grip, waddled across the marquee, and I'm pointing straight at Damian's triumphant little face.

'That's enough,' I snap. 'Nobody's going to die. Don't say that. You'll scare the others and it's not fair.'

Silenced by my outburst, Damian freezes. I turn to the others, softening my voice.

'It's just a thunderstorm. Thunder and lightning. It can't hurt you. Don't be scared. You'll be fine.'

The children stare at me, goggle-eyed, even Ethan who's still under the table. Suddenly, I realise there's no other noise in the marquee, nothing apart from the rain, and that's easing off. Everyone's silent, and I already know they're all staring at me. Great. I've gone and had a public outburst, on my wedding day ... in a cardigan.

'Auntie Maya's right.' Sara hoves into view. 'Don't scare the others, Damian. It's horrible.'

I'm aware of a hand at the base of my spine, that familiar tingling sensation every time he touches me.

'Wow,' Dan smiles. 'That was amazing.'

'Was it?'

I curl back into his arms. Now the anger's gone, fear's nudging its way back into my head. And I'm still shaking.

'The giant thunder tent thing must have worked.' He kisses the top of my head.

'I've just had a strop. That's not good.'

'Don't worry about it. Everyone's on your side.'

I wince, partly from embarrassment, partly because tiny arms and legs are on the move again.

'Are you okay?'

'Baby's getting comfortable.'

He puts a hand on my stomach.

'Don't mess with your mum,' he smiles. 'She's a force of nature when she gets going, far scarier than a thunderstorm.'

The hand moves to my chest. He places a palm over my heart and frowns.

'You should sit down for a while. No arguments.'

He guides me to a seat and waits for me to settle. A glass of orange juice is pressed into my hands, and then he sits next to me, stretching out his legs.

'What are you doing?'
'Looking after my wife.'
'You should be circulating, chatting with the guests.'
'They'll understand.'
'The thunder's gone. I'll be fine on my own. We've got a lifetime together, Dan. Go and do your duty.'
'What duty?'
'Just do it.'
With a sigh, he stands again, straightens his suit and saunters off. Picking up a glass of champagne from a passing tray, he eases himself into conversation with my dad. I miss him already, and I want him back. I'm about to follow and let him know I've changed my mind when I hear Lily's voice.
'Holding court?' She plants a dainty kiss on my cheek and takes the seat next to me.
'I'm under orders to sit down for a while.'
'I'm not surprised.'
'I feel like a sack of spanners.'
'You look absolutely beautiful.'
I can't believe the statement, but I thank her anyway. While Lily takes a few sips of champagne, I watch Dan as he laughs at something my dad says, and then moves on.
'What sort of dad do you think he'll make?' I ask.
She sucks at her lip.
'He may not have had a great role-model to begin with, but he'll do his best.' She turns to me. 'You're not worried, are you?'
'No. I just wonder how he'll take to it.'
'He's a quick learner. I think he'll be fine.' Her eyes darken. 'To think this might never have happened.'
I should have known this would come up. Lily's done her best to deal with the aftermath of Boyd, but it hasn't been easy for her.
'It's not worth thinking about.'
I watch her closely, spotting a tear in the corner of her eye. She wipes it away, quickly shaking herself back into public mode. I take her hand in mine and squeeze it.
'He didn't win. We won.'
'Still ...'
'It's done. The future's all that counts.'
I catch Lucy's eye, sending her a silent plea for help. Immediately, she breaks off from a chat with Gordon and swoops on us, thrusting a fresh glass of champagne into Lily's hands.
'Get that down you, Lil. I'm in the mood for partying, and you're

my perfect partner in crime. Come on.' She waves a hand impatiently and winks at me. 'Let's get down to business.'

'It looks like I've got no choice,' Lily grins at me.

'No, you've not. Good luck.'

Left alone for a minute, I gaze across the marquee to where Dan's sitting with his sisters. Looking completely relaxed and utterly gorgeous, he smiles at something Layla says, watching as her two boys whizz about in front of him. I decide to go over and join them, but Clive's next to me now, distinctly frazzled.

'How's the best man?' I ask.

'Coping.'

'Ready for your speech?'

'Cards.' He taps his pocket. 'I've made notes on cards.'

'You're doing a brilliant job.'

'You too.' He pauses. 'Listen, it seems that Damian's picked all the flowers off the cake. He ate most of them and then threw up outside. He's been suitably chastised, but I thought you should know.'

'He's the devil's spawn.'

'And dinner's about to be served.'

'Thank God.' I glance out of the marquee. It's stopped raining. Sunlight's glinting against the wet grass. 'You've been a massive help, Clive. Not just today. You've got Dan's back.'

'That's friendship for you.'

'But you always seem to be running around after him.'

'I owed him a few favours. He's helped me out in the past, more times than I care to remember. He deserves to be happy, and I've been only too glad to help.'

'You deserve to be happy too.'

'I am.' He nods towards Lucy. 'She's as mad as a badger, but I love her. She's letting loose today, and that's fine by me.'

'Be careful. You don't know how far it can go.'

'Oh believe me, I do. Now, let's get everyone into their places.'

Before long, the guests have been ushered into their seats, and I'm back with Dan. We're served by a succession of glum-looking, wet-haired teenagers, but dinner's amazing, and at least the morning sickness has gone for now, leaving me free to enjoy it all. As soon as the dessert plates are cleared away, I hear the tinkling of cutlery against a glass. I look up to find my dad's on his feet. And my heart sinks.

'This wasn't in the plan,' I whisper to Dan.

'He'll be alright,' Dan whispers back.

'He could barely get his dinner in his mouth, he's so drunk.'

Dan shrugs, and turns to listen to the speech.

'Quiet everyone!' Dad shouts. 'I'd like to say a few, er ... words.'

Resisting the urge to order him back into his seat, I smile sweetly as Dad blunders on about his beautiful daughter, his wonderful new son-in-law, and his forthcoming grandchild. Finally, he begins to ramble incoherently about plans for the new conservatory, at which point Mum tugs him back onto his chair.

'Bugger it.' I let my head fall, feel Dan's hand on mine, and look up again when Clive takes over.

'Ladies and gentlemen,' he begins, dropping his cards onto the table. 'Shit. Oh.'

He spends a few moments attempting to slot the cards back into the right order, with no evident success, before he proceeds to meander through the best man's speech entirely from memory, stumbling over a jumble of anecdotes and lame jokes, forgetting the punchline to every single one. At least he remembers to thank the maid of honour, rounding off the entire sorry episode with a toast to the bride and groom.

While Clive's clearly mortified by the whole experience, Dan hardly seems bothered. Holding my hand under the table, he thanks his friend, and then leans in to me.

'I'd say it's time to rescue the situation.'

He gets to his feet, immediately taking command of the marquee with a simple, calm authority. I'm impressed. It's a side of him I've never seen before, a side he must have used at Fosters time and time again.

'Ladies and gentlemen ...' He surveys our guests. 'I'd like to thank you all for being here with us to share our special day. And believe me, this is special. Thunder and lightning. There's never a dull moment in my wife's world.' He pauses. 'My wife. I'm so proud to be able to call her that.' He gives me a full-on, no holds barred smile. 'This beautiful, intelligent, talented, spirited woman is my wife.' He turns back to the audience. 'I am the luckiest man in the world. And I'm fully prepared to argue the toss over that one.'

There's a babble of laughter. He becomes serious.

'It's a miracle we ever got to this point. You all know what's happened over the last year, and that's the only reference I'm going to make to it. What you may not know is that when I first met Maya, the very first time I ever laid eyes on her, I knew ... I knew I'd be spending the rest of my life with her.' He takes in a breath and blinks. 'I was an idiot back then, didn't exactly go about things the usual way, but Maya stuck by me ... she saw the real me, she believed in me, and she had faith in us. I can't thank her enough for that.'

A round of applause interrupts his flow. He waits for silence to resume.

'We both grew up in the same town. In fact, we grew up on the same street. We hardly crossed paths back then, but years later, fate brought us together again.' He rubs his chin, gazing at the tablecloth for a moment before he goes on. 'The past is a difficult place for some of us, but if it weren't for our shared past, we wouldn't be here today. I needed to cope with my past, and Maya helped me to do that. I love this woman more than I can say. She's given me a life. She's given me love, hope, and a future. Ladies and gentlemen, I'd like you to raise a glass to the love of my life, my soul-mate, my other half.' He picks up his glass and looks at me, his eyes dancing with complete and utter happiness. 'Mrs Maya Foster.'

The last I saw Dan was about half an hour ago. I go in search of him, making my way through the orchard, no longer bothered that the bottom of my dress is splattered with mud. The sun's finally showed its face and, with the chairs wiped down, guests have migrated outside. This is nearer to what I'd imagined. I head towards Clive who's laughing with Gordon and his boyfriend. At the next table, Lucy and Lily are deep in a serious, drunken conversation with Sara, probably comparing notes on Boyd.

'Anybody seen my old man?' I ask.

'He went inside,' Clive grins. 'Said he fancied a cup of tea.'

I look towards the house.

'Tea?'

'Tea,' Clive confirms. 'Seems he's not into coffee these days.'

'Well, he doesn't have to make his own,' I mutter, wandering off to the house. 'We've got caterers.'

I head straight to the kitchen where I find him standing at the Aga, his back to me. He's jacketless now, still wearing his waistcoat. It accentuates those gorgeous hips, and I pause to admire him.

'What's going on?'

He turns and gives me the broadest smile.

'Making tea. I was just coming to find you.'

'It's your wedding day. You should be having a few beers.'

He lifts the lid on the Liberty teapot and checks the brew.

'I don't need beers.' He replaces the lid. 'My wife can't drink, and I'd like to stay relatively sober for her. And besides, I need to have her to myself for a little while.' He glances at me, his eyes twinkling and I'm wondering if he's planning on whisking me off to the

285

bedroom for an early honeymoon.

'You can't just abandon your guests,' I remind him.

'I know that. A little while. That's all.' Picking up the pot, he fills the sweet pea cups. 'Right.' He hands me a cup. 'Let's go.'

'Where?'

'You'll see.'

I follow him back out into the orchard, stopping here and there while Dan tells our guests we need a few minutes together, on our own. He leads me through into the kitchen garden, along the grass walkway between the vegetable patches, finally halting at the bench ... beneath the sweet peas. He takes my cup, waiting for me to settle on the bench. It's not easy, not with the bump and several thousand pounds worth of wedding dress. When I'm finally comfortable, he hands me back my cup and sits by my side.

'Remember our first time here?' he asks.

How could I ever forget?

'Of course.'

I sip at the tea, suppress a grimace at the metallic taste, and cast my mind back to that perfect evening when I first thought I'd got to the heart of him. And barring a few facts, perhaps I had ... sweet, kind, a little lost.

'You gave me a handful of sweet peas,' I prompt him, knowing what he wants to do.

He places his cup on the ground and turns away. In the few seconds it takes him to pick a handful of flowers, I grab my opportunity to throw the tea away. Turning back, he hands me the sweet peas, takes my empty cup and places it next to his.

'They're not the most expensive flowers in the world.' He squints into the sun. 'But they're the dearest to my heart.'

Because his adoptive parents sat out here every evening in the summer, hardly saying a word as they were so comfortable together.

'And to my heart too,' I add. 'Lucy thinks I've over-egged the pudding. Too many sweet peas.'

'Some puddings are better that way.'

He takes my hand, threading his fingers through mine, watching them, deep in thought.

'You drifted off when we were here,' he reminds me. 'I asked you what you were thinking about.'

'Penny for them.'

'You said they weren't worth that much. What were you thinking about? You can tell me now.'

'I was day-dreaming ... about being married to you, about sitting here and drinking tea, and watching the kids play.'

'That early on?'

'That early on,' I confirm. 'I didn't want to admit it.'

'Well, here we are, complete with child number one.' He rests his palm on my stomach and right on cue, child number one decides to stretch, forcing a foot into my diaphragm.

'Oooh,' I groan.

The baby moves again, shoving an elbow outwards. Dan feels it and smiles.

'When do you think we'll pop out child number two?'

'Excuse me, let's get this over with first. Slow down.' I arch my back. 'All I know is this. We've got six bedrooms, all freshly decorated. Leaving one for guests, that means we've got four bedrooms to fill.'

'Four?' He mouths the word with a look of mock terror.

I give him a look of real terror in return. What the hell have I just said? I want four children? I want morning sickness and stretch lines and indigestion four sodding times? I shake my head.

'Yes, four.'

'And what about your pelvic floor?'

I smile, recalling my drunken outburst at Harrods.

'You'll still love me when I'm incontinent.'

'You're a coarse woman, Mrs Foster.' Leaning in, he kisses me gently on the lips. 'But I wouldn't have it any other way. Have I told you your massive pregnant tits look wonderful in this dress?'

I pull back my head and give him a good dose of disgust.

'You're a dirty bugger, Mr Foster. But I wouldn't have it any other way. So, why are we here then?'

'Because I've got a few more vows for you, just as solemn as the ones we made in front of everyone ... but these are private.'

I'm intrigued.

'Go ahead.'

'Okay.' He rubs his chin. 'I've already done the love, honour and obey thing, till death us to part, etcetera. They're kind of umbrella vows, aren't they?'

'Get on with it.'

'Okay, so I hereby vow to stop steamrollering you into things.' He waves a hand and shrugs. 'Well, obviously, it's a bit of a habit, but just kick me if I start.'

'Understood.'

'And I also vow to consult you on every important decision I make.'

'Every important decision we make,' I correct him.

'Quite right. We.' He surveys the garden. 'I vow to support you and encourage you wherever it's necessary. I vow to listen to you and your every need ...'

'This sounds too perfect to be true.'

'Cynic,' he chides me. 'I'm still going to be pretty selfish in certain areas. For example, I'll probably get an erection in your presence when it's most inappropriate, and I'll have to fuck you senseless on an incredibly regular basis. But all in all, I'll be the best husband you could possibly wish for, the best dad to this little one, and any further inconveniences to your pelvic floor, planned or unplanned. Oh, and finally, I vow never to keep another secret from you.'

'Unless it's a good secret.'

'Which is?'

'Presents, umbrellas, that sort of thing.'

'Oh, I get it.' He nods. 'Good secrets.'

'So, I should make some vows to you.'

'You don't have to.'

'I want to. I vow to support you and encourage you where it's necessary. I vow to use my brain before my mouth and stop being so bloody stubborn. I vow never to run away from anything that scares me. I vow to face it all, head on, with you at my side. I vow to put all my dirty clothes in the washing basket. And I'll try to remember to put the lid on the toothpaste. Oh, and I vow to do a bit better with the cooking thing.'

'That pretty much covers all the bases.'

'So, it does.'

'Oi!' Lucy calls from the gate. 'What are you two doing in here?'

'Oi!' a second voice joins in.

Pushing past her, Lily staggers towards us, veers onto a vegetable patch and stumbles about amongst a forest of broccoli, sniggering uncontrollably.

'Oh for God's sake,' I mutter. 'That's my fault. I told Lucy to cheer her up.'

Sara appears by Lucy's side and pushes her headlong into the courgettes.

'Well, it seems to have worked,' Dan comments wryly. 'They're enjoying themselves.'

While Lucy wrestles with a massive courgette, Sara reaches down to help her back to her feet, loses her balance and joins her on the ground. The broccoli quivers. Lily's face appears for a second or two, then disappears again. It's not a ladylike display ... far from it.

'I just wanted today to be perfect,' I sigh.

'It is perfect.'

'Really? We got married in a downpour, and now everyone's covered in mud. I had a strop in a thunderstorm, my dress doesn't fit, I'm wearing a cardigan, I've got a foot in my ribs and I can't stop going to the toilet. And that lot are pissed out of their tiny minds.' I wave at the three women. Cackling like witches, they're busy throwing courgettes at each other. 'The kids are feral, the cake's ruined ...'

'Who cares?' Dan interrupts with a smile. 'I certainly don't.'

'I just wanted to do it right. I suppose I wanted to prove a point.'

'Which is?'

'That I'm not a complete disaster area, that I'm capable of organising things.'

He laughs.

'I didn't marry you for your organisational skills. If I remember rightly, you were the worst PA in the world. I married you because you're you. Chaos follows you everywhere, Maya, and I love it.' He stands and straightens his waistcoat. 'Now, if you'll excuse me for a minute, it seems I need to rescue three drunken women from a vegetable patch.'

Chapter Twenty-Seven

I pause outside Fosters Construction. The evening migration is well under way, surrounding me with a bustling, seething mass of office workers, most of them heading home. Standing my ground, I let the bodies filter round me, recalling the first time I ever stood here. Back then, I was riddled with anxiety, but there's barely a trace of it now. I know exactly why it's still hanging around, though. The winding-down operation is coming to an end, this is the last day that Fosters will be Fosters, and I can't help worrying that his soon to be ex-workforce will blame it all on me.

I look up at the fifteen storeys of darkened glass while the last of the October evening sunlight glints against the windows, and think of the man behind the façade. He's up there, waiting for me, counting on my support. And no matter how nervous I feel, I'm giving it to him. When I walk back out of here, I'll be by my husband's side, and neither of us will ever be coming back.

With a deep breath, I edge forward, nod a quick greeting to the doorman and manoeuvre the pushchair through the revolving door. Inside, the atrium's almost exactly as I remember it: an imposing space littered with plush leather chairs, coffee tables and pot plants. But the reception desk's abandoned now. Under Mrs Kavanagh's supervision, the blonde and brunette are busy laying out champagne flutes on tables. Avoiding their attention, I head straight for the lift, shoulders slumping in relief when the doors close behind me. As we begin to rise, I check on the pushchair's little passenger, finding a pair of bright blue eyes gazing back up at me. I smile at my son, suddenly strengthened by a rush of love for him. He's slept all the way down from Lambeth, allowing me to enjoy my walk in peace. But now we're here, he's wide awake again.

'Daddy's big day,' I tell him. 'Try not to be sick on him.'

His eyes spark and he lets out a gurgle.

The lift comes to a halt, the doors sliding open to reveal the swanky lobby on the top floor. I step out, taking in the huge pictures, the marble floor, the glass desk where Carla normally sits. She's not there now.

'Oh.' Coming out of the kitchen, she stops in her tracks, clapping her hands together. 'Can I have a hold?'

I gawp at Dan's personal assistant. We've barely ever talked and I certainly never had her down as the type to turn all mushy over a baby.

'He might throw up on you,' I warn her.

'That's okay.' She shrugs, half-embarrassed. 'I can take it.'

I unbuckle Jack, carefully retrieve him from the pushchair and hand him over. She takes him confidently, and pulls a face.

'Are you staying on here?' I ask tentatively.

'No, I've got a new job with Mr Watson. He's setting up an accountancy company.'

'I never knew,' I apologise, wishing I'd shown more interest before.

The truth is I've not been back here since I was on the receiving end of a good seeing-to and a strange proposal in the lift. Pregnancy, painting, house renovations, the wedding, a new baby – it's all distracted me from visiting Dan's workplace.

'You've had a lot on your mind.' She holds Jack under his arms, away from herself. 'He's absolutely gorgeous. Beautiful eyes. How old is he now?'

'Eight weeks.'

And a complete handful, I'd like to add. Although I couldn't love him more, and Dan's proved himself to be a thoroughly supportive and loving dad, true to Beefy's words the last few weeks have been a blur of nappies and feeding and soothing.

'Well, he's a stunner.' She offers him back and nods to the half-open door. 'Mr Foster's waiting for you.'

'Yes,' I mutter. 'Well ...' I rearrange Jack in my arms and plant a kiss on his forehead. 'This is it, then. I'm sorry,' I blurt, overwhelmed by guilt.

'What for?'

'This.' I wave my free hand in the air. 'If I hadn't turned up, he wouldn't have sold the company. You must all hate me.'

'Nobody hates you,' she reassures me, touching Jack on the cheek. 'It's just time for a change. I suppose the accident made him think.'

'I suppose so.'

In an instant, I decide to keep the truth to myself: that he'd already decided to move on, even before the accident. I've got a decent excuse, ready-made protection from blame, and I'm going to use it.

'To be honest,' Carla goes on, 'I've never seen him so relaxed ... so happy. I'm pleased for him, for all of you. Honestly. Now, go on.'

She motions to the doorway.

Leaving the pushchair in the lobby, I take the changing-bag and walk through into Dan's office. I find him standing by the window, gazing out over the Thames. He's jacketless, wearing charcoal grey trousers and a matching waistcoat, and he's every bit as delectable as the first time I ever laid eyes on him. I'm just admiring his backside when Jack lets out a squeal.

Dan turns.

'You took your time,' he grins, coming over to join us.

'Well, I would have been here earlier, but somebody decided to fill their nappy before we left.' I drop the bag on the floor. 'So, I changed their nappy, and then they filled it again.'

'Oh, oh.'

Slipping an arm around my waist, he delivers a kiss that would go on forever if it weren't for the baby wriggling in my arms. Dan pulls back, looks down and ruffles Jack's blond fluffy hair.

'Hello, little man. Have you been good for Mummy?'

Jack lifts his mouth into a lop-sided, gummy grin.

'I think that's a yes.' Taking the baby from me, he sinks onto a sofa. Immediately, Jack pushes himself to his feet.

'Two months old, and he's trying to walk,' I observe. 'He's got your genes. In a rush to do everything.'

'Determined,' Dan confirms, smiling at his son. 'You carry on like that and you'll get everything you want in life ... just like Daddy.'

With a delighted squawk, Jack tries to bounce, landing a foot on Dan's crotch in the process.

'Well, that's enough of that,' Dan winces, encouraging the baby back onto his bottom.

'All done?'

'All done.'

Completely oblivious to the fact that a tiny hand has managed to grab hold of his tie, he surveys the office, his desk, the sofas, the huge glass meeting table.

'Sixteen years,' he muses.

'Second thoughts?'

He shakes his head.

'I just don't know where the time's gone.' He looks round again. 'This place has some fond memories, but only from the last few months. I should have had the furniture put in storage, especially this couch.' He focusses back on Jack. 'This is Daddy's favourite couch. It should have a plaque.'

Because it was the site of our first full-on sexual encounter.

'There'll be other couches,' I smile.

'There certainly will. And desks. And windows. And maybe bathrooms. I'll have a great office at the new gallery.' He pulls a silly face at Jack. 'Mummy needs to come and see it ... all on her own.'

I sit next to Dan, and I just can't help it. Even now, at the eleventh hour, I'm still plagued by uncertainty.

'Was this the right thing to do?'

'Chill your beans, wife.' Carefully, he pulls his tie out of Jack's mouth. 'I'm finally getting to live the way I want to live. The galleries won't consume me, not like this place. I'll have more time with you and the milk monster.'

While Jack lurches forward, grabbing for his tie again, Dan locks eyes with me, and I gaze into those bright blue irises, reassured by their softness.

'I'll be right behind you.' I put a hand on his knee.

'And I'll be right behind you too. You need to get back to painting.'

He's right. I haven't touched a paintbrush since the birth.

'I'll do it soon, but I'm not having a nanny.'

'You don't need a nanny. I'll be around.'

Jack squeals again, this time through a mouthful of regurgitated milk and before I can do anything about it, Dan's trousers have been spattered.

'Oh God,' he groans. 'Wipes!'

Leaping up from the sofa, I scramble through the bag, pull out the wipes and offer them to him. Taking the pack, he lifts an eyebrow, refuses my help and does his best to clean up the mess, one-handed. There's no time to dry out the trousers and I know for a fact the spare suits have already been returned to the apartment. He'll just have to make his grand exit, looking like he's lost control of his bladder. He throws the used wipes onto the table and makes a face at Jack.

'Oh dear.' Clive's at the doorway now, with Lucy at his side. 'What's going on?'

'Baby sick all over Mr Mean and Hot and Moody,' I explain. 'All part and parcel of parenthood.'

While Dan frowns, evidently confused by my code name for him,

293

Clive approaches and holds out his hands.

'Come to your godfather.' He takes Jack and admires him. 'He looks more like you every day. It's a tiny Dan.'

'I should hope so, seeing as he is the dad,' Lucy adds, kissing Jack on the head. 'So, are you ready to stay the night with Uncle Clivey and Auntie Lucy?'

I sense a pang, deep down inside. I know it's Dan's big day – and he's determined for us to have a 'special evening' to celebrate – but I'm not sure I'm ready to let Jack go.

'I don't know about this,' I muse, gazing at him. 'He's so little.'

'He'll be fine,' Lucy counters.

'I just don't know …'

'He'll be fine,' she repeats, glaring at me. 'The trial run was a success.'

'That was an afternoon. This is a whole night.'

'Stop moaning. Me and Clivey are more than capable of looking after little Jack. It's not difficult. You put stuff in here.' She points at his mouth. 'And stuff comes out of here.' She pats his bottom.

He giggles.

'It's not that simple.'

'You've got to trust us. We've got everything we need for the night. We'll call you if there's a problem … but there won't be a problem.'

'He's hard work.'

'It doesn't matter. One day, I'm sure we'll be asking you to do the same for us.'

I glance at Clive. He doesn't seem to be the slightest bit put out by Lucy's statement.

'You're not pregnant, are you?'

She shakes her head. 'Some of us know how the pill works. We're getting married though,' she adds, throwing out the news as if it's of no importance whatsoever.

'What?' I gasp. 'Getting married?'

'Yeah.' A wicked grin creeps across her face.

'I'm sorry,' Clive intervenes. 'We didn't want to rain on Dan's parade, but seeing as Lucy's determined to let the cat out of the bag …'

'We're getting married,' she squeaks, jumping around like a lunatic. 'Clive asked me last night. It was so romantic.'

'Congratulations.' Getting up, Dan pats Clive on the back.

'Best man?' Clive asks.

'Of course, and I'll try not to give a shit speech.'

'Dan,' I admonish him. 'No swearing in front of your son.'

'But he's just a baby.'

'He's a sponge, that's what he is, soaking it all up. I don't want a foul-mouthed toddler.'

'Sorry, boss.'

Carla appears at the doorway.

'It's time. They're all waiting for you downstairs.'

Suddenly serious, Dan looks at his friend.

'I didn't want this, Clive. I just wanted to leave quietly.'

'And your staff want to say goodbye.'

'I have no idea why.'

'Well, I do.' Clive grins at Jack. 'Daddy's been a bad-tempered shi ... person most of the time.' He goes on in a sing-song voice. 'But he's worked hard for his employees, yes, he has. And anyone who wanted a voluntary redundancy had one, haven't they? And he's managed to sell the company in one piece.'

'Well,' Dan rubs his forehead. 'There's no telling how long it's going to stay that way.'

'It's out of your hands,' Clive tells him. 'You've done your bit and they appreciate it. So, go and say goodbye to them ... with your adoring wife and son at your side.'

'And a wet patch on your trousers,' I add for good measure.

With Jack returned to the pushchair, Dan says farewell to the fifteenth floor, and we all ride the lift in silence. As the numbers above the door count down, I check on my husband. Hands clenched, staring straight ahead at the door, he's deep in thought. I reach out and touch his arm, letting him know I'm here for him. He has just enough time to reward me with a thankful glimmer of the eyes before the door slides open onto the atrium.

It's transformed now, overflowing with smart, professional types. And they're all silent, staring at us, expectantly. With the mask back in place, Dan's first out of the lift, barely taking three steps before the applause begins, the sound of it echoing through the atrium. I watch as he weaves a path through the crowd, stopping to shake a hand or indulge in a quick chat, gradually relaxing.

Norman appears in front of me.

'Maya.' I'm given a big, teddy bear hug. 'And the little one.' He leans down and brushes a finger across Jack's chubby cheeks. 'It's a big day.'

'Another one.'

'Well,' he laughs, 'I never saw this coming when you walked into my office.'

'Neither did I.'

'No more big kahuna, eh?' He winks.

'Maybe that's not such a bad thing.'

'When will you be back down at the house?'

'Tomorrow evening, probably.'

'I'll tell Betty. She wants to do a nice casserole.'

And with that, Norman's gone.

Before I'm swamped by baby-admirers, I scan the atrium, spotting Dan over to the left. He's laughing with a group of people I've never seen before. Yet again, I find myself thinking of that first ever visit to Fosters. Completely out of my depth, I had no idea I was already tangled in Dan's web. I saw him as nothing more than an arrogant, power-hungry, domineering piece of work, but I couldn't have been more wrong. I didn't know him at all. But now I've peeled back his layers, I've got to the heart of Daniel Foster, and I know exactly who he is: a loving, faithful, caring and protective man.

And my heart swells with pride to think that he's all mine.

He brushes my hair, gently picking his way through the tangles. We're sitting on the bed, enjoying our own little bubble of peace and quiet. With Dan behind me, leaning against the headboard, a towel wrapped around his midriff, I'm positioned between his legs, naked, drifting further into a fug of post-bath calm.

'Do you need a sleep?' he asks at last.

'And waste precious time with you? I can sleep later.' I gaze at the empty cot. 'It feels weird without Jack here.'

'He'll be back tomorrow. And then we'll spend plenty of time with him ... together.'

'So, what's in store for tonight?'

'Dinner ... later.'

'And before that?'

'It's a secret.'

I turn to face him, waiting for more.

'A good secret,' he adds, holding the brush in mid-air.

'Where are we going?'

'Not far.'

'Where?'

'Across the hallway.'

'The room of kink?'

'Either that or the guest bedroom.' He motions for me to turn again, and goes back to brushing my hair. 'I've missed it.'

Since Jack was born, we haven't used it once, and I've missed it too, evidently more than I realised, because out of nowhere, excitement's bouncing around my stomach like a hyperactive toddler.

'What are we using?' I ask, unable to contain it any longer.

'Well, that all depends.' He throws the brush onto the bed. 'There. You're done.' A warm hand comes to my shoulder. 'Ready?'

'Ready.'

He urges me up from the bed and heads straight for the wardrobe. Opening a drawer, he picks out a lacy pair of knickers and then, taking my hand, leads me from the bedroom, across the hallway, and into the room of kink. Letting go of my hand, he saunters over to the spanking bench.

'That?' I ask.

'Maybe.'

'But, I thought ...'

'It was out of the question?'

I watch him closely, registering the slight changes that are beginning to appear. Lips straighten, eyes darken, shoulders arch, as if he's suddenly poised for action. I've seen it all before, and just like before, it sparks off a glow of anticipation deep in my groin. That's the dominant persona emerging from the shadows, and I've missed him too.

Slowly, he moves toward me. When he's close enough, he traces a fingertip across my stomach. I jolt at the contact, close my eyes and soak up the sensations.

'What are you doing?' I ask.

'Exactly what I want to do. As always.'

He begins to circle me, taking his time, surveying me, drawing his fingers across my flesh. At last, he comes to a halt behind me and I'm pulled in close, one hand on my waist, the other clamped around my right arm. He skims his mouth across my shoulder.

'You liked the dominant.'

It's not a question.

'It turned me on. You know it did.'

'Me too.'

I'm swamped in confusion. I have no idea where this is going.

'But ... you didn't want to be that person any more.'

'I didn't want to hide,' he whispers against my ear. 'And now there's nothing left to hide from.' He turns me to face him. 'I can bring out the dominant for you now, Maya, because it's only a game. And when we're finished, I can put him away again.' He takes hold of my chin. 'Care to play?'

'Bloody hell, yes.' I'm already struggling to control my breath. 'So, it's the bench?'

'There was no way I was ever going to spank you while you were pregnant ... or while pain was still an issue. It's not for me, not any more. Hasn't been for a long time. How about you?'

I open my mouth, but I'm not exactly sure where to start. He helps me out.

'I need to know. The loner who didn't fit in, the child with no self-confidence, the girl who was tormented by her sister.' Letting go of my chin, he brings a palm to my cheek. 'The woman who ran away and blocked things out, who felt she deserved punishment. Did you leave her back there on the beach?'

'Yes,' I whisper, holding his gaze. 'Haven't seen her for a while.'

He nods, blinks lazily. 'So, tell me. What are you?'

I falter.

'I don't understand.'

'What are you?' he asks again. 'I need you to tell me.'

'I don't know what you want me to say ...'

'The truth. What are you?'

'Well ...' I stammer. 'I'm a woman.'

'Definitely not a girl,' he smiles.

'Definitely not,' I smile back. 'I'm a wife and a mother and an artist.'

'Good. Now, try some adjectives.' He waits for a moment, his eyes dancing in the light. 'You do know what adjectives are, don't you?'

'Of course I do. Don't be a condescending twat. I just can't think of any.'

'Then allow me to help.' He takes a moment to study me. 'Beautiful.'

He pauses again, waiting for me to repeat the word.

'I don't know about that.' I glance down. 'Stretch marks.'

'They're a part of you now, just like my scars are a part of me. Life's made its mark on both of us. But you're still beautiful, and I want to hear you say it.'

'Okay then,' I mutter, more than slightly embarrassed. 'Beautiful.'

'Now give me some more.'

I blow out a breath. I want a session on that spanking bench, no doubt about it, and if I'm to get what I want, I need to do this right.

'Sexy?' I ask.

'Believe it,' he orders sternly.

'Okay, sexy. I'm sexy.'

'Well done. More.'

Shit. More?

'Brilliant,' I venture, 'talented … funny.'

His smile broadens with every word, egging me on.

'Intelligent … feisty … spunky.'

'Oh, I like that one.'

'So do I.' I tut. 'Be quiet. I'm on a roll. Talented. No, I've said that one. Strong. Caring. Faithful. Lucky. Fucking lucky.'

'Too right you are.'

'Happy now?'

I bloody hope so, seeing as I've just run out of adjectives.

'Yes, thank you.' He gives me a satisfied smile. 'So, if I were to spank you tonight, what would you get out of it?'

'Is this a test?'

'Of course. And you'd better pass.'

Another deep breath.

'It's not like that night.' I nod at the cross and he understands. 'Not even remotely like that. You once told me I'd enjoy a proper spanking, and I did. It was something else. A pure rush. It hurt for a bit, but then it didn't.' I hesitate for a moment, wondering how on Earth I'm going to explain this, and then I hear myself talking, confident, calm, determined. 'I liked the shock of it, the way it made me feel awake and alive. And when the endorphins kicked in, I felt supercharged. Everything was intense.' I raise my chin, proud now. 'If you were to spank me tonight, that's what I'd get out of it. Absolute pleasure … and a few fucking brilliant orgasms.'

He nods.

'Perfect. Ten out of ten.' He holds up the knickers. 'You'll be needing these then.'

Buzzing with anticipation, I take them from him, slip them on and wait for the next command.

He taps the padded rest, his eyes glistening with promise.

Immediately, I climb onto the bench, moving my arms and legs into position. As soon as I'm comfortable, a warm palm touches my left shoulder, slowly smoothing its way down my back, across my buttocks, leaving ruffles of pleasure wherever it goes. He repeats the process, two, three times before he removes the hand. I'm desperate for more, and not waiting for long. Almost immediately, he places both hands on my shoulders and begins to massage me with patient, gentle movements. I'm in a daze, completely relaxed, when he finally comes to a stop.

'How do you feel?'

'Great,' I murmur. 'Bloody wonderful.'

'Excellent. Let's get you strapped in.'

As ever, he takes his time fastening the bindings, concentrating fully on the job in hand. He wraps the leather cuffs around my wrists, and then my ankles, checking that I'm comfortable. When he's satisfied, he moves my hair out of my face.

'Ready?' he asks.

'Ready,' I confirm.

He plants a tender kiss on my forehead.

'It fucking turns me on to see you like this, Maya.'

'And I love it.'

I'm stating the ruddy obvious here. My breathing's already shallow, and my vagina's twitching for England. Suddenly, a finger probes me. I moan.

'You're wet.'

'I can't help it.'

He removes the finger and brings it to my mouth, running it firmly across my lips.

'Taste yourself.'

I do as I'm told, licking away the wetness.

'I'd love to gag you,' he murmurs. 'Then I'd have you completely.'

The words come quickly. I'm feeling reckless.

'Do it.'

'Next time, maybe. More practice first.'

He walks away. I hear the sound of the wardrobe door sliding open. He's fetching the flogger. It's not long before he returns, placing one hand on the small of my back, holding me firmly, the other on my right buttock.

'Warm up time,' he reminds me. 'Don't fight it. Concentrate on your breathing. Use your safeword if you change your mind.'

'Like that's going to happen.'

Immediately, he slaps me hard on the left buttock. I jolt in surprise.

'Behave yourself. No back-chat.'

He slaps my right buttock, a little less harshly this time, and then, without a break, he continues, alternating between the two, spanking lightly. Within seconds, my flesh comes alive with a stinging sensation. A minute or so later, he stops.

'Harder now,' he tells me.

The hand on my back presses down, and he begins to slap again, left and right, left and right, increasing the speed and intensity.

'No,' I gasp, although I have no idea why. I'm already loving it.

'You know what to say.'

'God.'

'And you'll never say it.' More slaps rain down. 'I wonder why that is.'

I squeeze my eyes shut, my flesh burning now, fists clenched. Growing steadily weaker under his control, I bite back the urge to yell for coffee. I know exactly where this is going, and there's no way I'm about to put a halt to it.

He pauses, pulls down my knickers and smooths a hand over my skin.

'Cooking nicely.' He tugs the knickers back into place. 'You're nearly there.'

A second long, hard session begins, fast at first, then slowing in pace. Eyes still closed, I make an effort to unclench my fists, silently willing my muscles to relax, focussing on my breathing, consciously keeping it under control as each glorious, stabbing dart of heat sears right to my core.

He comes to a halt. Slipping a finger into the top of my knickers, he rips them away, and skims a palm across my bare buttocks.

'Time for the endorphins.'

'Mmm, endorphins,' I murmur. 'Yummy.'

I hear him chuckle, feel the leather strands of the flogger against my skin. Over and over again, he draws them across my buttocks, up and down my back, covering every inch of flesh. Before long, I'm tingling, shimmering, glowing.

I hear a soft thud. The flogger's been dropped to the floor.

A finger comes to my clitoris, softly massaging me, patiently bringing me to the edge. I'm almost there when he launches into the next round of spanking: short upward slaps, maybe ten on each side. It doesn't last long. I'm still reeling at the shock when the finger returns to my clit, urging me back towards an orgasm. And then he slaps again, repeating the process, taking the air clean out of my lungs and forcing me to focus back on my breathing. It's not easy, but I'm finally rewarded. Pain begins to mutate, transforming into something different altogether, an all-consuming, delicious flood of pleasure that washes through me, body and mind. I'm on the verge of oblivion when he stops again, this time, pressing a finger against my clit, and sending waves of energy through my groin.

'Oh, Jesus, let me come.'

'All in good time.'

And now something new. He flicks the lengths of leather against my vagina and clit. Quick bites of pain skim across nerve endings, fizzling out into a sea of warmth.

'Oh fuck.'
'Like that?'
'Yes.'
'Want more?'
'Yes, please.'
He gives me more. I have no idea how long he spends flicking the flogger against me, but by the time he's finished, I'm close to bliss, or ecstasy … or complete madness.

He must have dropped the flogger again – this time I hear no thud – and a single, hard slap lands on my left buttock. I'm given time to soak up the sensation before the same happens to the right. And then he spanks my clitoris, this time with short sharp actions. Almost immediately, I come, every last muscle contracting and pulsating down below. I get no time to rest. A hand comes to the back of my neck, another to my right hip, and he's inside me, thrusting hard. Before the first orgasm's anywhere near finished, the pressure builds again, with a renewed intensity.

'Shit,' I scream.

The hand tightens on my neck, and he pounds harder, hitting the back of my vagina every single time, keeping to the same unforgiving rhythm. Muscles contract again, and before long I'm free-falling through a second orgasm. Finally, his grip becomes vice-like, the thrusts vicious, and I know he's there. At last, he comes, filling me quickly, withdrawing and slapping again, alternating between buttocks, much harder than before.

And I smile to myself because I'm totally exhausted, elated, cast away in a world of pleasure. I've got everything I could ever want or need … and it really can't get any better than this.

I'm returning to reality, coming down from the trance. We're back in bed together and he's holding me, gently smoothing my hair. Raindrops patter against the skylight above us. The world's a thousand miles away.

I could say anything now. I'm weak, suggestible, filters gone, all defences down.

'I love my old man.'
'Do you, now?'
'Yes.'
'Well, if we're using clichés,' he grins, 'I love my ball and chain.'
His lips brush against mine.
'That was perfect,' I murmur. 'I love a good spanking.'
'Glad to hear it.'

'I never thought we'd do it again.'

'We just had to wait for the right time, and let's face it, we were never going to hang the washing on that bench.'

He laces his fingers through mine.

'So, there'll be more?'

He gives me a look of total disbelief.

'Good God, yes. I'll still be spanking you when we're old and grey.'

'We'll never be grey,' I smile dreamily, and if ever there's been a time to throw out a mantra, then this is it. 'Because the colour's back.'

'Too right.' He locks eyes with me, and I lose myself in those irises. They're vibrant tonight, an intense sapphire blue. 'It's been back for a while now,' he whispers. 'And this time, it's here to stay.'

Chapter Twenty-Eight

Dan

There's nothing better than a morning in Bermuda. It's paradise, pure and simple. I'd love to take my wife down to the beach and add another notch to that sunbed. The air's fresh. The sun's low in the sky. Perfect conditions for a good fuck and a quick swim with the woman I love. But the days of carefree sexual marathons are on hold.

And I never thought I'd say this ... but I really don't mind.

'Emily?' I whisper. 'How about a pancake?'

Sitting at the veranda table, breakfast spread out in front of me, the next objective is to get some food into my two-year-old's stomach. She stirs, her face still dug into my T-shirt, and shakes her head emphatically.

'But you need some energy if you want to play in the sea.'

She pulls back her head and glares at me from behind a mess of wild blonde locks. I push back her hair and melt at the sight of those green eyes and that gorgeous little face, all screwed up into a scowl. Just like her Mum, she's a bundle of stubborn energy, a total handful, and a complete beauty.

'For Daddy?' I ask, giving her a smile. She's a Daddy's girl, one hundred percent, a fact I'll use shamelessly, whenever the need arises. 'Just a little bit? I can put some magic sauce on it.'

'Magic?' She rubs her eyes.

'Magic. It makes you ... whatever you want to be.'

'A fairy?'

'If you like.'

She stares at the table, and I bite back the urge to rush. If I've learned nothing else, it's that patience isn't just a virtue. It's an absolute bloody necessity when you've got kids. Holding Emily with one hand, I slice off a piece of pancake with the other, douse it in magic maple syrup, and spear it with a fork. I'm about to coax it into her mouth when I hear the sound of squealing from inside the guesthouse.

'Right,' Maya calls. 'Jack, go and get your breakfast. Now.'

There's a patter of tiny feet on tiles, the squeals grow in force, and Jack springs through the open window, ready for the day in his sun-resistant outfit.

'Daddy?' He swings to a halt by my side. 'Are we ...' He trails into silence, scanning the food laid out on the table. 'Are we going on a boat?'

'Yes, we are.'

I slip the pancake into Emily's tiny mouth.

'Will you swim with me?'

'Without a doubt.'

'And ... can I?' Another silence as he watches a bird wheel through the sky. 'Can I use the snorgel?'

I laugh quietly.

'Of course. We'll find some interesting fish.'

'A stripy one?'

'Definitely a stripy one.'

That should keep him more than happy. Five years old, and he's already thoroughly intrigued by the natural world, constantly asking questions about anything with a heartbeat. A mini David Attenborough, that's what Maya calls him. He climbs onto the chair next to me and while Emily reaches for another helping of pancake, I put down the fork and run my hand over his blond hair.

'Where's Mummy?'

'Putting Ruby's costume on.'

Pardon?

'But I already did that.'

My son shakes his head. I push a plate of fruit towards him and watch hopefully as he picks up a slice of mango. He's a fussy little chap, something I can't understand. Even though Maya's relaxed about the whole thing, I hate it when he doesn't eat.

'Mummy said you put it on upside-down.'

Emily shuffles about in my arms, dropping the pancake onto my lap. A pool of syrup spreads out across my crotch. I sigh and decide it doesn't matter. After all, I seem to spend virtually every day covered in stains of one sort or another.

'I'm sure I didn't put it on upside-down.'

Jack rolls his eyes, bites off a chunk of mango and chews on it thoughtfully. Thank God for that. It's the first thing to pass his lips this morning.

'Inside-out,' he says at last.

'Oh, inside-out,' I laugh. 'I'm sure I didn't.'

'Yes, you did, Daddy.'

'Oh well, I tried my best.'

I suppose that's what happens when you're dealing, single-handedly, with chaos and mayhem on a grand scale. Running a building company was nothing compared to sorting out three mini human spinning tops first thing in the morning. It didn't help that Ruby, my three-year-old wild-eyed beauty of a daughter, couldn't stand still for one minute while I was dressing her.

'Where's your brain?'

Maya's voice sends tingles right through me. I turn, and what I see threatens to give me the first hard-on of the day. Every bit as beautiful and delicious as the first time I ever saw her, her hair tumbles over her shoulders, her skin's lightly tanned from yesterday's session on the beach, and she's wearing a black bikini with a flowing flowery sarong tied at the hip. Eyes locked on her, I will the old fella to behave. Six years down the line, and I still have to pinch myself. But it's true – she's all mine.

'Did you dress Ruby in the dark?' she demands.

'I was a bit overwhelmed, darling. Jack was a good boy, weren't you?'

He nods emphatically, takes a small bite of mango and pulls a face as if he's just eaten dirt.

'He sorted himself out, but our two semi-feral daughters were a handful, to say the least.'

'You should have woken me up. I could have helped.'

'You deserved a lie-in. You didn't sleep too well last night.'

She arches an eyebrow and my cock threatens to kick off again.

'And whose fault was that?' She pulls out a chair.

'Daddy silly pants,' Ruby squeals, emerging through the doorway, giggling like a maniac and skittering off across the lawn. She finds the ball we were playing with last night and begins to throw it about.

Distracted, Jack drops his mango and follows suit.

'Come back here,' Maya orders. 'Hats.'

Obediently, the pair of whirlwinds return to us. They know better than to ignore their mum. Maya pops sunhats onto both little heads and they're off again.

'Sun cream?' she asks, narrowing her eyes at me.

'Already applied,' I return, brim-full of self-satisfaction.

'We need to pack the bags.'

'Already done. I let them watch telly for half an hour and got on with it.'

'You'll have forgotten something.'

'Come on, Maya. I've been doing this long enough.' I reach out and skim a finger down her cheek. 'Louis's sorting out the food and drink. Towels are over there. Arm bands. Deck shoes. The lot. You need to relax and let me take charge sometimes.' I lean in. 'Didn't I tell you that on our first date?'

Her lips curve upwards. She's clearly thinking back.

'I'm sorry,' she smiles. 'But just so we're clear about this, if you've forgotten anything, you can deal with the consequences.'

'It'll be my pleasure.' I plant a kiss on her cheek. Jesus, she smells good this morning. There's something about the Bermuda air that brings out the sweetness in her skin. If we weren't currently surrounded by antsy children, I'd have her back in that bedroom in a heartbeat. 'And I'm sorry I put Ruby's swimsuit on inside-out. She wouldn't stop dancing. And Emily needed a ...'

'Don't even say it.'

Emily wriggles about on my lap, slowly slipping towards the ground. She's interested in what Jack and Ruby are up to, and I'm about to get a break. Quickly, I grab her hat from the table and put it on her head. Immediately, she tries to take it off.

'Keep it on, Em. The sun's hot.'

'No.'

'For Daddy?'

She staggers about, her tiny frame wobbling, gives me a disgusted look and then totters out over the grass, running after the ball. As soon as we're alone, Maya leans over and whispers into my ear.

'I love you, shit head.'

I can't help the grin that spreads across my face.

'And I love you too, sweet pea.'

I brush my lips against hers. I'd go in for a full-on snog, but Maya turns away.

'Bill's here.'

I look up to find him making his way down the steps from the main house. He's getting old fast, struggling with every move.

'How's my favourite family?' he beams, finally reaching us and taking a seat. 'You all sleep well last night?'

I give Maya another knowing look.

'Yes, thanks.' She helps herself to toast and nods at the kids. 'We should get that lot to have breakfast.'

All three of them are busy scurrying after the ball, whooping and squealing and squawking.

'Sort yourself out first,' I tell her. 'I'll make sure they eat.'

But first I'll give them five more minutes in the sun, running off some of their endless reserves of energy, before I shepherd them back to the table.

'We missed you yesterday,' I tell Bill.

After arriving the previous evening, our first day was spent in the cove and generally relaxing around the house. Bill waves a hand.

'I had business to attend to. Solicitors. Dinner with associates. I'm sorry about that. Charles and Kathy looked after you though?'

'They did,' I confirm. 'We had a beautiful meal with them last night. Louis and his family too.'

'That's good.' He turns, squinting into the sun, watching the little ones. 'How was the flight?'

'Fine,' Maya lies, with a wry smile. 'Fourth visit with kids. I think we've got it sorted.'

In actual fact, it was trans-Atlantic torture. While Jack ploughed through an endless stream of films, or napped quietly in his seat, the two girls decided to fidget and complain and climb all over me for most of the six hours, much to Maya's amusement. For the first time ever, I'd begun to wonder if Cornwall wasn't a better idea.

'So how's it going, Dan?' Bill asks.

'How's what going?'

'The new gallery?'

Here we go. The yearly interrogation.

'Great. We've just finished off a new wing. It's light and airy. Some beautiful spaces. And Maya's new work fits in there just fine.'

I can't help it. I steal another look at my super-sexy wife. Good God, I'd love to peel that bikini off her.

'What are you painting now?' Bill asks her.

'A lot of portraits. I'm overwhelmed with commissions.'

'I'm surprised you get anything done, what with this little lot and Dan being so busy with the new gallery.'

I pour myself another coffee, one for Bill, and tea for Maya.

'Lucy runs Slaters all by herself,' I tell him. 'She's on maternity leave at the minute, but she'll be back soon. I've got good staff at the new gallery, and Gordon's a partner. I don't need to be hands-on. I still get time to help with looking after the kids.' I wave at them. 'Jack's already started school. Ruby's starting when we get back. Emily's in a great nursery. It's getting easier. Maya's got a reputation now. She's in demand. She needs to paint, and I do everything I can to make sure it happens.'

'You got yourself a good husband there,' Bill grins.

'The best,' Maya grins back.

And my heart swells.

Bill takes a sip of his coffee. 'Hey, I saw that spread in the Observer.'

My wife lets out a laugh: the most beautiful sound in the world.

'Apparently,' she chuckles, 'we're London's new 'power couple in the art world'.'

'Great photos.'

They certainly were. Me in a tux, Maya stunning in a black gown.

'Ooh, that was grim,' she frowns.

'How so?'

'I'm not really a natural when it comes to photo shoots. I can't do a normal smile.' She points at her lips. 'It's all so false.'

And that's why I had to pause the shoot, take her into my office and fuck her half way into next week. That certainly did the trick. Plenty of photos of her looking lovingly at her husband, and hey presto we were in business.

'Well, you looked natural to me,' Bill says.

'Just like those people in the perfume ads,' I quip.

She laughs again.

'Daddy?'

I look down to find Ruby at my side.

'What is it, Rubes?'

'I want a cake.'

'Ah, the monsters are getting hungry.'

I motion for her to climb onto the seat beside me and get her a pancake, drizzling it with syrup and passing the plate to her.

'How's your swimming costume?'

She ignores me and digs in.

'Did I really put it on inside-out?'

She nods.

'Daddy silly pants.'

With a snigger, she shoves a piece of pancake into her mouth. And now Emily's back, climbing onto my lap without a care in the world. A tiny elbow lands in exactly the wrong place. I wince, pick her up and carefully reposition her.

'Jack,' Maya calls out. 'Come and eat now, if you want to go swimming.'

Immediately, he drops the ball and returns to the veranda. And I relax. For the time being, they're all in the shade, all suddenly interested in food.

'Why don't you come out with us?' I ask Bill.

He watches as Jack helps himself to more fruit, and then shakes his head.

'I'll read the papers, sit in an air-conditioned room and sleep. You'll have fun with Louis and his family. You don't need an old man holding you up.'

'There's air-conditioning on the boat,' Maya prompts him.

Because it's more of a yacht than a boat, complete with galley, living area and two bedrooms, useful when you've got an exhausted, over-heating toddler on your hands.

'And it's Dan's birthday.'

Oh great. She had to go and mention that.

'Ah, happy birthday, Dan.' Bill takes another sip of coffee. 'You should have said. I haven't got you anything.'

I mumble a little. 'It's okay. I don't make a big deal of it.'

'But you should,' Maya interrupts.

Every single year, she insists I celebrate my birthday, and every single year I try to get away with it ... and fail. I might as well throw in the towel. She gets up and saunters into the house. I watch her go, mesmerised by her backside, half-wondering what she's up to now.

'Right,' she begins, returning with a handful of cards. 'Here you go.'

One by one, she hands the cards to the children, and finally, one to Bill.

'Aha,' the old man laughs. 'You think Maya would let this go? She emailed me last week and set this up.'

'Good secrets,' I murmur.

In turn, each of the children wish me a happy birthday and present me with their own hand-made card: Jack's adorned with a picture of a turtle; Ruby's with the words 'Dady sily ponts'; and Emily's with a random scribble. When I'm done, I open Bill's, and finally Maya's, closing it quickly when I spot the word 'spank.' My cock twitches. I'll read that one later. Slipping it back in its envelope and hiding it under a plate, I reward my distinctly naughty wife with a reprimanding look. With a smirk and a shrug, she arranges the rest of the cards in front of me on the table, moving plates and cups out of the way.

'Well, I'm one lucky man,' I beam. 'Thank you everyone. This is lovely. Now, let's eat.'

We set about the usual rigmarole of a family meal, calming

restless children, dealing with refusals to try something new, clearing up the constant mess. I never fail to be amazed by our wordless communication as we pass food and plates and juice cups between us, reading each other's mind every step of the way, acting as one. When everyone's settled, I finally dig in to my own plateful of pancakes.

'So,' Bill begins, pouring himself a second coffee. 'Yesterday, I was busy updating my Will.'

I stop, mid-chew, and eye my old friend. That's really put a slammer on the morning's happiness.

'I'm getting old, Dan. No family as such. I need to think about what should happen.'

And I'm pretty sure I know what's on his mind.

'What would you say if I left all this to you and Maya?'

I glance at my wife. She shakes her head, and I know she's on the same wavelength as me, as ever. I need to knock him back, but I need to do it gently.

'It's an honour you thought of us.'

He sits back, a slight smile playing on his lips.

'But?'

'We've got more than enough. Perhaps you could leave it to Charles and Kathy, Louis and his family? Maybe it's time to give someone else a break?'

'I thought you might say that. And you're right. I just didn't want you to think I'd overlooked you.'

'Don't worry about that,' I reassure him. 'We don't need anything else. I'm a lucky man. I have an incredible wife, three amazing children, great friends, a job I love, more money than anyone could ever need. What more could I want?'

'You should invest more of that money, play the market.'

'Why would I want to do that?'

'With what you've got, you could become seriously rich.'

'I'm already seriously rich. You're talking about ridiculously rich. There's no need for it, Bill. We don't need a house in every country, a private jet, a yacht in every port. People who live like that, they lose touch with reality, and it doesn't make them happy.'

I won't even start on how much we give to charity. Even though we've still got more than enough, he'd have a heart attack on the spot.

'It's nice to be fairly normal,' Maya cuts in, sliding a slice of toast onto Ruby's plate. 'And we don't want the kids growing up in some weird bubble.'

311

Bill raises an eyebrow.

'Bubble?'

'For example,' she explains patiently, 'Jack's in the local state school because it's perfectly decent and perfectly safe. He loves it. Ruby's starting there in the autumn.'

Bill pulls a face, as if he can't quite understand.

'We've got cleaners and gardeners and security, but we like to do normal things together, like shopping and cooking and washing the pots.'

'I cook the meals,' I mutter wryly. 'Health and safety, darling.'

That earns me a light slap on the thigh.

'We don't need people doing those things for us,' she goes on. 'We don't need to be mega-rich.'

'And we certainly don't want all the shit that comes with it,' I add.

'Dan!' Another quick slap. 'Language.'

'Sorry, boss.' I bite back a laugh. 'Look, I've got everything I want, Bill ... apart from maybe one more of these things.' I wave a hand at the children, and hear Maya sigh.

'Come on, woman. You're the one who said you wanted four.'

'Was I drunk?'

'Absolutely not. It was on our wedding day.'

'Oh, yeah.'

'One more. Please?'

'I'm quite enjoying the not being pregnant thing. There was barely space to breathe between Ruby and Emily.'

'And now you've had two years. Pretty please?'

'I'll think about it.'

'You do that.'

'I will.'

'But just remember, I always get what I want in the end.'

'No, you don't, Daddy,' Jack announces, looking up from his food. 'Mummy always gets what she wants.'

'Yes!' Ruby screams excitedly.

'Excuse me,' I grin, leaning forward and addressing them both. Emily wiggles in my arms. 'I'm the boss around here.'

'No, you're not!' Ruby squeals.

I raise an eyebrow, mock dramatic.

'Well, if I'm not the boss, who is?' I demand.

'Mummy!' she squeals again. 'She's the big ...' She comes to a halt and I chuckle. Time and time again, Maya's taught them the phrase, but they still can't get it right.

'The big kamuma,' Jack smiles, picking at his fruit.

'Big kamuma!' Ruby shouts, making Bill jump.

'Big!' Emily gurgles, trying her best to join in. I lean back and push her mop of hair out of her face.

'Of course she is,' I whisper, giving Emily a wink. 'But we don't go on about it.'

'I think you've been conquered,' Bill laughs.

Maybe. But only because it's what I want.

'Come on. Me and Jack are outnumbered,' I argue. 'We want another boy.'

'And what if you get another girl?' she demands, fixing me with those emerald eyes.

'Then we're stuffed,' I shrug.

'Stuffed!' Jack echoes.

Emily moves again, edging her way back off my knee, and I'm relieved. We might be in the shade, and it might be early morning, but I'm already feeling hot. And the look in Maya's eyes isn't helping much. I watch as Emily runs back out onto the lawn, almost falling over her own feet in the process, and picks up the ball. And then I lean across, snuggling my head against Maya's neck. I feel her tingle at my touch. It's a sure-fire way to get her on my side. I've used it right from the word go, and I'm not about to give up on a winning tactic now.

'Don't even try that,' she complains.

'Che la dura,' I mutter against her skin. 'One more. And then ...' I make a scissors shape with my fingers.

A day on the boat. It's enough to try the patience of a saint and the energy of a superhero, but somehow we've managed it. The clan are bathed and ready for bed. With Kathy and Charles playing with them in the living room, babysitting for a couple of hours, I'm free to indulge in my yearly treat.

We pick our way down the steps to the beach, Maya ahead of me, stunning in a flowing pink dress. I can barely take my eyes off her arse. It's a miracle I don't lose my footing and fall flat on my face. With trees hanging over us, I watch as she runs her hands across the flowers, stopping every now and then to admire the colours with her artist's eye. Suddenly, she turns back to me.

'I've been thinking.'

'Have you? Careful, that sort of thing's dangerous.'

'You can say that again.' She bites her lip. 'Anyway, I reckon my pelvic floor can deal with one more.'

'I knew you'd come round.'

She gives me a wicked grin, turns and walks on. Before long, the path gives way to the cove. She stops again, digging her bare feet into the pink sand, looking out over the waves at the setting sun.

'It's so beautiful,' she breathes. 'I love this place.'

'You and me, both.'

I take her by the hand and lead her over to the sunbeds. There's a blanket laid out on the sand, a picnic hamper ready, complete with a bottle of champagne and a couple of torches which I'll light when the sky darkens. In a while we'll dig into the food, prepared by Kathy, and drink a toast to us. She'll wish me a happy birthday and cuddle into my arms, and we'll chat: small talk, big talk, talk about the children, her plans for painting, the latest gossip in the art world, developments for the new gallery.

But before that, I have something else in mind. I pull my penknife out of my shorts pocket. Maya sees it and raises an eyebrow.

'Notches.' I wave it at my favourite sunbed.

'You keep on defacing Bill's expensive furniture, and you'll get in trouble.'

'He never comes down here. Remember?'

She makes her way over to the sunbed.

'Five,' she counts.

'So, let's make it six.' Dropping the knife onto the sand, I settle myself on the bed and wait for my favourite show.

Her eyes glisten in the dimming light. Her lips part.

And my cock goes on the rampage.

'Now ... strip for me.'

Author's note

Thank you for reading my book! I would love to hear from you. You can contact me on my Facebook page:

www.facebook.com/mandylee2015/

Or on my website:

http://www.mandy-lee.com

I certainly hope you had as much fun reading my book as I had writing it. If you liked it please tell a friend - or better yet, tell the world by writing a review on Amazon. Even a few short sentences are helpful. As an independently published author, I don't have a marketing department behind me. I have you, the reader. So please spread the word!

Thanks again.

All the best,

Mandy Lee